Finding Home

Book Three in the Caston Teacher Series

Margaret Standafer

Finding Home - Book Three in the Caston Teacher Series

By Margaret Standafer

ISBN-13: 978-1734800838

This book is a work of fiction. Names, characters, places, and incidents are either the product of the author's imagination or are used fictitiously. Any resemblance to actual persons, living or dead, business establishments, or locales is entirely coincidental.

Cover Art: Kristin Bryant, kristindesign100@gmail.com

For Teachers

Those that taught me
Those I can call relative or friend
Those I'll never have the chance to meet

You've made, and continue to make, a difference.
Thank you.

1

If there was anything better than flying down a country highway on a clear day, the windows open and the cool wind sending your hair swirling, Max certainly didn't know what it was. With her right wrist draped over the top of the steering wheel, her left arm out the window, fingers tapping and her head bopping along to the music that blasted, she checked the rearview mirror and when there wasn't another car in sight, followed the song's advice and put the pedal to the floor. After all, who was she to argue with Molly Hatchet?

The engine roared to life, as happy as she to let loose. It had been a long winter, and she and her baby had been separated for far too long.

Max grinned as she watched the farm fields, still frozen under clumps of stubborn snow, whiz past. It would be a couple of months yet until the farmers could get out into those fields, and the odds favored more heavy spring snow blanketing their land before that day came, but for now, she enjoyed the sun and the view. She lifted her hand in a greeting to the farmer she spotted leaning on his fence and gazing out over his land, dreaming along with her of the warmer days ahead.

If the past week had been what she'd needed to recharge her batteries, the past three hours were what she needed to recharge her soul. Being reunited with her beloved Stevie Ray, opening him up and letting him eat up the miles of road, was like breathing for the first time in seven months. And she told herself with Stevie Ray at her side, she'd get through the next two-and-a-half months a whole lot easier than she had the past seven.

Max sang along with the next tape she popped into the cassette player. It was a mix tape courtesy of Skeeter, one of the few people she could say she'd known most of her life. Most came and went as quickly as the cities and towns she'd found herself in over the years, but Skeeter showed up time and again. Seeing him, spending time talking with him, and tinkering together under Stevie Ray's hood had been the perfect soothing balm to counteract months of tension at the hands of a hundred-and-some middle schoolers.

Skeeter preferred the AM/FM radios that came with the vehicles he favored, conceding to cassette players occasionally. CDs were too new-fangled for him, and the mention of streaming services drew only a blank stare. Of course, Skeeter also wore nothing but Wrangler jeans, T-shirts or flannel depending upon the weather, and boots Max was certain were older than she was. He'd stopped acknowledging most technological and fashion advances sometime in the mid-1970s.

Smiling at the memory of time spent with the only man she'd ever really loved, Max didn't see the highway patrol until it was too late. When the car turned to follow her and its lights flashed, her spirits plummeted.

Seemed a bit unfair, she thought, to position yourself so a stack of straw bales that still sported the remains of a smiling jack-o'-lantern face hid you from view. She grumbled to herself as she slowed to a stop and mentally calculated how much her insurance rates were likely to rise with a speeding ticket.

Not wanting to appear either hysterical or confrontational, Max sat still in her seat, hands steady on the steering wheel, watching the highway patrolman through her rearview mirror. He approached slowly, studying her car as he did so. Before he made his way to the driver's-side door, he stopped and crouched, examining the tires, she thought, but maybe even looking underneath the car. A glimmer of hope flickered.

"Afternoon," he said with a nod when he finally reached the open window. "Know how fast you were going?"

He said what Max figured he always said, what he was supposed to say, but his eyes wandered over the interior of the car. It was normal, she supposed, to determine if she was alone, if there was anything suspicious inside the vehicle, but Max got the feeling he was a lot more interested in the car than who or what was inside.

"Hi," Max answered. "Sorry about that. I'm not sure how fast, but I'm guessing too fast, huh?"

"Um, yeah. Too fast. Almost eighty." He forced his attention on her.

"Yeah. Sorry." When the patrolman didn't respond, just continued his perusal of the car's interior, Max asked, "Did you want to see my license?"

He stood up straighter and cleared his throat. "Yes. License, proof of insurance, and registration."

"It's in my purse." Max indicated the bag next to her on the passenger seat.

The officer nodded. "Okay. This a '69?"

"Yep," Max replied, doing her best to hide her grin.

She handed him the documents, which he skimmed, but his attention had strayed to the exterior. Max was particularly proud of the near-perfect restoration job to the car's body, and she let him have his moment.

"Where are you headed in such a hurry, Ms. Simmons?"

"Caston."

He shook his head. "Almost there. Bit of bad luck we ran into one another when we did."

Max smiled and shrugged.

The officer seemed unable to get a handle on his curiosity. "How long have you had the car? I've never seen it around before today."

"Four years, but I'm new to Caston, and just bringing the car there now."

"Did you buy it in this condition?"

Max chuckled. "Hardly. It didn't run, it was rusted and missing a bumper, lots of interior damage. It's been a labor of love getting it back to its original glory."

The officer's eyebrows rose above the tops of his sunglasses. "You did the work?"

"A lot of it. I had help, mostly with the bodywork, but nothing happened without my elbow grease, or at least my input and my supervision."

"So that's what you do in Caston? You're a mechanic?"

"Wouldn't that be a dream? No, I'm a teacher. Middle school math."

"Ooh! Ouch. Got three of them myself. Middle schoolers, that is. Twin girls in eighth, a boy in sixth. Love them like crazy, but sometimes it's hard to like them, you know?"

Max nodded, and the two commiserated with a look.

"No wonder you need a car like this to get away," the patrolman said when he broke eye contact. His eyes roamed over the car. "I need to run this." He held up the documents Max had given him. "Sit tight."

While Max waited, her mind wandered to the next day. She hadn't done much of anything over spring break to prep for the return to school. Even so, she'd planned on taking a long route home, getting as much time behind the wheel as she could before she parked her Mustang and went back to her reliable Honda for everyday use. Now she supposed it made sense to head directly home, lick her wounds, hope her insurance rates didn't skyrocket, and start thinking about the coming week.

"Here you go, Ms. Simmons."

Max glanced at what he handed her. Her license and the paperwork she'd given him, but nothing else. She looked, but he didn't have any other paperwork in his hands.

"No ticket?"

"Nah. You're a middle school teacher. Time served, I'd say. Just take it easy, all right? Hate to see you damage this beauty."

It was tempting to tell him that the day she couldn't handle a car at eighty was the day she'd turn in her license, but she thought better of it.

"Thank you. I appreciate it, and I will take it easy."

He nodded and turned to go, but then turned again and faced her. "I don't suppose I could get a peek under the hood?"

Max smiled. "Sure."

She stayed closer to the speed limit for the rest of the twenty-mile drive back to Caston, figuring she'd pushed her luck enough for one day. Stevie Ray, for the most part, hummed along. He gave her a moment of concern when he sputtered after she slowed and stopped for a stop sign, but after a hiccup and a jolt, he roared back to life and cruised to the garage spot Max had begged and bartered for with her landlord.

When she'd moved to Caston, she'd decided against the apartment buildings with vacancies, choosing instead an apartment over the garage of a house owned by a crotchety widower, Fred Jenkins. The space suited her fine. It boasted a small kitchen/living area, a manageable bathroom, and a tiny bedroom separated from the rest of the space by a half-wall. The fact that it came with a parking spot in the three-car garage was its biggest selling point.

For her first seven months, the garage space had been convenient, keeping her Honda out of the rain and snow, and relatively warm over the long winter. Knowing she'd have Stevie Ray joining her after spring break, Max had begun working on Fred a couple of months ago.

The third stall of the garage was mostly empty, she'd pointed out. Fred had a spot for his car, and most of the stuff shoved into the third stall could be stored in the shed on the back of his property. He'd argued back that he needed the snow blower, the lawn mower, and the garden tools handy. Max had offered to relocate the items to the shed, telling Fred she'd retrieve whatever he needed, whenever he needed it, but it hadn't been until she'd found out his riding lawn mower hadn't worked for over a year and he'd been forced into hiring a neighbor to mow his lawn that she'd struck gold.

She'd offered to fix the mower in exchange for the extra garage spot and had added that if she couldn't fix it—provided it wasn't beyond repair—she'd buy him a comparable replacement. Fred had snickered and taken her up on her offer. Max got the mower humming in one dirty Saturday afternoon in late February, and had also made some adjustments to the snow blower, cleaned the weed whacker and replaced its air filter and trimmer line, and only just restrained herself when she wanted to pop the hood of Fred's ancient Oldsmobile and give it a tune-up.

The afternoon spent in the frigid garage was worth it when she pulled Stevie Ray into his new home. Though it was only her, and occasionally Fred in the garage, and she figured she wouldn't need to worry about accidental dings, she nonetheless retrieved the custom-made cover and made sure Stevie Ray was tucked in safe and sound before she hauled her duffel bag up the stairs to her apartment.

She stopped when she walked in the door and tried to decide if it felt like coming home. Seven months was longer than she'd stayed in most of the dozens of places she'd lived over her life, and she'd certainly put down more roots in Caston than she had most places, but she realized she wasn't sure if what she was feeling was a homey feeling since she didn't know what that felt like.

Max knew most people wouldn't understand her lifestyle. To be fair, if she hadn't grown up moving from one end of the country to the other and back again with hardly a thought, she probably wouldn't understand it either. She watched the movies, the commercials even, with stories of those returning home after years away, for a holiday, or even after a long day at work, and somehow that home working its magic and fixing everything that was wrong. She didn't know what that would feel like, but she guessed it had to differ from the mild feeling of familiarity that greeted her when she closed the door of her apartment behind her. If not, they wouldn't make commercials and movies about it.

Oh well, she thought, they also made movies about people who traveled the world, made fascinating discoveries, met new people, learned new customs, and before it got to be more than vaguely familiar, pulled up stakes and moved on to the next. Her kind of movies.

Max dumped her duffel on the couch and went for the fridge. She knew before she opened it there wouldn't be much there as she'd made it a point to leave as little as possible knowing she'd be away for over a week, but the empty sight was depressing. She'd been spoiled having Skeeter cook for her over the past week. Not that he was a gourmet chef, not by a long stretch, but the chili and the macaroni and cheese he made from scratch were as close to comfort food as Max had ever known. Her own dad, when he'd remembered to feed her, had done so from cans and boxes.

Deciding she'd put off grocery shopping until after school the next day, she picked up her phone to call for a pizza when it rang in her hand.

"Hey, Ellie. How was break?"

"Good, Max. Wonderful. How about yours?"

Ellie sounded bubblier than usual. Warning bells sounded in Max's head. "Good. What's up?"

"I knew you'd ignore my text, so I'm calling instead. Want to meet at Scooter's and grab a bite? Nicole is taking a couple of hours away from the puppy and said she can be there in thirty minutes."

"Why not? Sure, I'll be there in thirty. Is there a reason for this get-together?"

"Oh, Max, always so suspicious."

"You've given me plenty of reason to be."

"I'll see you at Scooter's," Ellie said before she disconnected.

"You're up to something, Oklahoma," Max muttered as she stuck her phone back in her pocket before looking down at her worn jeans and even more worn sweatshirt. Since changing seemed like far too much work, and since the clothes were clean, even if they didn't look it, Max decided they'd do for an evening at Scooter's.

When she got to the garage, she debated uncovering Stevie Ray but decided she wasn't up to the dozens of questions Nicole and Ellie would have, so settled for her much less flashy Honda. As she drove across town, she wracked her brain trying to come up with counterarguments to whatever it was Ellie was going to throw at them this time.

Max was the first to arrive, so she grabbed a booth in the corner. She munched on the complimentary popcorn and sipped water while she waited. Depending on what Ellie sprung on them, she'd move on to either a soda or something decidedly harder. Ellie had a way of making Max feel like she needed a drink.

Not that she didn't love her new friends. She did. And wasn't that something? Girlfriends. Who would have guessed that after all the years of being the odd one out at school, never sticking around long enough to have anyone she could call more than a casual acquaintance, she'd find herself, at twenty-six years of age, with girlfriends? The world was a strange place, indeed.

She looked around her at the place she and her girlfriends had made their gathering spot. It was comfortable, clean, and served good food. It was a step up from the places she'd grown up inside, yet at the heart of it, these sorts of places were all the same. There may be fewer fist fights at Scooter's than there were at Bottoms Up, or Lucky's, or any number of places that, as far as she knew didn't have a name except 'Bar,' but they all had in common their ability to bring a sense of comfort to their patrons, to provide an ear when one was needed, and to give a person the sense he or she wasn't alone in the world. Whether it be in Indiana, Florida, Texas, or North Carolina, they all existed with the goal of being a home away from home.

Max waved when she spotted Nicole, then marveled at the change in her friend over the past few months. From the tense, slightly resentful, self-confidence-lacking-but-smart-as-a-whip new teacher, she was poised, glowing, and calm, though when she got close enough, Max spotted a hint of the dark circles under Nicole's eyes that makeup didn't quite cover. The glowing, Max knew, was due to Brady. The dark circles, she guessed, were due to the puppy.

"Hi, Max. How was break?" Nicole dropped into the booth across from Max.

"Good. Yours?"

"Good. The puppy is keeping me busy, and keeping me awake, but it was good. I was in love with her before we got home."

"And Brady? In love with him too?"

Nicole blushed. "You knew the answer to that before I did, but yes. I am."

"I'm happy for you, Nic. I'm happy things are working out. How's your dad doing?"

"He's doing. Still not loving Cranberry Pointe, but not complaining quite as much. We actually have a conversation now and then about something other than how much he hates it there. I'm counting it as a win."

Before they could say any more, Max sensed the perkiness level in Scooter's rise.

"El's here," Max said.

"Do you know what this is about?" Nicole whispered before Ellie reached the table.

"No idea, but I'm sure it's something she'll force us to agree to and then immediately regret."

"Hi, y'all." Ellie bounced up to the table. Though there was still snow on the ground in Caston, the day had been relatively mild, yet Ellie was bundled in her bright pink jacket, had a scarf around her neck, and wore gloves on her hands. She didn't remove any of it before she sat down next to Nicole.

"There is heat in here, El. Maybe lose the jacket and gloves?"

"In a minute. I'm still freezing. Now, catch me up. The assembly on the last day of school before break seems like eons ago. What have y'all been up to?" Ellie turned to Nicole. "How's the puppy?"

"She's good. She was a little scared at first, but she's getting used to her new home."

"And speaking of new homes, did you make a decision?"

A jolt of something like anguish rocked Max. Nicole was leaving? Going back to law school? A few months ago, it would have been nothing but news. Now, it was a punch to the solar plexus. She felt the air being sucked right out of her.

"You're leaving?" Max managed, though it came out as a croak.

"Oh, that's right. We talked about it after you'd already left—" Ellie stopped. "Max, whatever is wrong? You look like you've just been told you have to sit in that dunk tank again."

"Nothing." Max sucked in a giant breath. "Nothing's wrong."

Ellie frowned but continued. "Anyway, Nicole is thinking about getting out of her apartment and buying a house, thinking it would be easier with a puppy if she wasn't living on the third floor."

"I did some looking," Nicole said. "Still haven't made up my mind."

"You'll figure it out," Ellie said, then she bounced in her seat. "Did y'all order anything yet? I think we should have a drink. Something festive."

Max may have recovered from the shock of thinking Nicole was leaving town, but her radar was back up. They were getting to the real reason for the last-minute get-together. The fact that Ellie looked equal parts excited and nervous told Max she wasn't going to like what she heard.

"What gives, Oklahoma? Why don't you spill whatever it is you have to tell us? Or ask us. I know it's going to be something awful, so you might as well rip off the bandage."

"Is it warm in here?" Ellie said, pulling at the scarf that was still around her neck. "It's definitely warm in here."

"You're wearing your jacket," Max said. "And a scarf, and gloves, and for the love of everything holy, tell us what you have to tell us."

Ellie pulled off the scarf, shrugged out of her jacket, then slowly pulled off one glove, stalling before pulling off the other.

"I don't think it's a bad thing, Max. In fact, I think it's a pretty amazing thing. I hope you're as excited as I am. Well, maybe not quite as excited, but I hope you're happy—"

Max threw up her hands. "What?"

Ellie pulled off her other glove with a flourish and stretched her hand out over the table. On the fourth finger, a huge diamond glittered. "Zeke proposed!"

Nicole gasped, then grabbed Ellie's hand for a closer look. "It's stunning," she said, turning Ellie's hand one way, then the other. "When? How? Details!"

"Wow," Max said, a mixture of emotions causing her reaction to be a little more subdued than Nicole's. "Congratulations. Wait, am I supposed to say congratulations to the woman? I never know how those things work."

"Tradition dictates you congratulate the man, and offer your best wishes to the woman, but I'm too darn excited to care about tradition. I'm getting married!"

"Then let me say that I'm happy for you, and I wish you all the best. You and Zeke are perfect for each other. I know you're going to be happy together."

"Thank you, Max. We are. Perfect for each other, and going to be happy. I just can hardly wait to be his wife."

"When?" Nicole asked. "Have you decided?"

At that, Ellie's face fell just a fraction. "Not exactly. Mama's pushing for us to get married at home, but I don't think I want to do that. I planned one wedding there already, Charlene is getting married there in just a few months, and I don't want my wedding to Zeke compared to any of that. I think I want to get married here, in Caston. Mama's still stewing over that, so until she calms down, we're holding off on choosing a date. The sooner, the better, though."

Max leaned back and watched Ellie and Nicole talk dates, colors, venues, and all manner of things. Max had nothing helpful to add. Instead, she watched her friends' faces. Ellie was glowing; Nicole wasn't far behind. If Nicole was thinking about buying a house, that meant she was thinking about staying in Caston, something a few months ago she would have fought tooth and nail. It also meant Brady must be thinking about staying in Caston. Honestly, if Nicole had announced that she and Brady were also engaged, Max wouldn't have been surprised.

Both of her friends would be married in the not-too-distant future, and would likely be calling Caston home, at least for a while. Max shifted uncomfortably in her seat. Seven months in the same place was long enough to make her antsy. She needed two years of teaching experience, but there was no requirement it be two years in the same school. When she'd taken the job in Caston, she'd fully intended on putting in one year, then moving on. She'd find something else, somewhere else, and she'd fulfill her obligation. Then she'd be off on her real adventure.

"Max! Max, whatever are you dreaming about? If you don't like pink, don't panic. It's not set in stone."

"Pink? Pink what?"

"Dresses, silly." Then Ellie frowned. "You will be my bridesmaid, won't you?"

"Bridesmaid? What?"

"Max, weren't you paying attention? I asked if you and Nicole would be bridesmaids. You will, won't you?"

"What? You're serious? Me?"

"Of course, you." Ellie reached across the table and took Max's hand. "You're one of my dearest friends. With everything that we've been through together, I feel like we have a bond that will last a lifetime. I can't think of two people I want standing next to me more than the two of you."

"I don't know how to be a bridesmaid," Max said. "I'll probably screw it up."

"There's not a lot to know, and I'm sure Nicole will be happy to answer any questions that pop up."

"I have a few bridesmaid gigs under my belt. I'll be happy to guide you, Max." Nicole winked and grinned at Max.

"But what were you saying about pink?" Max looked around the room. "And where in the world is our server?"

"When I came in, I asked that they give us a few minutes," Ellie said. "I didn't want us to be interrupted and risk giving you a chance to escape."

"Haha. Maybe you could relay whatever sort of bat signal you agreed upon and get someone over here?" Max pondered what might be strong enough to help her cope with the title of bridesmaid.

"Of course," Ellie said. She lifted her hand and waved at the greeter. "It should be just a minute."

"Champagne!" Nicole said. "We need to toast." She leaned over and hugged Ellie. "This is so exciting. I can't wait to start planning."

Planning? Ha! Max thought. More like praying. For an elopement.

2

It wasn't as terrifying as it had been at the beginning, and it wasn't as overwhelming now that she had her lesson planning and prep work down to something of a science, but Max's stomach still gave a lurch when she walked into her dark classroom after a week away. She flipped on the lights and tried to give herself a pep talk.

Only a couple more months and it would be summer. Three months with no school. The excitement Max felt at the thought of those long, glorious months, free to do as she chose, rivaled the feelings she'd had as a child when summer vacation approached. Back then, she'd never given a thought to how her teachers must feel, but now, being on the other side of the equation, she realized the prospect of three months away from school was possibly more exciting—certainly more deserved—than it had been all those years ago.

Since she had time before the first group of students arrived, Max grabbed the poster she'd ordered from an online teacher supply website from her bag. She looked around for the best spot to hang it. The decorating fairies hadn't paid her room a visit over break, so she had lots of options. The walls were mostly blank except for the few posters she'd hung before school started. One explained the order of operations, PEMDAS, with written as well as pictorial examples. Another spelled out divisibility rules, and she'd directed her students to it countless times over the past months. There were also a couple geared toward her engineering students that showcased engineering marvels throughout history, from the Egyptian pyramids and Stonehenge to the International Space Station and the dawn of the internet.

Today she added a large, bright poster that explained the difference between theoretical and experimental probability and how to calculate each. She'd be introducing a unit on probability toward the end of the year, and based on what she'd read about teaching the concept, she anticipated a lot of questions. Hoping the poster would help, she hung it on a bulletin board near her desk.

Before they got to probability, they'd have to tackle an introduction to algebra. Her first test on whether she'd be able to convey the concepts to squirrelly sixth graders would begin in just a few minutes.

Max turned toward the whiteboard. She gave herself a moment to take a deep breath and to go over the reasons in her mind why running from the room screaming would be a bad idea. When she turned back to face her students, she forced a smile.

"You're right, Jake, x did equal seven over here," Max pointed with her blue marker, "but that doesn't mean it will always equal seven. X is just a representation of a missing number. We could use any letter but x is the most common, so we'll stick with that for now."

"But if one is always one, and two is always two, why isn't x always seven?" Jake asked.

"Because seven is seven. In this problem," Max pointed again with her marker, "x equaled seven because that's what we needed to replace x with in order to make the equation true. Here," she pointed again, "x cannot equal seven or the equation won't be true. Can someone tell me what x needs to be in this equation?"

Max looked out at a sea of blank faces and tried to be patient. Though algebra made perfect sense to her, she knew that wasn't the case for a lot of people. Math had always been her favorite subject in school, but again, she knew that was definitely not the case for many. Unless she wanted to ensure she'd have thirty students who, after today, decided math was their least favorite, she needed to keep calm, try again, and wait for it to click.

So, she started over.

By the end of the day, Max was starting to wonder why she'd ever liked math. Seeing it through the eyes of her students, it was downright frustrating. Just when they'd gotten the hang of fractions and decimals, of exponents and square roots, they had letters thrown at them. Letters that equaled numbers, but not always the same number.

At some point during her third class, she'd realized a few of her students were viewing x as if it were part of a code. She'd never thought of it that way, but she sort of understood where they were coming from. If x equaled seven, then y probably equaled eight, or maybe six. When she tried to step back, to view the concept as if seeing it for the first time, it almost made sense.

Despite the frustrations, she felt she'd conveyed the idea of variables to most of her students. And all the talk of codes made her want to add a simple unit on cryptology where she could demonstrate the basics of codes and ciphers, but she was afraid it might lead to more confusion than anything.

Max gathered up her things, locked her room, and was in the parking lot as the buses were pulling away. She normally stuck around a while, whether to chat with Nicole and Ellie, to touch base with one of the other math teachers, or to spend some time on classwork, but today she needed to clear her head. It wasn't a good sign, she figured, that after only one day back from break she was already desperate for an escape, but she told herself the day had been an exceptionally trying one, and Stevie Ray was waiting to heal all that ailed her.

It was cooler than the day before, but the sun was shining, the roads were clear of snow and ice, and as Max sat behind the wheel and left Caston in her rearview mirror, she left the stress of the day with it. She took the same route she'd driven the day before and made sure to keep her speed in check. She didn't have a destination in mind, just the goal of covering enough miles that the day's events seemed less discouraging. With all the faith in the world that Stevie Ray would help her accomplish just that, she relaxed and hummed along to a song by her car's namesake on the tape from Skeeter.

When she was about twenty miles out of Caston, close to the spot where the day before she'd nearly gotten a speeding ticket, she noticed a turnoff she'd missed on her drive into Caston. Stevie Ray didn't have a fancy GPS but figuring she could rely on her phone if she got herself turned around, Max took the barely marked road.

She passed more farms, slowed when she came upon a small town that seemed to be nothing much but a garage with a gas pump out front, a church, and a bar, then inched the gas pedal farther down and relished the freedom of the open road.

She'd driven across South Dakota, Wyoming, and Montana, where the speed limit was eighty, and where she'd pushed it higher than that. She'd driven on the Autobahn in Germany where there was no speed limit and where even the rental cars handled like a dream, and she'd felt a rush second only to the time she'd spent behind the wheel of a race car. But there was something about a rural highway with its hills and curves that made the slower speeds worthwhile. Sometimes, anyway. Max loved discovering whatever surprise was over the next hill or around the next curve.

She spotted signs advertising a small town's summer festival and another's winter carnival. She smiled at the faded and crooked hand-painted sign lauding the state football champions of 1979 erected next to the 'Population 1052' sign as she entered a town called Rankin. She passed houses that still had Christmas lights hanging from the roofs, and houses where the owners were already scrubbing the winter grime from the windows, buffing them to gleaming. And when the sun started sinking lower and her stomach started rumbling, Max turned and headed back the way she'd come. Further exploring could wait for another day. For now, she'd take the sure route home.

Knowing she'd be pushing it to make it back to Caston on anything but fumes, Max pulled into the next gas station she came upon. While she was filling the tank, a highway patrol car pulled up alongside her. A familiar face smiled and waved a greeting.

"Ms. Simmons. What are the chances?" Like before, his eyes wandered over the car while he spoke to her.

"What are the chances, indeed? I guess I'm becoming a regular on your stretch of highway."

"It was a fine day. I can see why you'd want to take her for a spin."

"Him, but yeah, I couldn't pass up such a nice day. There's snow in the forecast for later this week."

"April snow." He shook his head. "Usually means accidents. People get spring fever, get used to driving on clear roads, then bam! Ice and snow and accidents. It's like they forget everything they did for the past five months."

"I'll be parking this one," Max patted the hood of the car. "Never take him out in the snow if I can help it."

"I wouldn't either. Sure is a beauty."

Max beamed. "Thank you. I agree."

The patrolman stepped forward and extended his hand. "Marty. Marty Francis. If we're going to keep running into each other, it seems like we should be acquainted."

"Nice to officially meet you, Marty. Call me Max."

"Max, nice to meet you. Keeping the speed in check today?"

"You know I am, Marty. Don't have to tell me twice."

Marty threw his head back and laughed. "The fact that you said that with a straight face makes me want to hand you an Oscar."

Max laughed along with him, deciding she liked the tall, lanky cop. He had a friendly smile and an easygoing manner. It made her wonder what it took to get him to flip the switch when the job demanded he lose that easygoing manner.

"I promise I wasn't going as fast as yesterday."

"I'm glad to hear it. Were the kids hard on you today? You needed to hit the road and burn off some steam?"

"How'd you know?"

"I recognize the signs. I think I told you I've got three at home. Sometimes I think that's three too many. Can't imagine what it's like having a couple hundred."

"I tried to teach them about variables in algebraic equations today. Let's just say I've had better days."

Marty laughed again. "I stopped helping the kids with math once they left elementary school. My wife handles math and science questions, I tackle the other stuff, and when we know it's one of those days when they're not going to listen to a thing we say no matter how hard we try to help, we lock ourselves in our room, turn on a movie, and let them figure it out for themselves."

"I'd say that's a pretty perfect way of handling it. Kudos to you and your wife."

"It's more a matter of survival than anything, but thank you. We try."

The door of the gas station swung open and a short, stocky man strolled up to Max and Marty. His eyes wandered from the car, to Max, to Marty, and back to the car.

"Marty. How ya doin'?"

"Can't complain. And you?"

"Not bad. Knee's actin' up, means there's snow comin'. You're gonna be busy."

"That's what I hear." Marty turned to Max. "Max, this is Tank. Tank, Max Simmons. She's a teacher over in Caston."

"Huh. That so? Whatcha doin' out here?"

"Just taking a drive, enjoying the weather before that snow comes."

Tank nodded. "It's comin', mark my word." He flexed his left knee a couple of times, but his eyes wandered back to Max's car. "This your car?"

"Yes."

"Huh." Tank forgot about his stiff knee and squatted to get a closer look at the wheels. His head tipped as he tried to look at the undercarriage. "What's a pretty thing like you doin' with a car like this?"

If Max hadn't grown up around Tank's type, if she hadn't heard it all a hundred times before, she might have been tempted to give him an earful, but she was used to the skeptical looks and the downright doubt. She knew Tank and most like him meant no disrespect, just weren't used to women knowing anything about cars. And in a lot of cases, more than they did.

"Today, I'm driving it," Max said. "A few years ago, I was rebuilding it. Most every day in between, I've been either tending to it or fretting over it. You got a wife, Tank?"

The question seemed to catch Tank off guard. He stood and gave Max an odd look before he answered, "Yeah."

"You love her? She the best thing that's ever happened to you?"

Tank's eyes narrowed as if he sensed he was stepping into a trap, but one he didn't quite understand. He gave Max a tentative, "Yeah..."

Max patted her hand on the roof of her car. "Then you have an idea of how I feel about Stevie Ray here."

Tank cracked the first hint of a smile. "Stevie Ray? Most people name their cars after a woman, but seein' as you are one, I guess Stevie Ray might make some sort of sense."

"Well, thank you, Tank, for the vote of confidence."

"Stevie Ray, like Stevie Ray Vaughn?" Marty asked.

"Yep. A friend of mine gave me a few cassette tapes after we finished working on Stevie Ray. The entire time we worked on the car, he tried to get me to take out the cassette player, said it wasn't original and didn't belong in a car like this. I kind of agreed, but it was already there, and I decided to keep it. Can't always pick up a decent radio station when you get outside the big cities, and I like music. Skeeter, my friend, finally relented, and then gave me the cassettes. They were heavy on blues rock. Very heavy on Stevie Ray Vaughn. I became a fan, and Stevie Ray here got his name."

"Then you and this Skeeter fella really rebuilt a '69 Mustang?"

"That we did, Tank, that we did."

Tank looked at Marty. "Woulda thought Beck woulda had his hands in something like this."

"Max is new to Caston."

"Ah," Tank said as if that explained everything.

"Who's Beck?" Max asked.

"A mechanic just outside Caston. According to most folks around here, the best mechanic you'll find here, or anywhere else for that matter," Marty said.

"Hmm," was Max's only reply.

Tank pulled a rag from his pocket and wiped his greasy hands. "Much as I'd like to get under the hood of Stevie Ray, you need any work, you'd best look up Beck. I mostly just do oil changes, air filters, that sort of thing now." Tank flexed the fingers on his hands, made fists, then stretched the fingers again. "Hands don't quite work like they once did."

"Sorry to hear that, Tank," Max said.

"Sorry enough to let me have a peek?" Tank gave her a crooked grin.

"Sorry enough."

For the second time in as many days, Max lifted the hood of Stevie Ray and talked classic cars with someone she'd just met.

3

There were days when having a prep period first hour was handy, but mostly Max found it annoying. She'd squeezed in a before-school dental appointment a couple of months ago, and there'd been days when she'd used the time to finish up a lesson plan or make copies of worksheets, but usually Max sat at her desk and watched the clock.

Today, once she put in her time as a hall monitor and the bell rang starting the school day, Max wandered the halls for a few minutes, pausing outside a few doors and catching a minute or two of a teacher's lesson. She picked up the stack of worksheets she'd had printed in the office, ignored the dirty looks from Cynthia—the school's secretary and self-appointed guardian of school supplies—when she reached into the cabinet and snagged a few highlighters and a box of paperclips, then headed back to her room. She figured she could pass the time by counting out enough worksheets for each class and paper-clipping them together.

She'd only just sat down at her desk when the school's PA system crackled to life. Principal Amanda's voice was slow and measured.

"Staff, this is a lockdown. Activate lockdown procedures immediately."

"Oh, crap," Max muttered to herself. How had she missed an email telling her they were having a lockdown drill? She tried to think if she'd checked her email the evening before.

Amanda's voice sounded again. This time, Max heard the slight tremor behind her words.

"Staff, this is a lockdown with intruder. Activate lockdown procedures immediately."

Max's insides felt like they were melting. It wasn't a drill. It was real. For a moment, she was unable to move. The practice drills, the staff meetings, and the training they'd done for just such a situation all jumbled together in her mind. Her students. She'd do anything to protect her students, but when she looked around, she remembered she didn't have anyone in the room with her.

It wasn't until she heard doors slam, and from the room above heard desks scrape over the floor that she jumped into action. The papers she'd been holding fluttered to the ground as she flew to her feet and ran toward her own door. She slammed it shut, locked it, then double-checked the lock. Before taking cover, she hesitated.

Maybe she was needed somewhere. Maybe there were students who hadn't been in a classroom when the alert sounded. What if there were kids walking the halls, hiding in the bathrooms, terrified and frozen, unsure where to go or what to do? Maybe she needed to check, to look, to help.

But no, they'd been told to never leave their rooms unless directed to do so by law enforcement or via the secure messaging app they all had installed on their phones. Max pulled her phone from her pocket. The only message she had read *This is not a drill. Begin lockdown procedure immediately.*

Her heart banged in her chest. She'd never been more scared or felt more helpless than she did at that moment.

Since the sounds of doors slamming and desks scraping, Max hadn't heard another peep. Silence in Caston Middle School was a rarity. Now, that silence was as loud as an off-key band performance at a school assembly. As terrifying as the silence was, Max was more terrified the sound of gunshots would break it.

Deciding the likelihood she'd be able to help anyone if she left her room was slim, and knowing it would be reckless and go against everything she'd been taught, Max started toward her heavy desk in the corner of the room, ready to hide underneath it. She'd only taken a few steps when she remembered the substitute teacher next door.

Kimberly Trainor, one of the other math teachers, had her baby over break and had started her maternity leave. The sub—Max couldn't remember her name—was on her second day in the school. There was a good chance she didn't know the lockdown procedure, and an excellent chance that she was petrified.

Max peeked out the window of her door. She could duck next door, try the door, and if it was locked, run back to her own room. If it wasn't locked, which she was very much afraid would be the case, she'd announce who she was, dart inside, and help Ms. Whatever get things under control.

Max's hand shook as she slowly and silently unlocked her door. She inched the door open. The crack allowed her to look to the left, but not to the right. It was silent in the hallway, so she dared push the door a little farther. When it was ripped from her hand and flung all the way open, Max tried to scream, but the sound wouldn't come.

A hand pushed her back into the room. Max stumbled as her feet at first refused to move but caught herself just before she fell. She heard her classroom door close, then lock.

Max forced herself to look at the person in the room with her.

It was a man, slightly under six feet, she guessed, wearing a black jacket, black pants, a black cap, and white tennis shoes. The shoes looked odd, so out of place, and for a moment, it was all Max could see. Why would a person wear all black, as if trying to hide in plain sight, and then add bright white shoes?

"Where is he?"

The voice was high-pitched, pleading almost, as if the man were as scared as she. Though the very idea made her sick, Max forced herself to study his face, telling herself she may need to give a description later.

Light brown hair escaped the cap and looked shaggy as if it badly needed a trim. The eyes were dark, and they darted around the room, never settling on anything for more than a fraction of a second. He was nervous. He hadn't shaved in a few days, and his whiskers were more grey than anything else. Thin lips, a nose that had clearly been broken at least once, and a scar along his jawline. Max was confident she'd never forget the face.

"I asked you where he is!"

This time the voice was louder, and Max jolted.

"Who?" Her voice wasn't much above a whisper.

"My son! Where is he?"

"I don't know."

He was a parent? Max couldn't recall what she'd eaten for breakfast, but whatever it was, it was on its way back up. She swallowed hard.

He moved closer, and that's when she saw the gun. Whether it had been in his hand the entire time, or he'd just pulled it from his pocket, she didn't know, but she knew the way he was waving it wasn't good.

Over the course of her twenty-six years, Max had seen plenty of people with guns. The vast majority of those people respected the gun they held. They used it for hunting, for target shooting, for sport, but never to frighten, or intimidate, or harm.

She'd also seen people waving a gun in rage. People who had no business being within miles of a gun. She'd learned that more often than not, those people were more dangerous to themselves than anyone, but she'd also learned to assume nothing when someone held a gun.

She knew she had some decisions to make. Life or death decisions.

"He's here. Don't tell me he's not. This is the math room, right?"

"Yes."

"I knew it. He likes math. He's in this room." The man moved his head slowly now, staring and taking in every corner of the room. "Did you hide them in the closet?"

There was a small storage closet along the wall. It wouldn't hold one student, let alone thirty, but Max wasn't about to point that out. She stayed silent while the man kept the gun pointed at her and walked backward to the closet. When he flung it open and found it empty, he seemed more confused than angry.

"Why isn't he here?"

"What's your son's name? Maybe I can help you find him."

When he lifted the gun higher, Max's heart stopped. She was desperately trying to figure out her next move when he finally answered.

"Caden. Caden Quinn. Where is he?"

Max didn't recognize the name. He wasn't one of her students, and based on the last name, wasn't a sibling of one of her students.

"I don't know your son. He's not one of my students."

The man looked around again. He mumbled to himself. Somehow, Max found the quiet muttering much more frightening than the shouting.

"Maybe this isn't the room. There was a poster. Einstein. You know, e=mc2? Yeah, I remember the poster. It must be the next room."

Max stood frozen while the man got closer as he headed back to the door. Her mind raced. She knew there was no way she could let him leave, let him go into another room, a room with kids. She weighed her options. None of them were appealing, but she knew she had to choose one.

As soon as the man got close enough, and before he could reach the door, she lunged.

She aimed for his legs, and that's where she caught him. The force knocked him off balance and sent both of them sprawling and sliding across the floor. Max heard the sickening clank and thud of his gun bouncing on the floor. She squeezed her eyes shut, waiting for the explosion she was all but certain would follow, but all she heard was the man's groan, followed by a rant that she couldn't have made sense of if she'd had hours to ponder it. She heard his son's name, she heard something about rights, and then she stopped listening.

His legs were pinned underneath her torso, and while he ranted, he didn't move them. Max knew the instant the shock wore off, though, because those legs began to bicycle as he tried to free himself. She pictured the white tennis shoe when it connected with her arm, then with the side of her head. She blinked against the stars that exploded behind her eyes. Still, she didn't loosen her grip.

"Please, let me help you," she grunted as she struggled to maintain her hold. "Maybe we can figure out where your son is. If you fight, if you scare people, you won't be able to see him."

It was a lie, but a lie born of desperation. She was no trained negotiator. Her only bargaining skills had been learned on the streets or in this very classroom. Still, she had to try. "Give me the gun. No one is going to listen to you if you're flashing a gun. Give it to me, then I'll do what I can to help you."

The sharp, single burst of a laugh shattered the eerie quiet of the room, of the entire building.

"Get in line, cuz people have been telling me for years they're gonna help me. No one's helped me yet."

"I'll try. I can promise that."

"Time for promises is over. Long over."

With a swift kick, one Max would long curse herself for not anticipating because she'd let her guard down, just a little, he connected with her wrist and freed his legs. Then with a speed she wouldn't have thought possible, he was on his feet and charging for the door.

Max followed, refusing to acknowledge the burning in her wrist, the stars that wanted to force her back to the ground when she got to her feet too fast. She tore after him, following him into the hallway.

Where were the police? The thought pounded in her brain. In all their training, police presence, in some form, had always been part of the equation, but she hadn't heard so much as a single siren, seen a single flashing light, heard a single bullhorn.

Maybe it was too soon. Maybe they were still en route. She knew she'd lost all sense of time. Or maybe they were being cautious, unsure of what was going on inside the building, and not wanting to put anyone at more risk than necessary.

Whatever the case, Max knew she didn't have any time to pause and think, to plan. When the man stopped at the first door and tried the knob only to find it securely locked, he raised his gun and aimed it at the knob.

Whether that really worked the way it did in the movies, a single shot taking out a doorknob and granting almost instant entry, Max didn't know, but she did know she wasn't going to wait around to find out. For the second time in a matter of minutes, she was airborne, diving at the man whose hands, she briefly registered, were shaking.

This time, she hit him at the waist and he crumpled. She was on top of him and, without letting herself think, she swung her fist at the hand that still held the gun. To her shock and delight, it flew out of his hand and skittered across the hallway.

Underneath her, the man bucked. He was larger than her, and in his confused state, she had no doubt he'd stop at nothing to free himself. Just as she felt the momentum, felt his leg swing and one of those tennis shoes connecting again, this time with her calf, she heard words that sent both relief and terror through her.

"Police! Freeze!"

The man did, for a second. He froze, except for his head, which whipped from side to side. Max felt hands grasp her shoulders and pull her quickly and roughly to her feet.

"Don't move! Hands in front of you!"

She couldn't speak, she could barely think. The terror, the shock, the crippling anxiety that she'd held at bay for the last few minutes, letting instead her adrenaline take charge, rocked her from head to toe. Before she could respond, before she could even attempt to tell them she was a teacher, arms grabbed her again and forced her down the hallway and around a corner.

She felt as if she were floating, as if she were watching the entire scene play out from high above. It wasn't really her, it was a movie, a terrible, terrible movie, and one she didn't want to watch. She closed her eyes. She felt herself fall back, then heard the clang of the metal lockers as her back met them with the force of all her weight. Still, her eyes wouldn't open.

She was vaguely aware of the ID badge she wore on a lanyard around her neck when she felt the tug as someone grabbed it, as she felt it fall again against her chest.

"Ms. Simmons? Ms. Simmons, are you okay?"

At once, the pain in her shoulder, her wrist, her leg, and worst, her head, screamed. That pain demanded her attention, and she started to sink to the floor, her back sliding down the lockers and her knees buckling. An instant later, she bolted back up and her eyes flew open.

"He has a gun! Where is he?" Max's head spun in one direction, then the other, before her eyes focused on the corner. He'd be coming around the corner any second and this time, she was going to be ready. She leaned toward the person standing alongside her but didn't break her stare that remained trained on the hallway. She lowered her voice to a whisper.

"He's got to be close. You have to help me. We have to—"

"Ms. Simmons, it's okay. You're okay. My partner has the man in handcuffs. You're safe."

Slowly, and with jerky movements, Max turned toward the voice. Her brain was foggy, nothing wanted to register, but some part of her mind noted the uniform, the badge, the thickness under the woman's shirt that indicated a bullet-proof vest.

Max exhaled what felt like a year's worth of breath. She felt dizzy and could tell she was tipping but didn't seem to be able to do anything to stop herself. A strong pair of hands righted her before pushing her into a chair that could have materialized out of thin air for all Max knew. She had no sense of anything happening around her. She leaned back in the chair and felt her head rest against the lockers. She closed her eyes and tried to breathe.

"Did he hurt anyone?"

"Not that we're aware of."

"And you've got him? You're sure?"

"Yes, I'm sure."

Max nodded, then she did something she hadn't done since she was six years old.

She sobbed.

She'd been in the faculty conference room on several occasions, but that afternoon as Max sat in there with the crowd of police officers, school and district personnel, and a crisis counselor, she pulled at the collar of her shirt and wondered how she'd never realized just how small the room was.

From all around her, she heard bits and pieces of conversations which, when jumbled together, made about as much sense as what had happened earlier that day. Max had been interviewed by two different police officers, she'd talked one-on-one with Amanda as well as the district superintendent, she'd been checked over by a paramedic, and she'd politely, but firmly, refused the services of the crisis counselor. Still, no matter how many times she relayed her story, it seemed like a bad dream, like a man hadn't really broken into the school and waved a gun in her face.

She knew a few things. The gunman, Arthur Quinn, did have a son named Caden, Caden had attended Caston Middle School, but Caden was now a junior in high school. A high school in Albuquerque, New Mexico. The police were still piecing together Arthur's history but knew he'd been stripped of his visitation rights with his son after a series of mental health issues that had led to him becoming disoriented and, at times, violent. There were still a lot of questions as to how Arthur got into the school, why he thought Caden would be there, and at least in Max's mind, whether he would have used the gun when he couldn't find Caden. That question, she knew, would likely never be answered, but it was the one she couldn't get off her mind.

Max also knew it was thanks to a quick-thinking seventh-grade boy who'd missed the bus that morning that the office staff knew of the intruder in the building. The boy, after checking in at the office and getting a pass to his first-hour class, had just started down the math hallway when he'd spotted a man who looked out of place. According to what Max had heard, the boy watched Arthur Quinn for a minute as the man fiddled with something in his pocket. When the student saw a flash of something metallic, he'd hurried back to the office where, thankfully, Cynthia had taken him seriously and had begun the protocol for just such an instance.

Max had been in the school office since the police officer who'd first pulled her away from Arthur Quinn escorted her there—something Max didn't remember happening but she'd been assured she'd walked as opposed to being carried—so she hadn't been part of getting the nearly eight hundred students calmed and loaded either onto buses or into a parent's car to take them home. But that didn't mean she hadn't seen the parade of buses and cars in and out of the parking lot, that she hadn't watched parents pull their children into fierce hugs while fighting tears and panic. Now the school had returned to its eerie silence. For as much as she sometimes longed for that kind of quiet, a reprieve from the dull roar that seemed to follow middle schoolers like a shadow, all she wanted at that moment was to hear some of that roar, some sign that things would return to normal.

She knew there'd be no school the following day in order to get counselors in place and up to speed to help any students or staff who wanted to talk come Thursday. Not that she was expected to be in school on Thursday. Every person she'd spoken with had told her, at least once, that she should take as much time as she needed.

What she needed was to go home, but it didn't appear that would happen any time soon.

Max watched Amanda pace, and the district superintendent mercilessly twist his knuckles until they cracked. They were waiting for the chief of police to give them the word on whether to send staff home or to keep them longer for more questioning.

A glance out the conference room's small window gave Max a clear view of the news vans parked in the circular drive in front of the school, and of the reporters talking into microphones while their camera people turned and positioned them to get the best backdrop. So far, the press had not been allowed into the building, nor been granted any official interviews. Aside from the police chief giving a brief statement saying that the situation was under control, that no one had been hurt, and that there was no further threat to students or the public, Max didn't think the press had been given any other information aside from what they'd probably gathered from parents and students as they'd filed out of the building.

She'd already asked if it would be possible to keep her name from the reporters but no one had given her a direct answer. She took that to mean no, and that she'd have reporters hounding her for an interview which she had no intention of granting.

Max felt impossibly tired. She understood mental trauma did that, made you feel as if you hadn't slept in a week, but combined with her aches and pains from twice diving and tackling an armed intruder, and from being kicked several times by that intruder, her level of exhaustion was fast approaching the point where she knew she'd need to lie down or she'd fall down.

As if reading her mind, Amanda waved at Max and motioned to the hallway. Amanda held the door, then led the way to her office. The police chief followed them.

"Please sit down, Max," Amanda said as she dropped into the chair behind her desk. Resting her elbows on the desk, she leaned her head into her hands, then used her fingers to massage her forehead and temples.

Max sat, then wondered if she'd need help to get back up.

"Max, I hardly know what to say." Amanda put a hand over her mouth and smothered a sob.

Max watched Amanda swallow several times before attempting to speak again. Up to that point, Amanda had seemed in complete control. A bit robotic, now that Max thought about it, but their principal hadn't cracked, as far as Max knew. Until now.

Amanda took a deep breath. She looked broken, defeated, and impossibly sad.

"I can't exactly tell you I'm glad you did what you did because you put yourself in such incredible danger, but I'd be lying if I said I wasn't grateful. And impressed. You were so brave, and we owe you such a debt of gratitude, I don't know how we'll ever repay it."

"You don't—"

"We do, Max. We do," Amanda said. "I'd like to think that if in your position, I would have been able to do the same thing, but I honestly don't know. The whole thing has left us all so frightened, and so angry, it's hard to think straight. You were able to put your fear aside and risk your safety for the safety of all of us. The next few days, weeks, are going to be chaotic. We'll have students who are frightened, we'll have staff who are frightened, and that's completely understandable. We will, of course, be reviewing our security procedures, as clearly we were lacking."

Amanda paused, put her hand over her mouth, and looked toward the ceiling. It was a moment before she could speak again. "We'll be dealing with the media, with parents, with other school districts all wanting information, or advice, or assurance. So, as I said, it will be chaotic and it might take a while, but I will find a way to acknowledge what you did. It will not go unnoticed. I want you to know that."

"I'd rather it did," Max said.

Amanda smiled, the first smile Max had seen from anyone since it all happened. "And how did I know you'd say that?"

"I'd really rather try to keep my name out of all of this," Max said. "Is that a possibility?"

Amanda deferred to the police chief.

"I understand wanting to avoid the spotlight, but I'm afraid your name is already out there. Once one or two got wind of what happened, the news spread like wildfire. I can speak for my department, and I think for the school district, when I say we have not released your name as of now, but I've heard from some of my officers that they've already been asked by the media when they can expect to hear from Ms. Simmons."

Max groaned. Everything hurt more than it had a minute earlier.

"I'm due to speak to the media again in a few minutes. I won't give them your name, but it's only a matter of time until they track you down. If they haven't already. If you'd like, I'll have an officer escort you home as I'd expect you'll find at least a few reporters camped out in front of your place. We can make sure you're not harassed."

The full impact was setting in, and it was daunting. "It's going to be that bad?" Max asked. "I need a police escort?"

"Until they get what they want, it's likely you'll have reporters calling, approaching you as you enter or leave your house, the school, anywhere else you frequent. They have a way of learning your habits pretty quickly. I'm sorry. I can tell that's not what you wanted to hear."

"No, it's not." Max sighed. "But I'll deal with it. I can always say, 'No comment,' right?"

"You can."

"Do you need me any longer, or can I go? I'm really tired."

"You're free to go. I'll want to talk to you again, but you've given us everything we need for now. Thank you. Your account of what happened was very thorough. Not everyone can recall so many details. You were very helpful."

Max shrugged. She was certain she'd never be able to forget a second of what happened. What happened after was still foggy, but as far as every detail of every second she'd spent with Arthur Quinn, that was etched in her brain.

"I'm glad I could help," Max said.

"I second what Principal Chapman said. We all owe you a tremendous amount of gratitude. Not everyone could have or would have done what you did today. On behalf of the Caston Police Department, and all of Caston, thank you."

He reached out his hand. Max did the same but felt as though everyone was making too big a deal out of something she'd done without really thinking. She wanted to tell them that if she had to do it again, she didn't know if she could.

"Just one more question before you go, Ms. Simmons." The police chief paused and seemed to choose his words carefully. "When you were with him, when you stopped him, did you get the feeling that he would have used the gun? That he would have fired on students?"

Max lifted her hands in a helpless sort of gesture. "I wanted to ask you that same question, and I hoped you'd be able to answer it because I just can't decide what I think."

"We may have to live without ever knowing the answer." He tipped his head toward her. "Let me know if you want that escort getting home. I'll be in the conference room for a few minutes until I address the media, but any of my officers will assist you if I'm not available. Thank you again, Ms. Simmons. I'll be in touch."

He nodded to Amanda, then slipped back into the hallway, closing the door behind him.

Max looked at Amanda, unsure of what to do next. She didn't want to be hounded by reporters, but a police escort seemed like overkill. Maybe she could get in her car and then lose anyone who was following her. She didn't have to go home. She could drive as long as she wanted, check into a motel somewhere, and not think about any of it until the next day.

Even as she planned, she knew it wouldn't work. Not that she wouldn't be able to lose some reporters, but she knew she'd never be able to lock herself into a motel room and expect to have everything miraculously go away for the night. Being alone in a strange motel with nothing to distract her would be far worse than being at home with reporters camped out in front of the house.

She almost smiled when she thought of Fred's reaction to vans parked in front of his place. He just might be grouchy enough to scare them away.

"If you want to take the police up on their offer to see you home, I think it's a good idea. However, I should tell you I've had to nearly barricade the doors to keep Ellie and Nicole out of the office. Every time I've addressed the staff, they've cornered me demanding to see you. I never knew Ellie Hawthorne could be quite so pushy."

Max's lips twitched with the beginnings of a grin. "She's relentless when she wants something."

"That's for sure. We haven't let anyone inside the building except for law enforcement and district personnel, but I happen to know that Zeke Fahrner and Brady Mason are both waiting outside and have also asked about you. Zeke Fahrner is Ellie's fiancé?"

Max nodded.

"Huh. And Brady Mason. It seems like months ago that he spoke to the students. Anyway, Ellie has instructed me, more than once, to tell you that the four of them are ready to see that you get wherever it is you want to go without any trouble. Yesterday I would have laughed at the idea of Ellie Hawthorne being anyone's bodyguard, but not any longer. I'm starting to think that sweet southern charm is just a front. She's fierce. And Nicole has been quoting all sorts of laws and things about victims' rights. You have quite the support team, Max."

Max nodded, and the hated tears pricked at the backs of her eyes.

"There's also a highway patrolman outside helping with crowd control and traffic flow." Amanda picked up a notepad from her desk. "Marty Francis. He relayed a message to me to let you know he's here, ready to help in any way that he can."

Max ran her fingers through her short, sleek hair. She slapped her leg and tapped her foot. She did everything she could to keep the tears at bay, but she felt a drop run down her cheek.

"Is it okay if I let Nicole and Ellie in? You can have my office for as long as you need it."

"Please," Max said as she sniffled and swiped at her cheek.

"I know you're in good hands, but you call me if you need anything. Anything at all. Any time. And as I told you, take as much time as you need."

"Thank you."

Amanda leaned down and hugged Max, then wiped tears of her own before leaving Max alone in the office.

4

Max sat at the table in Zeke's magazine-worthy kitchen and sipped tea, heavy on the brandy. It had been like something out of a Hollywood thriller getting her out of school undetected. The staff was dismissed, so most of the reporters were distracted, but Max had been warned that her school photo had leaked. To avoid detection, Brady backed his truck up to the loading dock, Max threw on an old jacket and safety vest Kent, one of the custodians, gave her, then she grabbed a dolly and a couple of boxes and scooted them, and herself, into the back of Brady's truck and under the safety of the truck's topper. Brady drove a few blocks, then rescued Max from the back and tucked her into the passenger seat. He'd driven straight to Zeke's house where Zeke, Ellie, Nicole, and a houseful of dogs were waiting.

It had taken a good part of the first hour to assure Ellie and Nicole she was okay. Ellie had turned her every which way, had asked a series of ridiculous questions to, Ellie said, ensure Max was thinking clearly and wasn't concussed, and had hugged her more times than Max could count. Nicole had fretted and fawned as well but was more business-like in her manner. She wanted as many details as Max was willing to provide and offered advice on what Max could expect from a legal standpoint. Max hadn't considered the possibility of the intruder suing her. The thought seemed laughable, but Nicole cautioned it was a possibility. In all likelihood it wouldn't happen, and even if Arthur Quinn attempted a lawsuit, chances were good it would be dismissed as frivolous, but there was always a chance. Nicole had then outlined countless reasons Max was well within her rights to defend herself and everyone else in the building from an armed intruder.

Max chose to let most of it go in one ear and out the other, but she hadn't stopped Nicole. It seemed to do her friend good to look at the situation analytically and to separate some of the personal from it.

Some of the tension slipped away as Max sipped. Warmth spread from her belly to her limbs, and by the second cup, she was able to quit clenching every muscle in her body. Zeke was at the stove warming up soup and had the homemade rolls he'd pulled from the freezer in the oven baking. Ellie had been working on a salad, but Zeke had gently taken the knife from her hands and relieved her of her duties when she couldn't stop looking over her shoulder at Max.

Max reached her free hand down and stroked Bowie's head. Trained as a therapy dog, and making frequent rounds in the hospital with Zeke, Bowie seemed to sense that Max needed comfort. He'd been at her side since she'd fallen into a chair at the kitchen table.

Ellie's dog, Boomer, sulked from his spot in front of the sliding door leading to the back yard. Much to Boomer's obvious dismay, Ellie had ordered him to stay put. He'd come a long way from the rambunctious terror Max had first met months ago and was mostly well-behaved, but he looked plenty ticked off that Bowie was allowed next to Max while he was relegated to a rug. And that was to say nothing of the puppy scampering and tumbling and commanding everyone's attention. Luna, Nicole's puppy, was a goofy ball of fluff, and young enough at only ten weeks to get a free pass on any naughty behavior. Max swore if Boomer could talk, he'd have plenty to say about the injustice of it all.

"Are you doing okay, Max? Can I get you anything? More tea?"

Max checked the clock on the microwave. Six minutes since Ellie had last asked. A personal best.

"No, I'm fine."

"Maybe some ice for your wrist? I noticed you wince when you reached to pet Bowie."

"It's okay, El. I'm okay. I promise."

Brady poked his head into the kitchen. "The local news comes on in a few minutes. They're going to lead with a story about what happened today. Do you want to watch, Max?"

She'd been debating that but didn't have an answer.

"You don't have to," Ellie said. "We can keep everything off, tune out everything for the night if that's what you want."

"I don't know. I should probably watch so I know what to expect when I'm eventually cornered by a reporter. Or a parent. Or anyone who's going to want to know what happened in there. I can understand, I guess. If I was on the outside with questions, I'd want answers too."

"You're probably right. People are going to want to hear from you. It's only natural to want a first-hand account, but you need to know that you don't have to give one if you don't want to. There's nothing that says you're required to talk to the press. You talked to the police, to the school staff, you cooperated and did everything you could to help them understand. That's as far as any obligation you may have goes." Nicole spread her feet slightly and crossed her arms over her chest. She looked ready to take on anyone who considered arguing with her.

"I know, but it's probably going to be easier to talk with someone and just get it over with." Max shrugged. "We'll see. I'm not making any decisions tonight."

"Of course you're not," Ellie said, coming to stand alongside her and put an arm around her shoulders. "How about a blanket? Are you chilly?"

Max patted Ellie's hand. "I think we should go watch the news. Let's see what they have to say. Maybe they have more information on the sh—" Max hadn't been able to utter the phrase, 'the shooter' to that point, and found she still couldn't. She, better than anyone, knew how real it was, but saying the words gave it another level of validity. "On Quinn."

Max stood, trying unsuccessfully to mask her groan when her aching muscles screamed. "Let's watch."

They filed into Zeke's living room, a cozy space with comfy leather couches and chairs, dark wood end tables and a matching coffee table, and bookshelves filled to bursting. With a quick scan, Max spotted everything from medical texts to travel books to best sellers. The fireplace crackled, the scent of burning wood comforting Max's tired soul almost as much as that of the bread baking in the kitchen.

Max noted the fuzzy, fleece blankets artfully flung across the arms of the chairs and the backs of the couches, the throw pillows that added a pop of color, the lush green plants, and wondered if Zeke had a flair for interior design or if Ellie had added touches to the room. When Max sat and spotted a photography book on the coffee table titled *The Best of Oklahoma in Pictures*, she had her answer.

The wall-mounted TV was tuned to a local channel. They were barely seated when the news broadcast started with overhead shots of

Caston Middle School showing crowds of students filing out of the building and rushing into the arms of frantic parents. Max did her best to brace herself for what was to come.

"A terrifying scene today at Caston Middle School, where an armed intruder entered the building just after the start of the school day. No injuries were reported, and once the police had the situation under control, they were quick to issue a statement saying there was no additional threat to the public. The identity of the shooter has not yet been released, but indications are it was a man, and perhaps a parent of a former student. At this time, no information has been provided as to how the man was able to enter the building undetected.

"One thing we do know is that if it were not for the quick thinking and bravery of a teacher at CMS, the outcome may have been very different."

The image changed, and Max's school picture filled the screen. She groaned. Any hope she'd been holding onto that she'd somehow manage to fly under the radar disappeared as fast as the newscaster's expression changed to one of glee at being able to relay the juicy details.

"According to reports from some students and staff leaving the school following this morning's incident, Maxine Simmons, a math teacher new to the school and to the district just this year, single-handedly subdued the intruder until law enforcement arrived on the scene. Neither school officials nor Chief of Police Schroder has provided details on what exactly happened, but by all indications, Ms. Simmons' selfless act ensured the safety of the hundreds of students and staff inside the building."

Max shifted in her seat, hating every word she heard about herself. *"Not much is known about Ms. Simmons."* She'd like nothing better than to keep it that way. *"Students seem in agreement that Ms. Simmons is a popular teacher at the school."* Huh. That was news to her.

"The parent of one of Ms. Simmons' students had the following to say."

A shot of a reporter standing just out of the school parking lot, the school providing a backdrop for the interview, came on the screen. The reporter held a microphone in front of a woman dressed in workout clothes and with a long blonde ponytail pulled through a baseball cap.

"My son is in Ms. Simmons' class, so I met her at conferences earlier this year. I can see her doing something like this. She seems like the type who wouldn't back down from a situation, no matter how frightening. My son tells me often that Ms. Simmons is one of those teachers who doesn't let them get away with anything. She always knows what's going on in her classroom, you know? I'm so thankful she was in the right place at the right time today. Who

knows how many lives she saved?"

At those words, the woman who'd looked thrilled at the idea of being interviewed seemed to consider what her words meant. The color drained from her face and Max saw her begin to tremble before the camera zoomed in on the reporter, taking the woman out of the shot.

Max had heard enough. The reports, the pictures, the interviews...it was as if she were listening to reports of something that happened on the other side of the world. Even though she'd been in the middle of it, hearing about the events of that morning on the news made the situation surreal.

She'd always hated that word. Surreal. It seemed everyone who was asked about something that happened to them fell back on that word. Just a couple of weeks ago, Tammy, one of the science teachers, had said that the surprise birthday party her husband threw for her was 'surreal.' The teen working at the grocery store check-out had told Max it was 'surreal' Max was buying eggs because just a minute ago, a customer had dropped a carton of eggs and they'd broken on the check-out conveyor belt.

Max often guessed people didn't really know what the word meant, just liked the sound of it. The fact that it had become something of a buzzword drove her crazy. Still, it was the only way she could describe the experience of watching people talk about her on the news. People she'd never met, people who had no idea what actually happened inside the school, people who wanted their ten minutes of fame.

They could have it. And hers.

"I think I've seen enough," Max said. "There's no new information, nothing that I didn't already hear from the police. I think I'll wait in the kitchen."

"We'll turn it off," Ellie said, jumping to her feet. "Zeke, we should turn it off."

"No, you go ahead and watch. El, you and Nic are just as much a part of this as I am. If I weren't here with you now, you'd be watching. I'll be in the other room. You can tell me if there's anything new."

"You're sure?" Nicole asked.

"I'm sure."

Zeke followed Max into the kitchen.

"Zeke, I'm okay."

"My rolls won't be if I don't keep an eye on them."

Max doubted attending to the rolls was critical, but let it slide. While he checked the rolls, stirred the soup, and busied himself at the stove, she wandered around his kitchen, reading the spines of the dozens of cookbooks that filled three shelves, and checking out the cabinets that were definitely custom-made to fit the kitchen. She couldn't claim to know much about cabinetmaking, or woodworking in general, but she knew quality, and she sensed the care that had gone into designing and finishing the kitchen that looked like it should be splayed across the pages of a glossy magazine.

Her phone's familiar ringtone sounded from across the room. Nicole had insisted Max set her phone aside, guessing it would be only a matter of time until her number leaked and the phone started ringing with interview requests. Since Zeke was closer, or maybe because he'd been instructed to do so, he picked it up before Max could decide whether she wanted to check it.

"Caller ID says Fred Jenkins," Zeke reported. "Want me to answer or let it go?"

"I'll take it. Fred's my landlord."

Zeke handed Max the phone

"Hey, Fred."

Max heard a sigh that sounded a lot like relief before Fred spoke.

"Max. I just heard your name on TV. Is all that stuff true?"

"Yeah, it is."

"Well, dang. Are you all right?"

"I'm okay."

"There's quite a commotion in front of the house. News trucks, people all over the place. They're ringing my doorbell, asking for you."

Max dropped her head into her hand. "Sorry. I hoped that wouldn't happen."

"Don't apologize. You didn't send them to my door."

"No, but I don't like that they're bothering you."

"Hah! It takes more than a few pesky reporters to bother me. Are you coming home soon?"

"Um, I'm not sure. My friends think I should stay overnight." Zeke was watching her. He nodded at her last statement.

"Probably a good idea. I think I'll see about getting rid of the crowd."

"How are you going to do that?"

"I have my ways," Fred said, and Max could picture his crooked grin. "Do you need anything?"

"No, but thanks."

"You let me know, you hear?"

"I will. Thank you."

"Take care of yourself."

Before Max could respond, Fred disconnected, and before she could set down her phone, it buzzed with a text. Only two words, but Skeeter was a man of few words.

'*You okay?*'

I'm okay. Thanks for checking on me, Max typed back. The response took a while, and Max could all but hear Skeeter cursing his stubby fingers as he struggled with texting.

'*Always. Call when you're ready.*'

I will, Max answered, then set down her phone. She wondered if she'd be hearing from her dad. Probably, but probably not for a while. She knew he was on the road, or maybe already working, but either way, he wouldn't be checking news out of Wisconsin anytime soon. Unless the story made national news, or unless someone got in touch with him, it could be days before he heard anything.

That was okay, Max decided. Theirs was a relationship that worked better when they talked shop, not personal things. Her dad would be concerned, of course, and he'd want to be sure she was safe, but once that was out of the way, he'd be eager to change the subject. That was just how it worked between them, and the way it had worked for twenty years.

Zeke waited until Max set down her phone. "People who saw the news?"

"Yeah, my landlord, and then a text from an old friend."

"Probably more of that coming. Did you talk to family before the news aired?"

It hadn't even crossed her mind, not that there was really anyone to contact.

"No, but it's just my dad and my grandma. My dad is on the road, I think, so it's unlikely he'll hear anything. My grandma is in a care facility in Indiana. We're not close, and she's not well. Even if she somehow heard a report, she probably wouldn't put two and two together."

Max could tell Zeke wanted to ask questions. It was normal. People with family, especially those with stable families, were always curious about those who came from something different. Even though Zeke had more than his share of issues with his brother, he had family, and he'd come from a safe, loving home. Now, with a career in medicine, the desire to help and to heal was woven into his being.

But Zeke didn't ask, only nodded, then pointed toward the rolls he'd just pulled from the oven. "Get 'em while they're hot."

Max hadn't eaten since breakfast. There'd been food in the conference room at school—a couple of the local restaurants had sent over pizzas and sandwiches—but food had been the last thing Max had wanted. Now, the smells had her stomach rumbling.

"Smells good. I guess I could eat."

"It'll do you good. Chicken noodle or tortilla soup?"

"Chicken noodle. Is it homemade?"

Zeke gave her a withering look. "You think I'd serve you soup from a can?"

"Soup from a can is good."

Zeke shushed her, then looked around his kitchen as if she'd somehow offended the room. "You can't say such things out loud."

Max snorted. "Sorry, chef. Should've known better."

"You're forgiven." Zeke lifted a steaming bowl and pointed Max back to the table. "You sit. I'll get what you need."

"I can help."

"Of course you can, but I don't want to risk the Wrath of Eleanore. Please sit."

"Fine." Max looked toward the living room. "Do you think they're still talking about it on the news?"

"It's a big story, this is a small-town news market, my guess is yes."

"How big do you think?"

"What do you mean?"

"I mean, you don't think it will make national news, do you?"

Zeke took the chair next to her. "I think you need to be prepared for the possibility. Probability. School shootings, and attempted school shootings, are news. Sad, horrifying news, but news all the same. When it hits a small, otherwise safe community, I think that makes it even more so. My guess is the fact that there were no casualties means the story won't make national headlines for long, but the community here has been shaken. It's going to be news for quite some time."

"I was afraid you were going to say that."

"Eat. Try to forget about it, at least for a while. I'm going to get the rest in here to join you."

Max did as she was told. Her first taste of Zeke's chicken noodle soup had her questioning how she'd ever thought the stuff in the can was good. Zeke's soup, with its thick, hearty noodles, generous chunks of shredded chicken, tender vegetables, and flavors she could only imagine came from a variety of spices and hours of simmering, had her blowing on her spoon, wanting to hurry the next spoonful into her mouth.

"You didn't miss much," Ellie said when she joined Max. "A lot of rehashing what they'd already said, a lot of speculation, and a lot of pictures of worried parents."

"Do you think parents are going to be reluctant to let their kids come back to school?"

"We were talking about that. This is going to come out wrong, I'm sure of it, but it's a bit like the dog day care mixing up Boomer and Bowie."

Max raised her eyebrows at Ellie.

"See, it sounds all wrong. I don't mean it's on the same scale as what happened today, but when it came time to send Boomer and Bowie back to Top Dog, Zeke and I agreed the staff would be extra careful and vigilant because of what happened. What I'm trying to get at is hopefully parents realize that the staff at school will be extra vigilant and their children will be safer than ever. Hopefully if they look at it that way, it will give them a small sense of comfort."

"I don't know, it's still going to be frightening, don't you think? For everyone?"

"Absolutely. I don't mean to imply it won't be. I guess I'm just hopeful we, as the staff at the school, will be able to reassure them their kids will be safe."

"Do you feel that way? Really? That you'll be safe?" Max asked.

Ellie put down her spoon. More like dropped it as it clattered in her bowl.

"It's what I'm trying to tell myself. It's not easy, but I know I have to be brave and calm or the kids never will be."

Nicole sat down. "Never will be what?"

"Oh, I'm trying to convince Max I'm not worried about going back to school. Mostly, I'm trying to convince myself."

"Do you think one day off is long enough?" Nicole asked. "I can't decide if it's better to take more time, to let things hopefully calm down some, to get some answers to reassure everyone, or if more time will be more harmful. Would more time send a message to the kids that we're worried and afraid about going back, and will that make them more worried than they already are?"

Max shook her head. "I have no idea. I don't know that there are a lot of rules when something like this happens. It's probably different depending on the circumstances. And don't ask me what sort of circumstances, and how they're interpreted, because I certainly don't know. The only thing I do know is that I'm glad it's not my decision."

"It could change," Brady said when he joined them. "I flipped channels for a minute and saw a report that claimed the return date is still up in the air."

"Really? I suppose we'll have some communication either from Amanda or the district tomorrow," Nicole said. "It's a tough call."

They sat in silence, looking at one another as if the answer was there, somewhere, and they just had to find it.

"What about tonight?" Ellie finally asked. "You'll stay here, right?"

Max sighed. "I planned on persuading you to take me home, but my landlord called a few minutes ago and told me there are reporters camped out in front of the house. So..."

"Good, then it's decided," Ellie said, her breath whooshing out. "I was afraid I'd have to fight you on it."

"Yesterday I would have laughed at that, but Amanda told me you," Max moved her gaze to Nicole, "and you, were pretty fierce in your demands earlier today. Thanks for that, and yeah, I guess I'll stay. Fred, my landlord, sounded kind of excited about the idea of chasing reporters away from the house, but I don't know if he'll be as successful as he hopes."

"Hey, everyone come in here for a minute," Zeke called from the living room.

"Zeke, we should give Max a break from the news," Ellie argued.

"I think she'll like this."

They gave each other curious looks but followed Zeke's voice to the living room. He held the remote in his hand, but the TV still played.

"I came in here to turn this off and to turn on some music, but they hinted at another angle to the story after this commercial."

"Zeke..." Ellie's protests grew more vocal.

"Just hold tight." Zeke put his arm around Ellie.

"But—"

"Trust me."

Ellie smiled up at him. "Always."

Max took a moment to roll her eyes before directing them back to the television. Zeke had her curious.

Once the commercial ended, the first thing Max noticed was the radiant smile on the newscaster's face and the gleam in her eye. Not the look Max would have chosen if she were on TV discussing a school shooting scare.

"While we were on-scene today at Caston Middle School, we were treated to a surprise. Just a couple of weeks ago, TV5 News reported exclusively that famous, and famously private, author B.L. Mason wowed the students at Caston Middle School with a surprise appearance at their assembly leading into spring break. Mr. Mason, the author of the wildly popular Dragonthea book series, had kept his identity under wraps until that appearance at CMS.

"Today, Mr. Mason was again spotted at the school, and while it appears he was trying his best to go unnoticed, our eagle-eyed reporter on the scene, Melinda Rivers, spotted him in the crowd."

The camera zoomed in on Brady. He wore a bulky jacket, a stocking cap pulled down to his eyes, and dark sunglasses.

Nicole chuckled. "Nice look, Brady."

Brady just grumbled in reply.

"While many members of the public gathered at the school as the terrifying and shocking events unfolded, we know that officers were trying to keep the crowd to only those with a connection to the school. We know that Mr. Mason has a niece who attends CMS, but it is unknown if he was there solely to check on her well-being or if he has other ties to the school. We send our best wishes to Mr. Mason, to his family, and, of course, to all those affected by today's tragic events."

"Hey, Mr. Mason," Max said. "I have an idea. Why don't you hold a press conference or something equally grand? Might take some of the heat off me."

"Oh, well, I...I suppose..." Brady stammered. He looked wildly from Max to Nicole and around the room. "I could..."

"Geez, relax!" Max said, slightly afraid Brady was ready to pass out. "I was only kidding."

"If you think it would help, I mean, if you're worried, I'll do whatever you need, Max. I have to talk to my agent, but I'm sure I could do something."

All around the room, laughter bubbled. After a day full of horrors the likes of which Max never dreamed she'd face, watching Brady panic and try to figure a way out of a public appearance seemed hysterical.

Max joined in. It felt good to laugh.

5

"You're sure you can drive a stick?" Max demanded. She chewed on the side of her thumb while she came up with a dozen reasons why handing over Stevie Ray's keys to Brady was a horrible idea.

"Of course, I can drive a stick."

"This isn't just any car, you know. It's a '69 Mustang with a V-8. It can be a little temperamental, but it packs a punch. You need to ease the engine into waking up. Stevie Ray and I sometimes disagree on whether it's time to rise and shine. He needs a gentle touch, not someone gunning the engine like a stupid teenager trying to drag race in his mom's car. You got that?"

Brady saluted. "Got it."

"This is no joke, Brady. I've put my blood, sweat, and tears into that car. Literally. I've let no one except the guy who helped me restore it behind the wheel. You get the car, you drive straight to your apartment, and as long as you're reasonably sure you weren't followed, you park and we swap places."

"We've been over it at least ten times, Max. I'm up for the challenge."

"Why do I get the feeling you're not taking this as seriously as you should be?"

"Sorry. I am taking it seriously. All of it. Driving your car—something I will enjoy only the appropriate amount—and keeping you away from the press. It will work." He winked at her. "Be right back. I'm going to check on the dogs."

Max hoped he was right. After spending the night at Zeke's, she was itching to get away. Not that she didn't appreciate her friends' efforts, she did, but she needed to work things out on her own and the best way she knew to do that was behind the wheel. If everything went according to plan and she was able to get out of Caston undetected, she had every confidence Stevie Ray would come through and begin to fix all that was wrong.

They'd hatched the plan sometime around midnight when they'd all still been wide awake, but exhausted and unable, or unwilling, to close their eyes and go to sleep. For her part, Max knew it was a fear of what awaited her in the form of nightmares. She figured it was the same for the others.

Brady and Nicole would drive to school, pick up Max's Honda she'd left there, and head back to Max's place with Nicole driving Max's car. The plan was Nicole would park the car in the street and if there were reporters waiting, she would distract them by giving a statement or answering their questions. While she did that, Brady would enter the garage from the back through the door Fred would open for him after making sure he was seen entering the garage. Brady would then leave in Stevie Ray, the hope being that anyone not already occupied with Nicole's interview wouldn't pay much attention to what they'd assume was Fred leaving his house. Brady would then meet Max, who'd be driving Brady's truck, a couple of blocks away.

Based on her conversation with Fred earlier that morning, Max figured the news people would be more than happy to see him leave. His gleeful reports on what he'd done to discourage them from camping out in front of his house had included everything from using the snowblower to blast the remaining snow piled at the end of his driveway directly at the news vans to running his hoses to the edge of the yard then hooking up his sprinklers and turning them on full blast.

Fred had also told Max he'd, with the assistance of a bullhorn he for some reason owned, informed the reporters that he lived alone, he had for sixteen years, and unless they were there to hear about his years working as an accountant, they should move along. And he'd actually giggled while telling her he'd started reading the accounting code of ethics through that same bullhorn.

At the time of her phone call with Fred, there were no reporters to be seen, but Max knew that was likely to change as they became more desperate for a comment from her.

"We just got an email from Amanda," Ellie said when she joined Max in the kitchen.

"What does it say? Anything new?"

"No new information on what happened, and she says they're

weighing when to reopen the school. A decision will come late morning or early afternoon."

"Then it might not be tomorrow." Max tried to figure out how she felt about that.

"You must have read the email from Amanda," Nicole said as she walked into the kitchen looking at her phone. "What do you think?"

Max shrugged. "Thankfully no one was injured. If that had been the case, we'd be looking at an entirely different situation. The way it is, maybe the sooner we go back, the better."

Ellie looked torn. "If we go back tomorrow, there may be families who choose to keep their kids out longer. That needs to be okay. They need to know they can do that. But for those who are ready, maybe tomorrow is best. I don't know."

"I don't think anyone knows," Nicole said.

"Amanda is supposed to call me this morning," Max said. "Maybe she'll have more information."

A night with her friends had helped, Max thought as she looked around the kitchen at those who had put their own lives on hold to try to help her, but it didn't solve the bigger problems. They had to go back to school, whether it be tomorrow or a week from tomorrow, and walk the hallways, and sit in the classroom where a man with a gun had threatened their safety. They had to trust they'd be safe in a place where someone had entered, undetected, with a gun. They had to try to get back to normal when everything they'd considered normal had changed.

It wouldn't be easy.

Max looked at Nicole and Ellie, and their frowns told her they were thinking along the same lines. They needed a change of subject.

"Did Zeke get out of here on time this morning?" Max asked.

Eventually, he'd gone up to bed to try to sleep and Brady had gone home. She, Ellie, and Nicole had spent a restless few hours in Zeke's living room, alternately dozing and waking, talking when they noted movement from the others. No one had gotten much sleep, but Zeke had a full day at the hospital ahead of him.

"He did. He called a few minutes ago to tell me he was there. He said he did his best to be quiet as he snuck out this morning, but I can't believe I didn't hear him."

"I guess we were all tired enough that we finally fell asleep," Nicole said. "But I'm still exhausted. How in the world is he going to work today?"

"He's used to functioning on little sleep. Comes with the territory, he tells me." Ellie yawned. "I guess that's one of the many reasons I'm not a doctor."

"Everyone ready to go?" Brady asked as he popped back in from the back yard. He rubbed his hands together like they were all conspirators in some elaborate plot. His enthusiasm had Max again worried for Stevie Ray.

"Are you sure you don't want to stay here?" Ellie asked. "Zeke told me again when he called that we're all welcome to stay as long as we want. We could cook something, we could play a game, we could do whatever you want, Max. Aren't you tired? Don't you think you'd rather stay here?"

"Thanks, El, and tell Zeke thanks, but I need to get away. Not from all of you," Max added when she saw Ellie's stricken look, "just away. I need to clear my head."

"Of course, but promise us that if you need us, you'll call. Or come over. Or let us know what we can do to help," Ellie said.

"Promise," Max said and to seal the deal, she drew a cross over her heart.

Forty minutes later, Max blew out a breath with the force of a hurricane. Breath she felt like she'd been holding for the past twenty-four hours.

Their plan, which now seemed like overkill, had gone off without a hitch, and Max was cruising out of Caston behind the wheel of her beloved car. The temperature had been dropping with each day, making the forecasted snow look more and more likely. Max didn't care if she froze. She opened the windows and sucked in gulps of the chilly air.

She wondered how she'd never before realized how good it felt just to breathe. One deep breath after another, tension escaping with each exhale, she knew without a doubt that for her, it was better than any medication, or any expensive therapy.

The more miles she put behind her, the better she felt. When she passed the gas station where she'd run into Marty and met Tank, she wondered if she'd cross paths with Marty again that morning. She hated the fact that her thoughts immediately went to what she could do to avoid him and thereby avoid any talk about the incident at school. She knew it was only postponing the inevitable, but to her, postponing sounded like a good option.

Max drove and tried not to think. She mostly succeeded until she needed every brain cell to fire on high.

She'd never had a car die on her in the middle of a highway. With no warning thunks or screeches, no high temperature or low fuel indicator light flashing, Max was taken by surprise when the engine suddenly quit and she found herself coasting. Trying to keep her cool, she turned the key in the ignition, then breathed a tentative sigh of relief when the engine roared back to life.

Still, it was unnerving.

"What's up, Stevie Ray? That's not like you."

Not wanting to get any farther from Caston, Max took the next opportunity to turn around. On the return trip, she hardly noticed the hawk that circled and dived just a few yards in front of her. She paid no attention to the young woman whose horse kicked up clods of mud as the woman coaxed the animal into a run to race the passing Mustang. She didn't so much as slow to get a better look at the 1950s Ford Pickup with a for sale sign parked in front of a sprawling, tidy farm dotted with pristine, white barns and a new silo. Instead, she looked, listened, smelled, and sensed everything happening inside the car for any indication of what might be wrong with the engine.

When the car died a second time, she held her breath. When it died a third time, she cursed and tried to remember the name of the mechanic Tank mentioned.

Not that she'd let him near Stevie Ray, but as she got closer to Caston, she planned out how she'd talk him into letting her use his shop and his tools to fix the car herself. He wouldn't want to, but after she got a read on him, she'd decide what track to take. If he was a friend of Tank's, he was probably around the same age. Max had a few names she could drop, people she'd met and even worked with over the years, that if he was truly as good a mechanic as Tank had made him out to be, might give her a leg up with him. If the place looked run-down, not especially busy, she could try offering him enough money to make it worth his while. If he was a fan of classic cars, especially classic Mustangs, she could, she supposed, offer to let him watch, even help. Though that would be a last resort.

But what was his name? It was something short, one syllable, she thought, like Tank. She ran through names, saying them out loud to see if anything rang a bell.

"Jake, Mike, Frank, Scott." She shook her head. They weren't right. It was something less common, she thought. She tried her trick of focusing on one letter at a time. "A," she mumbled and waited for inspiration. "B...C..." She got to G before something brought her back to B.

"B, b, b...Buck?" She turned it over in her head. "Buck. Beck?"

It sounded right when she said it, but she wasn't certain. Since she was just about to Caston, she pulled over but kept the engine running. Grabbing her phone, she did a quick search for auto repair shops and included 'Beck' in her search.

"Bingo," she said with a grin when the first result was Beck's Auto. The map told her she was only a few miles away. Relieved, she set off, practicing her pitch while she drove.

It looked clean. That was a plus. Though working on cars was a dirty business, Max had always felt that didn't mean the shop needed to be dirty. The brick building she looked at now had a waiting area with clean windows, a few signs advertising popular tire brands, and some of those tires stacked neatly along one wall. The parking lot, which was smooth blacktop, held several waiting cars. Max let her eyes roam over them. Mostly domestic, but also an Audi and a BMW. When she inched her car into a parking spot, she got a glimpse inside an open garage door and found an organized shop.

So far, so good.

She heard voices when she got out of the car, all coming from inside the shop. Skipping the waiting area, Max took a few steps inside the open garage door. She wouldn't go far inside, because she knew she'd hate it if someone did that to her, but she wanted to get a look before anyone knew she was looking.

A closer examination confirmed what she'd guessed from her glimpse. Neat, organized, relatively clean. Music played, and the blues rock sounded a lot like the cassettes that filled Stevie Ray's glove box. Another plus.

"Can I help you?"

Max jumped and hated herself for it. She didn't like being caught off guard, and more, she didn't want to appear out of her element inside the garage. She ordered herself to answer the man, who looked at her with the beginnings of a smirk, in a calm, confident voice.

"Yes. I'm looking for Beck."

He pulled a rag from his back pocket and wiped his hands. "I'm Beck. What can I do for you?"

All the calm and confidence went out the window. Max knew her jaw dropped, but she couldn't seem to do anything about it.

He had to be lying to her. He wasn't old, or limping, or round in the middle. He was none of the things Tank was, so none of the things she'd expected. Instead, he was tall, a few inches over six feet, and he was trim, but solid shoulders and muscled arms stretched the sleeves of his T-shirt. Where Tank had been mostly bald except for the buzzed grey that ringed his head, this man had thick, wavy dark hair, long enough, Max guessed, to pull back in a short tail if he chose to do so. His skin looked tanned, as if he'd recently spent time somewhere other than Caston. When Max didn't answer and the man cocked his head slightly, offering her a questioning smile, Max was nearly undone by the cleft that deepened in his chin.

"Uh, you're Beck?"

"I am. How can I help you?" He studied her as if trying to place her. It was unsettling.

"Oh." She took a breath and tried to gather her wits. Nothing she'd rehearsed on the drive seemed like it was going to work with the man standing in front of her. She had to adapt on the fly. "Nice place you've got here."

"Thanks. I like it."

"How long have you been in business?"

"I've had this place for about three years."

"And before that? How long have you been working on cars?"

"Are you interviewing me for a job I don't remember applying for?"

"No, sorry, no. Just curious."

Beck considered, but then, apparently deciding there was no harm in answering Max's questions, said, "Cars, in one way or another, are sort of a family thing."

That Max could relate to.

"What kind of cars?"

"Are you a reporter or something?"

Max flinched at the words. "No. Just curious."

"Do you need some work done? If not, I have to wonder what this is all about."

He was beginning to look more annoyed than curious. Max wanted to keep things friendly, but she still needed some information.

"My car's outside. It died on me a few times while I was driving today. It's a '69 Mustang." She saw his eyebrow inch up, and she noticed the other two men in the shop who'd been under the hood of a late-model Ford suddenly quiet and look in Max's direction. "First time it's happened. It was tuned up a week ago. Nothing worrisome at that time. Thoughts?"

Beck glanced out the open garage door, but Max knew he wouldn't catch a glimpse of the car from his angle. When he turned back to her, he looked curious.

"Points or electric ignition?"

He asked it with a barely concealed smirk, clearly expecting a blank look in response, but Max ignored the smirk and concentrated on the question. It's where she would have started.

"Electric. Converted when it was restored."

"That'd be where I'd start. You don't, by chance, have a dozen keychains hanging off the ignition, do you?"

The words on the tip of her tongue would likely have Beck throwing her out, so she bit them back. "No, I don't."

"Glad to hear it. I could take a look at it for you. Could probably get to it tomorrow."

That wouldn't do, but she knew she needed to tread carefully. "I don't know about leaving the car here, and I'm not sure how I'd get it back tomorrow. I have to work…"

The words caught in her throat when a sense of dread permeated every cell of her body. The sheer force of that dread shocked Max. She reached for something to hold, something to ground her, but her hand caught only air. Worried she was going to embarrass herself by passing out, she turned to leave.

"Hey! Hey, hold on."

She heard Beck, but her only thought was to get out as fast as she could. When she stumbled, a hand was there to steady her.

"Are you okay?"

"Fine. I need to go."

"I think you might need to sit." Beck whistled. "Jake. Bring me a chair and a water, will you?"

Max wanted to argue and wanted to pull free, but she didn't trust her legs to hold her.

"Everything okay, Beck?"

"I think so."

Max felt herself being guided into a chair. It was eerily similar to what happened in the school hallway just a little over twenty-four hours ago. Against her will, she shuddered as she sat.

"Why don't you finish up with the Ford, Jake?"

"Yeah?"

"Yeah. I've got this."

Beck pushed a water bottle into Max's hand. Careful not to meet his eyes, she took a grateful sip. Her gratitude increased when he didn't press her for an explanation. After a few more sips and a few deep breaths, Max pushed to her feet.

"Sorry about that. I'll get out of your way. Thanks for the water." She lifted the bottle in a toast but still didn't look Beck in the eye.

She took a half dozen steps before Beck spoke.

"You can't think I'm going to let you get behind the wheel, can you?"

She stopped, keeping her back to him. "I think it's none of your business."

"You almost collapsed. If you're not feeling well I can call someone, but I'm not letting you drive."

Now she did turn. "You're not letting me. Huh. And how do you suppose you're going to stop me?"

She may hate the smirk on Beck's face, may despise the way he sized her up, but she had to admit, the anger that surged inside her pushed away most of whatever it was that had brought her to her knees a few minutes earlier.

"Played some football in high school, then in college. I'm pretty good at open-field tackling."

Max snorted. "Ran some track in high school. I'm pretty good at speed."

Beck laughed. "As much as I'd like to see who'd come out on top, I'd feel better if you'd come to my office. Sit down for a while. Make sure you're okay to drive."

"I know when I'm okay to drive." She softened just a little. "But thanks."

"Then how about you let me take a look at that Mustang?"

It was a stall tactic, she knew that, but she also knew that however much her ego wanted her to deny it, it wouldn't be smart to get behind the wheel while she was still unsteady.

"I thought you couldn't get to it until tomorrow."

"That doesn't mean I can't look now."

"Fine." Max turned and headed outside. Careful to keep her back to Beck, she sucked in gulps of fresh, cold air. With each step, she regained some composure. By the time she reached her car, she felt almost like herself.

From behind her, Max heard a low whistle.

"It's a beauty. How'd you get your hands on it?" Beck's words came slowly as he circled the car, tipped his head, and studied it.

It was a long story, the chapters not all happy, but Max gave Beck the condensed version.

"A friend heard about it. One of those stories where a car is tucked away in a barn for years. The guy who inherited the farm inherited the car with it. He wasn't particularly interested in the car, and at the end of the day, we both left happy."

"How much work did it need?"

"A lot. It took the better part of a year to get both the engine and the body into shape. A lot of blood, sweat, and tears in there, but it was worth it, I think." Max ran her hand over the hood.

"You did the work?"

Max was used to the question. Most times, it was posed with a note of incredulity, sometimes downright scorn, occasionally confusion. Rarely, though, did she detect the trace of admiration she heard from Beck.

"I did. I had help at times, but it's my car, so it was my responsibility."

"Seems like I would have spotted it around town if you've had it for a few years."

"I just brought it to Caston, um, a few days ago." She had to pause. Had it really been only a few days? It seemed like weeks.

"Ah. And did you just bring yourself to Caston a few days ago too?"

"Last fall."

"Then that explains why I don't recognize either one of you. Although, you look kind of familiar. Maybe we've run into each other?"

"No, I don't think so. The only reason I know you're here is because I stopped for gas the other day and met Tank. He mentioned you, so when Stevie Ray started acting up I thought I'd check you, I mean your place, out."

"You met Tank? Let me guess. He gave you the weather forecast based on how his knee felt, he was itching to get a look under the hood, but could hardly bring himself to ask, and assuming you told him you did the engine overhaul, he didn't even try to hide his skepticism."

"That pretty much sums it up. After he did finally work his way around to asking for a look under the hood, we spent over half an hour talking engines."

Beck smiled. "Tank's a good guy once you get past his outer shell.

He doesn't often let anyone crack that shell, but I imagine this was a good icebreaker." Beck took his turn running his hand over the car. "Want to pop the hood?"

Max did, then stuck her hands in her pockets and forced herself to stand back and watch. She'd learn a lot in just a few minutes, and it would give her an idea of what sort of mechanic Beck was. She hoped it would also give her an idea of what it was going to take to persuade him to let her do the work herself in his garage.

Beck checked all the likeliest, and easiest, problem areas first. Max could have told him none was the culprit, but she appreciated the order in which he ticked off possibilities. He climbed behind the wheel and after allowing himself a minute to settle into the seat and grasp the steering wheel, another thing Max could appreciate and something that made her grin, he played around with the ignition.

Max waited, mentally composing the questions she'd ask if she were in Beck's spot, while he climbed back out of the car and again stuck his head under the hood.

When he stood, wiped his hands, and started asking questions, she answered them as she mentally nodded her approval.

"I'll need to take a closer look. I can squeeze it in tomorrow. Are you comfortable driving it home, or do you want to leave it here overnight?"

"I'll drive home, but I'm not sure about tomorrow." The uneasiness was back, but Max fought it. "I'm not sure about my schedule, or about getting someone to drive out here with me. I'll have to let you know."

"I'll give you my card. Just give me a call." Beck closed the hood, then indicated with a nod of his head that Max should follow him back inside, but she held her ground.

"You know, all I need is a spot in your garage and the use of a few of your tools. I'm sure I can figure out what's wrong, then you won't have to bother with it."

Beck looked at her as if she'd sprouted a tail. "You're not serious."

"Of course, I'm serious. I know what I'm doing."

He shook his head, not bothering to conceal the fact he found the whole thing ridiculous. "No can do, um…what's your name?"

"Max."

"No can do, Max. My garage, my tools. That means I do the work."

Beck turned and started walking. Behind his back, Max threw up her arms but followed him.

"I know my way around a car. I'm sure it won't take long. Once I figure out what's wrong, assuming I need parts, I'll move the car out of your way. It'll be like I'm not there. Like the car's not there."

He yanked open the door to his office with more force than Max thought necessary. She stole a quick look at the cramped space. A file cabinet, a smudged laptop open and with NASCAR wallpaper, a few NASCAR posters, a race schedule.

A fan. That may work in her favor.

"I'm running a business here, you know. There are insurance considerations. I have employees I interviewed, trained, and observed before letting them loose." He waved a hand toward the work area. "There's limited space that I like to reserve for actual paying customers. Sorry, but it's still no." He held out a card. "Call me when you want me to look at it. If you want me to look at it."

He sat and rifled through some grease-stained papers on his desk, clearly indicating he'd decided the conversation was over. Max wasn't ready to give up.

"I know what I'm doing. I've been around cars my entire life, and I've worked on them for almost that long. I've spent time under the hood of a car in more garages and driveways than I can count, from one side of the country to the other. I never expected to do this for free. If you let me use the space, the tools, of course I'll pay you. I hope it won't take long to figure out what's wrong, but if it turns out to be a bigger job than expected, we'll figure out where we go from there. We can make it work."

"What's with all the 'we's' you're throwing around? When did you decide this became some sort of partnership?"

"You want references? You want assurance that I'm not going to hurt myself, or damage your stuff? Rob you blind, or burn the place down? I can give you names. As many names as you want. Call them. They'll tell you what you want to hear."

"I'm not interviewing you, for crying out loud."

"Listen, this is important to me. I don't have the space, or the tools, to do this on my own. If I did, obviously I wouldn't be here. I just need a favor. Please?"

Beck inhaled so deeply, and blew out his breath so forcefully, he had to slap a hand down over the papers on his desk to keep them from scattering about the room.

"Tell me why I should believe you. Trust you. Tell me what you do. For a living. Obviously you're not a mechanic or you wouldn't be here, but from the way you talk, that's what you know. You said you're fairly new to Caston. What are you doing here? If you've been working on cars your entire life, you must have tools. Where are they? You're something of an enigma, Max."

She didn't want to tell him anything, it was none of his business, but the flicker of hope that he'd let her loose in his garage smothered that desire for privacy.

"I'm a teacher, but I grew up around cars. It's what my dad did, and since it was just the two of us, I learned like I would have learned a second language, or how to cook, or, heaven forbid, the ins and outs of the insurance business if any of those had been his thing. I'm in Caston for a job. Short term. A friend stored my car over the winter, but it's several hours' drive away and since I obviously can't drive hours to get to his place, I need to work on it here."

"A teacher? Doesn't really seem to fit. Do you teach shop—"

Beck pressed his lips together, effectively sealing them on his last syllable. His eyes narrowed, then widened before he caught himself. He shifted in his chair, he righted a few papers on his desk, and Max spotted a dozen different emotions in his posture, on his face, and when he looked up at her, in his eyes.

"You looked familiar. I didn't put it together until just now."

He didn't have to spell it out for Max to know he'd seen the news, seen her picture plastered over every broadcast during the past twenty-four hours. She turned to leave. She wouldn't sink so low as to play on his emotions to get what she wanted, no matter how badly she wanted it.

"Wait! Hold on a minute." When she turned back, he waved toward the only other chair in his office. "Will you sit? For just a minute? I promise I won't grill you."

She didn't know whether she could believe him, but she knew she didn't have to answer any of his questions. She shrugged and moved a stack of catalogs from the chair so she could sit. Since she didn't know what else to do with them, she dumped the catalogs on his desk, then stared at him, waiting.

"I'm sorry. It caught me off guard. I meant it when I said I won't grill you, but I have to ask. Are you okay? I assume what happened a few minutes ago had to do with what happened yesterday. Do you need anything? Something to eat? Need me to call someone?"

His obvious discomfort was mildly entertaining. "I'm fine."

"I doubt it, but okay." He looked at her warily, as if afraid she'd keel over at any moment. "Changing the subject then. I suppose I could let you use the space. After hours, though. I can't spare the space during the day. And I'm going to be here. The whole time. We'll work together, or if I'm convinced you're not going to trash the place, I'll watch you work, but I'll be here."

"Really? Perfect. How much?"

"How much what?"

"How much do you want for use of the space? Your stuff?"

"I don't know. Let's see how long it all takes."

"Fair enough." Itching to get started, Max's fingers skittered over her thighs as if she were playing the piano. "When? When can I start? Tonight?"

"Ah, not to sound insensitive, but do you think you're up for it? Earlier, when you mentioned work, I had to catch you to keep you from falling on your face. I understand now, but still, maybe you should take a little time, let things settle before you start using tools."

Why didn't he understand the only thing that would keep her from falling on her face was to do something she loved, something that would soothe, something familiar? There was a desperation in her voice when she spoke that sounded foreign to her.

"I'm fine. I told you that. I'm not some sort of lightweight who's going to faint if you say the wrong word. Call someone, I can give you names, they'll vouch for me, and for the fact that I'm level-headed, that I'm not going to fall on my face, as you put it, and that I can handle a simple car repair in my sleep. Call them, then let me get started. I really need to get started as soon as possible. Tonight. Tonight would be good." She dug in her purse and pulled out her phone. "Here. I have some numbers." She looked up at Beck. "Aren't you going to write this down?"

He held his hands up at his shoulders. "Whoa, easy. Let's slow down and talk logistics. Can you do that?"

Though her hands weren't quite steady, and though she had to hold her breath to keep from screaming, Max nodded.

"Okay, then. How far away do you live? Do you want to drive the car home and then drive back tonight—assuming I can make tonight work—or do you want to leave the car here and get a ride home and back?"

Max let out her breath slowly, determined not to huff. "I don't live far. Five miles, maybe." She looked over her shoulder toward the lot. Though she couldn't see her car from where she sat, it bought her a few seconds. "I suppose I could call for a ride, then get back here later. What time?"

Beck frowned and looked toward the ceiling. "I haven't agreed to anything yet. If we work on it in the evening, this evening or another one, is there someone who's going to be willing to get you back and forth? Are you going to need a ride?"

If possible, he looked even more dejected at the idea of having her in his car than he had at the idea of having her in his shop.

"I have another car. I can get myself back and forth."

"Good. It's supposed to snow later this week. You don't drive the Mustang in the snow, do you?" He cringed a little waiting for her response.

"As I said, I'm level-headed. Driving Stevie Ray in the snow would be decidedly non-level-headed."

One side of his mouth turned up in a grin, almost as if he were fighting it.

"Stevie Ray?"

"Yeah. Problem with that?"

"Nope. Story behind that?"

"Of course. Maybe it will give us something to talk about while I'm here working. Later tonight."

Beck dropped his elbow to the desk, then used his hand to knead his forehead. Max heard a low grumble from deep in his throat.

"Fine. Tonight. Seven o'clock. And I'm not staying here all night."

"It won't take all night."

Max reached her hand across the desk. Beck, somewhat reluctantly, shook it.

"Give me your phone number in case something comes up. And your last name. What's your last name?"

"Simmons. Max Simmons." She rattled off her number while Beck scribbled on a scrap of paper. "And a reference? Do you want a name and number to call to check on my sanity?"

"I don't doubt your sanity, Max Simmons, but yeah, give me a number. Maybe I'll make a call."

Max glanced again at the NASCAR posters.

"Jimmy Curtis, but he goes by Skeeter. Don't call him Jimmy, you'll just piss him off."

The pen Beck had been holding dropped from his hand, and he slowly raised his eyes.

"Or you can try Pete Fitzgibbons, but again, you'd best call him Fitz.

I have Kevin McIntyre's number too, he goes by—"

"Torque," Beck said, his voice and his expression giving Max the very clear impression that he was wavering between disbelief and awe. Perfect, she decided.

"Yeah. You want his number?"

He narrowed his eyes and studied her while he shook his head almost imperceptibly.

"Who did you say you were?"

"Max. Max Simmons. We've been over that."

"But how do you know Torque McIntyre? And Fitz, and Skeeter Curtis?"

"I told you, I've been around cars my whole life."

"Being around cars and knowing some of the biggest names in NASCAR are two very different things."

Max sighed. "My dad drove, for a while. I don't remember it, I was young, but once he quit, he stuck around the circuit. Pit crews at times, mechanic for several teams. He bounced around."

"Simmons." He said it slowly, and even more slowly, a devilish smile grew until it was wide enough to split his face in two. "This is unbelievable! Mad Max. You're Mad Max, aren't you?"

She'd thought throwing out some names he might recognize would help her cause. She'd never expected to be blindsided. It was a name she hadn't heard in years. Her brain raced, then, like a tsunami, it hit her. Her eyes flew from one side of the room to the other, they scanned his desk desperate for confirmation. Finally, at the top of an invoice, she spotted it, and instantly her cheeks heated.

She'd assumed Beck was a shortened form of his last name, or a nickname. The invoice, though, confirmed it. Beck Dawson. Why did the world have to be so stupidly small? She wished for the floor to open up and swallow her whole.

When she finally worked up the nerve to look at him, Beck was grinning like the proverbial Cheshire cat. She wanted to reach across the desk and wipe the insolent grin off his face, exactly the opposite of what she'd wanted to do with that face so many years ago.

"I can't believe this. What's it been? Twenty years? No, not that long, but fifteen for sure."

"I have no idea," Max mumbled. She jumped to her feet. "I'll let you get back to work. I'm going to call for a ride."

"No, no, sit. Please. We have a lot of catching up to do."

She remained standing. "We don't."

"Mad Max." He shook his head. "You grew up."

"Time has a way of making that happen."

"The last time I saw you, you had pigtails, skinned knees, and an attitude as big as the Grand Canyon."

"Last time I saw you, you had an ego the size of the Grand Canyon." And eyes that had reduced her to a puddle, a voice that she'd heard in her adolescent dreams. She stared at a poster rather than at him.

The phone on Beck's desk rang, as loud as a train whistle. Max jumped but breathed a sigh of relief at the interruption.

"Yeah, okay, be right there." He set down the phone with a clatter that had her jumping again. "Sorry, Mad Max, I've got a deadline and the guys need some help. Tonight? Seven o'clock?"

"Sure."

"And you can get a ride home? You're sure about that? If not, I can have Sven take you."

"No, that's not necessary. I'll see you later."

Max darted for the door. Outside in the crisp air and leaning against Stevie Ray, she cursed Tank for ever mentioning Beck, cursed Stevie Ray for acting up, and cursed the universe for putting Beck in the same small town where she, for the time being, was stuck.

6

"Why are you both here?" Max demanded as she hurried into the backseat of Nicole's car after finding the front already occupied by Ellie. She shot a look over her shoulder as they pulled out of Beck's parking lot, grateful beyond reason when she spotted no one.

"You're very welcome for the ride," Nicole said. "It was no problem."

"Sorry. Thanks for the ride. You found the place okay?"

"Yes. It's not a big town, Max," Nicole answered.

"I appreciate it, but really, why are you both here? You're not still worried about me, are you?"

"Of course, we're worried about you," Ellie replied as if Max had just uttered the most ridiculous words ever uttered. "But, I happened to be at Nicole's when you called, Boomer and Luna were playing, so I rode along."

Max didn't entirely believe it was nothing more than a dog playdate. She figured the more likely scenario involved the two of them watching the time, fretting over where Max was, and wondering how long they had to wait until they could call to check on her.

"What happened to your car?" Nicole asked.

When Max didn't immediately answer, Ellie asked, "Did you get in an accident?" She said it on a gasp as if terrified of the answer.

"No, I did not get in an accident," Max growled. As if. "Something with the engine. I don't think it's a big deal, but it needs to be fixed."

"How did you end up here?" Nicole asked with a glance of her own over her shoulder. "I didn't know this place was here, but that's not saying much. I was always more the type that puts gas in the car and assumes the rest just happens by magic."

60

"Hmpf. You should know the basics, at least." Max looked between Nicole and Ellie. "Both of you. Do you know how to change a flat? Change the oil?" At their blank looks, Max said, "*Check* the oil?"

"I did that once," Ellie announced with no small amount of pride. "Granddaddy showed me how when I got my license."

"Once. Wow. Well, you two are a problem for another day."

Max let her head drop back against the seat. The moment she did, it filled with thoughts of Beck. How could she not have recognized him? Because it had been eighteen years, that's why, and if she'd grown up, so had he.

Gone was the child-like roundness to his face, the shaggy hair that had made her eight-year-old self think he looked like a rock star, and the little gap between his front teeth. What remained was the annoying way he was able to raise one brow, only one, when he was surprised, or skeptical, or when it had come to her, annoyed. He'd been nearly a teenager that summer, still a couple of months away, but he'd liked to flaunt it, and she'd had her first crush.

Max cringed when she remembered how she'd followed him around, how she'd tried to act cool, say cool things, how she'd wished her hair was longer, that she knew how to curl it so it would bounce on her shoulders. And how she'd stood in front of the mirror for hours, trying over and over to get only one of her eyebrows to rise and disappear into her crooked bangs.

At times, he'd indulged her. They were the only two kids, after all, and though she was younger, he wasn't old enough that he didn't still want an occasional playmate. He'd let her try to beat him in pinball or foosball, they'd watch TV on the tiny set crammed in the corner of the office, Max laughing when Beck laughed even if she didn't understand the jokes.

Mostly, though, he'd ignored her, choosing instead to stick like glue to the mechanics with their heads under the hoods or their entire bodies under the race cars. He'd dreamt of driving, she knew, and when he had the chance, he'd sneak to the track to watch the drivers burn laps around the oval. What Beck didn't know was that Max had been there, hiding in the shadows, when a too-young and too-cocky-to-know-better driver had let Beck behind the wheel. Max had seen Beck's face when he'd finished his lap, his eyes wide and full of dreams. She didn't know if there'd been a repeat, she'd been too afraid to tell him she'd seen him so couldn't ask him about it, but she'd held onto that secret as if it were a gold chain bonding them together for life.

Even though it had been years, once he'd recognized her, once she'd heard the name Mad Max—a nickname she both hated and loved at the same time—she didn't know how she hadn't recognized him from the start.

"What utter bull," she muttered to herself.

"Hmm?" Ellie asked.

"Nothing. Hey, I purposely avoided my email all day. Are we going back to school tomorrow?"

Nicole and Ellie looked at each other, and though neither said a word, their silence could have filled novels.

"What? What happened?"

"Nothing happened," Ellie said. "Everything is fine."

"What aren't you telling me?"

"Did Amanda call you?" Nicole asked.

"No. Well, I guess I don't know." Max scrolled through her phone. "There are a couple of missed calls here, but not from school."

Ellie nodded. "Probably her cell phone. Is there voicemail?"

Max sighed. "Yeah, looks like it. I assumed it was a reporter."

"Maybe you should listen," Nicole suggested.

"I'm getting the feeling I'm not going to like it. Why don't you just tell me and get it over with?"

"Amanda called me earlier this afternoon. She said she'd tried to get in touch with you but hadn't yet. We're going back to school tomorrow. I mean, school will be in session tomorrow, but…"

Max narrowed her eyes at Ellie. "But what?"

"Amanda thinks you should take the rest of the week, at least."

Nicole's blunt voice seemed to reverberate in the car. Max might appreciate Nicole's directness—a far better alternative than waiting for Ellie to come up with a delicate and round-about way of saying the same thing—but that didn't mean she had to appreciate the words.

"What do you mean, *the rest of the week*? I can't go back? I'm perfectly capable of going back at the same time everyone else is." Max punched at her phone. "I'm calling Amanda right now."

"Max, hold on," Nicole said. "It wasn't just Amanda's decision. She has the backing of the superintendent as well as input from some, um, mental health professionals, I guess you'd call them."

"Mental health…oh, for crying out loud! I don't need any mental health professional, or anyone else, telling me when I'm ready to go back to my job!"

"It's only a couple of days. I'm sure you'll be cleared to go back by Monday."

Max saw Ellie wince, clearly regretting her choice of words, then brace herself for another barrage. Max wasn't about to disappoint her.

"Cleared? What in blazes is that supposed to mean? Cleared. I'll give them cleared. What do they think, I'm going to lie on a couch and cry about my sad childhood? Tell them sob stories about unrealized dreams? Beg for sleeping pills because I can't close my eyes for fear of seeing that face again?"

It wasn't until the car slowed, then stopped and Nicole turned around, joining Ellie in staring, that Max noted the horror and the pity on her friends' faces.

"Max?" Ellie whispered, and Max saw Ellie's fingers reach for Nicole's hand and grasp.

"Are you okay?" Nicole asked.

Max blew out a breath, then threw her head back against the seat. She squeezed her eyes shut and wished she could turn back time to undo the past couple of minutes. Humiliated didn't begin to describe what she was feeling.

"Fine. I'm fine. Tired, worried about my car, but fine. I was just trying to make a point. I don't need an evaluation, or whatever they want to call it. I need to go back to work."

Max didn't have to have her eyes open to know what was happening in the front seat. Ellie, her face pale and a portrait in worry, was looking at Nicole, whose brow was knit in concentration, trying to figure out the best way to handle their newly insane friend. Ellie would be thinking along the lines of a slumber party with wine, ridiculously sugary snacks, and girl talk into the wee hours. Nicole would be compiling a list of counter-arguments to Max's refusal to heed the advice of their principal and superintendent.

Max needed none of it, none of them, and nothing but time alone, and if she could snap her fingers and make it happen, she'd be sitting behind the wheel of Stevie Ray, and flying across Wyoming at eighty-five miles per hour. With the Tetons rising and tickling the clouds on one side, the vast expanse of nothing but wide open space on the other, and the wind in her hair, she'd be herself inside of an hour.

But that just made her think of engine trouble, and that made her think of Beck, and that had her grinding her teeth.

Because the car still wasn't moving, Max opened one eye. As expected, four stared back at her.

"You should have something to eat," Ellie said. "I'd suggest Scooter's, but you're likely to draw attention you don't want, so how about my place?"

"How about you tell me exactly what I can expect when I call Amanda?"

"I don't know exactly," Ellie said. "All I know is she called when she couldn't reach you, and she wanted Nicole and me to know about the decision in case you didn't call her back. She didn't want to put you in the position of heading to school in the morning, only to find that there was a sub in your room."

"I could have told the sub to go home."

"You know, taking a couple more days isn't that big of a deal," Nicole said. "In fact, I'd say it's pretty standard following a traumatic event. We talked about it, and we agreed, that it's good to get school back in session, to get the kids back, but I think it's also a good idea to let things sort of work themselves out for a couple of days before you're back and the subject of a million questions. By Monday, after the kids have had two days back at school, a lot of their questions already answered, and they've had a chance to start to process things with their friends, there will be a different vibe than there will be tomorrow. Give it until Monday, Max. It makes sense."

"Why didn't I have anything to say about it? Why was the decision made with no input whatsoever from me? The one affected?"

"I don't know, and I can say I don't agree with the way it was handled, but I think the outcome was the right one." Nicole held up a finger when Max opened her mouth. "Think about it. The police still want to talk to you, representatives from the district want to talk to you. There's a good chance, if you were in school tomorrow, you'd be pulled out of class more than once. You know how any disruption, anything out of the ordinary, upsets the precarious balance in the classroom. The kids don't need that right now. You don't need that right now."

Max grumbled because she knew Nicole was right. That didn't mean Amanda, and whomever else she had to talk to, wouldn't hear her thoughts on making the decision without her.

"Oh, whatever. I'm too tired to think about it right now."

"Do you think you'll be able to sleep tonight? You could stay at my place if you don't want to be alone. Zeke gave me the name of an over-the-counter sleep aid that he recommends. He said it won't leave you feeling fuzzy-headed the next day. Or, if you think you need something stronger, he can get you a prescription."

"I'm not taking sleeping pills, and I'll be fine at my place." Then she remembered. "Speaking of my place, any idea if there are still reporters around?"

"We drove by on the way to pick you up," Nicole said. "All clear."

"Small miracles," Max said. "Okay, then take me home. I need to eat, take a nap, and then I'm going back to Beck's to work on my car tonight."

"You're what?" Ellie said.

"I'm going to work on my car."

"You really know how to fix a car?" Ellie couldn't quite hide her shock, or disapproval, or whatever it was, and her nose wrinkled in that Ellie way.

"Yes, I know how to fix a car. I know how to rebuild an engine. I know what to do to an engine, and to a car, to get it to top out at 200 miles per hour. Wrinkle your nose all you want, Oklahoma. You're the one who thinks there's nothing weird about shoveling out a barn full of horse crap."

Nicole snickered. "You're both a little weird in my book, but we're getting off track. You sure you want to go home, Max?"

"I'm sure."

"Do you have anything to eat there, or should we stop and get something?"

"I'm planning on ordering a pizza. Comfort food seems like a good idea."

"If you're sure," Nicole said. When Max nodded, Nicole started the car again. "I can't claim to know anything about cars, but I do know something about business, and I'm confused about why you're going back to that garage to work on your car. It's that guy's business, isn't it? Why isn't he doing the work?"

"Because I don't trust him, that's why," Max replied with a huff. "Never did, never will," she added under her breath.

"Still, it doesn't make sense. A restaurant owner isn't going to let you bop into her kitchen and cook up your own dinner. A salon owner isn't going to let you put your friend in one of his chairs and give her foils. Why is this guy letting you in his place?"

"I'm paying him. And I sort of know him."

Ellie perked up. "You know him? How?"

"It's a long story, and I'm almost home."

"I can take the long way," Nicole said.

"Ooh, do that," Ellie told her. "Max?" She drew out the single syllable into something that sounded like a song lyric.

"You drive me crazy sometimes, you know that?"

Ellie smiled sweetly. "And you love every minute of it. Now dish."

"I knew him when I was a kid. When we were both kids. My dad spent a few months working for a race team in Alabama, and Beck's dad was working there at the same time. We got to know each other. Haven't seen him since, and didn't know Beck's Garage was this Beck, that's for sure."

"You didn't like him?" Ellie asked.

"I was eight years old. He was twelve. Mostly, he gave me a hard time. We were the only two kids around. I suppose I bugged him, but I was bored."

"That's what your dad does? He's a mechanic? Is that where you learned?"

"You could say that. My dad dreamed of racing cars, but an accident cost him most of the use of this right leg and brought that dream to an end, so he's spent his life since then hanging around racing teams, working on race cars, doing whatever he can to earn a few bucks and still pretend he's part of the game."

"That's why you grew up the way you did? Moving all over the country?" Nicole asked.

"Yeah. Sometimes it would be a year, sometimes a week. Met a lot of people, saw a lot of the country, and learned just about everything there is to know about cars and racing. So there you go, my life in two sentences."

"But what about—"

"Listen, El, I'm really tired, and I'm home. Another time, okay?"

"Of course. I didn't mean to push. You'll call if you need anything? Promise?"

"I promise. And thank you, both of you, for everything. I don't know how I would have made it through the past day and a half without you. And Zeke and Brady. Even if I don't always act like it, I do like having friends."

Ellie swiped at her eyes. "Oh, Max." She leaned between the seats and hugged Max. "We're here whenever you need us."

"She's right," Nicole said. "Whenever. Day or night. Even if it doesn't seem like it now, things might get rough tomorrow, or next week, or next month. You have to let us help."

"I will. And since the coast appears to be clear, I'm going to make a run for it. I'll talk to you tomorrow." Then, before Ellie could come up with something else to cry about, Max sprinted for the steps.

The first order of business was a shower. A long, hot shower. Slowly, some of the aches started to lessen, and some of the tension flowed away with the water down the drain. When the water cooled, Max shut off the faucet.

Once she'd bundled herself into cozy sweats and thick socks, she blasted her hair with a hair dryer, then ordered the pizza. Worried she might starve before it arrived, she scrounged around her meager kitchen until she found a bag of pretzels. While she munched on them, she dialed Skeeter.

She'd promised him a call, and she knew he'd be worried, but she also knew until days passed without hearing from her, he'd leave her alone and give her space until she was ready to talk.

He answered on the first ring, a very un-Skeeter-like thing to do.

"Max. You're okay?"

"I'm okay."

"Tell me."

So she did. He asked a question here and there but stuck to the facts, leaving the emotions out of the conversation unless she brought them up. He told her how proud he was, and just before they hung up, he asked the question she knew he'd been wanting to ask.

"Have you heard from him?"

"No, not yet."

"He probably hasn't heard. He's on the road."

"Yeah."

"Might not make the news where he is, and even if it does, it's unlikely he's watchin'."

"Probably. Did you try to call him?"

Skeeter hesitated, but Max knew he'd never lie to her. "Yeah. Couple times."

"Hmm."

"Went straight to voicemail. Probably not listenin' to his messages."

"Never does."

"Max, he'd call if he knew."

"Yeah. I 'spose. Hey, my pizza's here. I'll talk to you soon, okay?"

"Anytime, Max, you know that."

"I know. Thanks, Skeeter."

Refusing to give in to the hurt, Max took a swig from the beer she'd opened to wash down the pretzels, then collected her pizza. She'd eat, she'd take a nap, and she'd go work on her car. And if her dad never knew what happened, what did it matter, really?

Barks greeted her when she opened the door to Beck's Auto, and not the friendly kind. Figuring the dogs would give Beck all the notice he needed, she chose to wait on the safe side of the door rather than venture, unwelcome, into the work area. It didn't take long for the door to open. She barely had time to register the fact that there were two of them before the smaller one was airborne, coming straight for her.

Max threw her hands up in front of her face, but when the dog crashed into her chest, instinct had her reaching for it, holding on to it. After a fleeting second, once she realized what she was doing, she began to push the creature away, but a fleeting second was also all the time the dog needed to begin licking her face.

"Indie."

It sounded more like resignation than scolding, Max thought, and wondered how Beck ever had a return customer if they were all subjected to his insane pack of dogs. While she tried to peel the dog from her chest, it tried just as hard to find the spot it wanted, finally settling when it managed to tuck its head in the crook of Max's neck.

Something that felt as solid as a brick wall bumped her leg. When she looked down, she found the other one staring up at her, its huge brown eyes a mixture of mild curiosity and, she would have bet a year's wages, indecisiveness on whether to take a piece out of her leg.

"Is this how you welcome all your customers?"

"No, you're one of the lucky ones. During the day, if they're here, they're out back on their tie-outs. At night, they get the run of the place. They see it as their solemn responsibility to guard the place, and I'd like to think me, from all that goes bump in the night."

The dog still clung to her. "This is watchdog behavior?"

"No, actually Indie usually takes a good long while to warm up to someone. Not quite sure what's going on here."

"Lulling me into complacency, I'd guess, before moving in for the kill."

Max turned her head to see the dog's mouth in easy reach of her jugular. The one on the floor still stared up at her, probably waiting for her to make just one wrong move before switching to attack mode.

"One word from me is all it would take," Beck said, then grinned like a fool.

"Very funny. Want to get it off me?"

"Her, and yeah, sure."

Beck reached for the dog who released her death grip on Max, then leaped to the floor to jump on top of the other dog. Mayhem ensued while they barked, snapped, and tried to kill one another. At least that's how it looked to Max.

"Don't you need to do something about that?" she asked as she hopped and sidestepped what quickly became a blur of dog parts around and between her legs.

"Nah, they'll tire of it soon enough."

Max thought it more likely that one of them would kill the other one, but she decided it wasn't her problem as long as they stayed away from her.

"I pulled your car into the shop," Beck said.

"I noticed it wasn't in the lot."

It was the first thing she'd noticed, and before the dog attack, she'd planned on calling him on it. She hadn't given him permission to move it, though she knew it went with the territory, but her instincts told her if he'd started it, he'd likely done more than simply pull it into the garage.

The dogs lost interest in their all-out war once the door opened, and they darted ahead of her. Max took her turn through the door and, once inside the shop, bristled at the sight of the hood already open, a rag draped over the side, and a light hanging from the hood. He'd started without her? That she'd been clear on. She quickened her step and beat him to the car.

"What have you done? Did you take anything apart? I told you I wanted to do the work."

"Relax, Mad Max, all I did was pop the hood."

"And how far did you drive?" Max leaned inside to look at the odometer. She knew, within a few miles, what it had registered when she'd left it that afternoon.

"I'd guess about forty yards, but you should have seen me. I floored it, got it up to sixty, then slammed on the brakes and sent it skidding."

"You're a regular comedian, aren't you? Tell me the truth."

He did that thing with his eyebrow, and she had to look away. "I drove it from the parking lot to right here. If it had been any other car, I would have driven it for a while to see how it ran, see if it stalled, but I didn't want to face an angry Mad Max. Guess I made the right decision."

Max muttered under her breath but decided he was telling the truth after her check of the odometer. Lucky for him.

"You can stop calling me that any time."

"Mad Max? I kind of like it."

"I'm not eight years old any longer, and besides, it's just stupid."

"Is that why you used to blush every time I used it?"

She'd probably blushed every time he'd looked at her, certainly every time he spoke to her. Intending to change the subject, she looked around her. "Where did the dog posse go?"

"Probably the storeroom. It's warm, they've got beds and water in there, and contrary to the way they behaved a few minutes ago, they're actually pretty lazy."

"When they're not trying to kill each other. Or an unsuspecting customer."

"That only happens once a month or so."

Obviously he thought it was funny. She thought the dogs probably belonged in cages.

"Do you ever close the door, or put them in those dog cage things?"

"Don't bother anymore. Ace is a canine Houdini. He's gotten out of every room and every crate, he's opened doors and locks, he's escaped fences, he's opened cupboards and helped himself to whatever he wants. Indie couldn't work her way out of a cardboard box, but she's good at following Ace. Aside from trying to be sure they won't hurt themselves, I've more or less given up trying to contain them."

"Comforting." Max shot another look over her shoulder. "Can we look at the car, or is that going to somehow incite another riot?"

"I think we'll be okay." He switched on the light he'd hung from the hood. "I did some thinking after you left. It was summer, eighteen years ago, in Alabama. Talladega. My dad was still working for a tire manufacturer in R&D, and he spent that summer there testing new designs. He had me for the summer after my parents split. My sister was supposed to be there too, but she was fifteen, and the fit she threw? I bet it's still echoing off the walls of our old house in Akron."

Max tried to ignore him, but she was curious. If she'd known at the time that Beck's dad wasn't part of the big racing family the way her dad was, she didn't remember. At eight, she'd likely assumed everyone lived the way she and her dad did.

"It was fun. Looking back, I guess it was an odd way to spend a summer, but at the time, it was fun. Made me want to be a race car driver for a while."

Max kept her head under the hood, but couldn't keep her mouth closed. "I saw you, you know. I saw you drive a lap with that driver who was too green and too stupid to know better than to put a kid behind the wheel of a race car."

"Oh, man, that was one of the best nights of my life. You saw me? You never said anything. Or told on me."

"I've never been a snitch."

"Lucky for me. My dad would have skinned me alive, and chances are good he would have done the same to that driver. What was his name?"

"I don't remember. Wayne something?"

"I think you're right. He didn't stick around long, as I recall. Wonder whatever happened to him?"

"Probably got caught putting another kid behind the wheel and that kid's dad did skin him alive."

Beck laughed. The sound was a memory that rocketed straight to Max's belly and sent it fluttering much as it had done when she'd been eight. Thankfully her head was under the hood because she was certain the blush was back. She might as well be eight again, she thought, for as ridiculously as she was behaving. Before she'd completely recovered, Beck was leaning beside her.

"Sadly, my racing career didn't pan out, so here I am. Now, since you were able to start the car again, there's a good chance it's the fuel pressure. We can also check the battery, look at the alternator, even drain the fuel in case it's as simple as bad gas. You've never had the problem before?"

Talking cars rather than ancient history started to calm the crazed butterflies in her stomach.

"No. Not until today. And now you're using the 'we' you accused me of using earlier. I thought you said you'd let me handle this?"

"You wouldn't deprive me of the chance to work on a car like this, would you?"

"I can do it myself."

"I'm sure you can, but it'll be fun. Come on, let's get to work."

They worked, side by side, for over two hours without pinpointing the problem. It was nothing obvious, and it wasn't any of the things they could easily test. As frustrating as it was, Max enjoyed the puzzle. Had it been as simple as a bad battery connection, not only would she be back home, she would have been disappointed at being robbed of the chance to diagnose whatever was ailing Stevie Ray.

Max found it annoying that after eighteen years, Beck still had some kind of hold over her, something that made her have to prove herself to him. She tried to tell herself there was no reason to be nervous, but she found herself fumbling a tool more than once, and each time, hoping he wouldn't notice.

They chatted, but most of the conversation stayed focused on her car, or cars in general, so gradually, Max relaxed. Until Beck started asking questions.

"Is your dad still part of the NASCAR scene?"

"My dad is part of something different every few months. Always has been."

She hadn't meant for it to come out as bitter as it did. Beck noticed.

"Then he moves from one team to another?"

"He hasn't really been part of a team for a long time. He's done a hundred different things, always trying to work his way back to the big time."

"You said he drove?"

Max sighed. When she'd thought about what her evening would be like, it hadn't included her father's history. "He did, for a short time. Then he was injured, and that was the end of that."

"Injured? Oh, right. His leg. I'd forgotten about that. Did you bounce around with him as he moved from place to place?"

"Yep."

"What's your dad doing now?"

"Not sure. I saw him for a few days around Christmas, he was back in Wisconsin hanging around Skeeter's place, but he's off to the next big thing. I'm not sure where."

"Then you haven't heard from him? He didn't call you about… when…you know, the thing at school?"

"No."

He looked as if he expected her to elaborate. She had no intention of doing anything of the sort, so she grabbed a rag and began wiping her hands.

"As much as I'd like to keep working, I'm guessing you want to get home. You probably need to feed the beasts before they decide to eat you."

"You really don't like dogs, Mad Max?"

"Dogs are fine. I'm not sure what, exactly, you have."

As if on cue, the two came trotting from somewhere in the back of the garage. More accurately, the one Beck called Ace was trotting. The other one, the one she suspected might be part vampire, was charging at full speed. Max took two steps, putting the car between herself and the dog. Normally, she'd sacrifice herself to save Stevie Ray, but an errant golf ball, a kid out of control on a bike, even a lightning bolt, had nothing on the thing Beck called Indie.

Beck corralled the dog before she could leap. She snuggled into his arms, acting like the perfect, well-behaved pup.

"They're both a mixture of a bunch of different things. I did those dog DNA tests on them. I don't know if I believe the results any more than I believe the human test that told me I'm part Cherokee and part Bantu, but what are you gonna do?" He shrugged and rubbed Indie's head. "It said they have some American Staffordshire Terrier, some American Pit Bull Terrier, some lab, some boxer, I don't know, the list went on and on. Back in the day, I would have called them mutts, but that term earned me a, shall we say, less-than-friendly glare at the shelter. We'll go with mixed breeds."

"Shelter? You rescued them?"

"Yeah, seemed like they deserved a second chance. Or, in Indie's case, a third or fourth chance."

Against her will, Max felt her heart soften. "That was a nice thing to do. A responsible thing."

"I'll admit, there were moments when I was sure I'd made the biggest mistake of my life, but we've figured each other out. For the most part, anyway."

She wasn't about to admit it, but for years, Max had longed for a dog. 'Just a small one,' she'd begged, along with promises that she'd take care of it. A companion, something that would be a constant in the nomadic life they lived. No matter how long her list of reasons she needed—and deserved—one, her dad had never allowed it. His list of reasons why it wouldn't work had been just as long.

There'd often been dogs around where they stayed, and she'd made friends with most of them, but like her human friendships, the canine ones had been fleeting. She'd also learned a few tough lessons, one in particular when she'd tried to get too close to a dog who was more watchdog than pet. She had the scar on her left calf as a reminder in case she considered trying to hug a dog she didn't know.

"It's nice you gave them a home." Max reached a tentative hand down toward Ace, who was sniffing around her feet. "You're sure they're friendly?"

"With people. Not always with other dogs, or with each other, but they're more bark than bite."

"Comforting." Still, Max crouched and patted Ace. With his short, wiry hair she could give him a good scratch. She was shocked at how solid the dog was, feeling nothing but toned muscle under her fingers.

"When do you want to put some more time in on the car?" Beck asked.

"As soon as possible. I have some time this week, a lot of time actually, but I don't suppose you're going to change your mind and let me in here during the day?"

"No can do, but tomorrow evening works for me."

That came as a surprise. Max had figured there'd be someone waiting for him, or maybe several someones waiting their turn.

"Okay. Same time?"

"Sure." Then he studied her with what looked like a question on his lips, one he wondered whether he should ask.

"What?"

"I had the news on earlier. According to the report I heard, school's back in session tomorrow, but you said you're free during the day?"

"I've been told I need to *take the rest of the week off.*" She mimed air quotes. "Maybe longer, depending."

The words from the brief phone call with Amanda still rang in her ears. They'd made her angry enough that she hadn't been able to eat more than one slice of pizza, and now, among a host of other things, she was starving.

"I see," Beck said. "Based on your tone, I'm guessing you don't agree?"

"No, I don't agree. There's no reason I can't go back to my job when everyone else does."

"Everyone else didn't take down a shooter."

"Right place, right time. Or, maybe wrong place, wrong time, depending on how you want to look at it."

"I'd guess there's a building full of people, as well as an entire community, who'd go with right place, right time. And I'd guess they're pretty grateful you were brave enough to do what you did."

She'd heard it before, over and over, the gratitude and the thanks, but it had come from school staff and law enforcement, not from someone completely removed from the scene. She wasn't sure how to handle it when it came from Beck.

"It makes you uncomfortable? The attention?"

She shrugged with one shoulder while she bent over again to pet Ace and to avoid looking Beck in the eye.

"I asked that my name be kept out of the whole thing, but that didn't exactly happen. There were reporters camped out in front of my apartment until my landlord chased them away. I'm not looking for time in the spotlight."

He was quiet long enough that she stood and looked over at him. His head was tilted, and he was studying her with that one eyebrow raised.

"Eighteen years ago, you would have done anything to be in the spotlight. Remember when you talked your dad into getting you a baton? You twirled it from morning until night. Until the day you put a baton-sized dent and scratch into a fresh paint job. I never saw that baton again."

Max had forgotten all about that. Her performance had earned her an earful from her dad, and from the guys who'd just finished the paint job. Beck was right, that was the last she'd seen of the baton.

"How do you remember that?"

"I remember a lot about that summer. Someone had to keep an eye on you. Most of the time, it was me. Your dad should have paid me babysitting wages."

Max drew in a sharp breath and straightened her spine. "Babysitting! You weren't my *babysitter!*"

Beck laughed, a smooth-sounding laugh, the kind that makes it clear the one doing the laughing knows he's in charge. Max wanted to hate it but had to admit that had she not been the butt of the joke, she'd have found the sound pleasant. Alluring, even.

"Easy there, Mad Max, just joking around. You remember joking, don't you? I remember a lot of it from that summer."

She did too, but she didn't want to admit just how much she remembered. Back then, she'd been the target of a lot of the joking, but the times that they'd teamed up, whispered about someone else, secretly poked fun at something someone did as if they were a real team, were etched in her memory. When he'd spared her the time, Beck had made her feel special and important. Wanted.

"It was a long time ago."

"Do you still have a baton? Do I need to erect barriers in front of the cars?"

She tried not to laugh but failed. "No, that was the one and only baton I ever owned, and I never worked up the nerve to ask my dad if I could have it back."

"I'm pretty certain it was destroyed by committee."

"Probably. Well, I'm going to head out. Thanks again for tonight. You're sure tomorrow works for you? You don't have a hot date?"

"Jealous, Mad Max?" His cocky grin was as big as she'd seen it.

"Of what?"

He laughed again, but before she could slap back, a series of bangs sounded from the office area. Max looked down, suspecting the dogs, but Ace was sniffing around Stevie Ray, and Indie was still in Beck's arms.

"What's that?"

"Probably my dinner. I ordered Chinese. The guy who delivers knows he has to be loud if I'm going to hear him. I'll be right back."

He put Indie down before he jogged out of sight. Max watched Indie, but only out of the corner of her eye, figuring direct eye contact could only lead to trouble. Indie lunged at Ace but didn't follow through, almost as if she were testing him, seeing if she could scare him. Ace never flinched, probably used to her feints. Sensing Ace wasn't in the mood for her shenanigans, Indie chose Max. Like a shot, she covered the space between the two, then jumped.

Max had no idea a dog could jump so high. It was as if the dog had springs instead of legs. She bounded straight up in the air, high enough that she was eye-level with Max. Startled, Max jumped back.

"Geez, what is with you?"

Indie wasn't deterred. She stood at Max's feet and head-butted her legs until Max caved and bent to pet her. Indie relished it until she smelled food and turned her attention to Beck.

"Get down, you crazy thing." He lifted one arm and bent it at the elbow to protect the bags he carried, so Indie settled for circling his feet.

"I'll leave you to it," Max said.

"Unless you want to stay and eat. There's plenty."

"You're going to eat here?" She looked around. "Do you live here?"

"No, I don't live here, but sometimes it feels that way. That's why I usually bring these two with me. I don't like to leave them at home alone for twelve hours at a time."

"Don't like to, or don't dare to?"

"A little of both, I suppose. A couple of months ago, Ace got hold of a pan of brownies. I thought I'd tucked it away where he couldn't get to it, but he finds new ways of surprising me. He ate the whole thing. Chocolate brownies, with chocolate chips and chocolate frosting. The emergency vet bill was steep."

Max forgot she still hadn't made up her mind about the dogs and bent down to hug Ace. "I've heard chocolate isn't good for dogs. It's true, then?"

"True, and then some. His heart rate was skyrocketing, he was panting like he'd run a marathon, and things I'd rather forget were coming out both ends at alarming rates."

"Oh, you poor thing," Max said as she ran her hand from his head to his tail. "He's okay now?"

"Okay, but not any smarter, I'm afraid. Ate an entire bag of sour cream and onion chips the other day."

"You need to lock up your food."

"Or, I need smarter dogs."

"I'd say they're very smart. They're outsmarting you, aren't they?"

"Yeah, yeah. Do you want food? It's getting cold."

"Sure. I could eat."

7

Max blamed it on being too worked up about her upcoming talk with Amanda when she forgot to check for reporters before opening her door. A camera clicked at Mach speed, and a microphone was shoved in her face.

"Ms. Simmons, how are you feeling after the incident at school? Were you hurt when you took down the intruder?"

For a moment, all she could do was stare and think she had to be living someone else's life. People like her didn't have reporters waiting outside their doors. When she finally wrapped her mind around what was happening, she tried to side-step the reporter without answering, a difficult task given the narrow stairway leading from her apartment above the garage.

"Ms. Simmons, is it true you had to wrestle a gun away from the intruder? That he had the gun pointed at a student?"

They were trying to bait her, she knew that, but she couldn't seem to stop herself.

"I was not hurt. I did not wrestle a gun away from anyone."

She pushed past the woman with the camera, as well as a man with a monstrous video camera perched on his shoulder. They weren't to be deterred, however, and she heard the footsteps clambering down the steps behind her.

"Do you feel that you were adequately prepared to handle such an event? Do you feel the staff should have more training on dealing with violent situations?"

She paused, mid-step, and sensed the video camera come within inches of her shoulder before the operator was able to stop himself. Though every bit of common sense she possessed told her to keep her mouth shut and keep walking, it seemed she was willing to give that common sense the day off. She whirled.

"How can anyone ever be prepared for what happened inside Caston Middle School? No two situations are ever going to be the same. We can listen to policies and procedures, we can practice drills, we can read and study all the other horrific events that have taken place around the country and around the world, but be prepared? I can't speak for everyone at CMS, but no, I don't think I could have ever been prepared for what happened."

She spun on her heel and walked as fast as she could without running toward the garage door. The ground muffled the footsteps more than the wooden staircase, but she still heard them coming after her.

"Are you saying that the Caston school district doesn't adequately train employees? That students aren't safe within the schools?"

She dropped her head and sighed, knowing she should never have opened her mouth. She could already hear the sound bites they'd splice together, making it seem as though she'd just criticized the school district and everyone associated with it. Though she knew it was likely pointless, she turned one more time.

"I said no such thing. I said no one, besides perhaps military personnel or police officers, could ever be prepared for an intruder with a gun inside a school. Caston, Los Angeles, Pittsburgh, Seattle, it doesn't make a difference. Teachers are in school to teach, that's what we're trained to do. After that, we do whatever we can to ensure our students are safe, but the vast majority of us don't have military or law enforcement backgrounds. We do the best we can. I...I did the best I could."

She hated the fact that her voice cracked, that her eyes stung with unshed tears. Putting her hand over her mouth, both to hold back any more words she'd regret and the sob that was burning the back of her throat, she flung open the garage door, closed herself in her car, and hoped the three who'd been staring at her with their jaws hanging open were smart enough to stay out of the way.

"Based on your expressions, I guess I don't have to ask if you've seen it," Max said to Ellie and Nicole later that afternoon. She dropped her bag inside the door and threw herself face down on Ellie's couch. It had been a long, miserable day, but she'd promised Nicole and Ellie she'd meet them after school and she knew if she canceled, they'd just show up at her place.

"We saw it. Everyone saw it," Nicole said.

"Well, probably not *everyone*," Ellie added.

"They twisted my words," Max said. Her voice was muffled by the pillow, but she didn't have the energy to move.

"Of course they did. You wouldn't have said you thought the school district hadn't provided adequate training." Ellie was quiet—everything was eerily quiet—until Ellie finally added, "Would you?"

Max pushed herself upright. "No, Eleanore, I wouldn't, and I didn't. That's why I didn't want to talk to reporters. Why I shouldn't have talked to them. The story made it seem like I blamed the school administrators for what happened. I didn't. I don't."

Max grabbed the pillow, pressing it into her lap, then twisting it and sinking her fist into it. Maybe she should just leave. Fix Stevie Ray, pack up her few belongings, and leave. She needed another year of teaching under her belt, but it could be anywhere. Besides, she was good at leaving and starting over. She'd been doing it her entire life.

"We know that," Nicole said. "That poor pillow does too."

Max tossed aside the pillow. "You, yeah, but what about everyone else? I've been waiting for my phone to ring and to hear Amanda tell me I'm out of a job. Or to hear I'm being sued for slander, or whatever you call it when you say something that rips on someone else."

Nicole and Ellie looked at each other. Ellie's mouth twitched first, followed by Nicole's. Nicole laughed first. Ellie was right behind her. Max waited for them to share the punchline to whatever joke she'd missed. When neither bothered, she threw her hands in the air.

"What?"

"Do you want the honors?" Nicole asked Ellie.

"No, you go ahead."

Nicole nodded at Ellie and mouthed, "Thank you," then leveled her gaze at Max.

"First, everyone else feels the same way we do. At least everyone who matters. And by that, I mean your coworkers. Every single teacher I spoke with—and it was a lot of them because they all wanted to make sure the message got to you—was either outraged by the report or found it laughable. If anything, they're more proud of you, and impressed by you, than ever. Was it a weird day at school? Of course it was. Was everyone talking about you? Of course they were. But you know what? They all think you're a hero. Even more so than the other day, because they've had more time to think about it, to process what happened, and they are grateful, and they are indebted to you. Their words."

"But—"

Nicole waved a finger. "Not done. As you had to expect, you're the main topic of conversation among staff and students alike. And don't make that face at me. I know you don't like the attention, but it's unavoidable. It will fade, as everything does, but you're going to have to embrace it for the time being. Now, as far as that television report? The only surprise anyone expressed was that you actually spoke to the media. Word got around that you wanted to avoid that, so people were surprised to see and hear you on TV. As far as what you said, to anyone who listened carefully, your meaning was clear."

"Amanda…"

"I saw Amanda on my way out. The report must have aired after your meeting with her was over?"

Max nodded.

"Amanda brushed the entire thing aside. She mentioned that the district will be reviewing policies and training, but you already knew that. They have to, they know that, everyone knows that. Anytime something like this happens, or even happens somewhere else, it's only natural that policies and procedures are reevaluated. As for what you said, she actually kind of laughed at it. Not really laughed, because I don't think she's going to be able to truly laugh for a long while, but you know what I mean. It meant nothing to her, or to anyone else that matters."

Just the way Nicole spoke, the way she slipped into what Max thought of as lawyer mode, started to bring Max's heart rate down to somewhere around normal.

"What about—"

Again, Nicole interrupted Max before she could continue.

"The lawsuit? That actually is funny, Max. There's not a lot that could get me to laugh right now either, but the thought that you ever entertained the idea that you could be sued by the school district is laughable. You know better, so I'll just chalk this one up to exhaustion and stress. Slander? Really, Max. You spoke your mind, under duress, and even then, you said nothing slanderous. Trust me."

Max closed her eyes, and the tension began flowing out of her. She thought if she stayed there, she might melt right into the couch.

"You believe us, don't you Max?"

She didn't open her eyes. "Yeah, I guess I do, El. I had myself so worked up about the meeting, then it was even worse after I did what I swore I wouldn't do and spoke with the reporters. When I saw and heard myself on TV, it was like a really bad dream. Stuff like this doesn't happen to me, you know?" She pressed her fingers to her eyes for a moment before opening them. "If I ever wanted a do-over, it's now. I want to go back to before this all happened and somehow change it. Not just for me, but for everyone. How are the kids?"

"There were more absences than usual, but that didn't come as a surprise," Ellie said. "Parents have been encouraged to keep their kids home as long as they feel it's necessary, or as long as a student feels like they want to stay home. Those that were there handled it in different ways, just as they handle everything in different ways. I'm not going to sugarcoat it. Some seemed afraid, and some seemed angry. Some tried hard to act as if it was a day like any other. Some took advantage of the counselors, and I think that was a good thing. Just knowing the counselors were available was a good thing for a lot of them. Maybe a student didn't feel like she needed a counselor today, and maybe she won't tomorrow, but the counselors are going to stick around for a while, and I think that brings a sense of security knowing that even if it's a week or more from now, there will be someone there to talk to."

Max nodded. "I imagined so many scenarios, but I guess, deep down, I figured it would be about like you said. Lots of different emotions, lots of different levels of coping."

"They had a lot of questions about you," Nicole said. "They're not as oblivious as we might think they are. They know the three of us are close, so Ellie and I fielded a lot of questions."

"What did you tell them?"

"We reiterated what Amanda said at the morning assembly, that you were fine, but would be taking a couple of extra days off to help the police, and to talk to different people in the school district," Ellie said.

"Did they buy it?"

"Some of them," Ellie said. "Some of them looked skeptical, and asked follow-up questions, but for different reasons. Some were worried that you were hurt and no one wanted them to know, some were worried you'd never come back, and some wondered if their homework would still be due. You know how it is."

"I never asked. Who was my sub? That couldn't have been an easy job."

"I think everyone agreed on that, so they have a math teacher from the high school taking your classes and have a sub for her at the high school," Ellie said. "They didn't want to put a sub in the position of having to answer difficult questions, so they went with an experienced, well-liked, and respected teacher."

More calm settled over Max. She hadn't realized until then just how worried she'd been about her students. It felt good knowing they were in capable hands.

"Can we switch subjects and talk about your day?" Nicole asked. "Aside from the reporters, I mean. How did the meetings go?"

"You want to ask if I lost my cool, don't you?" When Nicole shrugged, Max added, "I didn't, but it wasn't easy. I told them I'm ready to go back to school tomorrow, they told me I wasn't, and things only got worse from there."

"Oh, Max, you didn't argue with them, did you?" Ellie asked. "They're only looking out for you, you know that."

"What I know is that I should be the one to decide when I'm ready to go back to work. If I felt I needed more time, I'd say so."

"Would you?" Ellie asked.

"Probably," Max said.

"What about your talk with the police? Did you learn anything new?"

"The guy is saying he doesn't remember anything about what he did. He doesn't remember going into the school, he doesn't remember having a gun, he doesn't remember talking to me. They've had different doctors and psychiatrists evaluate him, and while the police chief didn't come right out and say it, I think they're leaning toward believing him. What does that mean? He'll get off?"

"Unlikely," Nicole said. "His ultimate fate will depend on many factors. The first step will be to determine what to charge him with. Then, depending on the findings of the psych evals, there's the possibility of an insanity plea, meaning he could be found not guilty by reason of insanity. Sometimes, there's also a defense called diminished capacity, but some jurisdictions don't allow it, and in this case, since there's not a murder charge, I don't know that it would apply. It's tricky, and it's too early to know what will happen, but he's not going to walk out of jail a free man."

"The police had me go over every detail again today. They wanted to know exactly what he said, as best I could remember, and if he seemed afraid and unsure, or focused and intent. All sorts of questions like that. I don't know if I helped, or if I made things more unclear."

"They're trying to determine his mental state when he was inside the school. Just recount, as best you can, what happened. That's all you can do." Nicole sat alongside Max, then placed her hand on Max's arm. "And don't worry. This isn't all on you. The officers who were first on the scene will be asked to give their impressions of his behavior. They will also interview people who've interacted with him recently. Your input is important, but it's not the only input that matters."

"That's not how it felt today. It felt like the weight of the world was on my shoulders. I don't know when I've been so nervous. I don't usually get nervous, but sitting there, in that little room, with all those people looking at me, I could hardly think straight. I was so afraid I'd forget something, or I'd remember something the wrong way, or that I just wasn't giving them the information they wanted."

"Well, of course you were nervous," Ellie said. "As nervous as a turkey at Thanksgiving, I'd bet. I'm sure you did just fine. Now, you need to try to put it behind you."

"Put it behind me? How am I supposed to do that?"

"I don't mean what happened at school, I mean your talk with the police. They may want to talk again, to ask you more questions, but for now, you have to know that you did everything you could, and you need to put that part of it behind you."

"You weren't in that room. Easier said than done."

"I'm sure, sweetie, but you have to try. Ooh! You know what? We should do something fun. Something to take your mind off everything. What do y'all say? How about Saturday?"

"Good idea. Saturday works for me," Nicole said.

"I'm not going to the spa again," Max said. "That was the opposite of fun."

"It doesn't have to be the spa. You choose. Whatever you want."

"I don't know, I…"

A slow grin spread across Max's face. There was something she wanted to do with Nicole and Ellie. That something they'd promised her they'd do if she hated the spa. This just might be the perfect time.

"You know what? Maybe that is a good idea. Let's plan on Saturday afternoon. I have to make a couple of calls, but I think I can arrange it."

For as excited as she'd been, Ellie now looked nervous. "Arrange what? You're grinning, Max. You don't grin unless you're up to something."

"You said anything, Oklahoma. Wear comfortable clothes."

"Comfortable clothes? What does that mean? We'll be getting dirty? We'll be walking? It's still chilly outside. Do I need to dress for the cold?"

"Relax. Wear some jeans, some shoes without heels, bring a jacket, you'll be fine."

Ellie turned her attention to Nicole. "Nicole! Make her tell us."

"You're the one who said we'd do whatever she wants."

Ellie crossed her arms over her chest and looked between Max and Nicole while she chewed on her lip.

"I got some of the parts," Beck said as he pushed open the door for Max, "so we can try a few things, but the rest won't be in until tomorrow."

"Okay. And hello."

Beck grunted. "It's been a day. Do you want to work on your car, or not?" He turned and walked toward the shop.

Something inside Max snapped.

"Oh, had a bad day, did you? Did you walk out your door this morning and have a camera and a microphone shoved in your face? Did you have to sit in front of your boss, her boss, and a bunch of other people, and listen to a list of reasons why you can't go back to work? Did you have to be evaluated by a psychologist to determine whether you'll ever be fit to go back? Did you start to wonder whether they're right, that maybe you'll never be able to do your job again?"

Beck stopped and turned, but Max wasn't done.

"Did you have to recount for the police every second you spent with a crazed man pointing a gun at you? A crazed man who was threatening a school full of kids? Did you have to relive what it was like looking at that gun, wondering if he was going to pull the trigger? Did you spend every minute after wondering if you'd remembered enough that there'd be enough evidence to convict him?"

Max reached out her hand and pressed it against the wall, hoping it would keep her upright. "Did you spend your day praying that the very last thread holding you together wouldn't break and leave you in a million pieces, scattered on the floor like something to be swept up and tossed in the trash?"

"Geez, Max, I'm sorry. Sit down or something."

Beck was pale, his eyes wide, and he looked as though he'd rather break into a million pieces than have to deal with her. But he rolled a desk chair behind her until it hit her in the back of the knees. Since that left her with few options, she sat.

It was the second time she'd nearly collapsed in front of him. It was definitely an un-Max-like thing to do, and she was humiliated.

"Maybe tonight isn't such a good idea."

She tried to stand, but found Beck's hand firmly on her shoulder, keeping her from doing anything but sitting where she was.

"Maybe not, but neither is getting up just now. Sit. Breathe. Stick your head between your knees, or whatever you need to do so you don't pass out."

"I'm not going to pass out."

"Why do I keep having to worry about you doing just that?"

"Sorry to trouble you, Beck. If you let me up, I'll get out of your way."

"That's not what I meant. You're not troubling me, you're making me worry about you. I don't like worrying about people. And I'm sorry. I'm sorry you had the day you had. Want to talk about it or something?"

She lifted her head long enough to glance at him. Based on the look of sheer terror on his face, talking about it was the last thing he wanted to do.

"There's nothing to talk about. I had a crappy day, you had a crappy day, either we both get under the hood of a car and make our crappy days better, or we go home and drown our crappy days in junk food and beer. I'll leave it up to you."

"I like junk food and beer as much as the next guy, but I suppose the smarter choice would be to work on the car."

"Then let's do that."

This time when Max tried to stand, he let her, but he kept his hand close.

"You're sure?" Beck asked.

"Yep."

They walked in silence until they were alongside Stevie Ray. Beck handed her a rag, and she shoved it into her back pocket. She reached down to pop the hood, then asked Beck, "What parts did you get? What do you think we should try first?"

"You know you just asked my opinion about something to do with your car? It makes me think you're not quite as okay as you want me to believe. Did you really have to do all those things? Talk to all those people?"

"Yeah. I did."

"I saw the news. You looked ticked off. First at the reporters for bugging you, then at yourself for answering them."

Well, if that didn't sum things up in two sentences. How did someone she hadn't seen in nearly twenty years know her so well? She'd have to think about that later. "I never should have talked to them. What did you take away from what I said?"

"What do you mean? You didn't say all that much."

"Maybe not, but what do you remember?"

He gave her an odd look, but answered, "You said you didn't engage in a wrestling match with the guy, and you said that no teacher, no one in general, could ever be fully prepared for someone to show up with a gun. Unless you're a cop or trained military personnel. You added that. I liked that part."

"Then you don't think I called out the school district for not adequately preparing teachers?"

"I think that's what the reporter wanted everyone to believe, but if people paid attention, that's not what you said. You told the truth. You're not letting a news report bug you, are you, Mad Max?"

"Honestly, everything is bugging me right now. Including you. Are you ever going to quit with the Mad Max thing?"

"Probably not. Anyway, what was the verdict today? When do you go back to school?"

"Monday."

"That seems reasonable. Two days isn't that long."

"Maybe not to you. Hand me that wrench, will you?" Max indicated with a nod of her head. "I can't help but wonder if it's going to be harder going back on Monday than it would have been today. Everyone else will have already had two days to process, to ask questions, to walk down that hall for the first time. I'll be two days behind. I won't have that shared sense of security of dealing with all those firsts with everyone else."

"Did you tell them that today?"

"Not really. Mostly I just got mad that I didn't get my way."

Beck laughed long and hard. "Why does that sound familiar? Did you scrunch up your face and put your hands on your hips? Seriously, how can you expect me not to call you Mad Max?"

Max straightened and looked at Beck. She caught herself a second before she put her hands on her hips. Instead, she twisted the rag around them.

"That's where Mad Max came from?"

"Sure. You were always mad at someone. Usually your dad, as I recall, but anyone who dared say you couldn't do something because you were too young, or too small, or heaven forbid, because you were a girl, got a good, healthy dose of Mad Max. What did you think?"

"I thought...never mind."

She moved to lean back under the hood, but Beck caught her arm. "You thought what?"

He was close, his face only inches from hers, and she hated the fact that her pulse skittered under his touch. She hadn't let herself look into his eyes, but she couldn't avoid doing so now. While the rest of his face had changed from boy to man, his eyes were still the same fascinating combination of blue with golden-brown flecks. She'd never seen eyes quite like them, and they were no less intriguing than when she'd been eight and had first seen them.

The stubble on his chin was black, several shades darker than his dark brown hair. There was a scar on his chin. It stood out against his tanned skin, and she wondered where he'd gotten it. The scar and the tan. Since he made her wonder about a lot of things, she twisted her arm free.

"That movie. *Mad Max*. I thought it had something to do with that."

"You saw *Mad Max* when you were eight years old?"

She scoffed. "No, but I'd heard of it. Guys talked about it, I knew there was a lot of driving in it, lots of chases, lots of crashes. From what I gathered, Mad Max was the best of the bunch." She squared her shoulders. "I figured you knew that one day I'd be the best driver around, so you called me Mad Max."

Beck chuckled. "Sorry to burst your bubble. I wish I could tell you that was the case, but seriously? You think I would have given you a cool nickname? I was trying to insult you."

"I'll choose to remember it my way. It will let me feel a little better about myself."

She hadn't meant for it to come out sounding so pathetic. She cringed at the sound of her own words.

"Hey, I was a stupid kid. I'd never hurt your feelings like that now."

For as pathetic as her voice had sounded, Beck's sounded just as sincere. And what? Affectionate? More than that?

Obviously she was tired and not thinking clearly. They needed a new topic.

"Why are you tan?" Max wasn't sure it was a good topic, but it was the only thing she could think to ask.

"Noticing my tan, are you? And here I thought it was mostly faded."

"You know what? Never mind."

His low, rumbling chuckle was back. "Daytona. And then Phoenix."

She stood up so fast, she nearly hit her head on the hood of the car.

"Daytona? For the 500?"

"Yep. One of the best in years."

"I know. It's been so long…"

"How long?"

"Since Daytona? I was a junior in high school the last time I saw it in person. I've been to a few other races, but nowhere in the last four years."

"Why not?"

"School. Work. You know."

"I have work. I had school."

She stuck her head back under the hood. "It's not what I do anymore."

"You can still be a fan."

"I am still a fan. From a distance."

"Did you watch this year?"

"Of course, I watched. I'm not dead, am I? The crash, the finish, it was awesome."

"Better in person."

"Tell me."

For the next hour, he did. When they were wrapping up for the night, her phone rang. She was going to ignore it since it had been ringing off and on throughout the day. How reporters got her number, she had no idea, but they had, and they were relentless. Local, even national.

When she went to silence it, the number on the screen came as a surprise. Two days too late, but a surprise nonetheless.

"I'm going to take this. I'll be right back to help you clean up."

She didn't wait for Beck's reply, just hurried to the safety of his office and closed the door behind her.

"Hi, Dad."

"You're okay, Maxie Lou? You're really okay?"

Mad Max, Maxie Lou. It was like her past rising up and smacking her in the face.

"I'm okay."

"I'm sorry. I didn't know until just now. Saw you on the news. I've been driving, not paying much attention to what's going on in the world. I could hardly believe it when I saw your face on TV. Tell me, Maxie. Convince your old man you're okay."

So she did. She told him what happened, most of it, anyway. He asked questions, she answered, and like always, whatever hurt she'd felt at not hearing from him sooner, melted away as he worked his charm on her, the same way he did with racing teams from one coast to the other.

"Who would have thought that teaching would be more dangerous than driving? You want to take a break? Come stay with me for a while?"

"Where are you?"

"Talladega. Hitched up with Frankie."

"Talladega. Huh. Remember that summer we spent there when I was eight? There was that tire rep there, and he had his kid with him. Beck."

"Yeah. I remember. You had someone to play with for a change."

"Beck's got a garage in Caston. That's where I am right now. He's letting me work on Stevie Ray here at night."

"What's wrong with Stevie Ray?"

"Haven't figured that out yet." It irritated her to have to admit it, to her father, or to anyone. "Started stalling on me while I was driving."

"Check the starter? The line to the fuel pump?"

"Ruled out a few things, have a few more to check. I'll figure it out."

"So this kid, this guy, Beck. You stayed in touch with him? I didn't know that."

"Hah! Hardly. This was purely coincidental. Stevie Ray started acting up, I didn't have the space or the tools I needed, so I had to find someone who did. Ended up finding Beck. Small world."

"That it is. I meant it when I said you should come see me for a few days. Get away from everything that's going on there."

"I've been fighting with my principal and the superintendent to let me get back to my job sooner rather than later. They think I need time away. I don't. I can't leave now and let them think they were right."

"No, I don't suppose you can. You're tough, Maxie Lou, I've never doubted it, but if it gets to be too much, I'm here."

"I know, Dad. Thanks. Skeeter said the same thing."

"Take one of us up on our offer if you need to. You don't have to be tough all the time."

But she did, and they both knew it.

8

Friday had been filled with more meetings and more phone calls. There'd been some pushback about her return date from the superintendent after consulting with the psychologist assigned to Max, but Max had held her ground, and she'd be back in the classroom come Monday.

She didn't plan on admitting it to anyone, but Friday night had been the worst night she'd had since looking into the eyes of a potential shooter. She hadn't worked on her car, Beck had told her he had plans, so she'd been left with a long night alone. It wasn't until she'd tried to fill those hours, hours she'd already grown accustomed to spending with Beck and Stevie Ray, that Max had realized what a calming effect the duo had on her. Whether it was the familiarity of being under the hood of a car, or whether Beck had something to do with it, she hadn't decided, but without either of them, there'd been too much time to think.

Both Nicole and Ellie had offered to come over or to meet her for dinner. Ellie had, of course, suggested another sleepover, but Max knew she'd have to face an entire night alone sooner or later, so had declined. Instead, she'd spent the night pacing around her tiny apartment, inching the curtains aside to peer out the window, and much to her disgust, wondering what Beck was doing. A date, she supposed, although he hadn't offered details, and she hadn't asked.

Sleep hadn't come easy. For the first time in her life, Max was uneasy in her own bed. She refused to think of it as fear, but every creak, every thump, had her bolting upright and holding her breath. When a car backfired, the same car that she'd heard backfire at least once a week since she'd moved in, she'd thrown her hands over her head. She'd decided right then and there that she'd track down the owner and offer to fix the problem herself just so she wouldn't have to hear it again.

But it was a new day. No one had shoved a microphone in her face when she'd left her apartment. The sun was shining, the temperature had already warmed to the low forties, and the snow that had fallen overnight Thursday and into Friday was dripping from the roof and turning to slush on the sidewalk. Best of all, she had Nicole and Ellie at her mercy for the afternoon.

She'd made the phone calls, called in a couple of favors, and her friends were probably going to hate every second of what she'd arranged. Especially Ellie. The thought made Max smile.

Max was driving, for the same reason Nicole had insisted on driving to the spa, so they'd be sure to actually get to their destination. Ellie was tense and hadn't stopped asking questions since reluctantly climbing into the car.

"I wish you'd just tell us where we're going, Max. Is it far?"

"Depends what you consider far."

"How long will it take to get there?"

"No longer than it took to get to the spa."

"Nicole, what's within that distance that she could have dreamed up for us?"

"No idea. If it were August, maybe the state fair."

"It's not August, is it?" Ellie snapped. "What else?"

"I don't know, all right! Let's just wait and see."

Max put her hand over her mouth. Together with her oversized sunglasses, most of her face was hidden, but she wouldn't have cared if her friends had seen her laugh.

In the back seat, Ellie pouted. "It seems like now that we're in the car and can't back out, the least you could do would be to tell us where we're going."

"And ruin the surprise? Never." Then to save Ellie from further worry, Max chose the one subject sure to make the bride-to-be forget she had anything to worry about. "Hey, Ellie, have you made any decisions about the wedding yet?"

"As a matter of fact…"

Wedding talk got them the rest of the way.

"No way, Max. No way in the world I'm doing that."

"I think I'm with Ellie on this one," Nicole said. "I don't think I *can* do that."

"Of course you can. You both can. All you have to do is sit there."

"Sit there! Have you lost your mind? I'll die of fright! If you honestly think I'm getting in there, you're more than a few pickles short of a barrel."

"I love it when you go all Oklahoma on me."

A man emerged from the building at the edge of the parking area and waved.

"This guy is a friend of a friend, and he's doing me a big favor." Max wagged her finger between Ellie and Nicole. "Behave yourselves."

She heard Ellie whisper to Nicole, "Do you think if we don't behave, he'll make us leave?"

The man was in front of Max before she could warn Ellie again. He held out his hand.

"You must be Max Simmons," he said with a southern accent thicker than Ellie's.

Max shook his hand. "Nice to meet you, Mr. Bell."

"I knew your daddy years ago, even met you a time or two. 'Course, you wouldn't remember that, you were knee-high to a grasshopper and thin as a fiddle string. I recall pigtails and skinned knees. How is your daddy?"

"He's doing well. Down at Talladega right now, working with Frankie Payne."

"Frankie. Heck of a guy. Knows his way around a car, that's for certain. As I recall, your daddy always did too."

"Still does. Mr. Bell, this is Nicole, and this is Ellie."

"Pleased to meet you, ladies. And call me Coot. Everyone does."

"If I'm not mistaken, I'm hearing some Oklahoma. Where are y'all from, Coot?" Ellie asked when she shook his hand.

"Just outside Tulsa, but I'm sorry to say it's not really home anymore. I've moved around so much the moss has never had a chance to grow, I'll tell you that. I'll also tell you I miss Oklahoma like a cowboy misses his hat."

"Red Creek. And I know what you mean. I miss it every day."

"Last I knew, that was ranching country, not NASCAR country. How'd you come to be a fan?"

"Now that's something we need to talk about. You see, I'm not really—"

"My friends are new to all this, but they're excited to see what you've got in store for us. I appreciate you doing this, Coot."

He waved a hand and blushed under his bushy grey beard. "Ah, don't mention it. Skeeter and I go way back. He doesn't often ask for a favor, so when he does, I'm happy to oblige. Figure as I owe him more than I'll ever be able to repay. He speaks mighty highly of you, Max."

It was Max's turn to blush, though she dipped her head and tried to hide it. "I've known Skeeter my whole life. He practically raised me. It's possible he's a little biased."

"He raised—"

Max interrupted before Ellie could ask her question. "You've got a few drivers ready for us?"

"I've got two drivers ready for you," Coot said.

"Oh." Max swallowed her disappointment. "Then let's get Ellie and Nicole suited up, and get them out there."

"And you?" Coot asked.

"That's okay. I've done it hundreds of times. I can watch today."

"Then what am I going to do with the 32? I've got it fueled up and ready to go."

Max's heart exploded. Still, she hesitated, not quite ready to let herself believe he was offering what she hoped he was offering. "The 32?"

"Do you want to drive or not?"

"Yeah, I want to drive! You're sure, Coot?"

"Sure, I'm sure. Skeeter vouched for you. Said you coulda made it if you'd wanted it."

Max's fingers tingled, and it was all she could do not to grab Coot and hug him until he couldn't breathe.

"I don't know about that, but I'll treat the 32 like it's my baby."

"What are y'all talking about?" Ellie demanded. "What's the 32?"

When Max laughed, it was the laugh of her sixteen-year-old self being let loose for the first time behind the wheel at Daytona. She linked one arm with Ellie's and the other with Nicole's.

"Ready?"

"Not really," Nicole said.

"Not a chance," Ellie said.

"Ladies, you're not nervous, are you?" Coot asked. "750 horsepower, zero to sixty in three seconds, the track whizzing by at 200 miles per hour. What's not to love?"

"Mr. Coot, the only horses I want underneath me are the four-legged variety. I think, as a fellow Oklahoman, you'd understand and respect that."

"You ain't never tried out these horses. Give 'em a chance, Miss Ellie."

Max knew it was only Ellie's southern breeding that kept her from throwing a fit and refusing. For once, Max was grateful for that southern breeding.

Ten minutes later, they were wrapped in racing jackets splashed with logos, their hands gloved, and they stood, holding helmets, alongside three race cars. Max had a moment of regret that she didn't have her own gear with her, but it was packed away in a box now stored in Skeeter's attic and had been since she'd packed away that childhood dream.

"Okay, ladies," Coot directed his comments to Nicole and Ellie. "Don't you worry. You'll be perfectly safe. My drivers know what they're doing. They'll give you a NASCAR experience, but with none of the danger. You'll be secured in the seat with a harness. The cars you'll be riding in have been refitted with a passenger seat. Cars that race have only the driver's seat, but we use these to give folks like you a thrill you'll never forget."

"Why just a driver's seat?" Ellie asked.

"They're stripped of as much weight as possible to make them as fast as possible. If we don't need something, we leave it out."

Nicole studied the passenger side of the car. "There's no door."

"Nope," Coot said. "Don't need a door, don't have a door. Y'all will crawl right in the window." He turned to Ellie. "Think of it like mounting a horse."

"Hmm…" Ellie said. "Do you have a horse around here? I'd much rather do that."

Coot chuckled. "Now, Miss Ellie, you're going to love this. Trust me."

Ellie glared at Max. "Begging your pardon, sir, but I don't know that I can trust any one of y'all who does this," she stretched her arm out toward the track and twirled her finger in a circle, "for a living."

"You're going to be asking me when you can come back and do it again."

Both Ellie and Nicole gave Coot a very skeptical, "Hah!"

Coot reached inside the car closest to him and tapped. "There's a camera mounted inside here. It's going to film you while you're on your ride. I'd never be able to figure out how to do it, but Trish, who comes in to help me out with computer things, will send the video to the email address Max gave me."

"What? No! Coot, that's not a good idea. She'll do all manner of sneaky things with it. Use it to blackmail us, post embarrassing clips of us online."

This time, Coot threw his head back and let a laugh fly. "Max wouldn't do that, would you, Max?"

Max smiled. "Ready, ladies?"

"For the record, I'm scared to death," Nicole whispered to Max as she passed on her way to the car that Coot pointed out for her. Max watched Nicole look over her shoulder, open her mouth as if ready to say something, then hunch her shoulders and climb into the car.

Ellie didn't move. "I don't think I can do this."

"Of course you can. Get in, Oklahoma, engine's running."

"But—"

Max nudged Ellie closer to the car, then left her in Coot's care. Smiling, Max headed for the 32 car.

The vibration of the steering wheel beneath her gloved hands was like a lover's caress. The smell of the exhaust, the tightness of the harness, the roar when she tapped the gas…she'd had no idea how much she'd missed it. She closed her eyes and let herself soak it all in until Coot stood outside her window.

"Got 'em both ready. They're pretty white."

"You think I'm making a mistake?" Max asked.

"Nah. They'll be fine. Once they get going and get the first few laps out of the way, they'll love it."

"I hope so, or I'll be hearing about it for a good, long time."

"What about you? You ready?"

"Born ready, Coot."

"Ah, Max, I gotta ask. I saw the news. I wouldn't bring it up, and I'm not worried about the 32, but you need to convince me not to be worried about you. What you went through, well, it would shake anyone, maybe leave them a little distracted. There's no room for distraction on the track."

Max wanted to be angry, but Coot was right. "It shook me, but I'm okay." She squeezed her hands on the steering wheel. "This right here is the best therapy I can think of. I promise you, I'll be fine."

"Okay. I had to ask, but you're right about therapy." He slapped his hand on the roof. "Enjoy."

Max grinned when a green flag waved, then pressed the pedal to the floor.

* * *

Ellie said nothing for over a half hour on their drive back to Caston. Max chatted with Nicole who rode in the back seat this time, but whenever they tried to include Ellie, she shook her head or held up her hand, then stared out the window. Finally, Max couldn't take it any longer.

"Listen, Ellie, I'm sorry. I didn't think you'd hate it quite as much as you did. I shouldn't have forced you to do it."

Ellie looked at Max for what seemed like minutes without blinking. Then she drew in a deep breath and let out something between a sigh and a hum.

"You didn't force me. I could have refused. I'd like to think no one would have picked me up and shoved me into the car. You did pressure me, that much is true, but in the end, it was my decision."

"Well, still, I'm sorry you hated it and that you were scared."

"Scared? I wasn't scared, I was terrified. I had my eyes squeezed shut and was praying every prayer I could think of for the first few times around." She sighed again. "But, you told the truth about the spa, that you didn't completely hate it, so I have to tell the truth about today. I didn't hate it."

Max gasped, and her eyes rounded. Ellie, however, didn't give her a chance to speak.

"Before you start gloating, let me say I most certainly did not love it. I didn't even particularly like it, but there was something a little thrilling about it. In a horrifying way."

"Agreed," Nicole said. "The whole time I kept thinking that, assuming I didn't die, I couldn't wait to tell my brother. Nate's always loved going fast. Cars, boats, bikes, skis, whatever he could make go, he wanted to make go faster. He used to watch racing on TV. He's going to flip when I tell him what I did."

"I don't think my brothers will believe me. And there's no way I can let Mama find out. Her daughter in a race car? She'd faint dead away."

They were quiet for a couple of miles, the only sound the humming of the tires over the highway and the low bass coming from the car's stereo.

"Max, what did Coot mean when he said your friend told him you could have made it if you'd wanted it?" Ellie asked.

"Nothing. He was just talking."

"I don't think so," Nicole said. "You used to race, didn't you?"

It was Max's turn to sigh. "It was a long time ago."

"Oh, my stars! You really drove race cars?" Ellie said.

Max debated with herself but figured her friends had been good sports, for the most part, and deserved her honest answer. "Yes, I really drove race cars. For a while, it's what I thought I wanted to do."

"Wow. It seems so scary, but at the same time, kind of cool," Nicole said.

"It's definitely both. Cool doesn't begin to describe the feeling of crossing the finish line and seeing the checkered flag. And, yeah, it can be scary, but so is facing a room full of sixth graders. You have to overcome the fear if you're going to be any good. At either thing."

"And the friend, Skeeter, you said he practically raised you? What did you mean by that? Your daddy wasn't around?" Ellie hesitated but apparently decided she was on a roll. "And your mama? You've never told us anything about her. Anything about anyone in your family, for that matter."

"El, I don't want to get into all that."

"I didn't want to get into that car."

Max's eyes rolled upward, far enough that she glimpsed her car's light grey headliner. There was a tiny tear she'd been meaning to fix. A stain she'd been meaning to clean. There was plenty inside her car to distract her from Ellie's questions, but Max knew it wasn't fair to keep avoiding and changing the subject every time her friends asked about her past.

"Fine. My mom left when I was four. I barely remember her. She married my dad because she wanted to be married to a race car driver. My dad had a bad accident when I was very young. He hurt his leg pretty badly. He had surgeries, a lot of them, and for a long time, refused to give up on his dream of racing. When it became apparent it was never going to happen, and that his leg wouldn't allow him to even work on a pit crew, my mom took off. Since my dad didn't know anything but racing, he continued picking up jobs with one team or another. Sometimes, he was hired to work on the cars, but that didn't always work out, or last. He'd take jobs doing office work, promotions, even cleaning just to be around the track. We moved all over the country. Wherever he could find work. That's why I told you I never really had a place to call home, and why I never stayed in the same school long enough to make any real friends. My friends were the guys, and sometimes women, who were part of the racing world."

She sensed more than saw Ellie and Nicole share a look, but she definitely felt the tension crackle in the car like an electric shock in the dead of winter.

"And you've never seen your mom since?" Nicole asked.

"No."

"Do you know where she is?"

"No."

"It seems if she were still part of the racing world? Family? I don't know what you call it, but it seems like you would run into her, or at least hear something about her," Nicole said.

Max's laugh was a bitter one. "I think the racing world left her behind a long time ago. Let's just say my dad was a little more popular with that crowd than she was. I don't know the details because I stopped asking when my dad stopped answering, but Skeeter told me that for a time, when she was still trying to stick around and latch on to someone else, everyone made sure she got nowhere near me. If my dad and I were in the same town she was, they kept her away. I don't know how it all worked, but you were right when you called it a family. For me, anyway, that's what it was."

"Skeeter. You've mentioned him, and today you said he more or less raised you. What did you mean?"

"You never quit, do you El?"

Max wanted to be angry, but Ellie made it impossible. Max glanced at Ellie and saw the kind eyes, and she knew Ellie's kind spirit would accept whatever she heard and would help whenever her help was needed. It made Max uncomfortable because it was as foreign to her as the sushi she refused to eat. Though Max wanted to deny it, she knew Ellie—and Nicole—cared about her more than anyone, besides Skeeter, and her dad in his way, had in a long time.

"Fine," Max said when Ellie simply waited her out. "When I got older, when I didn't need constant looking after, my dad started to, how do I put it? Started to think his job as a parent was over. He'd take me with him when he worked, letting me run wild. If it hadn't been for Skeeter, I probably wouldn't have been in school unless the authorities finally caught up with my dad and forced the issue. Skeeter saw that I did my homework, that I had clothes that fit, that I had a decent meal once in a while. All that stuff. My dad loved me—loves me—but he's never been very good at showing it. His first and only real love is racing."

"Run wild? What does that mean? Did you get into trouble?" Alongside Max, Ellie shuddered.

"Our definitions of trouble are probably different, but no, not really.

I was a pretty good kid. Even though my dad wasn't always looking out for me, there were enough people around who were. Sometimes there'd be women around, whether they were working for a team or were the wives of the guys who were. Sometimes one of them would take me under her wing for a while, help me out with girl things. But even the guys, most of them were nice. Some of them didn't have the best judgment where a kid was concerned, but to me, it was fun. Learned to drive when I was twelve. Drove my first race car when I was thirteen. There were never many kids around, so I rubbed some of the guys the wrong way, but mostly, people were good to me. You know the saying, 'It takes a village to raise a child?' Well, I'm proof. There are hundreds of people I could credit with helping to raise me, but Skeeter was almost a constant. We weren't always in the same place, but we were often enough that he was like a grandpa to me. He's why I'm here. When he finally retired and settled, he came back to Wisconsin. He was born here, and he said it's the closest thing to home he knows, so I decided to make it the closest thing to home that I know, at least for the time being."

"I know it's easy to call my childhood sheltered because it was, but I knew life existed outside my bubble. Not everyone I knew had a life exactly like mine, but Max, I have to admit, I've never known anyone with a life like you've had. Until I left for college, I'd only ever lived in one town, in one house. I can't understand what it would be like to not have that sort of haven, that place where I knew I would always be safe and loved. It seems like it would have been easy for you to grow up jaded, angry at the world, but you're just the opposite. You're full of life, you're funny, you're a loyal friend, you're brave. Really, you're one of the most amazing people I've ever known, and the more I learn about you, the more I understand why you're such an amazing teacher. Not only have you lived all over the country, and gone to school with kids from all over the country, and from all sorts of backgrounds and situations, you've lived—and thrived—in all sorts of situations. It's made you understanding of, and in touch with, all different kinds of students. That's why they all love you. They can all relate to you because they can all see a little of themselves in you."

Max took her eyes off the road to look at Ellie. Dumbfounded didn't seem a strong enough word, but it was the only one Max could come up with that came close to describing how she felt. She'd expected to spend the drive home apologizing for making Ellie uncomfortable by forcing her inside a race car. She'd never expected to be the one left feeling uncomfortable. And again, uncomfortable didn't seem nearly strong enough.

Aside from compliments about the way she handled a car, compliments that came from those who hadn't refused to look the other way when a female was behind the wheel, Max wasn't used to being on the receiving end of any sort of praise.

"She's right, you know," Nicole said. "For months, I've been trying to figure out what it is you have that Ellie and I don't. The way you relate to the kids on a different sort of level. Now that Ellie put it into words, it seems so simple. So many different experiences, different parts of the country, and different people have made you the person you are, and as Ellie said, made you relatable to all of them. Though you've never talked about it, I've always had the feeling that teaching middle school wasn't your dream any more than it was my dream, but I think you've landed in exactly the right spot."

Max didn't know how to respond, so she clutched the steering wheel and stared out the windshield. Maybe if she ignored it, it would all go away. *Exactly the right spot*? That was so far from the truth, it was laughable. Just one more stop, one more step, on her way to the next thing. That's all teaching was to her. It didn't seem like what Nicole and Ellie wanted to hear, though, and Max certainly wasn't ready to get into the hows and whys of what she was doing in Caston, so she'd ignore that comment, for sure.

"Aren't you going to say anything?" Ellie demanded. "Most times, when a person is complimented, that person offers thanks or at least responds."

"Didn't we just establish that I grew up completely differently than you did? Maybe I learned to ignore compliments."

"Oh, Max." Ellie spoke and shook her head in a way that made it seem as if she were speaking to a small child. "Then just tell us one thing. When are we going to meet Skeeter? Because I have about a million questions."

9

She'd expected to be a little nervous, but the sweaty palms and the racing pulse as she walked across the parking lot of Caston Middle School came as a surprise. It was earlier than she normally arrived at school, but Amanda had requested a visit before Max began her day. When she noted how many cars were already in the parking lot, she figured it was going to be more than just a visit between the two of them, and probably a full staff meeting.

Nicole met her inside the door.

"I know you don't want me to ask you if you're okay, but are you okay? Are you sure you're ready?"

"I'm ready."

They walked down the hallway toward the office.

"Is there a staff meeting? Amanda said she wanted to talk to me, but it looks like everyone's here."

"Um..."

When they turned the corner and the commons came into view, Max stopped dead in her tracks. They were all there. Teachers, administrators, office staff, custodians, as well as some faces Max didn't recognize. She wanted to be angry, and she wanted to turn and run in the opposite direction, but she felt Nicole's hand on her arm moving her toward the crowd.

As she passed through the group and heard the words of encouragement, of support, of gratitude, realization smacked her in the face. She needed them. She needed the people surrounding her as she'd rarely needed anyone in her life. So used to doing things on her own and finding her own way, it wasn't natural to lean on others, but Max realized that's exactly what they wanted her to do, and what she needed to do. She'd get through the day, and all the days that followed, with them, because they were a team.

Teams, she understood.

It could have been any one of them who'd found themselves in Max's position. It was just timing and location. Max knew had the tables been turned, she'd do whatever she could to help the person who'd found themselves in a terrifying situation, so it was only fair that she accept help from them.

She'd walked partway through the group before it clicked that they were all wearing the same shirt. Blue shirts with silver lettering, *Caston Strong*. With Nicole urging her forward, she made it to the front of the room where Amanda was waiting. She handed Max an identical blue shirt.

"I know you never would have agreed to this if I'd told you, so, surprise! Really, though, we all want you to know that we're here for you. Whatever you need, whenever you need it. Just ask."

Max sensed movement at her side and turned to see Ellie. She grabbed Max's right arm. Nicole still held her left.

"I was going to meet you at the door, but Nicole said I'd never be able to keep a secret, so she made me wait in here. She's probably right, but I want you to know I was there in spirit."

"You always are, El. Both of you, you're always there. I'm starting to realize it's not such a bad thing." Max turned her attention to Amanda. "Thank you. You're right, I wouldn't have agreed to it, but I appreciate it."

"I'll be checking in throughout the day. Don't bother telling me it's unnecessary, because I'm going to do it anyway. If you need anything at all, call me, or call anyone in this room. Promise me that."

Max nodded. "Promise."

"Lunch in my office. I want to check in with you."

"Okay."

"Have a good day, Max."

Amanda leaned close and hugged Max. Max didn't know if she'd ever get used to people hugging her. Ellie did it all the time, Max had almost gotten used to that, but when near strangers or work colleagues did it, it was just plain strange. Shaking hands seemed to Max like a much more civilized way of handling things. Still, she forced a smile and used one arm to sort of hug back.

Nicole and Ellie led Max back through the crowd. More greetings, more thanks, and more hugs. Max smiled, offered thanks of her own to the good wishes, and was glad when the clear hallway was in front of her.

She may be ready to acknowledge the fact that she needed her coworkers, and she might even need friends, but enough was enough with all the touchy-feely stuff.

Nicole and Ellie kept hold of her arms and walked toward her classroom.

"Why are we going this way?" Max asked when they took a turn that would take them on the long route.

"It gets us to the same place," Nicole said.

Max barely had time to wonder what her friends were up to before they rounded the corner to find the hallway lined with her coworkers. How'd they gotten there so fast, Max had no idea, but there they were, forming a human shield and blocking the spot against the lockers where Max had collapsed after being pulled away from the gunman by a police officer. And the spot where she'd tackled that gunman. And the door next to hers where he'd tried to enter.

"You got this, Max."

"We're here for you."

"Whatever you need."

"We're proud of you, Max."

"Glad you're on our team."

Comments bombarded her from all sides as she, once again, walked between her fellow teachers, receiving their thanks and their support. As if they sensed she didn't know how to answer, as soon as she reached her classroom door, they melted away with waves and thumbs up.

But it didn't stop. When she flipped on the light in her room, she was met with hand-drawn posters and banners, balloons, and a giant bouquet of what looked to be every kind of flower in existence.

"This is the kids' doing," Nicole said. "All on their own. They started asking what they could do as soon as they came back to school."

Max had to turn away, so she pretended to study the flowers.

"They all love you," Ellie said. "They hung up signs and posters after school on Friday, then a few made arrangements with Amanda to come in early this morning to drop off the balloons and flowers."

"I appreciate it, all of it, but it can't go on. We have to get back to normal, don't we?"

"We will," Nicole said. "It will take some time, but we'll get there.

This is part of the process. It's as much for them as it is for you. It helps the kids feel like they have some power, some control over something that was so out of their control."

It made sense, Max knew that, but since she'd hung up her racing jacket years ago, she'd done her best to stay out of the spotlight. It was never really for her. This was far too much attention, so she decided it was time to deflect. She pulled the T-shirt Amanda had given her over the white blouse she was wearing, then turned to Ellie.

"El, you realize you're wearing a T-shirt, right? To school? Not a flowery dress, or wool pants and a cashmere sweater, but a plain old T-shirt? It hasn't even been bedazzled or be-flowered, or whatever it was you did to that pi day shirt you wore last month."

Ellie flinched as if she'd been slapped. She looked down at her T-shirt. "Of course, I realize that. Only for you, Max, only for you."

Right then and there, Max decided if the day got to be too much, she'd remember the look on Ellie's face and it would get her through.

With teachers dropping in to see how she was doing, with encouraging emails and texts popping up throughout the day, and with Amanda spending part of the day in the classroom with her, the day flew by. Amanda, a former math teacher, shocked Max and her students by sharing a rap about solving an equation with a variable that she'd used when she taught math. If seeing their principal rapping, as well as executing some hip-hop dance moves, didn't help the kids remember how to solve for x, Max didn't know if anything would.

When the room cleared out after the last bell, Max looked around her. Her desk was covered with plates of cookies and bars, cards decorated the previously empty bulletin boards, small gifts were scattered from one side of the room to the other, and the dry-erase boards were filled with messages. Her students had flooded her with good wishes and thanks.

She picked up a peanut butter cookie off a gorgeous ceramic platter with 'Thank You' written in a fancy script and took a bite. Amanda had provided lunch when they'd met in her office, but Max had been too wound up to do more than pick at the salad. It was in the refrigerator, she might eat it for dinner, but for now, a cookie hit the spot far better than lettuce ever could.

She picked up and set down some of the gifts her students had given her. It felt odd, and maybe wrong, to accept them, but after the first couple, when she'd realized Nicole was right, that the students needed it as much as Max did, she'd smiled and gratefully accepted each and every one of them.

"Oh, my stars!" Ellie said. "Would y'all look at this!"

"A bit much, isn't it?" Max said.

"Not at all. I told you, they love you."

Not wanting to go down that road again, Max scanned the pile of gifts and homed in on the purple bag.

"Hey, El, check this out." Max pulled out an object wrapped in lavender tissue paper. "You know those signs, Don't Mess with Texas?"

"Humpf. Don't mess with Texas," Ellie muttered. "More like, don't mess with Oklahoma. Which team is on a four-game head-to-head winning streak, I ask you?"

"I don't know, but I'm guessing Oklahoma?" Max said.

"A bit of history," Nicole interrupted. "Did either of you know that 'Don't Mess with Texas' was a slogan coined by the Texas Department of Transportation as part of an anti-littering campaign, and that the first time it was aired on television was during the 1986 Cotton Bowl? The commercial featured Stevie Ray Vaughn playing *The Eyes of Texas*, then at the end, looking into the camera and saying, 'Don't mess with Texas.'"

"Really? Stevie Ray Vaughn?" Max said.

"How do you know that? Why do you know that?" Ellie said.

"Yes, really, and I know it because I read about some trademark infringement lawsuits regarding the phrase."

"Trademark infringement? Huh. Then I suppose this is illegal?"

Max unwrapped what was inside the paper and held it up for Nicole and Ellie to see. *Don't Mess with Max-S* was burned into a piece of wood shaped like the state of Wisconsin.

"That's fabulous!" Nicole said. "Max, Max-S, like Tex-as. Get it, Ellie?"

"I get it." Ellie came closer and ran her finger over the letters. "It's so well made, and it's a very cute idea, but it's going to make me think of Texas every time I see it. If you hang it up in here, I might try *not* to see it." She leaned over some of the other gift bags and peeked inside. "Are these all gifts from your students?"

"Yeah. Everything from fruit to nuts. For real. There's a fruit basket over there," Max pointed to the counter on the far wall, "and there's a tin of nuts on my desk. Does it seem kind of weird?"

"It seems sweet," Ellie said. "May I?" She pointed at a tray of cookies.

"Sure. There's plenty."

Ellie plucked a cookie from the platter, then took a tiny bite. "Mmm, these are good."

"Take them. I have dozens more."

"I couldn't. I shouldn't. Wedding dress shopping is next weekend." Ellie did her wiggle she did when she was too excited to stand still.

Max spun to face Ellie. "Wedding dress? Wait, what? Shopping? For a wedding dress? Um, did I agree? I mean, am I..." She looked at Nicole for help. "Are we going with you? Did I forget?"

"Goodness, Max, don't look so scared. Mama and my sisters are coming for the weekend. Mama, of course, wanted me to come home and shop there, but since I'll need fittings and all, it makes more sense to do it here. I've found a few shops within driving distance that seem like possibilities. You and Nicole are more than welcome to come along. In fact, I think it would be fun for you to get to know Mama and my sisters, but I'll understand if you'd rather not, or if you can't."

"Understand? Does that mean you'll be upset if we don't go with you?"

"I promise it does not. It means whatever you choose will be fine. I'm just so excited for Mama to visit, and for Charlene and Hayley to see where I live, I won't have time to fret about it if you're not there."

Max wasn't sure, and based on the expression on Nicole's face, she wasn't alone. Max crossed her fingers and hoped that she'd be able to get out of a weekend of wedding dress shopping without hurting Ellie's feelings. The look she shared with Nicole promised they'd discuss it later.

"Now," Ellie said, "tell us about your day."

As tired as she was of talking about her day, and about her feelings, and just talking in general, it was safer than the topic of wedding dress shopping, so Max dove in.

She hadn't talked to Beck about stopping by, but once Max got home, she found she didn't know what to do with herself. The notes from the sub had been thorough; she'd covered everything Max had hoped to cover, and with a quiz scheduled in her math classes the next day, there wasn't much lesson planning to do. Her engineering class was in the middle of preparing for their upcoming project, so the next day would be an in-class research day. Nothing to prep for that, either.

That left her with too much time on her hands, and too much time to think. If she had Stevie Ray, she'd go for a drive. Since she didn't, she did the next best thing.

"Hey, Beck," Max said when she let herself in the open door and found him under the hood of a Chevy that had seen better days.

"What are you doing here, Max? Did we make plans for tonight?" He turned his head in her direction but didn't come out from under the hood.

"No, I just wanted to visit Stevie Ray. I haven't been here since Thursday. I need to make sure he's safe."

"And what do you think is going to happen?"

"I don't know. You could have a fire, you could be robbed, you could sell Stevie Ray to cover your massive gambling debts."

"When I gamble, I win, so you can cross that worry off your list."

"Why is it so quiet in here? Where are Sven and Jake?"

"Sven has the day off, and Jake called in sick."

"Ow. That's not very good timing, boss."

"No kidding. I'm swamped. Sven asked for the day off weeks ago. Jake never gets sick, but a girl he's dating talked him into sushi last night and today he has food poisoning."

"Of course he does. That's exactly why I will never eat sushi. What is it with people and raw fish? I don't get it."

Max wandered around the shop, peering under the hood of a Toyota Camry, checking the tire tread on a Ford Edge, and ended up back alongside the Chevy, where Beck was now cursing under his breath.

"Problems?"

"I've been resuscitating this one for three years. The owner could afford twenty new cars but refuses to buy one. I'll spend a few hours patching it up and getting it running and in less than six months, it'll be back in here and we'll do it all again. I don't have time to play that game today. Too much work to do."

Max looked at the Toyota, then the Ford, and then drummed her fingers on her thigh.

"I could help."

"Help with what?"

"With your workload. What's up with the Ford? Tell me why it's in here, and I'll take care of it."

Now Beck did emerge from under the hood. "Get out of my garage, Mad Max. I'm busy."

"Which is exactly why I offered to help."

"You don't work here."

"The guys who do aren't here. Or maybe you enjoy calling your customers and telling them you can't have their cars ready as promised. Hmm?"

"I'm beginning to think you're more annoying now than you were when you were eight."

"Very funny, Beck. Fine, then I'll just be going, though I can tell from here that the Edge needs new tires, and since I spotted four standing outside the door, I would assume they're the lucky winners. Four tires. I could have it done in under forty minutes, but if you don't need my help…"

He looked at her as if she'd lost her mind. *"You don't work here!"*

"Doesn't mean I can't work here this afternoon."

"Why?"

"I told you, because you need the help."

Beck leaned his hip against the car and wiped his arm across his forehead. "Why?" he repeated.

Max growled, then spun on her heel so she wasn't facing Beck.

"Because I need something to do. I need to stay busy. If I'm not busy, I start to think, and that leads to worry, and I'm not good at worrying. Gives me a stomachache." She paced around the garage but kept her back to Beck. "It was a bizarre day, a day I had no control over whatsoever. I need to do something that I can control, something where I'll know the outcome."

He stayed quiet for so long, she had no choice but to turn toward him. "What?"

"You had a rough day. I'm sorry. Was it hard being back there? Back inside the school?"

"It was fine." She picked up the jacket she'd tossed on a chair. "I'll get out of your way. Can I come back later in the week to work on my car?"

"Max. Tell me."

"Tell you what?"

He shook his head. "You know very well what. Tell me what happened."

"Why?"

"Because you'll feel better? Because you want to? I don't know, just tell me."

"While I install four new tires?"

"You really are more annoying than you were when you were eight. Fine. On one condition. No, two. One, you hurt yourself, you lie and say you did it somewhere else."

"I'm a good liar."

"And two, get me something to eat. I had a piece of toast at six o'clock this morning and nothing since. I'm starving."

Max grinned. She hadn't unloaded her car. "That, I can do, as long as you're up for cookies, banana bread, a selection of meats and cheeses, your pick from a fruit basket, or chocolate. So much chocolate."

"Huh?"

"You'll see," Max said, as she nearly skipped out of the garage.

Max had never been particularly fond of spring. At least not when she was in a northern climate where spring was more idea than fact. That night, with only a sliver of moon, clouds blotting out most of the stars, and no snow to reflect the glow of the one stingy lightbulb on the outside of the garage, it was blacker than ink as she felt more than saw her way up the stairs to her apartment. She debated grabbing her phone and using it to light her way, but figured she could make it up twelve steps faster than she could get her phone out of her purse and fumble with it to turn on the flashlight.

As she approached the small landing outside the door, she thought she saw the shadows move. Fear sent shock waves from her center to the tips of her fingers and toes. She stopped mid-step and listened. Her breath came fast and loud, blocking out any noise an intruder would have made while lying in wait for her.

She held her breath and told herself she was being ridiculous, that there was no one there, but flashes of the man in her classroom, his crazed eyes, his shaking hand holding a gun filled her senses until she was certain she could not only see him, but hear him, smell him, and feel him getting closer.

It was only her imagination, the odd reflection from the light below causing the shadows to shift, she tried to tell herself. She would back down the stairs, get her phone out of her purse, and then light the way so she could be certain. She'd only taken one step backward when she couldn't deny that the shadow was more than a shadow, because it moved, and it spoke.

Max turned to run. She'd almost made it to the bottom of the stairs when she heard the voice again.

"Maxine? Hello, Maxine."

Though she hadn't heard the voice in over twenty years, some part of her remembered it, no matter how much she didn't want to remember. The only difference was the last time she'd heard that voice, it had told her goodbye.

10

"Hey, Maxine, it's me. It's your mom."

The voice was shaky, insecure, and Max heard the long hiss of an inhale before she had time to notice the cigarette smell or the glow of the burning ash.

Max almost wished it was a madman waiting on her doorstep. Fighting him off, running, screaming, all would have been options. Instead, she was left wondering what sort of options she had with a woman calling herself mom.

"What are you doing here?"

A laugh, but a nervous one, answered her. Laughing was the last thing on Max's mind.

"Oh, Maxine, is that any way to greet your old mother?"

Max didn't think she'd consciously made the decision, but apparently part of her had decided to take the angry track.

"I don't have a mother."

"Of course you do, honey. I'm right here, aren't I?"

Max still couldn't see the woman who hadn't moved from the landing. The glow of the cigarette moved up and down, and the smell became all Max could focus on. She wanted to gag.

"Mothers don't disappear for over twenty years, then show up and act as if nothing happened."

"I know we have some things to talk about, but why don't we do that inside? It's cold out here. Besides, I want to get a good look at my baby."

Max wanted to scream. "I don't think so. It's been a long day, I'm tired, and I have to work in the morning. You should leave."

"Just a few minutes? It's been so long. I want to know how you're doing."

"Seems like you could have found a few minutes sometime over the past twenty years to ask."

"You're right. I made a lot of mistakes. Can't we try to move forward? Forget about the past?"

Max's anger spiked. "Forget about the past? Are you serious? I'm supposed to forget that my mother walked out on me when I was four years old and never bothered to contact me? Not once? Not one phone call, not one birthday card, nothing? Do you honestly think you can still call yourself my mother?"

Max heard the sharp intake of breath as the woman sucked furiously on her cigarette until there was nothing left. Max watched the faint glow as it dropped to the ground, then heard the scratching sound as the woman twisted her toe to crush it.

"I know words don't make up for everything that happened, but can't it be a start? And, Maxine, there were—"

"Stop calling me Maxine. It's Max."

"Of course. Max. Can't we go inside, Max? Just for a few minutes?"

"Why now? After all these years, why now?"

The woman hesitated. "It just seemed like time. Time to try to make up for my mistakes."

"It's going to take more than showing up at my door to make up for all your mistakes. I can't do this tonight. You need to leave."

"Tomorrow? I could come back tomorrow."

"No, not tomorrow. Not ever. Just leave."

When the woman started down the stairs, Max realized the two of them would nearly touch if she stayed where she was in the middle of the staircase, so she hurried down to the bottom, then stepped to the side. Though there was plenty of room, the woman drew closer when she reached the bottom. The light from the garage provided enough of a glow, and Max couldn't help but look.

Her hair was still dark, about shoulder length, but it looked lifeless. Wrinkles creased her face; more, Max thought, than a woman her age should have. They told the tale of a hard life, and Max guessed the tale was probably true. She wore glasses, and the light reflected off them so that Max couldn't get a good look at the woman's eyes. Too bad, Max thought, because she'd always been able to read a person based on their eyes.

The woman looked thin, though she was bundled in a heavy jacket. When she reached toward Max, Max took another step away, but not before she noticed the tremor in the woman's gloved hand.

Though it infuriated her, Max couldn't help but compare the woman in front of her to the single picture she'd kept since she was four years old. She'd looked at it every day when she'd been young, certain her mom would be back soon and Max didn't want to risk not recognizing her. When she'd been ten, she'd tried to tear up the photo, but she hadn't been able to do it. Instead, she'd folded it and tucked it inside a deck of cards she kept in a box of treasures that, no matter where they moved, always came with her. Though she hadn't looked at it in years, the picture was ingrained in her memory.

That woman had bouncy hair, lively blue eyes, and a smile that made her look like a movie star. Over the years, Max had picked up bits and pieces of information about her mom, and she figured out her mother had used that smile when it pleased her, and when it could get her what she wanted.

There was no mistaking it was the same woman, it was her mother, but the years hadn't been kind.

"I've missed you, baby," the woman whispered. "I've missed you so much."

Max didn't answer. If the woman who called herself her mother expected Max to fall into her arms and profess her love, she had another thing coming.

Without a word, Max headed up the stairs and let herself into her apartment.

She never looked back.

Sometime during the long hours she'd stared at the ceiling, Max had decided she'd ask Nicole and Ellie for their take on the mom situation. She figured Ellie would tell her to give her mom a chance, because for Ellie, family was what mattered, and Ellie didn't have much experience with family dysfunction. Nicole would be more analytical in her assessment, but would probably side with Ellie in the end, telling Max she should at least speak with her mom. Max told herself she'd listen to their arguments, but she'd still have the final word.

She fully expected that word to be no.

Max suffered through an endless school day, during which she was distracted and irritable. The fact that no one called her on it, just smiled and attributed her lousy mood and short temper to the circumstances of the previous week made her even more irritable.

When the day finally ended, when it came time to spill her pathetic story to her friends, she found she couldn't do it.

It was too personal, she decided, and she was too crabby to listen to anything they'd have to say. Instead, when they gathered in Ellie's room at the end of the day in their attempt to get back to something approaching normal, Max kept her contributions to the conversation to topics regarding her car.

Ellie tried to steer the conversation to wedding plans but finally gave in when Max steered harder in the other direction.

"Now that I have experience with race cars, I think you should let me drive your car when it's fixed."

It might have been the best thing anyone could have said because Max laughed harder than she'd laughed in a week.

"I don't think it's that funny," Ellie said as her mouth turned down in a scowl.

"Oh, it's more than funny," Max said, gulping for air. "It's hysterical. You could write a comedy routine around it and perform at open mic night at a comedy club. You'd bring down the house."

Ellie rolled her eyes and huffed. "There's no talking to you sometimes, Max."

"Do you know how many people have driven my car?" Max asked. She didn't wait for an answer. "Three. Me, Skeeter, and Brady the other day when he brought it to me. Well, technically, I guess Beck drove it because he had to move it into his shop, but that doesn't really count. No one drives my car. No one."

Ellie acted like she hadn't heard a thing Max said, and when Ellie got that look in her eyes that told Max something she'd hate was on the way, she braced for the worst.

"I know! You should let us borrow it for our wedding. We could drive it from the church to the reception. We'd decorate it with signs and tie cans on the back. Mama and Daddy drove in a Mustang all decorated like that. I've seen the pictures countless times and I know I could recreate it. It was so sweet. Of course, theirs was a convertible. Even so, yours would be okay, and Mama and Daddy would love it. Almost like my 'something borrowed.' The car would be borrowed, of course, but can an idea be borrowed?" Ellie paused to wrinkle her nose and consider. Then she shrugged. "You know, Zeke was just talking about finding a fun car for our wedding day. I don't know why I didn't think to mention yours."

Max felt dizzy. As a bridesmaid, was that something she was expected to do? Let them use her car? What in blazes had she agreed to? Cans tied to the bumper? And signs? Did that mean tape? On Stevie Ray? Being a bridesmaid should come with a blasted handbook. She would have read every single word in that book before agreeing to anything.

"Oh, but that means you'll have to be able to fix it. Do you think you'll be able to fix it, Max?" Ellie asked, syrup dripping from her words. "I know you said you know how to do things like that, but maybe this is too big a job? Just to be sure it's fixed and running properly, maybe you should consider taking it to an expert. A real expert, I mean. I'm sure if we ask around, we could find someone."

If the saying was true and you could actually blow your top, Max figured Nicole and Ellie were in for a show.

"I am perfectly capable of fixing my car! I don't need your so-called experts, I'm an expert! I can fix a car——"

It was hard to see through the red haze, and even more difficult to hear over the roaring in her ears, but somehow Max realized both Nicole and Ellie were laughing. At her.

"What?"

It was Ellie's turn to gulp for air. "It's just so darn much fun to tease you. You get as worked up as my sister, Charlene. She never could take a joke. She'd run straight to Mama and tell on us every time."

"A joke? Which part was the joke?"

Nicole giggled, so Max turned toward her but angled her thumb toward Ellie.

"You have some sense. Tell me what she's talking about."

Nicole kept laughing. "Some sense? Gee, thanks. We know you can fix your car. At least, we think you can. That was a joke."

"I can fix my car," Max hissed.

Ellie was still carrying on, laughing and doing some weird mimicking thing that Max supposed was meant to look like her. Ellie didn't quit until her phone buzzed. When Ellie looked at it, smiled, and answered it, Max seized her opportunity.

Whispering to Nicole, she asked, "What about the car at the wedding? Was that part of the joke, or is that a bridesmaid thing? Do I need to let her use my car if she asks?"

Max figured it was the sheer panic seeping from her pores that made Nicole stop laughing and take pity on Max.

"That part was a joke too. You don't have to let her use the car. You could *offer* to let her use it, or you could offer to drive them, either would be appropriate, but there is no bridesmaid rule regarding the use of a classic car. You really don't have a clue about this stuff, do you?"

The relief was as real as standing in front of an open freezer on a blisteringly hot day. Max allowed herself a moment to revel in it.

"No, Nicole, I do not have a clue. Not a single one." Then a bit of the tension eked back in when Max considered all that her lack of experience entailed. "You're sure she was serious when she said she didn't mind if we didn't go dress shopping with her?"

Nicole grabbed a lock of her hair and twirled it around her finger.

"That one's a little tougher than the car question. I think she was serious, but I'm not certain. I know she's over the moon that her mom and sisters will be here, so maybe she'd like to spend the day with family only. Then again, she may have said that just to give us an out."

Max stole a quick look over her shoulder. Ellie was still on the phone, smiling the smile that told Max it was Zeke. Max took advantage of the time she had.

"Then what do we do? I don't want to hurt her feelings, but..."

"But you don't want to go dress shopping."

"I do not. What possible help would I be?"

"Honestly, I think you'd be a big help. You have an excellent sense of style. It may not be the same as Ellie's style, but you know what to wear and how to wear it. If Ellie's mom and sister are just like her, it's possible they could use another opinion."

Max's heart plummeted to somewhere around her knees. All hope wasn't lost, but it was close.

"Do we ask her again? Do we wait and see if she brings it up?" Max held her breath, waiting for Nicole's answer.

"I'll take care of it. I'll talk to her and find out."

"Okay. Then there's still a chance I'll be shopping for wedding dresses on Saturday?"

"I suppose there's a chance."

Before Max could fully process the horror that would be dress shopping, Ellie finished her phone call.

"Ma-ax," Ellie sing-songed. "Is there something you haven't told us about this man who's letting you use his garage for your car?"

"No."

Ellie shook her head slowly and clucked her tongue three times.

"I don't think that's true."

"Why don't you just get to the point, Oklahoma?"

"Very well. I was talking to Zeke, I said something about your car and how we were teasing you, and Zeke told me he overheard a couple of the nurses talking during his lunch break today. He heard the name Beck, and since I've mentioned your friend to him, and since Beck isn't a common name, he listened for a minute. One of the nurses said her friend told her that her sister-in-law just had her car in for some work and the man who worked on it was drop-dead gorgeous. Zeke was woefully lacking in specifics, but I figured out that the nurse's friend's sister-in-law is single, she made it rather obvious she was interested, but Beck was all business. When she finally asked him out, point blank, he turned her down, telling her he was seeing someone. The nurse's friend's sister-in-law made a comment to the effect of, 'I hope she knows how lucky she is,' to which he replied, 'she will.'"

Ellie paused to cross her arms across her chest and jut out her hip.

"Now, I repeat, is there something you haven't told us?"

All Max could do was stare. She'd heard Zeke's name, she'd heard Beck's name, but beyond that, nothing Ellie'd said made the least bit of sense. Something about Beck's sister? Or maybe his sister-in-law? She didn't think he had a brother, but maybe she'd forgotten.

"So?" Ellie prompted.

"So what?"

"What's going on with Beck?"

"Today? I don't know."

"Do you always have to be so difficult? Was she talking about you?"

"Was who talking about me?"

Ellie looked at Nicole. "Is she doing this on purpose?"

"I don't think so. You might have lost her with all the sister-in-law of a friend of a nurse Zeke knows."

Ellie threw one hand triumphantly in Nicole's direction while she stared impatiently at Max. "She got it. It wasn't that complicated."

"You're giving me a headache. I'm going home. Nicole, you'll call me later?"

"Hold on there, Missy!" Ellie demanded. "I asked you a question, as plain as the nose on my face. I'd appreciate an answer."

"If there was a question in there, I have no idea what it was. Talk so a normal person can understand you, or don't talk at all. *Missy.*"

"Are you the one Beck is dating? Or is interested in dating?"

Again, Max could only stare. Sometimes she was almost convinced Ellie was a different species. If it turned out Max had to spend Saturday dress shopping with Ellie and three more women who were probably just like her, Max was going to need to talk to Zeke about some tranquilizers.

"I'd laugh if I thought you were kidding, but for some insane reason, you seem to be serious," Max said. "I am not dating Beck. I have never dated Beck. I have no intention of dating Beck. Does that answer your convoluted question?"

Ellie was undeterred. She smiled. "That's what I thought. I'm happy for you, Max."

Max closed her eyes and rubbed her temples. "I'm going home."

"That's fine, you can tell us more about it later."

Max didn't bother turning around. She quickened her steps when she heard Ellie call, "Wait! What was that about Nicole calling you later?"

All day, Max had been waffling between feeling certain her mother would be waiting outside her door once again and being convinced the woman had paid attention and crawled back into whatever hole she'd crawled out of. When Max pulled up in front of her home, the coast looked blessedly clear.

She made it inside without anyone, relative or reporter, stopping her. Since her regrettable responses to the reporter the week before, there'd only been one other time when she'd let her guard down and been blindsided by a reporter. That time, she'd kept her wits about her and hadn't uttered a word.

The phone calls continued with requests for interviews. Max no longer answered her phone. More frustrating were the requests filling her inbox on her school email account. It wasn't difficult to obtain her email address, all school district employee email addresses followed the same pattern, so anyone who wanted to could attempt to contact her that way. It had become part of her evening ritual to weed through the long list and determine which were legitimate emails from students and parents, and which she needed to delete without opening.

Max spent a couple of hours preparing lesson plans and grading quizzes. When she was absorbed in her work, she could pretend she was just like any other teacher: planning lessons, grading work, reading and answering emails, searching for tips to engage her students, adding meetings to her calendar. When she had too much time on her hands, she knew she wasn't like other teachers. She had come face to face with a man holding a gun, and that would likely

119

affect her for the rest of her life.

Angry that someone had that sort of control over her life, Max tapped her fingers on her tiny kitchen table and tried to think of something to occupy her mind. The idea came quickly, but it was an idea that terrified her.

One letter at a time, Max typed into her search engine, 'What does a bridesmaid do?'

The screen filled with article after article full of advice and pictures of perfectly put-together, laughing women.

"As if," Max muttered.

With great trepidation, she clicked on one of the articles that showed a checklist rather than a gaggle of color-coordinated women.

Congratulations! You have the honor of standing alongside your friend, or your sister, or your cousin on the biggest day of her life. So, what does that mean for you? It means the next few months are going to be busy. And expensive.

"Great," Max groaned and went to get the bag of cheese puffs she kept for emergencies. If this didn't qualify, she didn't know what did. She shoved a few in her mouth, then braved the computer screen.

Some of your first duties will likely come soon after you're asked to be a bridesmaid. Often, the bride will ask you to come along as she begins shopping for her wedding dress. This can be a fun day, and a day you get to know the other bridesmaids because chances are, some of you will not have met before.

"Well, that wasn't what I was hoping for," Max mumbled, her mouth full of cheese puffs.

Even if you don't go along when she shops for her dress, unless you're out of town, you can expect to go along when she shops for bridesmaids' dresses. This is a good time to learn how to keep your mouth shut when it comes to the bride's vision for her wedding. If she chooses dresses that look like pink cotton candy, complete with a bow on the butt, you're going to smile and tell her you think it's perfect. Only if she asks for your input, and only if you're certain beyond a shadow of a doubt that she wants it, should you offer any sort of feedback on the dress selection other than professing your undying love for her choice. You also will not complain about the price of the dress. You'll get a second job and suck it up.

"Oh, good lord," Max said. She went to the refrigerator and grabbed a beer. She skimmed the article to a part that didn't talk about shopping.

As a bridesmaid, you will also be responsible for planning, and paying for, a shower and a bachelorette party. The maid-of-honor should take the reins here, but you'll play an important support role. If the bride has her heart set on a trip to Napa Valley for her bachelorette party, you will plan a trip to Napa Valley. You will purchase and transport all the party trimmings. You've seen them: the bridal tiara, the sash, the matching shirts for the attendees... you get the picture. This is also going to be expensive. Unless it's simply out of the question for you financially, you will not complain. See above re: second job.

Other expenses you should be prepared for include shoes and jewelry to coordinate with the dress you'll be wearing, hair and makeup on the wedding day, gifts for the shower, the bachelorette party, and the wedding. Yes, the expenses can seem monumental. Try to remember that one day, you'll ask the same of your friend/sister/cousin.

Aside from financial obligations, there will be other expectations. A big one, and one that shouldn't cost much other than maybe a bottle of wine or some really good chocolate, is being there for the bride. This is going to be a stressful and emotional time for her. She's going to need to vent, or cry, and you're going to be there for her.

Max wanted to vent and cry. Did women really enjoy doing this, or was it all a big act? Opening a bottle of wine and listening to Ellie vent didn't sound that bad, as long as Nicole was there too, but the rest sounded like torture. When she'd given it a few moments thought, Max had figured she'd buy a dress, probably one she hated, and then show up at the wedding in said dress. All the other stuff hadn't even been on her radar. Of course, she'd never been to a wedding, let alone been involved in one, so she cut herself some slack as far as her naïveté went.

With another handful of cheese puffs for courage, Max skipped ahead to the section of the article devoted to obligations on her time.

Aside from planning the shower and the bachelorette party, you will also attend both. This could mean a couple of afternoons, or it could mean several days. Be prepared. You will also be expected to attend the rehearsal, the rehearsal dinner, and, of course, the wedding and reception. You'll be up bright and early on the wedding day, ready for a full day of hair, makeup, dressing with the bridal party, pictures, the ceremony, and the reception. Will you be tired? Of course. Will you show up late or leave early? You will not.

In fact, a big part of your responsibility at the reception will be to see that the party is just that. A party. If things are a bit lackluster, if no one is eager to get out on the dance floor, you will get the party started. Grab a groomsman and boogie like there's no tomorrow.

"Not a snowball's chance," Max said to her now-empty bottle of beer.

You'll also attend to the bride's needs throughout the day. Keep her fed and hydrated while she's getting ready. Things can get hectic, and she will likely forget to eat. It's your job to make sure she doesn't collapse while she's walking down the aisle.

Max perked up. She could do that. She'd pack some protein bars, sports drinks, and water, and she'd make sure Ellie ate and drank. Max grabbed a notepad and pen and made a list. She gave herself a congratulatory fist bump when she added, 'No chocolate, no red drinks.' Even she knew a spill of either on a white dress would spell disaster.

When she got to the part about being the bride's bathroom buddy, Max closed her computer. She wasn't entirely sure what the job of bathroom buddy entailed, but she refused to ponder the details. It was definitely a job for a sister, and Ellie had two of those.

Max got up to pace. When five of her long strides got her across the room, she realized that for the first time, she felt cooped up in her own home. Trapped, like a lion in a zoo who walked in dizzying circles along the perimeter of his far-too-small cage.

Small quarters had never bothered her. More often than not, while growing up, she and her dad had shared a tiny, one-room apartment, often over a garage, and almost identical to the one she now realized she hated. How was she supposed to properly pace when she had to turn and change direction so often she got dizzy?

Maybe it was time for a different place. Maybe a real place, with a bedroom that wasn't practically part of the kitchen/living room. It wouldn't hurt to look around, find a place where she could sign a short-term lease.

She gave her head a shake. It wasn't something she could think about at the moment. She had far bigger fish to fry. Namely, how was she ever going to be the kind of bridesmaid Ellie wanted? Expected? Deserved?

The financial strains the article detailed would be a pain, sure, but nothing compared to the demands on her sanity. Plan a shower? Not a chance. Sit through hours of hair, and makeup, and nails, and, lord help her, waxing, without complaining? Impossible. Smile when Ellie opened a plate, a bath mat, a pot holder, and act like it was the most amazing gift ever bestowed upon a bride-to-be? She'd rather be drawn and quartered.

Max wished she could meet the author of that article, the one who thought she was so cute, so funny, detailing all the…

Then it hit her. She circled back to the word funny. The author was trying to be funny! It was a joke, satire, an exaggeration, at the very least. That had to be it. Max felt her chest loosen, and the furrows in her brow ease. She dropped back down in her chair and breathed easier.

But the feeling didn't last. Doubt crept in, followed by a sneaking fear that the article *wasn't* a joke. She had to know, so she scooped up her phone.

"Hi, Max, what's—"

"Nic, you need to tell me straight. No matter how horrible the answer, I need to know the truth. I read this article…"

Max detailed what she'd read, not holding back a single horrid detail. Nicole didn't say a word until Max stopped and gasped for breath.

"Well, some of it will depend on the bride," Nicole said, but she didn't need to continue. Max knew from the tone of Nicole's voice that every nightmarish scenario was, in fact, likely to play out in real life.

"I don't know how to do that stuff, Nic. I don't know how to plan a shower, I've never even been to a shower. I know nothing about games, and party favors, and all the other crap I read about. And I really can't say that I hate a dress if I really hate a dress? What if she tells us she wants the truth?"

"You tell the truth only if the truth matches what Ellie wants to hear. I'm afraid the article had it right, Max. You're going to need to grin and bear it for the next few months."

She shouldn't have eaten half a bag of cheese puffs. Every last one of them was doing the Cha Cha in her stomach.

"I'll help you."

"Yeah, thanks, but still, this really isn't my thing."

"I know that, and Ellie knows that, but she loves you. It means the world to her that you're willing to do this for her."

Max groaned. "So there's no backing out?"

"You don't want to back out. I know it seems like a lot, but you'll mostly just have to show up. We'll throw a shower for Ellie here, with friends from school and any of Zeke's relatives that might be around, but Ellie's sisters are going to handle a lot of the other details."

"Wait, you've talked to them? To Ellie's sisters? You didn't tell me that."

There was a drawn-out silence, followed by a sigh. Max knew things were about to get worse.

"I did. Last week. With everything that happened, I haven't wanted to add to your stress level, but there's something I have to tell you."

The cheese puffs formed a conga line.

"Her family is coming this weekend. All of them. It's not just her mom and sisters to go dress shopping, it's a surprise engagement party for Ellie and Zeke, and they're all coming. Including her grandparents and her brother who lives in New York. Even Zeke's parents are flying in from Florida. Ellie and Zeke have no idea. It's all supposed to be a surprise, and her sister said they want us at the engagement party. It's Friday night in the party room at the hotel where they're staying."

"And so it begins," Max said as a sick feeling of resignation washed over her. "What do I have to do?"

"The plans are all taken care of, according to Charlene. All we have to do is show up. Ellie's mom has already invited Ellie and Zeke to dinner at the hotel. When they arrive, the group will be waiting to surprise them."

"Fine," Max said. "Tell me what to wear."

"A dress would be nice."

"Fine. What time?"

"Seven o'clock."

"Fine. Is that all?"

"Well, there's just one more little thing."

Max dropped her head and let it bounce off the table.

"Max?"

"What?"

"What was that noise?"

"Nothing. Tell me what you don't want to tell me."

"It's just, well, Ellie's sister is expecting you to bring a date. Ellie told her I'm seeing Brady, and I guess Charlene just assumed you'd probably have, you know, that there'd be someone…you probably don't have to, I just wanted to tell you…"

She could probably still try to make it as a race car driver. She'd felt good behind the wheel of the 32. Driving had felt as natural as breathing. She'd start at the bottom, of course, and she was behind on all the changes and new technology, but she could give it a try. She could call Skeeter, ask him to put out some feelers. She could get in touch with a couple of drivers who wouldn't mince words, who'd give it to her straight when she asked if she stood a chance.

"Max? Max, are you still there? Answer me."

"I'm still here."

"It's not that bad, you know. Women do this sort of thing all the time. You might find that you like it."

"Yeah, and Ellie might trade her cowboy boots for a racing jacket. My head hurts. I'm hanging up now."

"Max—"

But Max didn't hear the rest. She disconnected, let her phone fall to the floor, and reached for the cheese puffs.

11

She put it off for two days, hoping that somehow it had all been a bad dream, but by Thursday, Max figured she had to prepare for the worst and give some thought to the following night and the engagement party. Nicole had purchased a gift and told Max it was from both of them. Max knew she'd never have thought to buy a gift, so handing over some cash to cover half the cost felt like winning the lottery.

Since she didn't have a dress she figured would be appropriate, she'd ordered one and had it express-shipped. She'd had it delivered to school, not wanting to risk someone happening by and deciding the box in front of Max's door was fair game. As she drove home from school on Thursday afternoon, she watched the box out of the corner of her eye. The dress hadn't looked all that bad online, but since everything looked not that bad online, Max was dreading what the result would be when she tried it on. And if it didn't look good with the only pair of heels she owned, she was in trouble.

Or not. If all she had were a pair of jeans and a sweater, then so be it. She probably wasn't the only one who'd be happier if she wore a pair of jeans and a sweater.

Having a date, she'd decided, was ridiculous. She wasn't dating anyone, so asking someone merely to fill a spot seemed pointless. Though it would probably throw the seating arrangement into chaos, Ellie's sisters would just have to figure out how to deal with an odd number of people.

She was staring at the box, almost afraid it would rear back and attack her, so when she didn't notice the person waiting outside the garage, she told herself that was why.

In the daylight, her mother looked even worse. The lines on her face

"Found a job."

"Teaching. I'm proud of you. That's a good job. A hard job, but a good job."

Max was on alert. "How do you know I'm a teacher?"

Her mother squirmed. "Oh, I don't…" She shook her head, then looked around the small space. Her eyes landed on one of the two photos Max had framed and propped on a shelf. "Skeeter. How is he?"

"Skeeter's fine. How did you find me? It couldn't have been through Skeeter." Then it hit her. The news. Her mother had seen the news stories.

"You're kind of famous, Max. On the news and everything."

There was an odd gleam in her mother's eyes, a gleam that told Max there was more to this visit than catching up with her daughter.

"I'm not famous."

Her mother's look changed to one of concern. Real or show, Max wasn't sure.

"Are you okay? Were you hurt?"

"I'm fine. I wasn't hurt."

"Maybe not physically, but there are other ways to be hurt."

"Tell me about it."

Her mother winced. "Sometimes, after such a traumatic event, things happen later. Things you don't expect. Are you sleeping okay? Are you having panic attacks? Anything like that?"

"What are you, some sort of therapist?"

"No, I'm just worried about you. You were so brave to do what you did. I'd hate to think that you're paying for it now."

"I'm fine. No issues."

"That's good. Will you tell me about it?"

"Why?"

"Because I'm curious. Because when I heard the news stories, I imagined the worst. I'd like to hear from you what happened."

Max was already tired of the conversation. She figured she had three choices. She could end it now and show her mother the door. She could continue with the short answers, and they'd continue to go around in circles. Or she could give her mother answers with some substance and see where it led.

She didn't love any of her options, but really, how much worse could things—and her life in general—get?

"It was scary. Terrifying. If you're hoping I'll say I did what I did because I knew I was the only hope for everyone in the school, that I was willing to risk my life to save the lives of others, that I didn't give a second thought to what might happen to me, you're going to be disappointed. I acted, yes, but if I had to do it again, I'm not sure what I'd do. The look in his eyes…"

Max closed her own eyes for a moment, and she saw the man's face, the desperation in his eyes, and she knew, as she'd known then, that he wasn't going to stop because she asked nicely that he do so.

"He was desperate. He wanted something, and he wasn't going to stop until he got it. Whether that meant he was willing to use the gun, I honestly don't know. I'd like to think not, that it was, in his mind, merely a way of making his point, but I don't know. That's for psychologists to determine. All I know is I was scared senseless, but something made me act. I'm glad I did, but I think most people in my position would have done the same."

"Oh, baby." Victoria reached her hand across the small table but pulled it back before she touched Max's arm. "I'm sorry you were so scared. I'm sorry you were ever in that position. But you were so brave, and I am proud of you. So very proud of you."

It was Max's turn to ask questions, and she did so before she could think about how she'd feel when she heard the answer.

"Is that why you're here? Because you saw me on the news? Would you ever have looked for me if you hadn't seen me on TV?"

The slight hesitation was all the answer Max needed. She started to stand, but this time when Victoria reached for her, she put her hand over Max's arm.

"I've thought about looking for you so many times over the years. That's the truth. But I was afraid. Afraid too much time had passed and that you'd want nothing to do with me."

Victoria glanced up at Max as if afraid Max would confirm that fear. Max was about to but Victoria continued.

"When you were young and you and your dad were traveling around the country, I used to hear things about you. That you were smart, so smart, and were giving all those car guys a run for their money when you were barely a teenager. I heard about the time you figured out what was wrong with…oh, what was his name? I can't remember, but the driver who won at Daytona about ten years back. You figured out what was going on with his car, why it wasn't doing something it was supposed to be doing, and when they finally listened to you, he won."

Sandy, Max thought. The driver was Sandy, and it hadn't been

Daytona, but most of the rest was right.

"And I knew that you were kind, always looking out for any other kids that were new to the circuit. You showed them the ropes, made sure they stayed out of trouble, and were a big sister to anyone who needed one. I knew you had chicken pox when you were six, and that you broke your arm when you were twelve.

"If I asked direct questions, I rarely got an answer. That's a tight-knit community, and you and your dad ranked a lot higher than I did. Most people were pretty tight-lipped if I came right out and asked, but I learned to listen, and by listening, I was able to learn some things about your life and feel like I was a part of it, in a very small way."

"You chose to *not* be part of it. You left. If you cared about me, about what happened to me, it seems like sticking around would have been a better idea than taking off."

"I can't change the past. All I can say is that there are things you don't know. It wasn't easy for me to leave. Since then, I've spent my life regretting that decision."

Max could argue that Victoria had had years to right her mistake, but figured there wasn't any point. Instead, she picked up her phone and checked the time. They'd agreed on an hour. Max didn't intend to go past.

"Is my time up?"

"Half of it."

"I said I'd make you something to eat. The offer still holds."

"I'm not hungry." It was a lie. She was starving, but she wasn't about to admit it.

"You're sure? I could whip up something and if you're not hungry now, you could eat it later."

They had twenty-nine minutes. Eating probably wouldn't hurt anything, but she wasn't about to let her mother cook. That was far too cozy.

"I've got some leftover lasagna. I can nuke it."

"I'm happy to cook something—"

Max stood, her chair scraping over the floor and drowning out the rest of Victoria's words. After Max pressed the buttons on the microwave, Victoria tried again.

"You made lasagna? Do you do a lot of cooking?"

Max saw Victoria take another look around the small space, answering her own question.

"No," Max said. The night before, she'd heated the lasagna, one of the half dozen things Ellie had shoved in Max's freezer following the incident at school. It was as close to cooking as she'd come in weeks.

It only took a minute for the smell to get Max's stomach growling. She'd skipped lunch again, and since she couldn't remember what she'd eaten for breakfast, figured it must have been another one of the protein bars she kept in her desk at school. She needed to do better, she told herself for the hundredth time.

When the lasagna was hot, Max put a hunk on each of the two plates she grabbed from the cupboard. She added forks, and because she didn't have any napkins, a couple of folded paper towels.

"It looks good," Victoria said when Max set the plates on the table. "Is lasagna your specialty?"

Max dropped her fork to the table with a clatter. The hand in her lap clenched in a fist, and though she tried to fight it, her words came out through gritted teeth.

"A friend made it. I haven't cooked anything in weeks. I'm not much for domesticity, as should be evident if you take a look around. And so we can get this over with sooner rather than later, what else?"

There was a flash of temper in Victoria's eyes before it was quickly masked and replaced with a defeated look.

"I only wanted to get to know you. I didn't realize asking a few questions in conversation would come across as rude or prying. I'm sorry if I've upset you."

Max wanted to scream, but again, she harnessed her emotions.

"You didn't upset me, you just have me wondering where all this is leading. Are you planning on sticking around? I can't see you loving a town like Caston. Not nearly glamorous enough for you."

"I don't need glamor, Max, and I don't know yet what my long-term plans are. It will depend on you, in part."

On her? Oh, no way was she going to let Victoria put that sort of pressure on a daughter she hadn't seen in over twenty years. Before Max could bark out her retort, it was as if Victoria had read her mind.

"I don't mean to make it sound as though I'm putting pressure on you, that I expect you to welcome me with open arms, but I'm hoping that with time, we can develop some sort of relationship. I'd like to be a part of your life, Maxine."

It was the eyes. It was always the eyes, and right now, Victoria's looked sincere. Whether Max was falling under some sort of spell the woman was casting remained to be seen, but for the time being, she had to believe Victoria.

132

"I can't just start acting like I have a mother, like you've been there all the time but were, I don't know, out of the country for a while. It's not like that," Max said, only to see hurt fill those eyes. "It has to be slow. Very slow."

The eyes flew upward and locked on Max's. "Slow. Of course. It will take time, and we'll take it slow." Victoria stood. "And right now, my time for today is up. I won't overstay my welcome."

Max stood and faced Victoria.

"This weekend? Are you free? We could, I don't know, go for a walk. You could show me around town. We could grab a pizza. Whatever you want."

"I have some plans this weekend," Max said and saw the doubt in Victoria's eyes. "Friday night. Maybe Saturday. I don't know about that yet."

Then, for reasons unknown to her, Max felt the urge to explain.

"I have a friend, Ellie, she's getting married, and I'm sort of a bridesmaid. Well, I guess I am a bridesmaid. First time for me, so I'm still trying to figure out what it entails, but part of it is an engagement party on Friday, and maybe," Max couldn't stop the shudder, "dress shopping on Saturday."

Victoria smiled, and it transformed her face. With that smile, a genuine smile, Victoria looked younger, prettier.

"A bridesmaid? Oh, Max, how wonderful. You'll be a beautiful bridesmaid. I know the bridesmaids aren't supposed to upstage the bride, but that will be difficult in your case." Victoria's hand reached out again, toward Max's hair, but stopped short of touching it. "Your hair is like your father's, that glossy black I always envied. You have his eyes, too. The shape, I mean. So big and beautiful. I don't know where that vivid emerald came from, though."

Victoria tilted her head. "I am going to take credit for your complexion. It may be hard to believe, but I used to have that dewy, creamy skin. Take care of it, baby, or one day you'll wake up and look like this."

Victoria flicked her wrist under her chin and frowned.

"You don't, I mean, you…"

"Oh, baby, say it like it is. I'm old. I look old." Victoria shrugged. "Hopefully time doesn't catch up with you quite as quickly as it did me." Then Victoria shook her head. "No, I can tell you take care of yourself. Look at you, you could be a model. For anything, I suppose, but you'd be the perfect fit for an athletic clothing line. Some of those fancy leggings and tank tops I've seen, and now, seeing you? I swear that stuff was made for you to wear it."

Never comfortable with compliments, but even less so, it seemed, when they came from Victoria, Max scrambled to put an end to the conversation.

"Yeah, well, I have some things to do this evening…"

"Of course, of course. We agreed on an hour, didn't we?"

Victoria smiled again, but it looked forced, not the genuine smile Max had seen a few minutes earlier. When Max found herself missing the real smile, she turned away and yanked open the door, then waited impatiently while Victoria bundled into her jacket.

"Thank you, Max. This was, well, it was more than I dared dream of. I left my phone number on the table. If you have some time, and if you want to get together, just call. Or text. Any time. I hope I hear from you soon."

Since she didn't want to face her mother, Max looked toward the table, where she spotted the small slip of pink paper. It only took an instant for her knees to turn to jello. She had to grab onto the door to keep herself upright.

"Max? Maxine, are you okay? What is it?"

"It's nothing. Sorry, just tired, I guess. I'll try to call…"

"It doesn't look like nothing. You look ill. Let me help you to the couch."

"No." Max spoke with more force and strength than she would have guessed she could muster, but it served the purpose of getting Victoria to back off.

"Oh. Okay, then. Well, take care of yourself, and call. Please call."

"Yeah," Max muttered as she closed the door. If Victoria stood there looking at the door, if she debated knocking, still unsure if Max was really okay, or if she simply turned and headed down the stairs, Max didn't know, because once the door closed, her knees did give out. With her back to the door, she slid down until she ended up on the floor, her eyes glued to a simple piece of pink paper.

An hour later, Max drove to Beck's, hoping to spend some time working on her car. She turned up the music in an attempt to drown out any memory of her ridiculous reaction to a piece of paper. She wouldn't let herself think of anything but the beat of the music.

When her phone rang, she fully intended on ignoring it but then glanced and saw Skeeter's name on the screen. Just the sight of his name did more to calm her than the deep breathing, the long shower, and the eardrum-shattering music.

"Skeeter," Max said, his name coming out like a giant sigh of relief.

"Kiddo, what's up? You don't sound like yourself."

Neither did he, Max thought, and that had her antenna up.

"I'm fine, just a long day."

"Not more problems at school, I hope?"

"Nothing like you're thinking. Honestly," she added because she knew he'd wonder. She also knew he'd accept her answer, and wouldn't push any further, so she turned the tables. "You're back home?"

"Just got in this afternoon. Good trip, but better to be back."

"Buy anything?"

"Few things. Come visit, you'll like some of it."

"I'll try to do that soon. Maybe in a couple of weeks. Are you going to put me to work?"

"When I've got the best in my garage, yeah, I'm gonna put her to work."

Max's reply got caught in her throat, so she settled for swallowing and waiting for Skeeter to get to the reason for the call. He wasn't the chatty type, so she knew the wait wouldn't be long.

"Got some news when I got back."

"Yeah?"

"Yeah. You're not gonna like it, and I'm sorry about that, but it's only right I tell you. Victoria's been askin' about you."

A couple of days ago, the news would have come as a shock, probably enough of a shock to make Max consider taking steps to make herself harder to find. The way it was, she felt worse for Skeeter than she did herself.

"You're not going to like what I have to say either, Skeet. She's here. In Caston. Showed up a few days ago."

Max waited again, this time while Skeeter uttered a stream of oaths he reserved for the times that really called for them.

"I'm sorry I didn't get to you sooner. Before she did. Are you okay?"

"I'm okay."

"What did she want? Did she, ah, ask you for anything?"

"Said she wants to get to know me. Not sure why she picked now after all these years, and I asked her as much. She claims to have seen me on TV and didn't want any more time to pass before she tried to, I don't know, be a part of my life again? Something to that effect, I guess."

"Saw you on TV?"

"Most people did, Skeeter."

"I suppose."

"What do you know that you don't want to tell me?"

"Don't know that I know anything, it's just that with Victoria, there's usually an angle. She usually wants something. Don't mean to sound negative, and if you want her back in your life, that's your business. I just want you to be careful, is all."

He knew more than he was saying, but Max knew she wouldn't get any more from him, at least not over the phone. If they were face to face, if she could look into his eyes, she might, but Skeeter refused to acknowledge FaceTime was a thing, so if she wanted more, she'd have to make a trip to see him.

"I didn't say I want her back in my life. I told her as much, but she's sticking around."

"Okay. Be careful, girl."

"I will. And I'm coming to see you. Soon."

"You do that. One of those things I bought is a '71 Mustang Mach 1. Figure with all the experience between us, we'll have her runnin' in no time."

Max moaned. "You're killing me, Skeeter."

When she got to Beck's she was torn between irritation with Victoria, homesickness for Skeeter and the closest thing she had to home, an itching to get to work on the car Skeeter bought, and a lingering horror at her reaction to the note Victoria left on the table. Hanging over all of it, like a giant umbrella, was the frustration that she felt stuck right where she was, like putty waiting to be molded by all the outside forces: the whims of her mother, the upcoming weekend with Ellie's family, the need to be something she knew she wasn't.

She didn't bother knocking or calling out, just stomped back to the garage where she heard the low hum of country music, and the even lower hum of Beck joining in with Alan Jackson on an oldie. The sound, and the idea of Beck singing along with anything, started to crack the shell she'd built around herself in her attempt to get through the night, the coming weekend, and the foreseeable future.

"Mind if I spend some time on my car?"

If he was surprised or embarrassed to be caught singing, he covered it well. Of course, he had a minute before he had to face her while he eased out from underneath a Chevy pickup.

"Didn't expect you tonight, but no, I don't mind."

"Good."

She stomped again, this time to grab a light and a few tools, and then to stand in front of her car.

"Nice to see you're in a good mood."

"Mood's fine."

Max slammed the light into place with enough force to send it rocking. She winced. She might be angry with the entire world, but Stevie Ray didn't deserve her wrath.

"Sorry," she mumbled to her car as she straightened the light, then bent under the hood. Before she could pick up the first tool, Beck was standing alongside her.

"Bad day?"

"No worse than most."

"That's a sad way to look at life."

"Yeah, well, live a few days of my life and see how you like it."

"Didn't know this was going to be a pity party. I would have picked up a cake."

"If you don't want me here, say so, and I'll leave. Otherwise, leave me alone and let me work."

Max slanted her eyes toward Beck in time to see him lift his hands to his shoulders.

"Fine. Leaving you alone, but take it easy. Ticked off plus tools too often equals an accident. I told you, you're not an employee, I'm not insured—"

"Oh, for crying out loud. What do you think I'm going to do, cut off my hand? Let me do what I do best, Beck, and see if my mood doesn't improve."

He didn't bother answering, just shook his head and went back to his own work. Max fumed while she attacked the spark plugs. She'd already checked them, more than once, but she needed to do something she could do in her sleep, something where she didn't have to think.

They both worked in their own space, the only sound in the cavernous room the music which Beck had on a country playlist, and the occasional clang or squeak of tools and metal. Instead of clearing her head, working on simple tasks did just the opposite and left Max with too much time to think.

Was she a fool for even considering meeting with her mother again?

Skeeter knew more than he'd said, of that Max was certain, and if he knew something about Victoria, Max wanted to know what it was.

'There's usually an angle. She usually wants something.' Skeeter's words replayed in Max's head. Was that it? Victoria wanted something from Max, something other than a relationship? Money? Maybe, Max thought, but if that was it, Victoria was going to be disappointed. A place to stay? To live, even? If that had been the goal, Victoria should have been smart enough to turn around and head for greener pastures when she'd first tracked down Max and found her address was an apartment over a garage.

Max stood and tapped a wrench in her hand. A way to her father? Was it possible Victoria thought she could get to Bo Simmons through Max? After all these years, would she even want to? Doubtful, but Max was out of other ideas. If only Skeeter would have given her the whole story.

"Hah," she muttered to herself. That was only one of a long list of 'If onlys.'

If only people at school would stop treating her like she was made of glass and going to shatter at a moment's notice. If only she didn't have to go to an engagement party, and worse, wedding dress shopping. If only Victoria had never shown up on her doorstep. If only she could figure out what was wrong with her car. If only she'd get the letter she was waiting for and she could put Caston and all that went with it behind her.

She pushed harder on the wrench when a bolt wouldn't budge. When it stayed stubbornly in place, she slammed the heel of her hand into the boxed end of the wrench. At least that's what she tried to do. When her hand missed and slid over the wrench, she lost her balance and gasped. When she felt her hand strike metal, and then felt that metal slice her hand, she whimpered.

"Oh, oh no."

She pulled her hand toward her midsection and buried it, clasping the uninjured one over it. Max was afraid to look, but it only took a few seconds for her to know what she'd see when she did. The warm, wet flow turned her hand slick and oozed between her fingers.

Her breath came in shallow gasps. There was no pain, but Max knew it would follow in a minute, as soon as her brain caught up with what was happening with her hand.

"Beck?"

Even though Max knew she'd uttered that single syllable, she didn't recognize her own voice. It was distant, maybe coming from inside a cave. She tried again.

"Um, Beck?"

Even worse. High-pitched and even farther away. Still, she figured Beck heard something because before she could try again, he was standing in front of her.

"Sorry, Mad Max, I don't have time tonight, I've... What? What is it? Max?"

She watched as his eyes traveled from her face to her midsection. Then she watched as the color drained from his face.

"What happened? Geez, I told you to be careful. My insurance—"

"I think it's bad" Max managed before she started sinking.

Beck cursed under his breath. Max knew he was livid, but still, she felt his arms go around her to keep her from hitting the floor.

"Okay. You're going to be okay. Can I look?"

The hands pressed tight to her belly shook. "I can't, Beck, I can't look."

"You don't have to. Hang on."

He sprinted across the room, was back in a flash with a stack of clean towels, then reached for her hands.

"Turn away if you want, but I need to look."

Max gave one quick nod, then squeezed her eyes shut and turned her head as far as it would turn.

This time it was Beck who gasped.

"Okay," he said. "We're going to need to take a little trip."

Max sensed more than felt her hand being bundled into the towels.

"Is it gone? Is my hand gone? My fingers?"

Her whole body started to shake. There was only a throbbing where her hand should be.

Beck's hand cupped her chin and turned her head until she faced him. "It's not gone. Your hand is there, your fingers are there, but you're going to need some stitches. We need to get you to the hospital."

His voice was level, calm. He was steady when he rose from his crouch and took her with him. Max couldn't decide if he was really that calm, or if it was an act. And if so, was it for her benefit, or his?

"Beck..."

"Not now. Can you climb up into my truck or do you want me to drive your car?"

She felt light-headed, and the question seemed like such a hard one.

"Um, I don't know…"

"Let's get you in the truck. I'll help you."

She might have nodded, she wasn't sure, but she knew her feet were moving, though how remained a mystery.

"I don't like blood."

"No kidding?"

"I mean, I really don't like blood. Once in school, I threw up when a kid fell and smacked his head outside on the playground. I passed out during a movie…"

"You're not going to throw up now, because you're not going to look." He boosted her up into the truck. "You're going to sit here and tell me about your day."

Max heard the door close, then watched him run around to the driver's side. He reached across and strapped the seat belt over her, then did the same to himself, and all the while kept talking.

"What happened at school today?"

Now that she was seated, the truck was moving, and she had a minute to think about where they were headed, she remembered she liked hospitals less than she liked the sight of blood. And with that thought, some of the fight came back.

"I don't think I need a hospital. You could probably bandage it for me. The hospital seems a bit extreme."

Beck glanced her way. Though it was too dark to read his expression, she sensed enough to know she hadn't changed his mind.

"School? Any good stories?"

An old memory surfaced, and Max ignored Beck's questions.

"Once I cut my leg, I think I was about seven, and this driver…what was his name? Rook, that's right, everyone called him Rook. Not sure what that was short for, or if it was a nickname where it came from, but Rook it was. Anyway, he put four stitches in my leg. He had this spray that sort of numbed the area. He cleaned the cut and then sewed it right up. Still have a little scar just above my knee."

Max paused. "Hmm. Now that I think about it, I wonder why some driver stitched up my leg. Seems kind of odd, doesn't it?"

"Yeah, to say the least. Where was your dad?"

"No idea. I can't remember if he knew about it before it happened, or after the fact. Either way, still odd. If he knew before, why did he let some twenty-year-old race car driver sew up his daughter's leg? And if he didn't know, why don't I remember him throwing a holy fit when he found out?"

"I don't know, Mad Max. It's quite a mystery, isn't it?"

"Kind of makes me angry. I hadn't thought about it in years, but now, I feel like my dad owes me some kind of explanation. Don't you agree? Who hands their seven-year-old over to some guy who drives cars for a living but happens to have a needle handy?"

"You should probably ask him about that, but not right now. Right now, we're going to go in there."

Max looked where Beck's finger pointed. *Emergency* glowed red over the double glass doors. Before she could argue, Beck was opening her door and reaching to release her seatbelt.

"You okay to walk?"

"Of course, I can walk, I just don't think I want to."

"You're not afraid of hospitals too, are you?"

"I'm not afraid..." The glow from the hospital lights provided enough light that she could see his grin. "Shut up, Beck."

"Ooh, now she's getting feisty. Must be feeling better."

Max looked down at the ridiculously huge bundle of towels wrapped around her hand. It looked like she was wearing a giant boxing glove. For a split second, she considered using it on Beck's chin.

When she didn't move, the teasing disappeared from Beck's voice.

"Seriously, are you feeling okay?"

"Yeah, I'm okay."

"Good. Let me help you down."

She didn't want to but knew she had precious few options. She could probably force Beck to take her to Zeke's and try to get him to stitch her up, thereby avoiding the hospital, but for all she knew, he was inside the building in front of her. Besides, expecting him to deal with her...

Her brain stopped working when she realized she didn't know what she was dealing with. Didn't know how serious the injury was.

"Fine," she grumbled and climbed from the truck.

"Keep your hand up," Beck said. "It will slow the bleeding and help with the pain."

Max didn't answer, just did as she was told, and let herself be led to the entrance. When they got inside, Beck nudged her toward the check-in desk. Inspiration struck, and she dug in her heels.

"I don't have my purse, my identification, insurance information, any of that stuff. We need to go back and get it."

Beck lifted his arm. Her purse dangled from the crook of his elbow.

"Oh."

He turned to the nurse at the desk. "She cut her hand. It's, ah, it's pretty deep."

The nurse turned his attention toward Max. "Are you feeling light-headed? I can grab a wheelchair."

Max rolled her eyes, though regretted it when she nearly lost her balance.

"I'm fine," she said through gritted teeth.

"Of course." Without saying more, he rose from his chair, circled the desk, and pushed a wheelchair toward Max.

"I don't need that. Tell me where to go, and I'll walk."

"I'm afraid it's not optional. Have a seat. I'll get you back to an exam room."

Max looked to Beck hoping for support, but he simply nodded toward the chair. With a huff, Max sat. She closed her eyes when the chair began moving. It would be easy to take a nap, she thought, just a short one, just enough to get back some of her strength. She tuned out the conversation behind her.

"Try to keep your eyes open, Max."

It could have been a second, it could have been an hour, Max had no idea, but she jerked awake as if someone had shot off a firecracker under her chair.

"Good, that's good. Do you think you can stand and move over to the exam table?"

"I suppose," Max said, a bit disoriented. She saw a bed covered with paper and headed for it. She felt a steady set of hands ensuring she made it.

The bed was reclined enough that though it was hard, it was still comfortable. She closed her eyes again, then tried to position her throbbing hand on her stomach where it was at least somewhat protected.

"I'm going to put this over you," the voice said. "It will keep away the chill. I'm going to move your arm out of the way."

Before she could protest, she felt her arm being carefully lifted out of the way, a deliciously warm blanket spread over her, and then her arm returned to its spot over her stomach.

"Mmm." Max couldn't stop the sigh. It was so warm, so comforting, she wanted to drift off to a place where nothing hurt, where the sun warmed her, and best of all, where no one knew her and what had happened at school.

"Max? Max, another nurse will be in here in just a minute. Joanna will get a look at your hand, and a doctor will follow. Joanna will also need some information from you. Do you feel like you can answer a few questions?"

"Hmm, I suppose. I'm tired."

"I know. Go ahead and rest while you wait for Joanna."

Max made a noise. She wasn't sure what she'd tried to say, but it didn't matter. She heard a low rumble of voices in the background, but that didn't matter either. She'd rest as she'd been told, and…

"Maxine? How are you feeling? I'm Joanna. Do you think you can answer a few questions for me?"

Max squinted against the bright lights. The woman next to her bed was tiny, smaller than Ellie, and like Ellie, Joanna had a head full of blonde hair she'd pulled back in a ponytail that bounced every time she moved. And she moved a lot. She reached toward a cart with medical supplies Max had no interest in knowing the function of, grabbed a couple of things and pushed them into the pocket of her pink scrubs, then picked up what looked like an iPad.

Joanna tapped away at the tablet, and since Max figured it wasn't to play games, she guessed it was probably used to record whatever information Max provided. The last time she'd been in a hospital, things had been done with paper, pens, and manila folders. Somehow, Max thought she'd feel better if the nurse held a manila folder.

"And how are we feeling?" Joanna asked, and with those five words, had a huge deck stacked against her.

'We?' Was Joanna lying on a bed, in a hospital, her hand wrapped in rags plucked from a shelf in an auto repair shop, and throbbing with every heartbeat? No, she most certainly was not.

"I'm okay, can't answer for you, though," Max replied, pleased that the combination of the nurse's stupid question and the nap—had she napped?—served to put some fire back in her.

Her comment earned her a "Now, now" from Beck, but Joanna merely smiled and continued typing on the tablet. Weird. Maybe she was playing a game.

"Okay, Maxine, can you tell me—"

"Max. If we're going to get along, you're going to need to call me Max."

"Of course. Max. Can you tell me what happened?"

Max explained though she didn't want to. She wanted to go home, away from the smells, the sounds, and the very experience of the hospital.

"And your pain? On a scale of one to ten, how bad would you say it is?"

"Well, I don't know how to answer that as that question has never made much sense to me. How do I know where it falls on a scale of one to ten? It hurts, sure, it hurts like hellfire, but how do I know there won't come a day when something will hurt a whole lot more? Am I supposed to save ten, maybe nine, eight even, for that day? What if I have a kid? I've heard that hurts, and what if I've already used up my ten? What then? When the nurse asks me how bad it is, on a scale of one to ten, what do I say then? Eleven? Is that an option?"

Joanna smiled, but apparently she'd had enough of Max's ranting because she directed her next questions to Beck. "Were you there when it happened?"

"I was."

"And how long ago was it?"

Beck's eyes shifted to the clock on the wall. "About an hour ago."

"Did you see the injury? Were you the one to wrap it?"

"I did, and I was." Beck's eyes darted toward Max, then back to the nurse. "It didn't look good, the cut is deep. I told Max she needed to go to the emergency room. She disagreed."

At this, the nurse snorted and mumbled what sounded a lot like, 'Big surprise.'

"When she stood up, she almost fainted. She's been a little light-headed."

The nurse nodded.

"Okay, Max, I'm going to take a look. If you don't want to see, I suggest you turn your head. It can be difficult to see your own injury."

Max's eyes disobeyed and fell to the bundle of towels cradled on her lap. Spots of blood dotted the white mass. This time instead of a smart answer, Max drew in a shaky breath and looked away. If the towel looked that bad, she most definitely did not want to see what was left of her fingers.

As she felt the towel loosen, she clutched Beck's arm with her other hand and blinked furiously to keep the tears out of her eyes. At this point, it wasn't pain as much as fear that had the tears threatening. What if the cuts were so deep she lost her fingers? Or the use of her fingers? Would she be able to do her job if she couldn't type well, if she had to do everything one-handed? And what about her dream? The reason she was putting in two years teaching middle school students. What if that was snatched away?

It was enough to make her forget about the pain. Then, a bigger horror. Would she be able to drive her car? What if she could never drive Stevie Ray again? It required two hands. She couldn't sell the car. No way. She'd put too much work, and too much time into it to ever part with it, but what? She'd look at it? Ride along while someone else drove?

Giving into the light-headedness, Max leaned back against the bed and closed her eyes.

"Max? Max? Are you still with me?"

Max opened one eye to find the nurse hovering only inches from her face.

"Yeah," Max said, and realized she must have fallen asleep again. Strange flashes, just split-second images of vivid dreams raced through her mind, only to maddeningly disappear before Max could even begin to decipher them.

"Good. You gave me a little scare. Are you feeling steadier now?"

Max opened both eyes. "Steadier?"

Chilled again, Max looked down to see the blanket on the floor. And everything felt just a little off. She hadn't been so far down on the bed before, and Beck had been sitting on a chair scooted up next to the bed. That chair was now tipped over and on top of Max's blanket. Weird.

"Did something—"

"Don't worry about a thing," Joanna said. "Your hand will be cleaned up in just a minute, and then the doctor will be in."

"How bad is it?" Though she wanted an answer to her question, there was no way she could look for herself. She again turned her head to look at the opposite wall.

"Dr. Tanaka will discuss that with you."

"Give me a hint."

She got a pat on the shoulder instead. "The doctor will be in shortly. Are you warm enough? Would you like me to bring you another blanket?"

"I'm kind of cold."

She looked again at the blanket in a tangle on the floor. Her forehead wrinkled as she tried to recall tossing it off of herself. Before she could ask about it, Joanna said, "Just relax."

Joanna stood, straightened things on her cart of horrors, threw away some blood-soaked gauze which caused Max's stomach to do a triple flip, then tapped again at her tablet. All the while, Max felt as though one of Joanna's eyes never left her patient. In a flash, Joanna ducked

145

into the hall, found a blanket, and spread it over Max. She then reached below the bed. Something made a clicking sound, then a railing appeared alongside Max. Joanna clicked it into place before repeating the same process on the other side of the bed.

Max felt like she was in a crib and wanted to argue, but decided it wasn't worth a fight and chose, instead, to enjoy the warmth of the blanket. As her shivering slowly subsided, Max turned her attention to Beck. "How bad is it?"

"Do you think I watched?"

"You must have some idea."

"I'm ninety-nine percent certain you'll live."

"Funny," Max replied but didn't find any of it funny. "Why did she ask me if I was steadier?"

"Are you serious?"

"Of course, I'm serious."

"I don't know how to put this delicately, but you passed out, Mad Max. Just collapsed over to the side. This way." Beck pointed to the side of the bed opposite from where the nurse had sat. "I only just caught you or you would have ended up on the floor. Then you could add your head to your list of things to worry about."

Max sunk deeper into the bed, not an easy task on a surface that felt like concrete. She rounded her shoulders and tucked in her chin.

"I did not," she whispered.

"You did."

"And you caught me?" Could things get any more humiliating?

"Wasn't easy. You ever try to catch someone who has passed out and is falling off a bed? Dead weight. You did nothing to help me, you know."

"Oh, man."

Max used her good hand to pull the blanket up over her face. Aside from the debacle in high school health class, she had never passed out in her life before the aftermath of the incident at school. And now she'd done it again? Twice within a few weeks? She knew if she didn't have her hand to worry about, she'd be plenty worried there was something wrong with her brain.

"Max, hello, I'm Dr. Tanaka."

A petite woman smiled at Max. Her face was warm, her eyes kind, and she exuded confidence. For the first time since her injury, Max felt a hint of calm wash over her.

"Hello."

"I understand you had an accident."

"Yeah, a stupid one."

"We could argue all accidents are stupid, just as we could argue all accidents happen for a reason. For now, how about I look at your hand, and we save the philosophical questions for another time?"

"Okay."

Joanna appeared behind Dr. Tanaka and handed the doctor the tablet. They talked, and Max understood the meaning of enough of the words, and more, the tone of Joanna's voice, to be convinced the injury was serious.

"How bad is it?" Max asked.

"That's still to be determined."

Dr. Tanaka smiled again, and gently reached for Max's hand which was now re-wrapped, courtesy of Joanna. While it looked neater than Beck's attempt with the towels, and while the bandaging was nowhere near as big and bulky, her hand was still wrapped in white gauze, the appearance of which did nothing to calm Max's fears.

When Dr. Tanaka began unwrapping, Max turned her head. She looked at Beck, who did the same. She couldn't expect him to want to watch, but the fact that he looked pale provided further fuel for her certainty that she was going to lose at least one finger. If she hadn't already.

"Okay, Max," Dr. Tanaka said after what seemed an alarmingly short amount of time. "You've got a minor laceration on one finger, and deep lacerations on two others. On one of those, stitches won't be sufficient. You're going to need surgery to repair the damage, but the surgery will be quick, and I'm confident you will have full use of your fingers once you heal."

Max heard nothing more. Surgery had never crossed her mind.

For the next hour, she answered questions, then a minute later remembered neither the question nor her answer. She was poked and prodded, undressed and nearly unhinged, until the needle went into her arm and she slipped into blessed oblivion.

12

"Am I okay?"

Max was certain she spoke, but when the shape slumped in the chair next to her bed didn't respond, she closed her eyes.

When she opened them again, she didn't know if a minute or an hour had passed, and she realized she was getting sick of that feeling.

"Am I okay?" she said again.

"Hey, Max. You're awake."

The shape rose and stretched. There was only a dim light in the room, but Max knew it was Beck. She told herself it was his voice she recognized, not the broad shoulders, trim waist, and long legs.

"Am I?"

"Are you what?"

"Awake. And okay."

"Both. I thought you were going to wake up a couple of times earlier, but you were surprisingly resistant. Glad to see you've stopped fighting."

"Fighting? I didn't know I was fighting. I think I tried…"

She realized it all was foggy, so she gave up trying to remember. But then she did remember her hand. She lifted it to find three fingers wrapped with gauze and securely taped. A splint kept her index finger from bending.

She turned her hand one way, then the other, then held it toward Beck.

"This doesn't look okay."

"Doc said it will be."

Before he could elaborate, and before she could demand more information, a nurse bustled into the room, raising the lights as she did so.

"I thought I heard voices in here. I'm glad to see you're awake."

"I keep hearing that. Was I supposed to wake up earlier?"

The nurse smiled. "You did wake up, you just didn't want to stay awake. That's not unusual. Anesthesia affects everyone differently. As long as you woke up once and answered a couple of questions, which you did, we were happy to let you sleep."

"How long?"

"You got out of surgery about three hours ago."

"Three hours? I've been sleeping for three hours?"

Max tried to work out what time it must be. It was dark outside, but it had been dark when she'd arrived, so that was no help.

"Three hours isn't that long," the nurse said while she checked machines and made notes on yet another iPad. "How are you feeling?"

"Um…" Max took inventory. She was tired, she felt a little dizzy, and her hand felt…like nothing. Like it wasn't there. "My hand…"

"Feels a little funny, doesn't it? Numb?"

"Yeah, I guess. Kind of like it's not there."

"That will wear off. I wish I could tell you your hand won't hurt when it does, but I'm afraid you're going to have some discomfort for a few days."

Discomfort she could live with. Not being able to use her fingers was another matter entirely.

"And long term? Will my fingers work like they're supposed to work?"

"Dr. Tanaka was very pleased with the outcome. She'd like to see you this afternoon for a follow-up. She'll be able to tell you more then."

"But my fingers. You didn't answer my question."

"Your fingers are all there. The cuts on two of them were quite deep. Dr. Tanaka had to reshape one, here," she indicated the finger with the splint, "and you may have some continued numbness due to the nerves being affected by both the injury and the surgery, but the hope is that all the feeling comes back in time."

Max leaned back and closed her eyes. Words like 'reshape' and 'hope' didn't instill much confidence. She had a hundred more questions, but she was so tired.

"Sleep is the best medicine right now," the nurse said as if reading Max's mind. "The paperwork is ready for your discharge, so as soon as you're ready, you're free to go, provided you don't do the driving.

Leave that to your boyfriend."

"My what?"

The nurse acted like she didn't hear, and Max was again left wondering if she was actually speaking or if she only thought she was.

"There's a prescription here for pain medication. Take it. Don't try to tough it out, at least not at first."

"Mm hmm, fine," Max muttered, or at least thought she did. When she tried to open her eyes, the room spun.

"Your clothes are on the table. Take it slow. Let him help you. I'll be right back with some paperwork."

Max found if she opened only one eye, the room didn't spin quite as fast.

"What's she talking about? Boyfriend?"

"Uh, that would be me."

"What?"

"You get chatty when you're drugged up. Did you know that?"

"What?"

"Chatty, Max. You talk. A lot."

Dread crept over her, blanketing her like a shadow. "No, I don't."

"Yes, you do."

"And what, exactly, are you claiming I said?"

"You called me honey, for starters."

Now she knew he was lying. Or teasing. Or whatever he wanted to call it.

"I did not."

"Oh, but you did. It was cute, in your slurred voice."

"Seriously, Beck, you're not funny. Get out of here so I can get dressed."

He raised his brow in his maddening way, and if he was trying to conceal his smirk, he was doing a terrible job of it.

"How are you going to do that when you can barely open your eyes without the room spinning faster than a carnival ride?"

"How do you...never mind. I'll manage just fine. Get out."

"As you wish." He bowed like a prince in a Disney movie, then strolled toward the hall.

Max sat up, but no matter how slowly she tried to move, the spinning continued. An inch at a time, she swung her feet over the side of the bed, then used her good hand to hold tight to the railing when the spinning turned into a tornado. She moved to put her other hand over her mouth when her stomach heaved, only to smack herself in the face with the unwieldy bandages.

Something between an oath and a pathetic moan escaped her lips before she could stop it. Beck was back so quickly, she was certain he'd never actually left.

"Stay put. The dizziness will pass, it just takes some time. You need to work the meds out of your system. Do you feel like you can drink some water?"

His voice was kind. Gone was any trace of teasing, and in its place was what sounded like genuine concern crossed with some firsthand knowledge.

"Water sounds good."

He produced a cup with a straw, and she drank.

"Slow," he reminded her.

It tasted so good, she wanted to gulp, but recalling the turmoil in her stomach just a moment earlier, heeded Beck's advice. She took a couple more small sips, then nodded.

"Thanks."

"You're welcome, Mad Max. Now, let's see about getting you dressed."

"I'm perfectly capable of dressing myself."

"I thought we went over it, but maybe your brain is still a little fuzzy. You just tried that, remember? You couldn't get off the bed."

"I can now."

To prove it, Max scooted forward on the bed until her feet hit the floor. With a deep breath and one hand on the railing, she stood.

And then she fell.

At least she fell back onto the bed, but that didn't stop the gasp she heard from Beck, and it didn't stop his arms from going around her. Max shifted, he tried to follow, and they ended up as tangled as if they were playing Twister.

"How many more times am I going to have to catch you, do you suppose?"

"Zero more times."

"You say that now, but without leaving a hospital bed, I've had to catch you twice. That doesn't bode well for the drive home and the journey into your apartment."

"Yeah, well, once I get out of here and get some fresh air, I'll be fine." In what came out as more a growl than words, she added, "I might need a little help."

"Wait, I thought I heard something. No, maybe I got a whiff of that stuff they gave you because I swear I heard you say you need help."

"Can you knock it off and help me? Please?"

His serious voice made a return. "Of course I can. And I meant it when I told you that you'll feel better as soon as all that stuff is out of your system."

"What makes you such an expert?"

He blew out a breath, then held up one hand and pointed with the other. Max gaped at the scar that ran the width of his index finger just above his middle knuckle.

"About a year ago. Almost lost it. Had it sewn back together during surgery that I imagine was similar to what you just had."

Without realizing she was doing it, Max lifted her arms and let Beck slip off her hospital gown.

"How?"

"Working on a 2014 Camaro. A buddy of mine owns it but is a disaster when it comes to taking care of it. I go see him every once in a while as a courtesy to the car. It deserves better than Tibbs."

Max lifted her arms again as a T-shirt came over her head. It barely registered that Beck was helping her and that he was taking great care to avoid her hand. "Tibbs?"

"My friend, Kurt Tibbets, but I don't know that I've ever heard anyone call him Kurt except his mom. Even his dad calls him Tibbs."

"A 2014 Camaro. Great car. Can he drive it?"

"He can drive it, he handles it well, but he doesn't give a thought to what it takes to make the car perform and handle the way it does. He's one of those who puts in gas and thinks he's done his job."

Max scoffed. "A lot of those around. And your hand? It was bad?"

"Pretty bad. Tibbs had to drive me to the emergency room. It was thirty minutes away. I passed out before we got there."

"Geez, Beck. You could have died."

Beck shrugged. "Yeah, but I didn't."

"Still…"

"Lots of things could happen every day, and they don't. I don't suppose you expected to be here."

"No." Then, because it seemed important, she said, "This is the first time I've hurt myself like this while working on a car. I don't make mistakes. I'm careful."

"So am I, but…" He held up his hand again. "Guess that's why they're called accidents. Can you stand?"

"Huh?"

"I asked if you can stand. I don't think I can zip your jeans with you sitting on the bed."

"My jeans?"

Max was mortified. How had they gotten to that point? He'd dressed her, and she hadn't so much as flinched. He'd distracted her, that's how. Probably made up the story about his finger. Probably cut it slicing a bagel.

"Here."

Beck held out his arm so she could steady herself. Max avoided all eye contact and focused instead on his arm. Only his arm. Once she stood, and once she had her balance, he zipped and buttoned and acted as if he did it every day. Maybe he did. Who knew?

"Good," Beck said. "Now, sit down again and we'll tackle your shoes."

Max groaned, but again, did as he said. It was either that or wait for the nurse and ask her for help. When she glanced down to watch Beck tie her shoes, she noticed the T-shirt she was wearing. It was bright green, there was writing across the chest, and it most certainly wasn't hers. She grabbed the hem with her good fingers.

"All done." Beck exaggerated wiping his forearm across his brow.

"What is this?" Max asked when Beck stood.

"A shirt."

"Where did it come from? And where's my shirt?"

"Your shirt is in a bag over there." Beck nodded toward a small table next to the chair where he'd been sitting. "Let's just say it's going to need some stain remover. The shirt you're wearing is a gift from the hospital staff. I'm not positive, but I think the word with all the consonants is some kind of anxiety medication. Or maybe it's high blood pressure."

The shirt was ugly, her favorite Talladega T-shirt was probably ruined, but when Max looked at Beck, she realized she had bigger things to worry about.

"Why did you stay?"

"At the hospital?"

"Yes, at the hospital. Why did you stay and wait for me?"

"What was I supposed to do? Leave you here alone?"

"You could have called Ellie or Nicole. They would have come."

"I don't know how to get in touch with your friends. Besides, I had already posed as your boyfriend. It would have looked a little odd had I taken off."

"Speaking of that, they just took your word that you're my boyfriend? Just discussed my injury with you? Doesn't seem like the epitome of patient confidentiality, does it? Aren't there laws about that kind of stuff?"

"I told you, dear, you called me honey."

"I did not, but we'll circle back to your penchant for lying. You could have been some weirdo who spotted me injured on the street, picked me up, and brought me to the hospital. Either a good Samaritan or a total freak."

"I suppose that's true, but once they realized who you were, it seemed they were inclined to believe me and to try to do their best by you."

"Who I was? What does that mean?"

But then she realized what it meant. They knew her as the teacher who'd stopped a school shooter. She groaned, and hoped now that she was awake and mostly alert, she wouldn't have to answer a bunch of questions.

"You look so much better. Getting out of a hospital gown and into your own clothes has that effect. How are you feeling?"

"Better," Max told the nurse.

"The dizziness is gone?"

"Mostly."

"Good. You'll feel like yourself in no time. Here's your prescription, and some information on caring for your wounds. There's also a card with the time for your appointment with Dr. Tanaka this afternoon. She'll have much more information for you when you meet with her."

The nurse looked at Beck. "Will you be able to take her to her appointment? She can't be driving when she's on medication."

"I can probably swing it," Beck said and winked at Max.

"Or I can ask a friend." But she remembered it was a school day, and her only friends would be at work.

"Either way, just no driving until you're off the medication."

"How long will that be?"

"Dr. Tanaka will discuss all that with you. You know, you're very fortunate the accident happened when it did. We always have an orthopedic surgeon on call, but it's not always our hand specialist. All the doctors are capable, of course, and your injury wasn't so serious that you absolutely needed a hand specialist, but Dr. Tanaka is the best, and she did a remarkable job."

In some convoluted way, Max supposed what the nurse said made sense, but it seemed to Max lucky would have been not having the accident at all. Still, she tried to smile.

"Someone will be here with a wheelchair in just a minute. I talked to Beck earlier and explained that it's best if you're not alone right away when you get home. He assured me he'd be able to stay with you."

"But—"

"Let him help. You don't have to do everything by yourself." The nurse handed Max some papers. "Take these things, go see Dr. Tanaka later this afternoon, and be well, Max. I'm glad you're okay."

"Thank you. Me too."

The nurse smiled, looked like she wanted to hug Max but thought better of it, then scurried out of the room.

"Well, dear, it looks like we'll be spending some more time together."

"You really are not funny, you know that?"

"Now, dear…"

"Not funny, Beck, not funny. Wait! That's it! I didn't say honey, I bet I said funny. As in 'you're not funny.' You said I wasn't speaking very clearly. It probably only sounded like honey."

Max shivered, but Beck just grinned.

"Sure, we'll go with that. Whatever helps you sleep at night, Mad Max."

Max fumed and scowled at Beck's back when he headed out of the room to retrieve his truck from the lot. Belinda, a cheery nursing assistant, helped Max into a wheelchair, then pushed her to the exit. Beck was still grinning when he got out of his truck to meet her.

"Take care, Ms. Simmons," Belinda said

"Thanks."

Max was quiet while Beck helped her into the truck. They'd driven a mile on the deserted street before Beck broke the silence.

"You know, speaking of your anesthesia-induced mumblings," he began.

"Were we?"

"We were. Did you know you also talk in your sleep?"

"I most certainly do not."

Beck chuckled. "I was there, Mad Max, and you most certainly do."

If she threw herself out the door of the truck, hobbled home on whatever body parts she didn't injure too severely in the fall, got home to find Fred had changed the locks and kicked her out of her apartment forcing her to walk until she found a hotel, it probably wouldn't be worse than listening to whatever Beck was going to tell her.

"Aren't you curious about what you said?"

"Not in the least." And that was the biggest lie she'd told in a long time.

"I think you are, and to satisfy your curiosity while allowing you to hang on to what's left of your dignity, I'll just tell you without you having to beg."

Max's good hand reached for the door handle.

"You asked me to go with you to a party. An engagement party, I think, though you weren't always easy to understand. I figured it's a party for Ellie and Zeke. You kind of begged. Something about not wanting to be the only one there alone, and something about a seating chart. That part may have been about school, I don't know, but I do know that you were very clear about wanting me to be your date. Actually, you promised all sorts of things if I'd agree."

Max had told herself she'd stay quiet, that she wouldn't give him the satisfaction of a reaction, but at his last comment, she couldn't hold her tongue.

"No way. You're full of it, Beck, and I'm not falling for your stupid jokes."

"Well then, riddle me this, Batman. How did I know about the party? If you weren't talking about it and begging me to go with you, how did I know there was a party to go to?"

Max's teeth ached, she clenched her jaw so tightly.

"I may have said something about the party, but that's only because I'm dreading it. That doesn't mean I *begged* you to come with me."

"Deny it all you want, but I know what I heard."

Max clamped her mouth shut.

"When is it?"

"Friday."

"Friday, as in today, Friday?"

"It's Friday? It is, isn't it? Then I guess it's today."

"Do you think you can go? Do you think you should go? Your hand can't feel good, and it's going to get worse before it gets better."

She had her out. No way anyone could expect her to go to a party mere hours after having surgery. For about a minute, she felt lighter, the weight of some of all that had happened in the last twenty-four hours lifted from her shoulders. But it didn't last. Unless things took a serious turn, she was perfectly capable of attending a party. She may not be the life of that party, but she wouldn't have been anyway, and she may not feel like staying long, but that was a plus as far as she was concerned. Still, provided Dr. Tanaka gave her the okay, there was nothing preventing her from going and making Ellie happy.

"I'll probably go," Max said. "I bought a dress, after all."

Why had she said that? She wanted to pull the gauze from her fingers and stuff it in her mouth to prevent her from saying anything else stupid because, if Beck could be believed, there seemed to be a pattern developing.

"What kind of dress?"

She tried not to look but couldn't stop herself and caught a glimpse of Beck wiggling his eyebrows in a way that would have left Groucho Marx envious.

"You're impossible."

"I've been called worse."

"I'm sure you have."

They drove in silence for a couple of minutes until Beck said, "So, do you want me to go with you?"

She knew the fact that she did would keep her mind busy for hours.

She was supposed to meet the doctor in person, an appointment she'd forgotten about until she got home and saw the reminder note taped to the refrigerator door. Since she couldn't drive, she texted and asked if they could do it over the phone. The doctor settled for a virtual meeting, and Max made sure Beck left long before the appointment time.

Her hand hurt enough to keep her from really relaxing, so though she was exhausted, Max paced as she waited for ten o'clock. When Dr. Mallick joined the video call, he looked as relaxed as ever in his usual sweater over a dress shirt and tie, and his wire-rimmed glasses that magnified his patient, grey eyes.

"Hello, Max. How are you?"

"I'm fine. Good. Well, I guess not so good."

She held up her hand, and Dr. Mallick drew back from the screen.

"What happened?"

"An accident last night. I was working on my car, my hand slipped, and after some apparently successful surgery, I'm told it should be good as new. With time."

"I'm sorry. Are you sure you're up for our meeting? When you requested a virtual session because you weren't feeling well, I assumed you had a cold."

"I'm okay. I'd rather do this today when I'm already out of school than have to reschedule and miss even more time at school."

"Have you been missing a lot?"

And so it began, Max thought.

"No, just for our meetings, but I don't like being away."

"That's understandable. Aside from having to miss some time, how are things at school?"

Max talked; he listened. Occasionally, he asked another question or asked her to elaborate, but mostly, he listened. It was unnerving the way he sat so calmly and just listened.

"And outside of school? You said you've been working on your car. Any other activities, get-togethers, outings?"

"Not really. Lunch with Ellie and Nic. I'm supposed to go to an engagement party tonight for Ellie and Zeke."

Dr. Mallick smiled. "You rolled your eyes."

"Did I? I didn't mean to."

"You don't want to go?"

"Would you want to go?"

"An engagement party for some of my close friends? Yes, I think I would."

"Yeah, I suppose it's not so much that I don't want to go, it's that I don't want to be the center of attention."

"You think you'll be the center of attention instead of the couple?"

"That sounded wrong, arrogant or something, didn't it? It's not what I meant. It's just that I guess I don't want to have to answer a lot of questions from Ellie's family. If they're like her, they'll have a million, and it will get awkward."

"You don't have to answer any questions you don't want to answer. You know that. On the other hand, it would be, as you say, awkward, if they avoided the topic entirely. Their daughter, their sister, was involved. They may look at it as though you saved her life."

"And that's what I don't want. I don't like to be put in that spotlight. I didn't do anything special."

"People have different definitions of what's special. Saving a daughter's life is going to seem special to a mother or a father."

Max closed her eyes for a moment so she wouldn't be tempted to roll them again. When she brought her hand up to her eyes without thinking, she winced.

"It hurts. We can cut this short if you want to rest."

"It hurts, yeah, but it'll hurt whether I'm talking to you or not."

"How did it happen? I know you said you were working on your car, but what happened?"

"An accident. A stupid accident. I was careless, distracted."

Before the words were out of her mouth, she regretted them. As expected, Dr. Mallick pounced, but like always, in his calm way that made it seem as if his question was as simple as one about the weather.

"Distracted? Was there a reason?"

She knew she could lie, make up something she knew he'd like to hear. Maybe that she saw someone on the drive to Beck's that reminded her of Albert Quinn. Or maybe how the shadow when she lifted her tool looked like a gun. Anything to avoid the truth, but she decided against it. If she had to suffer through the mandated sessions, she might as well make Dr. Mallick earn his paycheck.

"My mother showed up."

His eyebrows rose ever so slightly above the rims of his glasses.

"You've never talked about your mother except to say she's not part of your life. Now she's here?"

"Isn't that a kick in the head? Yeah, she showed up out of the blue. She claims she saw stories about me on the news and it made her finally decide to get in touch. After all these years," Max added under her breath.

"How do you feel about that?"

She knew the question was coming, but she didn't know how to answer it. Not exactly, anyway, because she didn't know how she felt.

"I don't know. I was angry at first. Angry that after walking out on us when I was four years old, she strolled back in like she'd gone out to buy milk."

"Is that how she acted?"

"No, not really. She kept saying she was sorry—for leaving, and for waiting so long—and that she just wants a chance to try to get to know me."

"And you don't want that?"

Max used her good hand to rake through her hair. "I don't know. At first I didn't, absolutely didn't, but she seems sincere, I guess, though I don't know how I'm supposed to believe anything a woman who claims to be a mother but can walk out on a four-year-old says."

"That's something you'll have to figure out and determine for yourself. No one can tell you the right thing to do."

"I figured you'd say as much."

Dr. Mallick cracked a hint of a smile. "Am I so predictable?"

"You are. Maybe one day we'll turn the tables and I'll ask the questions. Show you what I've learned."

At that, he chuckled.

"So you were distracted after seeing your mother, and you think that played a part in your accident."

"I've never had an accident before. I'm careful, and I know what I'm doing."

"Careful people who know what they're doing have accidents every day."

"Yeah, yeah."

"Was there anything else that could have distracted you or upset you?"

Max chewed on her lip before she answered. She knew she wasn't fooling him, and that if she said there was nothing, he'd know she was lying. Still, saying it out loud made it seem even more pathetic than it was.

"We've talked about the fact that you can tell me anything. I don't judge, I don't correct, I only try to help you understand why things affect you the way they do."

"A piece of paper. A stupid piece of pink paper. What do you think about that? A piece of paper had me on my knees, Doc, hardly able to breathe for the better part of an hour."

Dr. Mallick nodded so slowly Max wasn't certain his head was really moving.

"It said something that upset you? It reminded you of something?"

Max looked down at her bandaged hand that rested in her lap. Though it made her stomach roil, anything was better than looking Dr. Mallick in the eye.

"When she left, all those years ago, she left a note. I don't remember a lot from that time, but I remember that. A few lines on a piece of pink paper, like an afterthought. She'd told me goodbye, but I didn't understand what she meant. Later, when I found the note on the kitchen table, I showed it to my dad. He cried. I'd never seen him cry before; I've never seen him cry since. She wrote, 'Maxine, I love you. I'll miss you. Be a good girl for your daddy.' That's it. No explanation, no promises that she'd be back, that she'd visit me, nothing but a few stupid words. Yesterday, when she left my apartment, she left her phone number on a slip of pink paper. Left it on the kitchen table."

"You were very young. Do you think maybe it said more than your father told you?"

A vise tightened around Max's heart.

"I found it years later when I could read. It was folded up and tucked inside my dad's wallet. That's all it said."

"Memories, good and bad, can be powerful things. It's not uncommon to have a strong reaction when you're caught off guard by an especially painful memory. I don't think your reaction was unusual at all. Certainly nothing to worry about."

"Well, it made me feel like a fool. Weak." Then her words came in a rush. "If I crumble at the sight of a piece of paper, what's going to happen if I let her back in and she walks out again?"

Shocked, she clamped her good hand over her mouth. Underneath her hand, she felt her cheeks heat to burning.

"It's nothing to be ashamed of, Max. The fear of getting hurt is part of the human makeup. As is the instinct to protect ourselves from that kind of hurt. It's a matter of deciding whether the potential reward is worth the risk."

"I'm an adult, not a four-year-old girl. I'd like to think I could handle it this time."

"I'm sure you could, but that doesn't mean you want to have to find out."

"You're not going to tell me what to do, are you?"

"You know I'm not. In this case, it's up to you, and only you, to decide how to handle things. You'll know what's right, and you'll make the right decision."

"How do you know?"

"Easy. You've made a lot of right decisions already. It's what you do. It's who you are."

Later, by the time Beck picked her up for her appointment with Dr. Tanaka, Max had managed to get a couple hours of sleep, had struggled through an awkward, one-handed shower, and had fielded calls and emails from Nicole and Ellie. Max felt better, but only slightly, and not all her discomfort was physical.

Following her appointment with Dr. Tanaka, it was mostly physical. Unwrapping and re-wrapping her hand, the exercises she'd been assigned, it all hurt, and it put her in a bad mood. Beck was the unlucky recipient of that bad mood.

"You didn't have to come in with me," Max grumbled to Beck as he drove her home from the appointment.

"As your boyfriend, it seemed only right. They said it was good if someone else knew how to care for the wounds."

Under normal circumstances, Max would have shuddered at the reminder of the mess that was her fingers, but she was too irritated.

"Are you ever going to quit with that?"

"With what?"

"You know with what. With the boyfriend nonsense."

"You asked me out on a date. What else am I supposed to think?"

"And that too. You can quit with that too."

"I only speak the truth. You asked me to go with you. Begged, actually."

Max wanted to argue but knew it would get her nowhere. Besides, the fact that he wouldn't relent had her curious.

"Why would I do that? Why would I ask you to go with me to an event I don't even want to go to?"

"Probably for that reason. So you're not going alone."

Max stared out the window while she drummed the fingers of her good hand on her thigh. As much as it pained her to do so, she felt boxed in and as if she didn't have a choice.

"According to the doc, I'm not supposed to drive. I'm perfectly capable of driving, but whatever." Max slanted her eyes toward Beck. She had to give him credit for the way he kept his face expressionless. "I suppose if you're not busy, and if you feel like a free meal, and if you're willing to drive, and if you want to go, well, I suppose that would work."

He pressed his hand to his heart and sighed dramatically. "I don't know when I've been more touched by an invitation. How can I possibly say no?"

He was infuriating. There was no other way to describe him. Max had a million retorts on the tip of her tongue, but instead closed her eyes and told herself it was only one night. And that she'd make sure it was a short one.

"We need to be there at six-thirty. Pick me up at six-fifteen. Wear a suit." She opened her eyes long enough to glance over at him. "You do have a suit, don't you?"

"Believe it or not, I do. I even have a tie and dress shoes. Once when no one was looking, I snuck out of the garage and crashed a wedding. Figured I should dress the part."

Part of her almost believed him. The other part bit her lip so she wouldn't laugh.

"It's an engagement party, right?"

"Right."

"I've never been to one of those."

"Do you think I have?"

"How do I know?"

"I have not."

Beck was quiet for a minute. "Are there special rules, or expectations, or requirements at an engagement party?"

"How should I know? I told you, I've never been to one."

"I thought you might have some intel. Didn't the bride tell you what to expect?"

"It's a surprise engagement party. Ellie doesn't know."

"A surprise? Huh. That changes things, doesn't it?"

"I don't know, does it?"

"Well, then it's up to someone else to decide the theme of the party. Who's planning it?"

"Her sisters, I guess. They're all coming up from Oklahoma."

"Oklahoma? This just keeps getting better. Why didn't you lead with that? I love Oklahoma."

"What do you know about Oklahoma?"

"Went to school there. College. Played some football."

Max slammed her head back against the seat. "Please tell me you're kidding."

"Nope. Why? Don't I look like I could play football?"

Max didn't bother looking. "Crap. Ellie's going to love you. They're all going to love you."

13

Max fidgeted in her seat. Her feet already hurt, and the dress that, with all the chaos of the past twenty-four hours she hadn't tried on until she'd put it on twenty minutes ago, was inching up her thighs. On top of that, her hand ached, and she was flat-out refusing to take anything stronger than the ibuprofen she'd found in her medicine cabinet.

"The Wilmont Club is pretty swanky," Beck said as they drove out of Caston. "Ever been there?"

Max snorted. "No. Why would I go somewhere swanky?"

"I don't know, a date? It's pretty popular with guys trying to impress their dates."

Another snort. "Then that's a double no. What about you? How many girls have you tried to impress?"

He shook his head. "I don't have to try when it comes so easily."

She didn't bother replying.

"But since you asked, I've only been there once, and it was for lunch with a business partner. He chose the place."

"Business partner? I thought you owned your business. You have a partner?"

"Had. Very briefly. It didn't work out. Do you think this party is going to be a surprise for your friends?"

Though Beck's obvious attempt at changing the subject didn't escape her, she decided to let it slide. If he didn't want to talk about it, that was his choice.

"I don't know. Probably. Ellie called three times after school, checking up on me and wanting to come over. I had to concoct a story with Nic in which Nic said she'd handle things tonight since Ellie had her mom and sisters in town and had dinner plans. It took some convincing, and honestly, until I got into your truck, I half expected El to show up at my door. She's not easily deterred. And that was a roundabout way of saying that yes, I think she'll be surprised because she was too distracted with worrying about me to give tonight much thought."

"Is she going to like it? Not everyone likes surprises."

"She'll love it. Ellie loves surprises, and more than that, she loves her family. With all of them there, she wouldn't care if she showed up in jeans and a sweatshirt. Actually, I take that back. She would care, but she'd make everyone hold off on starting the party, or having any fun, or probably even talking, until she could rush home and change."

Beck laughed.

"You think I'm kidding? Just wait until you meet her, you'll see."

"Now I'm kind of afraid."

It was Max's turn to laugh. "You have nothing to worry about. Mostly because you'll love her. Everyone loves Ellie, and she loves everyone. But if somehow things start to go off course, just mention Oklahoma football and she'll kiss the very ground you walk on."

They were the last to arrive, it appeared, but they beat Ellie and Zeke, so the room was still a flurry of activity. Swanky was one term to describe the place, Max supposed, but it also felt warm and inviting. She hadn't expected that. The few times she'd been in places that anyone could describe as swanky, she'd felt as out of place as Ellie had at the race track. Here, it was the opposite. It was as if the room wanted to give her a hug.

On one wall, a long bar stretched under hanging lights that gave the copper bar top a warm glow. A bartender in black pants and a crisp white shirt used a rag to polish the copper to gleaming. Tables dotted the floor, all draped in white linen and topped with riotous bouquets boasting all sorts of out-of-season flowers that Max guessed were Ellie's favorites. At one table, a woman who was a slightly older-looking version of Ellie fussed with a pink tulip that dared droop. The wide-planked wood floor absorbed some of the clicking from the sky-high heels on the women Max knew had to be Ellie's sisters and her sister-in-law.

It was the back wall, though, that drew Max. Dominated by a huge fireplace where a cheery fire crackled and popped and took away the chill Max felt, even with her coat on, the warm brick soared to the ceiling interrupted only by a rough-hewn mantle that held copper urns full of greenery and more flowers. Floor-to-ceiling windows bordered the fireplace and provided a jaw-dropping view of a wooded area lit with thousands upon thousands of white fairy lights. The towering pines glowed like Christmas and just the sight of them helped dispel more of the chill.

She felt a hand at her shoulder. "Can I take your coat?" Beck asked.

"Sure. Thanks."

Somewhat gingerly, Max slipped from her coat, trying her best to prevent it from hitting her fingers. Beck did what he could to help. Once the coat was off and draped over his arm, he aimed a low whistle at Max.

"That's some dress, Mad Max."

It was tighter and shorter than she'd expected, though she supposed she was lucky it fit at all. It was emerald green with a plunging neckline that Max had tried to disguise with a necklace but now wondered if all she'd succeeded in doing was drawing more attention to it.

"It's the perfect color for you. Matches your eyes," Beck said.

When Max saw he was looking into her eyes instead of any of the places the dress hugged, the last of the chill she felt melted away.

He stepped closer and touched the zipper that ran most of the length of Max's back.

"How did you manage that by yourself with your hand?"

"Once in a while, being an engineer comes in handy. A piece of string, a paper clip, and..." Max snapped the fingers that were still capable of snapping.

"Clever."

Beck got closer still, and Max was ready to close the small distance that was still between them when a tornado blew up beside her.

"You must be Max."

With whatever sort of madness that had overtaken her effectively banished, Max gave her head a shake, then turned to the woman beside her.

She was taller than Ellie, and with her four-inch heels was nearly as tall as Max, who wore much more reasonable heels. The woman's hair was blonder, her nails longer and shinier, her voice louder and more assertive, and her smile definitely more devilish. Everything about her was just a little more, but there was no doubt she was Ellie's sister.

"Hayley. It's nice to meet you."

"Y'all know my name? Isn't that just the sweetest?"

"Ellie talks a lot about all of you."

"Well, she talks about you too."

Hayley poo-pooed the hand Max held out and instead wrapped Max in a hug.

"I just hardly know what to say to you. If it weren't for you, we might not be standing here tonight. You're so brave to have done what you did. We're forever grateful to you."

"Oh, well," Max patted Hayley's back, then managed to wriggle free from the hug.

"Whatever happened to your hand?"

"It's nothing."

"It doesn't look like nothing." Hayley's eyes turned to saucers and her mouth opened into an O. "Is it from that day? Did he hurt you?"

"No, no, it happened yesterday. An accident. Nothing to worry about."

Before Hayley could demand more information, she was joined by her parents, who introduced themselves and repeated much of what Hayley had said. Ellie's mom blinked back tears as she clung to Max.

"Now, Genevieve, let the woman breathe," Ellie's dad said. He put a gentle hand on Genevieve's arm and eased her away from Max.

"We are very grateful to you, Max."

"Thank you, Mr. Hawthorne, but I only did what anyone in my place would have done."

"Charles. Please call me Charles. And no, I don't believe that's the case. You risked your safety for that of a school full of others. That takes a special kind of person."

Alongside him, Genevieve nodded. "If there's ever anything you need, anything we can do for you, please ask. Whatever it is, it's not too big."

Max wanted to argue, but settled for, "Thank you."

Ellie's siblings joined the group and all took a turn echoing the sentiments of their parents and Hayley. They introduced themselves, but Max didn't need the introductions. Ellie had described them perfectly.

Just as Max started looking around the room for Beck, or Nicole, or anyone to come and rescue her, Ellie's sister, Charlene, tapped her watch.

"Ellie and Zeke will be here any minute. We should get in our places."

"Our places?" Max asked.

"We thought we'd stand just over there," Charlene pointed toward the bar. "That way, when they come in, they won't see us right away. Ellie will see the tables, and the flowers, and wonder for a minute what's going on, then we'll shout, 'Surprise!' and she'll be so excited."

Max knew she'd hate it, and hoped no one ever planned something like it for her, but she agreed with Charlene that Ellie would love it.

Max took her place near the bar and while they waited in silence, her eyes connected with Nicole's.

"Okay?" Nicole mouthed and tapped the fingers on one hand with those of the other.

Max nodded. Nicole looked doubtful.

Alongside Nicole, Brady looked amused by everything he saw. He grinned, his eyes wandering from one person to the next. Max briefly wondered if he got ideas for his Dragonthea book series by watching people, or if perhaps he was planning for a different type of story because it certainly looked to her like he was sizing up everyone and taking mental notes.

"Zeke, what—"

"Surprise!"

No matter how badly her feet hurt, not to mention her hand, and no matter how much she'd rather be at home curled up with some hot chocolate and a movie, Max forgot all of that when she saw Ellie's face. Confusion first when she didn't know where to look, then shock as it began to register, followed by pure joy when, one by one, Ellie spotted everyone.

"Mama? Daddy? You're here too?" Ellie's hands flew to her mouth. "Trip? Trav? Oh, my stars! Coltie!"

The tears were flowing as Ellie dashed across the room. Max saw Ellie's indecision, trying to decide where to go first for a hug. Her family saved her from making the decision when they engulfed her. With Colt the only one shorter, Ellie was swallowed, but her voice carried as she repeated the names of her family over and over.

When they finally eased back and Ellie emerged, the shock still evident on her face, Ellie found Max and made a beeline for her. The words came fast.

"Max, you're here? Why are you here? You should be home taking care of yourself. Unless that was all part of this? Did y'all go so far as to concoct some crazy story to keep my mind off tonight?"

Without pausing for a breath, Ellie's eyes cut toward Max's hand. "Oh, but no, look at you! Max, does it hurt? You should go home and rest. But no, don't go, I'm just so glad you're here. I'm so glad everyone's here. This is just unbelievable. Y'all are the sweetest, and I'm the luckiest girl in the whole world."

By the time Ellie did finally stop long enough to take a breath, Max could only nod and mutter, "I'm fine."

"You're not, that much is clear. You'll tell me all about it, but would you mind terribly if I just said a few more hellos first?"

"Go, El, go talk to everyone. It's your night. Enjoy it."

Another hug. Max wondered if she'd been hugged as much in the previous twenty years as she had been already that night.

"I just love you so much, Max. Thank you."

Ellie darted away, but stopped on a dime and whirled around. For the first time, she took notice of Beck, and suddenly everything slowed down. Ellie took five slow steps back toward Max, her eyes on Beck the entire time.

"Forgive me. I was impossibly rude. Please introduce me, Max."

Max's eyes went to the ceiling.

"Ellie Hawthorne, this is Beck Dawson. Beck, the bride-to-be, and my friend, Ellie."

Ellie didn't so much as glance at Max. Instead, she put on her sweetest southern charm and gushed over Beck.

"It is just so good to meet you, Beck. I understand you took good care of our Max last night. Thank you for being such a gentleman and seeing that she got to the hospital and then back home safely."

"It's a pleasure to meet you," Beck said. "And you're welcome. She can be an ornery one, our Max. She fought me about going to the hospital, but I'm afraid I had to insist. Now, I can't claim to be a doctor, but I knew she needed tending to, and well, I couldn't leave her to her own devices, or who knows what she might have done."

"Isn't that the truth? She can be a bit careless when it comes to tending to herself, that's a fact. Max tells me the two of you know each other from way back."

"I–" Max managed only one syllable before Beck spoke over her.

"That's a fact. I knew Max when she was just a little thing, running wild and telling everyone she was either going to be an acrobat in the circus or a race car driver."

Ellie laughed. "That sounds just like Max. And now, you're reunited. It's a small world, isn't it?"

"That it is," Beck said, "that it is."

"I'm happy that you're here with her tonight. I've been saying, and

Max has been denying—"

Max had enough. "Beck played football for the Sooners."

Max swore the entire room went silent. Even Ellie, who was never silent, was rendered speechless. Max watched with no small amount of amusement as Ellie's mouth opened, then closed, opened again, and still, no sound came out.

"It was a long time ago," Beck said.

"It's true?" Ellie whispered.

"Yes ma'am, it's true, but I was never a starter. I didn't play all that much."

"But you were a Sooner." Ellie said it with the sort of awe one might bestow upon a famous actor or the hottest rock star. Max laughed behind her hand.

Ellie turned, Max assumed to announce the news to the rest of her family, but most of them were already standing behind her. She grabbed her father's arm.

"Beck played football for the Sooners, Daddy. *The Sooners*!"

"I thought that's what I heard."

The crowd grew bigger, and Beck rubbed at his throat as if in desperate need of a drink. Max laughed, punched him in the shoulder, and whispered, "Have fun," as she sauntered away.

She was still laughing and heading toward Nicole and Brady when she spotted the only member of Ellie's family who hadn't yet joined the crowd around Beck.

He wore a black suit and a cowboy hat. He was of average height, and stocky in a fit sort of way. When he headed toward her, Max noted he was slightly bow-legged. His face was ruddy and wrinkled, with skin that comes from years of blistering sun and harsh winter winds, and when he smiled, every one of those wrinkles deepened and set his electric blue eyes sparkling with mischief. The way he carried himself told Max he was a man used to getting what he wanted. His face told her he wasn't afraid of hard work. And his eyes told her that he could go from tough rancher to tender grandfather in the blink of an eye.

Max couldn't have refused returning his smile for all the steak in Oklahoma.

"You must be Ellie's grandfather."

He tipped his hat and nodded his head. "One of my many titles, but one of my favorites."

"I'm Ellie's friend, Max. We teach together."

"Ah, yes, I know who you are, and let me say that I'm very glad to know you. You can call me Joe."

He held out his hand and Max took it. She appreciated it when he didn't fawn all over her as the others had done, but she also realized that he said more with his handshake and with his eyes than the others had done with their endless words.

Max fell a little bit in love.

"What happened to your hand, darlin'?"

"Just a little accident. It's nothing."

Those blue eyes studied her. "You winced a minute ago when Colt brushed up against you. I don't think it's nothing."

There was no point in lying, or even skirting the truth. "Cut three fingers while I was working on my car. Had surgery on two of them last night, but the doctor promises they'll be as good as new."

"You taking any medications?"

Max was a little taken aback. "Um, no, I'm not. Well, an over-the-counter pain reliever, but not the stuff they gave me in the hospital." When Joe grinned, Max added, "Why?"

"How 'bout we see if they have any decent Scotch in this place?"

He held out his arm, and Max linked hers in his.

"I can't think of anything I'd like better."

A Scotch, and then another one, helped ease the ache in Max's hand, but, she thought, might have contributed to the odd and completely unexpected one in her heart. In all her life, she'd never spent an evening like the one she was part of that night. Three generations of family, all of them laughing, smiling, hugging, and telling stories, and all of them as welcoming to Max and the other three outsiders—as well as to Zeke's parents—as if they were all long lost family. She'd expected to hate it, or at the very least, feel out of place, but she was swept up in the love and the genuine joy that spending time with one another brought to the family.

Nicole, Brady, and Beck handled it all in stride, but Max knew a big family gathering wasn't as foreign to them as it was to her. Aside from her dad and Skeeter, Max had no one who was family to her. There were acquaintances and friends, lots of them and some of them close, but nothing like Ellie's family. Max didn't have years' worth of stories about Sundays spent at her grandparents' homes, about the schemes six siblings were capable of dreaming up, about the weddings and the funerals, about the good times and the bad. Instead, Max had fleeting memories of race tracks from one side of the country to the other, of celebrations when the driver her dad was working with won a race, and of packing up and moving when that driver, and that team, lost too many in a row. Her holidays were spent wherever they happened to be, and with whomever they happened to be with. Sometimes Santa Claus and the Easter Bunny found her, and sometimes they didn't.

The laughter and the stories continued through dinner. Max thought about making her escape as soon as the dessert dishes were cleared, but Ellie's family had other plans.

A microphone appeared, and speeches by anyone who wanted to take a turn at the microphone had Max's emotions getting the better of her. She was laughing one minute as Trip told a story of Ellie trying to sneak a nest full of baby birds into her bedroom. Ellie had given herself away when she'd innocently asked their mother if worms should be cooked in the microwave or in the oven. Then Max found herself blinking back tears when Colt took a turn and talked about the best big sister, the one who helped him successfully sneak a litter of kittens into his room, and who he missed every day. When Colt straightened to his full four-and-a-half feet and looked Zeke in the eye, telling him that he liked him well enough, but that if he was ever mean to Ellie, Colt would get on his horse and come to Wisconsin to find him, Max wasn't the only one drying tears.

And then the music started. Max knew enough to know about wedding dances, but engagement party dances? That was uncharted territory. She looked around to see if anyone else seemed surprised, but no one else seemed the least bit fazed by the development.

Ellie looked like she was floating as Zeke whirled her around the dance floor. Max was certain Ellie hadn't known about the party, even a Hollywood actress wasn't that good, but Ellie couldn't have chosen a more perfect dress for the occasion. What seemed like yards of midnight blue swirled and billowed around her legs and matched Zeke's tie as if Ellie herself had chosen the combination. How Ellie could walk, let alone dance, in the sky-high, skinny heels was a puzzle, but she not only managed it, she made it look as if she were wearing sneakers. She matched Zeke step for step, or maybe Zeke matched Ellie, as he didn't seem nearly as comfortable as Ellie did. Her feet skittered and seemed to barely touch the floor while she never took her eyes off Zeke. Ellie had left her hair down, and her blonde curls bounced and swayed right along with her. It was Ellie's smile, though, that held Max's attention. Ellie radiated happiness and love, and the longer Max watched, the more she started to believe in those things.

Shocked at herself, she pulled her eyes away and took a drink of her water, purposely letting an ice cube flow into her mouth where she crunched it in the hopes it would jolt her back to her senses.

"Will you dance with me, Max?"

In her Scotch- and family-induced halcyon daydream, Max had forgotten Beck was sitting alongside her.

"Dance? I don't dance."

"Everyone dances."

"You're wrong there. Everyone may try, the stupid fools, but not everyone dances."

"Do you mean you're admitting there's something you can't do?"

He'd known just the thing to say, but she wasn't falling for it.

"Fine. There's something I can't do. I can't dance. Happy?"

"Not at all. I want to dance."

"There are other women here. Ask one of them."

"I want to dance with you."

She hated the fluttering in her heart, it was downright embarrassing, so she played with the condensation on the outside of her glass until her pulse slowed.

"Come on. If it ends in disaster, you can blame your injured hand."

"What does my hand have to do with dancing?"

"Oh, Mad Max, you really don't know how to dance, do you?"

Beck stood, bowed theatrically, then held out his hand.

"May I have this dance?"

"Oh, for crying out loud. Fine."

Max let him take her hand and lead her to the dance floor. While she knew it probably wasn't true, it felt like every pair of eyes in the place was on her.

Beck kept Max's right hand in his but turned her so she was facing him. Awkwardly, Max put her left hand at his waist, trying to make contact only with her wrist and prevent any bumping of her fingers.

They'd barely started moving when the song changed. Unsurprisingly, the playlist was all country, but Max didn't pay much attention to the lyrics at first, instead focusing her attention on not stomping on Beck's feet.

It wasn't like she'd never danced. She had. And it wasn't like she was a complete klutz with no rhythm. She wasn't. But she was far from comfortable, especially when Beck's arms seemed to tighten around her.

"Believe it or not, it's easier if you don't look at your feet."

"Easy for you to say."

"Listen to the music and let your body move with it. Overthinking it makes it harder."

"And how do you know all this?"

"Dance classes."

Max pulled back so she could see his face.

"No way."

"Afraid so. My mom insisted."

"So, ballet? Jazz? Tap?"

Beck chuckled. "No, just a few sessions of ballroom dancing. My mom insisted I learned to waltz. Any other kind of dancing, she said, was up to me, but she was adamant that when I took a girl to a dance, I'd be able to lead on the dance floor."

Max tried to picture a much younger Beck, stiff arms reaching toward a girl a head taller than he, and rocking back and forth to *The Blue Danube Waltz*. Imagining him stepping on her toes, and casting pleading glances at his mother who was likely watching from the sidelines, relaxed her enough that she didn't realize Beck was leading her into a spin until it was over.

"I think you were holding out on me. You can dance."

"It must be my partner," Max said, then regretted her words when Beck grinned.

She looked the other way, and for the first time, listened to the song. It didn't take her long to recognize it. All about searching, looking for love, passing through town after town, making mistakes and moving on.

Since Max knew the song, she knew what was coming next, so when Beck started to softly sing along, she started running through numbers in her head. *Ten squared, one hundred. Eleven squared, one hundred twenty-one. Twelve squared, one hundred forty-four.*

When he sang about signs and broken paths, Max wanted to shout. *Thirteen squared, one hundred sixty-nine. Fourteen squared, one hundred ninety-six.*

Then he bent his head and sang the last words into her ear.

The whole 'legs turning to jelly' thing had always seemed stupid to Max, but she knew that at that moment if Beck hadn't been holding her up, her legs would never have been up to the job. The legs that had run a marathon just a few months ago, the legs that had earned her a top-five finish in the state track meet the year they'd actually been in one place long enough for her to join the team, the legs that had helped her fight off a school shooter, now useless at the sound of a man singing a few stupid words.

Except they weren't stupid. They felt somehow true. Hadn't she spent her life just passing through? Hadn't she had her share of long-lost dreams? But what, they'd led her here? To Caston? To Beck?

The song ended, but Beck didn't let her go right away. She stood, frozen, certain this time that all eyes really were on them until she felt a hand on her arm.

"Mind if I have the next dance, Beck?"

"Not at all, sir."

Beck took Max's hand and put it in Joe's.

"I've lost a step or two over the years, but I can still show a lady around the dance floor."

"I'm sure you can," Max said, so grateful for the interruption it was all she could do not to do the very thing she hated and hug Ellie's grandfather.

The next song was a little faster, and Joe kept up the chatter. Before long, Max managed to forget about the crazy thoughts she'd had while dancing with Beck and remind herself of her goals.

"I told her I'd love to see her come home, but it seems maybe she's found a new home here," Joe said.

Max hadn't been paying much attention but knew he was talking about Ellie.

"She does seem happy here. It seems like so long ago that the school year started and the three of us—Ellie, Nicole, and I—were all brand new at the teaching thing. Ellie was the most confident of all of us. More than once, she kept Nic and me sane, kept us from taking off in the middle of the night for parts unknown. I think you're right. She seems at home here."

"She's something special, isn't she? They all are, all my grandchildren, and I'd never admit to having a favorite, but Ellie has always had me wrapped around her finger. She has about the kindest heart of anyone I've ever known. She'd do anything for a friend, or for someone she just met, for that matter."

"I've seen that first-hand."

Joe nodded. "She was nearly destroyed when that no-good ex-fiancé of hers did what he did. I think it hurt me as much as it hurt her. It took all my willpower, as well as a few stern words from my wife, to keep me from marching right up to that skunk's door. Not sure what I would have done once I got there, probably would've let my old

Winchester do the talking for me."

Max chuckled. Joe wouldn't hurt a fly, any more than his granddaughter would, but she understood the sentiment.

"This Zeke, he's a good one?"

"He is. He's a lot like Ellie in that he'd do anything for anyone. It's his story to tell if he chooses, and I don't know all the details, but I do know there was some trouble in his family. Zeke took the fall for his brother, and it was a pretty steep fall. No, he'd never hurt Ellie. Just the opposite. Of that, we can both be certain."

"I like knowing you're here to watch over her when I can't, Max."

The knife already in her heart twisted. "And I like knowing she's got you in her corner, Joe."

"That's what family does. It's the most important thing in the world to me. There's nothing I wouldn't do for mine. We need to cherish every minute we have with them."

Later, after Beck dropped her off at home, it wasn't the moment on the dance floor with him that replayed in her mind, but Ellie's grandfather's words. It was late, but she picked up her phone, scrolled to find the number, and sent a text.

If you're free tomorrow, we could meet for lunch. Noon. Scooter's on Third Street.

14

The fact that she was nervous made her angry, and the fact that she was angry made her scowl, and without thinking, drum her fingers on the table. And that just hurt.

It wasn't like she could forget about the bandages and splints on her fingers. That morning, she'd had to unwrap and clean the wounds as she'd been taught by the assistant in Dr. Tanaka's office. It had taken her forty minutes to work up the nerve to take off all the bandages and to look at her fingers. Then it had taken another fifteen minutes before she could bring herself to soak those fingers and swish them around in a bowl of water. Trying to bandage them again with one hand had almost proven too much, but somewhat sloppily, she'd finally succeeded.

Maybe Victoria wouldn't show. Max knew, if forced to wager, she'd bet that way. It still didn't make sense that Victoria truly wanted to reconnect. Cursing the warm and fuzzy feeling she'd gotten after spending an evening with Ellie's family, and telling herself she should have known better than to send the text, Max stood only to see Victoria walk in the door. Max lifted her hand when Victoria scanned the room, and Victoria haltingly made her way to Max's table.

Victoria looked as nervous as Max felt. What a pair they made.

"Hi, Max. This place is nice."

"It's comfortable."

Victoria shivered. "It's chilly for spring, isn't it?"

"Not so chilly for Wisconsin," Max said, hating small talk as much as always. "Sit."

Victoria did but kept her coat wrapped around her. Her eyes wandered around the restaurant before returning to Max and eventually landing on the hand Max had tried to keep out of sight.

"What in the world happened to your hand?"

"It's nothing. I don't want to talk about it."

It was clear in the way Victoria shifted in her seat and tried to get a better look that she'd much prefer to talk about it at length. Victoria studied the bandaged hand as if searching for an explanation.

"Hungry?" Max asked, handing her mother a menu.

Victoria tore her gaze from Max's hand and focused on the menu. "I am. What's good here?"

"Everything I've tried, but I'm partial to their pizza."

"Pizza sounds good. What kind do you like?"

Victoria's eyes flew up from the menu and looked terrified. A mother who didn't know what kind of pizza her daughter liked. Max wondered how many of those kinds of mothers were haunting the streets of Caston.

"All kinds. You?"

"Whatever you like."

"Then we should get the Scoot the Moon. It's a little of this, a little of that, but never quite the same as the last time."

Max smiled at the memory of the first time she'd eaten it with Nicole and Ellie. Max had loved it, as had Nicole. Ellie had politely picked off half the toppings and pronounced it perfect.

"Sounds good," Victoria said.

"I'd like a beer with it," Max said. "Do you drink beer?"

"Um, sure, sometimes. That sounds good."

Though Max wasn't usually one to rely on anything to relax her, she thought in this case, a glass might do them both good. After they'd placed their order, they sat, staring at one another.

"So," Max said. "You wanted to get together."

"I did. Of course, I did. I want to spend time with you. I want to get to know my daughter."

Max could snap back that a mother shouldn't have to get to know her adult daughter, but what would be the point? They'd go around in circles, much as they'd done the other day.

"What do you want to know?"

"Tell me more about yourself. About college, about how you got into teaching, if you think you'll stay here in Caston, if there's a special someone in your life. Whatever you want to tell me, I want to hear."

That wasn't true, Max thought. Victoria definitely wouldn't want to hear some of the things Max wanted to tell her, but Max decided to keep the snide remarks to herself. Instead, she tried to figure out how to tell someone about herself, someone who should already know all there is to know, in a few sentences.

"College was the longest I ever stayed in one place. I went to two different schools, but the two-and-a-half years I spent at the second school was the longest continuous stretch I've spent anywhere. Teaching wasn't planned, it just happened. I have degrees in engineering and math and hope to put them into practice after I put in some time teaching. As far as staying in Caston? Doubtful. I don't stay anywhere for long."

Even as she said the words, a strange ache had Max rubbing her fist over her heart.

"You and your dad moved around a lot."

It was a statement, not a question, and Max wondered how often Victoria had sought out information on Max's life.

"We did. I have a feeling you knew that."

Victoria shrugged. "Maybe some, but usually not where you were at any given time."

"Did you care?"

"Oh, Max, of course I cared."

"Funny way of showing it."

"I cared. I failed as a mother, but I never stopped caring."

"Then why? Why did you leave? Why didn't you come back?" Max noticed heads turn in her direction and lowered her voice. "If you cared, you could have come back."

"It wasn't that easy. It was never that easy. After I was gone for a while, out of your lives, I didn't know how to come back. I knew I wouldn't be welcomed with open arms. I feared I wouldn't be welcomed at all. I didn't know if I could stand the pain if your father turned me away, if he didn't let me see you."

"So, because you were afraid of something that might have happened, you never once made an effort to contact your daughter?"

Victoria looked hurt. "That's not quite fair. I admit I didn't try to see you, but you can't say I didn't contact you. There were the birthday cards and the Christmas gifts. I know I didn't do as much as I should have, but I…"

Victoria looked curiously at Max, and the hurt turned to genuine shock. Her words were so soft, so slow, Max could barely make them out. "He didn't tell you? Your father didn't give you the things I sent?" Her voice dropped even lower. "None of them?"

It was Max's turn to be shocked. As far as she knew, there had not been one thing in all those years from her mother. No cards, no gifts, nothing. Her father had kept them from her? Max's shock turned to crushing pain, then before the pain could swallow her, she channeled it into bubbling anger. Like a pot on the stove, too full and boiling too hard, the bubbles rose to the surface and threatened to spill over.

Max grabbed the edge of the table to keep her good hand from doing something she'd regret. Her knuckles turned white as she contemplated what it all meant. One finger at a time, she released the table, ready to reach for her phone, when their server set drinks on the table. Behind him, another server carried the pizza.

Max sat as rigid as a statue while the server cleared a spot for the pizza, then pulled silverware wrapped in napkins from the pocket on his apron. Coasters followed, and he moved the glasses on top of them. She knew he was talking while he worked, she knew Victoria talked back, but Max heard nothing but a buzz like a hive of bees in her head.

When he left, instead of reaching for her phone, she reached for her glass and downed half of it without stopping for a breath. When she slapped it back down on the table, Victoria's eyes were wide and wary.

"Are you okay, Max?"

"Okay?" A wild bark of laughter escaped before Max could stop it. "I am so not okay. I'm livid. I feel like my life was some sort of elaborate lie. I thought he was the one I could trust, and now I find he lied to me for most of my life? About everything? I guess I'll never know the truth about anything, will I?"

Max picked up her glass and took another gulp, then swiped the back of her hand across her mouth.

"Didn't you wonder why I never sent you a thank you? Or acknowledged the gift in any way? Didn't you ask him about it? Or did he lie to you too?"

"Max, calm down. It was a long time ago. I don't know that it matters all that much now."

"It doesn't matter?" Max's voice rose with every word. "I'd say it matters. One of my parents took off when I was hardly more than a baby. The other one spent his life lying to me, keeping things from me. My whole life is one big lie!"

"It's not. You were loved, Max, remember that. Your father loved you, loves you, I know that. I made it a point to know that. He always did, from the second he laid eyes on you. You were his world. As you grew up, he may not have shown it in the same ways other parents did, but he never stopped. If he didn't tell you about those things I sent, that was him looking out for you."

"Hah!" Max muttered into her beer.

"No, the more I think about it, the more I realize he did the right thing. Honestly, I suppose I should have suspected that's exactly how he'd handle it. Max, if he'd given you the cards, the letters, the gifts, you would have had a million questions. You'd have wanted to know where I was, why I didn't come to see you, why you couldn't go see me, and you would have blamed your father. He didn't deserve your blame, I did. I guess looking at it in that light, I should never have done it. I shouldn't have sent things and forced him to make that decision, one I'm sure wasn't easy, and force him to be the bad guy." Victoria dropped her head. "I was the bad guy, not your father."

Some of Max's anger began waning. She wanted it back. She needed it.

"Maybe when I was young, but when I got older, that should have been my decision, not his. It's not right that he kept things from me, that I never had a say in any of it. Who knows? Maybe I would have tossed whatever it was straight in the trash without looking at it. Maybe I wouldn't have cared one way or the other if you sent me a birthday card. Still, it should have been up to me to decide." Though she tried to fight it, her anger petered out. "He didn't have the right to make those decisions for me," Max added, but the fight was gone.

"Maybe he didn't, but we can't change the past. Believe me, I know that."

Victoria busied herself unwrapping the silverware, then arranging it carefully on the napkins, first Max's, then her own. With her arms crossed over her chest, Max watched with indifference.

"Eat some pizza. It smells so good." Victoria reached for a slice, then pulled her hand back. "Is that an egg?"

"It is. You never know what you'll find on a Scoot the Moon."

"I see. Well, let's give it a try, shall we?"

Max grabbed a slice and tore into it like a starving wolf. Somehow the act of ripping at the pizza helped further calm her anger.

"I think I should call him and give him a piece of my mind," Max said, but resignation had replaced the anger in her voice. Still, she reached in her bag for her phone. As she picked it up, it buzzed with a text. Though it was the last thing she felt like doing, Max couldn't help but smile when she looked at the picture on the phone screen.

"What is it? Good news?" Victoria sounded relieved.

"Ellie, the friend I told you about who's getting married, is dress shopping today. She's sending me pictures of dresses she's trying on and asking my opinion."

"That's right. You mentioned shopping with her. Why aren't you there?"

"Her mom, her future mother-in-law, her sisters, and both her grandmothers are here. She has enough help."

Max scrolled through the pictures. Ellie couldn't be serious about wanting an opinion from Max, could she? Despite what Nicole might think, Max knew she was woefully unqualified to have anything of value to offer on the subject.

"May I see?"

"Sure." Max reached across the table with her phone and let her mother look. "Ellie seems to think I'll have an opinion."

"Don't you?" Victoria looked at Max, then back at the phone. She pointed at the dress in the current photo. "She's such a little thing, she gets lost in all those ruffles. Look." Victoria tapped the phone and Max looked. "See how all that fabric swallows Ellie?"

"Yeah, I guess you're right. She should have something less, um, less fluffy and more, I don't know, sleek? Is that the right word?"

"Exactly." Victoria smiled and nodded. "She wants people to see her, not just the dress. Something graceful with delicate lace, but no ruffles."

"I can see that."

Max scrolled to the next picture.

"Oh, my!" her mother choked on her pizza and had to take a sip of beer. "She can't be serious."

Max laughed. "I don't think she is." Max turned the phone to study the picture. The dress was knee-length, the skirt made entirely of what looked like feathers, and the top, which was what Max thought was called a crop top, had more feathers on the shoulders. "At least, I hope she's not."

Victoria looked frightened. "You need to tell her, Max. Tell her it's horrible. She can't wear that on her wedding day."

"I'm sure she's kidding. She's a very proper southern lady, surrounded by a gaggle of very proper southern ladies. Well, her sister Hayley might not fit the bill entirely, but the rest do. Ellie has to be kidding."

Victoria didn't look convinced but nodded.

Max turned the phone back toward her mother and kept scrolling, realizing that she and her mother were, what? Bonding? Laughing, anyway, and agreeing on what suited Ellie and what didn't. Never in her wildest dreams would she have thought she'd be sitting in a restaurant, eating pizza and drinking beer with her mother, and laughing over Ellie in wedding dresses. It was madness.

The string of pictures seemed endless. Ellie must have tried on a hundred dresses. Max found herself thinking she'd much rather be right where she was than at some frilly dress shop trying to smile at dress after dress.

There were a few more photos, all of them very tame and not a feather in sight, when the screen changed and there was a picture of Max and Beck from the night before.

"Who is that?" Victoria asked before Max could skip past the picture.

"Just a guy. Beck."

"Beck. Last night? Your hand was bandaged, so it must have been last night. The engagement party? He went with you?"

Max wondered why she wasn't irritated by the question, but couldn't come up with a good answer.

"Yeah. He's the guy who took me to the hospital when I hurt my hand. I guess I asked him to go with me when I was drugged up. At least that's how he tells it."

Victoria put one elbow on the table and dropped her chin into it. She smiled at Max, and her eyes danced. She looked almost like a teenager and nothing like the beaten-down woman who'd shown up on Max's doorstep a few days earlier.

"You like him."

"I do not."

"Oh, you do, I can tell. All women get that look in their eye when they're interested in a man." Victoria tilted her head one way, then the other. "He must be intelligent, definitely funny, kind, and probably as fiercely independent as you."

"I..." Since she had no idea how to respond, Max clapped her mouth shut.

"It's okay. Let it sink in." Victoria picked up her beer and sipped. "Now, are you ready to tell me about your hand?"

When she poked her head into Ellie's room on Monday morning, Max was reminded of the dress full of feathers. Watching Ellie float around the room, stopping to twirl every few steps, made Max wonder if the swan dress wouldn't have been just the thing for Ellie.

"Max, you're here. Good." Ellie floated across the room and threw her arms around Max. "How was the rest of your weekend?"

Those may have been the words she spoke, but her expression screamed, 'What's the story with Beck?' Max chose to ignore the unspoken.

"It was fine."

Ellie grew serious. "And how's your hand? Are you sure you should be here today?"

"I'm sure. It's nothing but a nuisance now. The pain is gone." Max turned when she heard footsteps behind her. "Morning, Nic."

"Good morning. Did I overhear you saying your hand is better?"

"You did. It's fine."

Nicole nodded, then turned her attention to Ellie. "So? Did you choose one?"

Ellie clasped her hands together. "I did!"

"A dress?" Max asked.

"Of course, silly, what else would I be talking about?"

"I don't know. The next book you assign the kids to read?"

"Oh, Max, you do like to tease, don't you?"

"Which one? Which one?" Nicole pleaded.

"It was such a hard decision, but then, it wasn't. Once I was home and had time to think about it, it was as clear as the nose on my face."

"And…" Nicole prompted.

"And the sheath with the lace appliqués down the back and on the train." Ellie collapsed into her chair. "It's so beautiful, and so perfect, and I can't wait to wear it."

"I knew it!" Nicole's arms shot into the air. "I knew it as soon as I saw it. It's the perfect dress for your size and shape. Ellie, you're going to be stunning on your wedding day."

"I hope so. I hope Zeke likes it."

"Like it? El, he's going to love it. Your only concern is going to be him holding it together while you walk down the aisle."

Ellie sighed. "Do you think?"

"I know."

"What's a sheath?" Max asked.

Nicole and Ellie stopped their girl talk long enough to turn and look at her. Then they looked back at each other in the way the two of them had that drove Max crazy. The way that meant it was time to take pity on their poor, lost friend.

"Fine. It's not like I care what a sheath is. I was only being polite. I have work to do."

Max turned to leave, but both Nicole and Ellie called after her.

"Wait, Max," Nicole said. "A sheath is a straight, fitted dress. No billowy skirt, just long, clean lines."

"Okay." Max had told the truth when she said she didn't care. "I do have to go. Catch-up work from Friday."

"Of course," Ellie said, then rushed to Max's side. "I know dress shopping isn't your favorite, and I have the feeling you weren't exactly sad not to go along on Saturday, but I want you to know how much it meant to me when you texted back after looking at the dresses I tried. Your opinions were a breath of fresh air."

"I suppose that means what I had to say wasn't worth much, but you got a laugh out of it?"

Ellie drew in a sharp breath. "Not at all. Mama, and my sisters, and my grandmamas? I don't think any of them would have had the nerve to tell me I looked like I was squeezed into a sausage casing, or that the swirling ruffles were going to make people dizzy looking at me. Well, Hayley might have, but I know Mama threatened her with all sorts of horrible things if she didn't behave."

"Then I'm glad I could help. Now, I really have to go."

"Fine, but after school? I have a long list of questions for you about Mr. Beck Dawson."

"I'll probably be busy after school."

"No way, Max. Right here, right after the last bell."

"We'll see," Max said as she stepped into the hallway. Then she turned and stuck her head back in the room. "That dress with the feathers? That was a joke, right?"

Ellie giggled. "Hayley dared me to try that one and act as though I loved it. Mama nearly had a stroke. Hayley laughed her head off. It was Hayley's way of getting back at Mama."

As Max walked to her own room, she imagined sitting at a bridal shop, surrounded by all the women in her family, teasing, and joking, and crying over dresses. She couldn't, not really, but when she let herself look at the imaginary group surrounding her, one of the faces in the group of otherwise faceless women looked a lot like Victoria.

Max watched Reid, one of the brightest students in her engineering class, but one of the most timid and socially awkward. He was new to Caston and three-fourths of the way into the school year, didn't have many friends. Max knew what it was like to be the new kid, and her heart ached for him.

She'd tried to engage him in class. He answered when called upon, and he always had the correct answer, but getting him to elaborate, or to offer any of his own ideas past the standard book answer, was impossible. The work he turned in made it clear he had a thorough understanding of the concepts they covered. Max understood his reluctance to speak up and risk being labeled as the brainy one, or the teacher's pet. If you were popular and you spoke up, everyone listened. If you weren't so popular, they snickered.

Middle school was a minefield.

Max wandered the room, stopping to check her students' progress on their balloon-powered cars. She answered questions, offered advice, or in the case of Trevor, just shook her head at the 'Terror Wagon' he was designing. It had wheels that turned, it had a body made from one of the items Max had given them to choose from, and it had a balloon to power it. He'd met all the criteria. But instead of focusing on making his vehicle travel farther, which was the goal of the project, he was busy painting flames on the sides and making the front look like a mouth with jagged teeth and dripping blood.

Sometimes, she'd learned, a teacher had to choose her battles.

When she got to Reid's desk, she watched him. He was meticulous in his work, carefully measuring and balancing the car's components. He selected then discarded bottle cap wheels when they weren't perfectly round.

"How's it going, Reid?"

"Oh, fine."

"Your car's looking good."

"Thanks."

He had his skewers set aside, and Max knew he'd previously had them in place. "What's your plan for the axles?"

Reid looked around and lowered his voice. "I was wondering if it's allowed to use lubricant on the axle. If it spins easier, it will reduce the friction and the car should travel farther."

Max wanted to clap, to give him a big gold star, to have him stand up and explain his theory to the class. Instead, she bit her tongue.

"That's an excellent idea, but you can't use anything other than the objects I provided. Sorry, those are the rules."

"You have pencils in there. Some people tried to use them as axles." He gave his head a shake. "They're too heavy. Since the pencils are technically something you provided, can I color on the skewers with a pencil? The graphite might work as a lubricant."

"Very clever, Reid, very clever. Yes, you can do that."

He tried to fight it, but he couldn't quite hold back his smile. "Thanks."

"Don't thank me, it was your idea."

She wanted to talk more with him, to encourage him, but she knew unease when she saw it. Besides, even without looking, she knew Aiden was on the move.

"Let me know if you have any other questions. And good job, Reid."

On a good day, she spoke with Aiden once or twice about his behavior. There weren't many good days.

She feigned heading to her desk, then came up behind him just as he was about to pull the chair out from underneath Matt, who'd stood to reach for a bottle cap that had rolled away from him.

"If you move that chair, you're going to be moving all of them after school today."

Aiden flinched, but Max had to give him credit for thinking on the spot.

"I was just making sure it didn't tip over when Matt stood up."

"Ah, well then, I'm glad you're making good choices. I'm sure you'll make more good choices and see that the wad of gum in your hand doesn't end up on his chair."

"Yep. I was just gonna throw this away."

Aiden held up an astonishingly large wad of bright green gum as he walked backward toward the garbage can near the door. The green apple smell carried the six-foot distance between the two of them.

Max thought back to the many schools she'd attended that hadn't allowed gum in class. At the time, she'd thought it one of the dumbest rules teachers had ever come up with. Now, she considered suggesting it at the next staff meeting.

She watched until Aiden dropped the gum in the waste basket. Deciding that fire was, for the moment, extinguished, she continued her circuit of the room. Many of her students were putting considerable effort into the project. It was rewarding and fun watching them try different materials, make changes to their car's design, and then test and retest, trying to determine whether their car would travel the required five feet once they powered it with a balloon.

Not all the projects she'd attempted with her class had been successful, so finding one that was felt good. She believed in hands-on learning when it came to engineering. Try, fail, try again. It was the best way to learn. Some kids were easily frustrated or didn't have the patience to try something a half dozen times and still not succeed. Most thirteen-year-olds had little patience for anything, and not all were destined to become engineers. That was okay. Even if the class wasn't their favorite, even if they did only the minimum, they'd take away some basic knowledge that would serve them down the road.

"Time to clean up," Max announced. "Make sure you put all the supplies you need in your bin and put those you don't need back for someone else to use. Remember, tomorrow is the last class day to work on your cars. Wednesday we'll test them."

A barely organized chaos reigned for a few minutes while students packed up their belongings. Just as the bell rang, Max heard the squeak of the cabinet door where she kept emergency supplies and extra cleaning products. She didn't bother turning around, but her voice carried over the din.

"Aiden, remember our discussion. If you hide Matt's project again, you'll be scrubbing all the work tables every day for a week."

The door banged shut. She looked over her shoulder to see Aiden scamper from the room, probably chasing Matt and certainly unfazed by her warning. How Matt continued to be Aiden's best friend was another middle school puzzle Max knew she'd never solve.

With a prep period the next hour, Max wasn't in a hurry to finish the organizing the kids hadn't quite finished. She wandered to the closest work table and only then realized Reid was still in the room.

"Reid, did you forget something?"

"Um, no, I wondered if um, if I can…" His eyes darted around the room before landing on his car. "If I can take my car home with me to be sure it doesn't get broken."

He didn't make eye contact, which wasn't unusual, but he rocked from one foot to the other and Max saw the fingers on his free hand tap a wild staccato beat against his thumb.

"I think it will be safe here. I can put it on top of the cabinet if you're worried about it." Max pointed to the cabinet against the back wall.

"Oh, um, okay, I guess that'll work."

His fingers moved even faster. Not wanting to pressure him, Max took her time gathering his bin and moving it to the top of the cabinet.

"How far do you think your car will go?"

"I don't know. At least five feet, though."

"I know it will go that far. You followed the directions and didn't add anything that could keep it from rolling smoothly."

"Yeah." He looked at her for the first time.

"Is there something else, Reid?"

His eyes darted again before landing on her bandaged hand.

"What happened to your hand?"

She'd given all her classes a shortened version of the accident, leaving out most of the gory details.

"As I said, I slipped when I was working on my car and cut it pretty badly."

Reid nodded. "Were you being careful?"

Max allowed herself a little smile. "Like I tell everyone else, over and over? No, probably not, at least not as careful as I should have been. I was distracted, and that leads to accidents."

"Has anyone ever gotten hurt in your class?"

"No, and let's hope it stays that way."

Reid spoke slowly and seemed to choose his words carefully. "If we see someone doing something that's not safe, do you want us to tell you?"

Interesting, Max thought. They might be getting somewhere.

"I do. It could be private. I wouldn't tell anyone who told me."

Reid nodded again, and though he looked like he wanted to say more, did not.

"If you saw someone in class doing something that you thought looked unsafe, you can tell me. You should tell me. I don't want anyone to get hurt."

His head shake was vigorous enough to make Max feel dizzy for him.

"I didn't. Honest."

"Okay."

"I was just wondering, in case I do. See something…someone, I mean. Or maybe hear something."

"Okay," Max repeated.

The bell rang to start the next hour. Reid's face turned red.

"I'm going to be late for science."

"Who's your teacher?"

"Mr. Boston."

"I'll write you a pass. It won't be a problem."

Reid let out a breath. "Thanks."

"You're welcome." Max scribbled a pass and handed it to him. "Here you go."

Reid grabbed it. "Thanks, Ms. Simmons," he said as he darted toward the door, looking like he couldn't get out of the room fast enough.

Weird. That had been one of the stranger conversations she'd had with a student, and she'd had plenty of strange ones. Max grinned while she straightened the room recalling Mackenzie's story about not getting her assignment done because she'd been at a wedding. Max had been prepared to extend the deadline for Mackenzie and was making a note in Mackenzie's folder when the poor girl had gotten so flustered, she'd woven a wild tale about a wedding for a relative, but she wasn't sure how she was related, that took place on a Monday in a town she couldn't recall the name of, and that had a dance that lasted late into the night so her family had stayed an extra day because they'd been too tired to drive home. Once she'd gotten herself in that far, it was as if Mackenzie couldn't stop herself. She'd added details about the wedding dinner making guests sick, about an uncle and an aunt getting lost so the wedding had to start late, and about some cousins getting in a fight. By the time she'd stopped for a breath, Mackenzie had looked so terrified, Max had been afraid the girl was going to collapse.

And all Max had said was, 'How was the wedding?'

There'd also been tales about home break-ins, lost pets, devastating injuries, and sick grandparents. So many sick grandparents.

Max was good at knowing when a student was lying to her. Reid wasn't flat-out lying, but he was holding something back, and wondering what occupied Max's mind the rest of the day.

15

"I was about ready to come looking for you," Ellie said.

"I told you I'd be too busy to sit around and gossip with you," Max said.

"It's not gossiping if it's about yourself," Ellie said with a smile, "or if it's true. So let's not beat around the bush. Tell us about Beck."

Ellie sat with her hands neatly folded in her lap, leaning forward in her chair as if she couldn't quite contain her excitement. Nicole at least tried for decorum, though Max read the curiosity in Nicole's eyes the same as she did in Ellie's.

"What am I supposed to tell you that I haven't already? You know as much about him as I do. Maybe more, based on the way you grilled him Friday night."

"I still can't get over the fact that he played for the Sooners. It's all my brothers could talk about the rest of the weekend. Beck seemed uncomfortable talking about his playing days, and he kept stressing that he didn't play much before getting injured. I didn't want to pry, but do you know what happened?"

Ellie not want to pry. And here Max thought she wouldn't laugh all afternoon. She bit her lip. "I don't know. Something with his knee, I think."

Ellie nodded with all the wisdom of a top orthopedic surgeon. "It's always the knees. Still, he had some fascinating stories about practices and team bonding activities, and he even shared some inside information. You must love to sit and listen to his stories."

This time, Max laughed out loud. "Oh, yeah, that's my favorite thing to do."

Ellie looked as if she couldn't quite decide if Max was teasing or was serious. Ellie settled for a shrug of her shoulders. Max decided to try to change the subject.

"Were you surprised and not just acting like it?"

"About the engagement party? Oh, my stars, I was thunderstruck. I had no idea. Y'all did such a good job of keeping a secret. I still can hardly believe everyone was here. It was…"

Ellie turned her head and dabbed at her eyes.

"It was wonderful, and now it's hard that they're gone," Nicole finished for Ellie.

Ellie nodded.

"How did you spend the rest of your time with everyone?" Nicole asked.

"Saturday, after shopping, Zeke had everyone over to his place. We ordered food so no one had to worry about cooking. We talked, and laughed, and played games, and had the best time. I love that my family was able to get to know Zeke better. And his parents. They joined us for a while until they went to meet some friends. Zeke was so gracious in opening his home to everyone. Mama and my Grans went wild over his kitchen."

"His home, his kitchen," Max said. "Haven't you started thinking of it as yours?"

"You decided? You're going to live there after you're married?" Nicole asked.

"I think so. No, I know so. I love the house, Zeke loves it, there's plenty of space for us, the two dogs, and hopefully one day for kids. It would be silly to look for something else. Wouldn't it?"

"You don't sound convinced," Max said.

Ellie waved her hand. "I am, I am, it's just, oh, it sounds so silly, but when I came to Caston, and I bought my own house, and I fixed it up, made it my home, I felt like for the first time in my life, I'd done something all on my own. If I move into Zeke's place, is that like taking a step backward?" Ellie shook her head. "That didn't come out right. I love Zeke, and I can't wait to marry him, but my house feels like a part of me. Before I came to Caston, before I had the courage to do any of the things I've done in the last couple of years, I wouldn't have blinked at the notion of moving into my new husband's house. Now, I don't know. What's wrong with me? Why is it even an issue? Why am I giving it a thought?"

"Because you're a different person than you were back then. You're brave, and you're independent, and you know you can do things on your own, that you don't need a man behind you backing you up," Nicole said.

Ellie's spine stiffened. "But I like having Zeke behind me backing me up. I don't think there's anything wrong with that."

"Of course, there's nothing wrong with that. But you're equals. I get the feeling you didn't see yourself that way in your relationship with Vincent," Nicole said. "And that's the person Zeke fell in love with. The brave and independent one. Moving into his house doesn't make you any less those things."

Ellie was quiet for a moment. "You're right about how I saw myself when I was with Vincent. I didn't realize it at the time, and probably not for some time after, but no, I don't think I ever saw us as equals. I know he didn't. And you're right about Zeke's house. Our future home. Four walls and a roof don't make a home. It's what's inside that makes a home, and we'll fill it together, with love and with things that we love. It will be ours, not his or mine, but ours. Right?"

"Exactly right."

Max wasn't sure how the conversation turned from her to Ellie, but she was more than okay with it. Now, if she could only make her getaway.

"I think I'll get going. I need to go through all the cleaning and bandaging nonsense with my hand. It'll take me the rest of the afternoon." Max began backing away. "See you tomorrow."

"Oh no, you don't. Get right back here and tell me about the rest of *your* weekend. Don't think I don't know what you did, asking me about my family, and how we spent our time together. You may have distracted me, but you didn't make me forget. Sit."

Ellie pointed to a chair. Max grumbled but sat.

"Very good," Ellie said. "Now, about Beck. Was Friday evening your first date, or have you been holding out on us?"

"It wasn't a date."

Ellie chuckled. "Oh, Max, you say the darnedest things. Did Beck pick you up?"

"Yes."

"And were you at the same place, at the same time, you in a dress and Beck in a suit?"

"Yes," Max sighed, already tired of Ellie's game, but knowing Ellie was only getting started.

"And did you have a meal together?"

"You know we did."

"And did you dance with Beck?"

Max's belly did a somersault at the mention of the dance, but she thought she did a good job of covering. "If you want to call it that."

"And did Beck drive you home?"

"Of course he did. I couldn't very well walk."

"And did he kiss you goodnight?"

Ellie asked all her questions in rapid-fire succession, hoping, Max knew, to catch her off guard. Ellie was going to be disappointed.

"He did not."

Ellie's shoulders slumped. "Oh. Well, it was still most definitely a date. Right, Nic?"

"Sounds like a date to me. What about the rest of the weekend? Did you see him again?"

Max had debated with herself on what she'd tell Nicole and Ellie about her mother. Since she didn't know herself where things were headed, her logical side told her to keep it to herself. More and more, though, she was finding she actually had an emotional side, and, as frustrating as it was to her, that emotional side was winning out more and more.

"Sunday, yes, we finished up with my car. Saturday I had lunch with my mom."

"You finished up with your car." Ellie tilted her head and smiled. "Is that your way of saying—"

Max knew her words finally caught up with Ellie because Ellie sat bolt upright in her chair and her head spun in Nicole's direction, then back to Max.

"Did you say you had lunch with your mama? Your *mama*?"

"Yeah, that's what I said."

"But...but you never...you said..."

Ellie at a loss for words was almost as entertaining as some of the stories Max's students dreamed up.

"You've never spoken about your mother except to tell us she left when you were young," Nicole said. "I didn't think you had any contact with her."

"I didn't until last week when she showed up at my door."

"She just showed up? What did she say? Where has she been? Why didn't..." Ellie put her fingers over her lips. "I'm sorry, Max, that was rude of me. Tell us what you want to tell us. We're here to listen."

"It's okay. Ask what you want. I don't know that I'll have too many answers." When Nicole and Ellie merely waited, Max continued. "I didn't ask where she's been for over twenty years, because at this point, I don't care. She claims she wanted to contact me for years, but the more time that passed, the more difficult it was. Then, when she saw the news stories, she decided it was time. Maybe it scared her, I don't know."

"I bet it did scare her, though I'm sorry that's what it took for her to contact you," Ellie said. "How is it, being with her?"

"It's weird. I don't know how I'm supposed to forget that she walked out on me when I was hardly more than a baby."

"You're not expected to forget that," Nicole said. "Take it one day at a time. If you decide you want to have a relationship with her, then hopefully you'll put that behind you, but if not, that's your decision."

"What did y'all talk about?"

"She asked about what happened here, of course, and a lot of the general stuff you'd talk about when you meet someone for the first time. We avoided most of the more difficult topics. Then, we were having lunch, and the texts started coming of you in all those wedding dresses. That sort of broke the ice, and we actually laughed some, and talked about things I never would have dreamed I'd talk with my mother about."

"Is she still in town?"

"Yes. I don't know how long she's staying. I don't even know where she's staying. I didn't ask too many questions, probably because I didn't want to know the answers."

Max felt her phone vibrate. She glanced at the screen, then with a scowl, declined the call.

"You're still getting calls from news people?" Nicole asked.

"Wouldn't you think it would be old news by now?" Max said.

"It's a big story, with a happy ending. Not all of those types of stories end the way ours did," Nicole said.

"I know, and I sort of understand, but I don't want to be interviewed, I don't want to be on the radio or TV. Can you even imagine?"

"It's not for me either," Nicole agreed, "but there are a lot of people who would jump at the opportunity to have their moment of fame."

"I'm not one of them. How much longer until they figure that out, do you suppose?"

Nicole shrugged.

"For your sake, I hope it's soon," Ellie said.

And on that note, Max decided it was as good a time as any to make her escape before Ellie remembered she'd been grilling Max about Beck. Besides, she did have a mountain of work waiting.

"I need to run." She stood to do just that, but then sat again. "Before I go, I need some advice."

Ellie beamed with that told-you-so look in her eyes.

"Teacher advice," Max said.

"Oh." Ellie tried, unsuccessfully, to hide her disappointment behind a furrowed brow.

"What's up?" Nicole asked.

"I have a student, Reid. He's a seventh grader, so I don't expect either of you to know him. I got a strange vibe from him today. He's a bright kid, but very shy. He's new to the school this year and hasn't made many friends from what I can tell. Today he stayed after class and asked me some strange questions about my injury, about unsafe conditions, and about what to do if he sees someone doing something unsafe. We spend a lot of time in class talking about safety, so it wouldn't have been that strange if I thought he was referring to something he saw during class, but I got the feeling it was more than that."

"And he didn't say anything more? He didn't give you any idea who or what he might be talking about?" Nicole asked.

Max shook her head. "I tried to get him to talk, but he wouldn't elaborate."

"He probably saw someone in the bathroom, or outside school doing something he knew was against the rules," Ellie said.

"Maybe, but it seemed like more. I can't put my finger on it, but he seemed afraid."

"He trusts you, Max. I'm no expert, but I say keep trying and hope he trusts you enough to tell you if there's something he feels needs to be told," Nicole said.

As Max drove home, her friends' words played on repeat in her mind.

Hope you can work things out with your mom and put the past behind you.

Hope Reid trusts you enough to tell you what's bothering him.

Hope the news people lose interest in your story.

She added to the list.

Hope her hand would be okay.

Hope Skeeter wasn't keeping something important from her.

Then, her biggest hope.

Hope the letter, or the email, or the phone call that she'd expected weeks ago came soon, so she could stop thinking about most of the rest of the list.

She wasn't used to hoping for things, or for that matter, worrying about things. If things got tough, if she felt stuck, she picked up and moved on. Now, it seemed everything was coming at her at once, and hope didn't seem a strong enough word for the feeling that she needed to somehow fix things. Things that she couldn't quite define.

The urge to cut the ties that suddenly felt like hundred-pound chains was almost more than Max could bear. She signaled to take a left, a turn that would lead her to the Interstate and away from Caston. But when the light turned green, she flicked the blinker off and went straight.

At home that evening, Max was restless. The idea that she had too many people relying on her, that she was tying herself irreversibly to Caston, gnawed at her until neither pacing, eating junk food, nor blasting the music could ease her mind. Throwing herself on the couch, she sat and stared out the window.

Spring was coming. The days were longer, the smell of new growth was in the air, and the robins that had taken off the previous fall were back in force, chirping and hopping everywhere she looked.

The world was starting over. Why shouldn't she?

Nicole and Ellie might be the closest things to friends she'd ever had, but that didn't mean she owed them the rest of her life. Circumstances changed, people came and went. They could stay in touch. Texting was easy. Max could even relent and accept one of the requests Ellie kept sending to be 'friends' on some social media site or another.

Or, they'd lose touch, like so often happened when life got busy. Max would bet good money that Ellie and Zeke would start a family within a year of getting married. Nicole, whether she knew it yet or not, wouldn't be far behind. Brady had cornered Max a couple of times already and quizzed her in what he may have thought was a casual and just-making-conversation kind of way, but that Max saw through from a mile away. A guy didn't ask about where a girl had her first date, about whether she'd had her heart broken, about places around town that held bad memories, unless that guy was getting ready to propose and didn't want to screw it up.

Both of her friends would find their lives changing, their priorities changing, and while Max wasn't foolish enough, or self-pitying enough, to think they'd forget about her entirely, things wouldn't be the same.

Deciding it was time for action, or at least to start thinking about taking some action, she grabbed her computer. There had to be other schools that needed math and engineering teachers. Maybe some place warm. Maybe some place closer to a big-time race track.

She sat up straighter and propped her feet on the coffee table. A bit of that familiar feeling of excitement at the idea of something new started to awaken her nerve endings, and she felt a tingle in her fingers as she pecked, one-handed, at the computer keys.

Maybe South Carolina. She'd always liked it there. She found the website for a school district close to Darlington Raceway, then drummed her fingers on the keyboard while she waited for it to open. Impatient, she clicked to open her email while the website took its sweet time.

Her heart lurched in her chest, giving such a thump, it was almost painful. Her hand trembled as she clicked to open the email.

There it was. Her eyes flew over the words in front of her, most not registering, but the important ones sinking in. *Congratulations. Welcome. Rwanda.*

Max dropped her head back and closed her eyes. The program in Rwanda was what she'd been most hoping for. An opportunity to help bring drinking water to people who often didn't have it, to instruct farmers on things like drip irrigation systems, to study the feasibility of dams. Most of all, to do something new.

It was the news she'd been waiting for. The news she'd started to think she'd never get. It was her ticket out of Caston.

Dozens of questions swirled in Max's mind, everything from the logistics of traveling to Africa, to training before she left, to how she'd get through the additional year of teaching she needed to fulfill the requirement without losing her mind.

But she kept coming back to one question, and it was one she never dreamt she'd ask herself.

Why didn't she feel the sort of elation she'd expected at the news?

16

It didn't exactly come as a surprise, still Max was impressed by the speed with which Ellie knew something was off.

"You may as well tell me now and save us both some time and energy," Ellie said with a bored look. "I'll ask, you'll deny, I'll ask again, you'll deny again, and we'll go round and round like a carousel until you finally spill the beans."

Max wasn't ready to spill these particular beans. Until she figured out her own feelings, she didn't need Ellie's, and then Nicole's, factoring into the mix.

So, she bluffed.

"It's my mom. She wants to spend more time together, and I can't decide how I feel about it."

Based on the look on Ellie's face, Max hadn't lost her touch.

"I'm sorry I made light of it. I thought maybe it was something to do with Beck, in which case I was prepared to give you a push in the right direction. As far as your mama, I don't know what to tell you."

"I didn't expect you would. If I can't figure it out, how can you?"

"I wish I could offer some advice, but I'm not sure what to tell you."

"I know. You don't have any experience in the area of family dysfunction."

Ellie looked hurt. "I'm sorry. I might not have any great wisdom to impart, but I'm your friend, and I'm here for you."

Max felt like a jerk. "I'm the one who's sorry. I didn't mean what I said. You are a friend, a wonderful friend, and I know you're there if I need you."

Ellie nodded once. "Which way are you leaning? Do you think you'll see her again?"

Max glanced at the clock. She had less than five minutes before Ellie would need to head to her own room. Max knew she could stall, or change the subject, but even though the topic of her mother wasn't what was foremost on her mind, it was still on her mind, and maybe some input from a friend wasn't such a bad thing.

"Let's see if I can explain it as you would," Max said. "It's as if I'm on a see-saw and as soon as I start going one direction, the see-saw tips and I'm heading the other way before my feet have a chance to touch the ground."

Ellie smiled. "I understand exactly what you mean. Your entire world is turned topsy-turvy. Max, I can't tell you what to do, but I can tell you that whatever you choose, it will be the right choice. You are so strong, and so brave, that no matter what you decide, it will end up being the right thing. You'll see that it is."

Ellie's words popped into Max's mind a dozen times during the day. At first, Max was annoyed by the words. Ellie was wrong, Max decided. It would be entirely possible, maybe even likely, that Max would make the wrong decision and once that happened, she wouldn't be strong enough, or brave enough, to fix it. After pondering the words for a few hours, Max reluctantly concluded that her friend was right. As much as Max wanted to believe there was always one, and only one, right answer, Ellie firmly believed the opposite. In any situation, any decision could be turned into the right one with the right attitude and a little work.

So Max took her friend's wisdom to heart.

After the third time she spotted Reid looking her way with what was clearly fear clouded with uncertainty, she asked him to stay after class. And once her school day finally ended, she texted her mother and made plans for the coming weekend.

Though Reid hadn't bared his soul, he'd come closer to telling Max what was troubling him. Max had put her superpower for bull detection to work and had determined he was telling her the truth, but also that he wasn't telling her everything. She felt fairly certain that it wasn't someone or something in their class, or even their school, that was worrying him. She also didn't think it was an issue at home. Past that, she wasn't sure. He'd been too vague and too evasive for her to zero in on the source of his ever-growing anxiety.

The text to her mother had been answered almost before Max hit send. Her mother was eager to get together again and had suggested

Max's place so they could talk uninterrupted. Victoria had suggested Friday afternoon and had offered to bring lunch. Max didn't need to lift a finger, according to Victoria. Food, drinks, dessert, as well as everything they'd need as far as dishes, silverware, drinkware, napkins, and whatever else could possibly be involved in what Max had hoped would be a simple meal, would be taken care of.

Her mother's enthusiasm, combined with Reid's distress, left Max a jumble of nerves. When her phone rang she was tempted to ignore it, but since without thinking through all the ramifications she'd given Reid her number, there was an outside chance it was him. She glanced at the table where she'd dropped her phone.

Beck.

How so many different feelings could assail her at once was a mystery, but the bigger mystery was why, as she stood staring at her phone and one by one those feelings came and went, the one that stuck around was some kind of warm fuzzy feeling that, if questioned, she'd deny even under torture.

It rang four times before she answered.

"Thought you might be screening your calls and I didn't make the cut."

"I was, and you barely did."

Beck chuckled. "I wasn't able to put my finger on it until now, but there it is. That friendly personality. That's what I've missed without you in the shop every evening."

He missed her? In order to quash the warm fuzzies that were attempting a return, Max worked out a long division problem in her head. *Two-thousand six hundred ninety-eight divided by seven; seven goes into twenty-six three times, twenty-six minus twenty-one is—*

"So, what do you say?"

"Huh? What do I say about what?"

This time, he sighed. "You're going to make this difficult, I see. Fine. Max, would you like to go to dinner with me? Real dinner, not take out in the garage."

A date? "Um…" Max could already hear Ellie's questions. "I don't know. When?"

"Did you hear nothing I said, or are you determined to make this difficult? Tonight. I asked if you want to go to dinner tonight."

Startled, Max pulled the phone away from her ear and looked at the time. Not even six o'clock. Why had she thought it was later? Probably because the day had seemed interminable.

Did she want to go to dinner with him? As distracted as she was worrying about Reid and about her mother, she'd probably be lousy company. Still, maybe having someone to talk to would help. Maybe not help her figure out her problems, but maybe help the evening pass quicker than it would if she sat and stared at her four walls.

"I sense you're hesitating. Seems like an evening out with me should be enough of an incentive, but I'll sweeten the deal. I have a Mustang in the shop right now, a 2015 so a different animal than yours, but it's got transmission issues. I can't quite put my finger on the problem."

He had her attention. "Manual transmission?"

"Yeah."

"There have been complaints since 2010 about problems with the transmission. Slips, jerks, difficult shifting until finally the transmission fails. There's a class action lawsuit alleging Ford knew about the problem."

"I know. It's not that. How about I tell you more over a steak?"

"Steak? Really?"

"Is that so strange?"

"I expected pizza. Maybe a burger."

"We can do that if you want."

"No. A steak sounds good."

And it did. Max realized she was starving. Meals had been hit or miss, and mostly miss, over the past few days. The past few weeks, really.

"Good. I'll be there in twenty minutes. Does that work?"

"It works."

She heard the grin in his voice. "Then see you in twenty, Mad Max."

She didn't fret over her outfit, exactly, but Ellie had wormed her way so far into Max's head that a simple dinner turned into a reason to give some thought to what she'd wear. The jeans and faded sweatshirt she was wearing—the sweatshirt she'd had since she'd been to Daytona ten years earlier—didn't seem appropriate. Then again, neither did anything too fussy. She didn't want it to look like she'd put too much thought into it. In the end, she settled on a nicer pair of jeans, a green cashmere sweater, and a pair of black suede ankle boots. At the last minute, she added a gold necklace and a pair of gold earrings.

She heard Beck's truck in the driveway, so hurried down the stairs from her apartment before he could come up to knock. That would seem too much like a date, and over the last twenty minutes, Max had convinced herself it was more of a business meeting than a date. Beck needed to consult on a business-related matter, she had knowledge and experience to offer feasible solutions, so getting together to discuss that matter was nothing more than good business sense.

Did they have fun when they were together? Usually. Did they have a lot in common? Of course. Were they friends? Sure. Were they more than friends?

That's where Max got stuck. She didn't have a lot of experience with 'more than friends,' so didn't know how to answer that question. She did her best to put it out of her mind but found that was hard when Beck jumped from the driver's seat and hurried around his truck to open the door for her. Did business associates, or even friends, do that? She didn't think so.

"I would have come to the door," Beck said as Max climbed into the cab of the truck.

"I heard you pull into the driveway. No reason for you to come up just so you can go back down."

Beck gave her an odd look as he closed the door and circled around back to his side.

"How was your day?" Beck asked.

"Why?"

"Why? Why not? People ask each other about their days all the time. It's called conversation."

"My day was..." Max debated adjectives. She could fall back on 'fine' and return the question. She could say it was difficult and she'd rather forget about it. Or she could tell him the truth and see if he, as an outsider, had any input. She decided on, "Odd."

"How so?"

"I have a student who wants to tell me something, something he's worried about, or afraid of, but so far he hasn't taken the final step and spilled."

"What do you think it is?"

"I'm not sure."

"Do kids often tell you about things that are worrying them?"

"No. This is a first. Then again, I don't have much experience. I suppose with other teachers, better teachers, students are more likely to talk."

"More experience doesn't always mean better. I have a feeling you're a good teacher."

Max shifted so she faced Beck. "What makes you say that?"

"You have a way of relating to people that's natural, comfortable. Even when you know far more about a subject than someone else, you don't talk down to them. I heard you with the Nissan in need of a brake job. Though you wanted to, you didn't tell the owner that riding the brakes and getting too close to the car ahead then slamming on the brakes, were likely the reasons he needed new brake pads so soon, and not that the previous ones were faulty."

"You heard me?"

Max hadn't known that. She'd arrived to work on her car before Beck closed for the day. He'd been on a phone call when a Nissan pulled into the lot and the owner, assuming Max worked there, had inquired about an estimate on the brakes. Beck was right. She'd had to bite her tongue to keep from telling the guy how to drive. Instead, she'd answered a few of his questions, then told him to hang on until Beck could talk to him.

"Yeah, I heard you, and I saw your jaw clench."

"Well, I saw him pull into the lot and slam on the brakes. If he drives like that all the time, you're going to have a regular customer."

"Anyway," Beck said, "it just goes to show that, when you want, you know how to relate to people. Your students know they'll get a straight answer from you, that you won't belittle them, but you also won't sugar-coat it if they need to hear something they may not like."

"Maybe."

"And, also important when it comes to being a good teacher? You see right through the bull. Your students know that. They're a little afraid of you, but they respect you."

"You know all of this how?"

"I'm an observer. I've watched you in action, and I've got you figured out."

"Hah! You'd like to think so."

"That's a conversation for another time. Back to your student. He has you worried."

"He does. It's something big, at least to him. From what I know of him, he's level-headed, not likely to overreact, so I have to believe it might actually be something big."

"Are you worried about his safety? Is it something you need to report?"

"No, not in the way I think you mean. I don't get the feeling it's something directly related to him, rather something he knows about and he's struggling whether to tell."

"If I remember middle school, being labeled a tattle-tale wasn't what a kid strived for."

"A tattle-tale? Still not a goal of most middle schoolers, but times have changed, so it depends on the situation. We stress, 'See something, say something' with the kids…"

When Max couldn't finish her thought, she turned her head to look out the dark window, hoping Beck would change the subject. Instead, she felt his hand gingerly close over hers, which were tightly clasped in her lap.

"I'm sorry. I should have put two and two together."

"Nothing to be sorry for. I don't expect," Max paused and corrected herself. "I don't *want* everyone to feel like they have to tiptoe around me and watch every word they say. I'm not going to fall apart because of something someone says that could maybe, possibly, be interpreted as having some sort of far-flung tie to what happened. It's nonsense."

"Got it. No tiptoeing."

Despite everything, Max laughed. Before she could come up with a safer topic of conversation, they were pulling into the parking lot of a restaurant she'd never seen.

"Where are we?"

"About ten miles outside of Caston. The town's called Oak Grove, the restaurant is called The Grove."

"Clever." Max looked around at the unfamiliar surroundings. If she'd driven through Oak Grove, chances are good she would have missed The Grove. Like the spa, and the hotel where she'd been for Ellie and Zeke's engagement party, and like so many other places she'd seen since arriving in Wisconsin, the style was what she'd termed 'rustic cabin.' And The Grove might have outdone all its competition. Unless you were looking for it, the building almost disappeared into the forest that surrounded it.

Max sidestepped puddles and potholes left over from the long winter as Beck steered her toward the restaurant. What looked like huge Lincoln Logs were stacked atop one another to create an actual log cabin. She and Beck climbed stone steps to a porch that wrapped around the restaurant and, Max guessed, in the warmer months, held tables. Now, huge copper urns filled with pine boughs and birch logs, and wrapped in white lights, framed the giant double doors and dotted the rest of the porch to brighten the dark night and welcome diners. With the weather warming, they'd need to update their decor sooner rather than later.

When Beck pulled open the door, a blast of warm air filled with the mouth-watering aroma of grilled meat greeted them. While Beck checked in, Max looked around. The inside was as rustic as the outside. And like the outside, the inside was all exposed logs that seemed to glow under the light from the chandeliers that held what looked like real candles and that hung above every table. Max looked closer and determined the candles were electric, but it didn't diminish their effect. Every table, though, had a candle glowing in its center.

The ceiling featured huge beams that came to a peak so high Max had to tilt her head back to see it. The engineer in her studied the ridge beam and began calculating angles.

As they were led to their table, Max noted the white linens. She decided if she'd given it thought before seeing it, she would have said the fancy linens would seem out of place. Now, she decided they softened the look of the room and added a touch of elegance. From around the room, glass clinked, and a fire crackled behind the soft murmur of conversation.

They were seated at a table next to a window that looked out into the expanse of forest. Spotlights at ground level illuminated towering pines. Max was still trying to gauge the scope of the forest when Beck whispered, "Look."

She followed the finger he pointed out the window to a herd of deer at the edge of the trees. Gracefully, and Max imagined silently, they stepped their way over roots and branches, stopping to bend their heads and search for food.

"Do they eat pine trees?" Max asked.

"They will if it's all they can find. At this point, it's been a long winter, food is scarce, and they're hungry. They'll eat branches, dried grass, seeds, anything they can find." He paused and glanced at the closest tables, then lowered his voice. "I happen to know that the owner of The Grove tells his chefs to put out extra fruits and vegetables, and that he also puts out acorns and sometimes cuts high branches and leaves them on the ground where the deer can reach them."

Their server arrived with menus and a wine list. When Beck asked what she liked, Max waved her hand and deferred. Choosing wine wasn't her strong suit. While Beck discussed and debated with the server, Max watched the deer until they wandered out of sight.

Beck opened his menu, then looked at Max over the top. "What sounds good?"

"You promised steak."

"I did, though I'd be negligent if I didn't tell you that the walleye is the best you'll find for miles, the roasted chicken is always delicious, and the venison is fresh."

"I still think I'll..." Max gasped and whipped her head around to look out the window. "Venison? You don't mean..."

When Beck chuckled, she wanted to be annoyed, but mostly she just felt relief.

"Not funny."

"Actually, from where I'm sitting, it was pretty funny."

Before replying, Max let her eyes wander over the menu, wanting to be certain venison wasn't listed. Once she assured herself it wasn't, she closed her menu, set it down on the table, and leaned forward, resting her elbows on the table and folding her hands.

"Hold on to that feeling. When I get you back, you'll need to remember this moment."

"So noted."

Their server brought the wine. Max watched while Beck went through the ritual of nodding his approval at the label, inspecting the cork, then sniffing and tasting the sip the server poured into his glass. When Beck pronounced it acceptable, the server poured a glass for Max, then filled Beck's.

Once the server left, Beck lifted his glass. "To holding onto the feeling."

He said it with a grin, but behind his grin, Max was certain she detected a deeper meaning. A little unsteady, she lifted her glass and clinked it against his.

The wine was smooth, and it eased her suddenly tight throat. She took a second sip.

"It's good," she managed. "Are you some kind of wine expert?"

"Hardly. If I don't recognize any of the wines on the menu, which I normally don't, I go middle-of-the-road and then bluff my way through all the sniffing and tasting." He shrugged. "It usually works."

"I'm familiar with your bluffing skills. Don't forget I witnessed firsthand your attempts to convince your dad you hadn't already eaten a half dozen ice cream bars and you should be able to have just one before bed."

"I'd forgotten about that." Beck's eyes took on a faraway look, and a smile slowly bloomed, eventually reaching those eyes.

"You must have eaten your weight in ice cream that summer."

Beck returned his attention to Max. "You remember that?"

"I remember a lot about that summer," she said without thinking. "I mean, since I've run into you and have had reason to give it some thought. You know," she added lamely.

Thankfully, Beck didn't seem to notice her discomfort. Instead, he was lost in ice cream fantasies. "I'm not sure what anyone expected. I mean, it was right there, a chest full of ice cream bars. It was hot, no one was paying any attention to what I did, it would have been weird if I hadn't eaten about ten a day."

"I didn't eat ten a day."

"You didn't? Well, you were kind of weird back then, Mad Max. You were more interested in watching the mechanics than most anything else."

Most anything else, Max thought. "One might say the kid who tried to learn something about cars when surrounded by them was less weird than the kid who tried to learn how many ice cream sandwiches he could eat."

Beck dipped his head. "Touché."

"Some of it must have rubbed off given your current profession. I never asked when you decided that's what you wanted to do."

"I suppose it was when I realized I couldn't make a living winning ice cream eating contests." When Max rolled her eyes, he added, "Okay, in all seriousness, it probably wasn't long after that summer when my interest was piqued. My dad spent his career researching how to make tires better, faster. I don't mean to say I found it boring, but, well, I found it boring. Tires. How exciting can a piece of rubber really be?"

"Quite exciting, actually. Tires are critical to a race car's performance. Different tracks cause tires to wear differently, so the composition of a tire is extremely important. If—"

Beck feigned a yawn. "Anyway..." he said, talking over her, "I guess cars, in one way or another, are in my family's blood much like they're in yours. My dad grew up in Caston. When I spent the summer with him, we usually spent at least a few weeks in Caston visiting my grandparents. My grandpa had a small auto repair shop. I started hanging around and watching what he did, learning a few things."

Max wondered why it warmed her heart, picturing Beck standing alongside his grandfather, handing him tools, asking him questions. She took another sip of wine in hopes of cooling those warm feelings.

"Then, the summer before I started college, Dad had a stint at a test track. My parents agreed I could tag along, provided I had a job. So, I cleaned garages, hauled trash, mowed lawns, and did some office work, but that summer I paid more attention to what was happening in the garages. They couldn't test tires without working cars and trucks. Since I had some know-how from the time spent with my grandpa, I found it a lot more fascinating than I had at Talladega when I was twelve. I hung around whenever I could. I watched mechanics work magic, tweaking things to get more out of an engine. I was hooked."

"So your place was your grandfather's?"

"No. His business was more of a hobby than anything. After he retired, he started working on cars as a way to pass the time. He did all the work out of his garage."

"So you didn't take over his business, and you're not from Caston, yet you're here. Why?"

"I'd always liked the town. When I decided I wanted my own place, I wasn't tied to anywhere in particular. My parents both left Akron once I graduated from high school, so I didn't feel any pull to go back there. I liked Oklahoma but didn't want to settle there. When my grandma passed away, a year after my grandpa, I came back to Caston with my dad to take care of her affairs. I looked around, realized there wasn't much in the way of competition, and I decided to stay. I had a few friends I'd made when I spent time here in the summer, so it wasn't as though I plopped myself down where I didn't know a soul."

"Huh. Interesting." Max realized that if she were pressed to choose a place to settle, she had no idea where it would be.

"But before that, you went to college." Knowing she'd have to report back to Ellie, Max added, "Did you think you'd play football professionally?"

"I suppose every kid who is even marginally good dreams of the NFL, but it didn't take long for that dream to fade. Once I got hurt, I focused on school and got a business degree. I also got a part-time job at a garage where I learned lessons as valuable as what I learned in school. Maybe more so."

"I'd imagine the business degree has helped with running your own business."

"Yes, so eventually I had to stop being mad at my parents for forcing me to stay in school once the football gig ended. It took a few years, though."

"I'd say you got the best of both worlds. Education is important.

Even if it didn't seem like you were learning anything that was going to help you do what you thought you wanted to do, you can't say you wish you'd never received the education. Just like someone forced to take piano lessons. They may hate every second of it, complain about going to every lesson, throw a fit when it's time to practice, but down the road when they know how to play the piano? They'll never say, 'Gee, I wish I didn't know how to play the piano.' Know what I mean?"

Beck's eyebrow inched up. "Sounds personal. You play the piano?"

"Not well, but yes, though I haven't in years, and it's the sort of thing that requires practice to be any good."

"Still, I'm impressed. And curious. From what you've told me, you moved around. A lot. How did piano lessons factor into that sort of lifestyle?"

"One place where we were for, oh I don't know, maybe a year-and-a-half? There was an old piano in an unused office at the track. I was fooling around on it one day and a woman who worked there sat down next to me, showed me a few things, and before I knew it, my dad had made arrangements with her to give me lessons."

Max allowed herself a smile at the memory. "Mrs. Covington. I've often thought of looking her up and sending her a thank you note. She put up with a lot from me. I didn't want anything to do with lessons, even when she told me I had a knack for it and that she was surprised at how easy it was for me. I don't know if that was true, but I never thought learning the notes and learning what to do with my hands was particularly difficult. The touch needed, the feel for it, that wasn't quite so easy. Still, she taught me a great deal. When we moved on, my dad bought a second-hand keyboard and it was one of the few things we lugged along wherever we went. He always managed to find someone who'd work with me for a few bucks. Honestly, I think it was cheaper than a babysitter." Max shrugged. "Whatever the case, I learned how to play. Sort of. And to my point, though I hated it, I've never said I wish I didn't know how to play."

Beck spent a minute just looking at her, his face a mixture of curiosity and confusion.

"What?" Max finally asked.

"You surprise me, that's what. Not only because of all the things you seem to know about and how to do, but maybe more so because you told me. I've gotten the feeling you don't often tell anyone much about yourself."

Max was shocked by his observation and was glad she was saved from responding by their server. By the time he'd refilled their water glasses, topped off their wine, and taken their orders, she'd regained her composure. Still, unless he went back to the subject, she was happy to let it drop.

A minute later, she wished she'd delved neck-deep into it.

"And what else? What else was bothering you when I picked you up? I understand your concern for your student, but there's more. Do you want to talk about it?"

"I swear, between the therapist I'm forced to meet with, my principal and just about everyone else at school, of course Nicole and Ellie, and now you, all anyone wants me to do is talk about what's bothering me. Whatever happened to talking about the weather, or what's in the news, or the latest celebrity dating scandal?"

Beck reached into his pocket and pulled out his phone. "I suppose I could search 'celebrity scandals' and find more than enough to get us through dinner."

Max crossed her arms and scowled. "You know what I mean."

"Not really, but if you don't want to talk about anything more serious than the weather, that's fine. I was simply offering an impartial ear in the event you need one."

Maybe she did. Without giving herself time to consider the ramifications, she blurted, "My mom showed up in town and is trying to have some kind of relationship with me." She paused for a half second to gauge Beck's reaction. Except for one of his brows twitching ever so slightly, his expression remained remarkably neutral. "She wants to get together again this weekend, and I can't decide how I feel about it."

The gulp of wine she took was larger than she'd intended and led to a coughing fit. Though she didn't, Beck kept his composure, calmly handing her a napkin, but otherwise barely moving, and keeping his eyes locked on hers.

When she finally quit coughing, he said, "Understandable, considering you haven't seen her for most of your life. It's one of the things I remember best about you from back then."

"What do you mean?"

"I remember it quite clearly. We hadn't been there more than a day or two when I realized you didn't have a mom around. Neither did I. I assumed your parents were divorced, like mine, and that it was your dad's summer to have you, like it was mine. When you're a twelve-year-old boy, you don't give much thought to what happens in other families or even with other kids unless it directly affects you, but something about you was different, so I asked a couple of questions. I was told, in no uncertain terms, that I was never to ask you about your mother or even bring up the subject of your mother again. With anyone. Period. I wish I could say it was out of concern for you, but it was more my arrogance that had me asking another couple of questions. All I learned was that your mother left, and should she decide to show up again, she wouldn't find anyone rolling out the welcome mat. They were looking out for you, Max. All of them. Everyone around you."

She'd known it, but hearing it from Beck made it seem like new information. The people surrounding her had taken their job of protecting her so seriously they'd warned a kid about bringing up the subject of her mother? She realized she hadn't known the scope and depth of the circle around her. A little part of her wondered what that circle would do now if they knew Victoria had shown up and inserted herself into Max's life.

"Your silence tells me maybe I should heed that old advice and back off."

Max took a deep breath, letting it out slowly while she considered. "No, I think you're right, and I could use an impartial opinion."

"I promised to listen. Given the subject, I don't know that I'll have an opinion that's worth sharing."

Max shrugged. "It's worth a try."

Max launched into the story of how Victoria had shown up, unannounced, at her door and had since managed to get an invitation inside her apartment, and to somehow finagle a lunch. She told Beck everything; how she'd felt at seeing her mother, how rude she'd been, and then how uncomfortable she'd been, yet how they'd somehow shared laughs over lunch at Scooter's. When she got to the coming weekend, her words slowed.

"So, I guess what I need to decide is if I'm willing to take a chance on her. Thoughts?"

"Can I ask a couple of questions first?"

Max tipped her wine glass toward Beck and nodded.

"Have you had any contact at all with her since she left?"

"No. Well, I guess she sent cards and gifts while I was growing up, but I never knew about it. My dad never told me, or gave me, any of it."

"Huh. That opens up another can of worms, but we'll table it for the time being."

"Fine."

"Do you know where she was and what she was doing for all those years?"

"Not really."

"Do you want to know?"

Max tapped her nail against her wine glass. "Yes and no. I'm curious what was so much better than being a mother, but at the same time, I don't want to know."

Beck nodded. "Makes sense. Does your gut tell you she's being honest with you? That what she's told you is the truth? I think you're a pretty good judge of character."

"It seems that when it comes to my mother, my gut fails me. Or maybe my gut is being overridden by my heart. As embarrassing as it is, it seems on some level the idea of a mother is, I don't know, appealing? Comforting?" Max shook her head. "Whatever."

"It's nothing to be embarrassed about. Even the toughest sometimes need their moms."

Max rolled her eyes. "So? Do I agree to this lunch, or not?"

"I can't tell you what to do. I can tell you that should things take a turn, I'm here for you. Whenever you need me."

He said it with such sincerity that Max swore she felt her heart melting in her chest.

She played with her silverware, she swirled the wine in her glass, she dropped her napkin just so she'd have a reason to bend over and pick it up. When she ran out of stall tactics and looked at Beck, she saw what she'd been afraid she'd see. Never before had she seen that look in a man's eyes when they'd been pointed in her direction. That didn't mean she didn't recognize the look. And that sent a shockwave through her, stronger than the time she'd plugged in a curling iron while standing in a puddle in a middle school locker room.

Hadn't she seen Zeke look at Ellie that way? And hadn't she seen Ellie return that look? Only about a million times. A career as an author may make Brady an expert at observing others and seeing past the facade, but it did not make him an expert at hiding behind his own. Cartoon hearts practically shot from his eyes when he looked at Nicole. Nicole was a little tougher to read—regardless of what she said, Max felt certain her friend would have made an outstanding trial lawyer— but when Nicole thought no one was looking, she turned to mush when she looked at Brady.

Yes, Max had enough experience recognizing *the look,* but having it directed at her was as foreign as Swahili.

So, she did what she did best, and ignored it entirely.

"I'm starving." She turned her head toward the kitchen. "Do you think our food will be out soon? Maybe we should have ordered an appetizer."

Max heard Beck click his tongue at her. "You are a champion at avoidance, aren't you?"

"And what is that supposed to mean? Avoiding what?"

"Oh, Max, what don't you avoid when it comes to uncomfortable topics and situations?"

"I don't avoid, I move on. There's a difference."

"I'd argue it amounts to the same thing. You don't always have to move on, you know."

Didn't she? Regardless of what Beck meant by move on, though she suspected his words held a double meaning, she realized she wasn't so sure anymore. It had always been the answer, her way out of what Beck would call uncomfortable situations, or even tiresome situations, but maybe a zebra could change its stripes. Or a leopard could change its spots. Or whatever the saying was.

Maybe Max could change. Maybe she was ready for a change and that was why she hadn't immediately emailed back about the position in Rwanda.

Maybe she no longer recognized herself.

"You'll make the right decision where your mother is concerned. You'll figure out whatever is going on with your student. Know that you don't always have to do everything on your own, though, so remember what I said. I'm here. If you need me, I'm here."

Max nodded.

"Now, did you see the forecast? It's supposed to be nearly fifty tomorrow. Maybe warmer by the weekend."

Max laughed, and the worry melted away.

The rest of the evening, they talked of nothing more serious than the weather, the NASCAR schedule, and the Mustang in Beck's garage. Max relaxed, but she couldn't quite rid herself of the memory of the look she'd seen in Beck's eyes.

They lingered over desserts, sharing a brownie with homemade vanilla ice cream and hot fudge sauce, and a slice of the best banana cream pie Max had ever tasted. When they were finally ready to leave, she considered asking Beck to roll her across the parking lot.

Their easy conversation continued on the drive home. Beck told stories of his college days, and about starting his business. Max talked of some of the places she'd lived, and some of the people she'd known. Occasionally, they found they had an acquaintance in common.

All too soon, they were in the driveway below Max's apartment. Before she could gather her purse and open her door, Beck was outside opening it for her.

"Thanks for tonight. It was exactly what I needed."

"You're welcome. I'm glad you said yes. I figured the odds were about fifty / fifty."

"You're probably right. Not smart to bet on me, one way or the other."

He stepped closer and reached toward her. His hand brushed back her hair that the wind had ruffled and left in her eyes. "I don't know, I think you're a smart bet." He stepped even closer.

It might have been the wine since she'd let Beck refill her glass when he'd said, as the driver, he'd had enough. It might have been the meal, the hours of relaxed conversation, or even the full moon overhead. It might have even been the memory of the look in Beck's eyes, or all of it combined, but when Beck leaned toward her to kiss her, she didn't protest, or make a stupid joke, or simply run. She kissed him back.

Just like that, she was back in that middle school locker room, every nerve ending on alert, and wondering if a person's hair really could start on fire.

The jolt was just as real. But this time, in a good way.

17

For two weeks, life was good. The weather was typical for spring in Wisconsin, teasing summer one day, threatening winter the next. The temperatures rose then plummeted, but Max took advantage of every warm day and got outside for long runs. No matter how many miles she logged on a treadmill, it was never the same as feeling the pavement under her feet, the breeze in her face, and even the raindrops pelting her when she got caught in a spring shower.

School rolled along, most often smoothly, with only the occasional bump in the road. The kids grew more and more antsy as the weather warmed, the promise of summer vacation dangling like a carrot in front of them, but since Max couldn't blame them, she cut them some slack. Reid didn't make any more strange remarks and seemed more relaxed in class. He even bonded with Jeremy, the second-place finisher in the balloon-powered car race, and Max spotted the two together in the lunchroom and in the halls.

Max saw her mother a few times. They shared the lunch Victoria had been determined to provide. They met for coffee on a Saturday morning. They took a walk around the lake on a particularly warm evening. They chatted, they got to know one another on the surface, but they both refrained from going too deep.

And she and Beck dated. At least that's what Ellie insisted on calling it. Max termed it hanging out, but when Ellie methodically pointed out that going to a movie together, going to lunch or dinner, taking her car and exploring the area on the weekends, even cooking for one another, were the sorts of things people did when they were dating, Max gave up arguing. She also refrained from pointing out that she and Nicole and Ellie did all those same things, and let Ellie have the win. Fine. She

216

and Beck were dating.

Probably because things were so good, Max was blindsided when Arthur Quinn appeared in court and restated his plea of not guilty. The precarious balance they'd achieved in school was shattered as the news coverage brought the day back to the forefront, and students and staff alike were on edge. Absences soared, crisis counselors were called back to duty, students argued one minute, cried the next, and Max realized the damage caused that day may have been treated with a Band-aid, but a Band-aid wasn't going to heal the wound.

Once again, her phone began ringing, and reporters hounded her outside her apartment and on her walk across the school parking lot. Requests for comments, for interviews, for appearances on talk shows came all day, all night.

And in between all of it, the decision still hung over her head. She vacillated between lunging for her computer and typing out a heartfelt acceptance letter, to not only deleting the acceptance letter but breaking out in a sweat at the thought of leaving Caston. A stranger experience she'd never had. Deep down, she knew that her indecision in answering *was* her answer, but still, she didn't reply to the email. They'd given her a deadline. She was down to three days.

It was a Friday, and a beautiful one. Warm sunshine, tulips poking through the soil of the neglected garden behind her garage apartment, a sky so blue it didn't look real. Victoria had texted earlier in the week asking if they could get together after school on Friday. Max had agreed, and since the weather was too nice to sit inside her small apartment, when she got home, she hosed off the patio furniture Fred had uncovered the week before. She hauled cushions from the garage, dropped the umbrella in its stand, and when she dropped herself into a chair, decided she'd have to make it a point to sit outside more often.

Max stretched out her legs and rested them on the chair across from her. The sun's rays warmed her all the way through, and she sighed. Leaning her head back, she closed her eyes and tried to clear her mind, but it proved impossible.

She still hadn't told a soul about the job offer. Not Nicole and Ellie, who she knew would be hurt when they learned she'd kept it from them. Not Beck, who may understand her need to keep moving, keep searching for the next adventure, but who may, with whatever was happening between them, not understand the way he would have a month ago. Not her father, who would only tell her to do what she wanted to do, then change the subject. And not her mother.

Did she want to tell Victoria? Some days she did. They may be mother and daughter, but they didn't know each other well, and Victoria didn't know who Max had been before coming to Caston. Knowing only the Max of today might make Victoria the best impartial voice. Then again, there may be some maternal instincts, no matter how deeply buried, that would lead her to discourage Max.

No closer to a decision, about the job or even about discussing it with Victoria, Max found even the sunshine could no longer relax her. She pulled her phone from her pocket to check the time. She'd no sooner glanced at the time to determine she had about fifteen minutes until her mother was due to arrive when a text from her mother came through.

We're still on, right? I'm on my way!

"What is going on with you?" Max said to her phone. Since she and her mother had made their plans, Max had gotten a daily text reminding her of the date and time. It wasn't like Max had forgotten other plans or had even changed them last minute, so the constant checking didn't make any sense to her. Her mother had also insisted she'd provide snacks and drinks. That, too, didn't make much sense, but Max wasn't about to turn down whatever Victoria provided, knowing it would become dinner and would save Max from cooking. She never loved cooking, especially not on a Friday after a stressful few days.

Unable to sit, Max wandered the yard, pulling weeds from between the tulips, as well as those poking up in the landscaping rocks. She found herself imagining how she'd change the yard if it were hers. Clean up the garden, for starters, but also add some shrubs along the back fence, something with color, put a fresh coat of paint on the shed, replace the cracked paver blocks, maybe even a few bird houses and one of those bird baths, or a fountain.

Shocked, she stopped in her tracks. Since when did she give thought to planning out a back yard? To having a back yard?

She wiped her hands on her cutoff shorts, then shook her head to rid it of domestic dreams. When she sat again, she faced the house, deciding it was safer to stare at the faded siding than at the bewitching yard.

Victoria's car announced itself from a block away. The muffler was shot. Max had offered to take care of it, but Victoria had declined. Max guessed her mother was afraid of the bill. Though they hadn't gotten into many specifics, Max did know Victoria was sleeping on the couch in the basement of a friend of a friend's house. It bothered Max, but the relationship wasn't to the point where it seemed like it was her business to comment.

She heard the car stop, the doors open and close, and what sounded like muffled conversation before Victoria rounded the corner of the house, her arms loaded down with bags. Max briefly wondered who her mother talked to, if she had friends, even a boyfriend, somewhere.

"I'm over here," Max called when Victoria headed for the stairs.

Her mother squinted into the sun. "Outside?" Victoria looked over her shoulder and seemed unsure of the seating arrangement.

"It's nice out." Max frowned at her mother's outfit. "Though you look like you're dressed for some kind of gala Ellie would throw."

Her mother looked down at her blue dress. "Oh, I just threw this on."

She hadn't. It was clearly new, and Victoria was clearly self-conscious about it. Max reached to take a bag from her mother.

"Are you okay sitting out here? It's warm on the patio."

Victoria threw another glance over her shoulder. "Oh, um, sure, I guess that will work." She forced a smile. "It will be nice." Then the smile disappeared. "You're wearing shorts. Cutoffs."

"Yeah. I told you, it's warm. School was past warm and downright hot. I couldn't wait to get out of my slacks and blouse." Max set the bags on the table. "What is all this?"

"A little of this, a little of that. Are you hungry?"

"I am. I usually forget to eat during the day."

Victoria opened bags and set out plates of cheeses and thinly sliced meats, bowls with crackers and fruit, a tray with vegetables of every color. From an insulated bag, she pulled a bottle of wine along with two glasses. Max watched while her mother arranged the plates and bowls precisely on the table. She added serving utensils and brightly colored plates and napkins. It seemed like overkill to Max, but as long as there was food at the end of the production, she didn't much care how much of a fuss her mother made.

Victoria straightened, then fussed with her dress before smiling down at the table.

"Help yourself. Should I open the wine?"

"Sure." Max grabbed a plate and filled it, popping a cracker into her mouth while she selected meats and cheeses, pickles and olives.

Victoria made conversation, asking about Ellie's wedding plans, Nicole's father, and sprinkling in questions about Beck. Max answered, but with each question from Victoria, Max sensed her mother's growing unease. It seemed sitting outside made Victoria nervous. She looked over her shoulder, she shifted her chair an inch one way, two inches back. It nearly drove Max crazy. When Victoria turned the conversation toward school, she seemed even more agitated.

"And how are things at school? With Quinn making his first court appearance, it must have brought emotions to the surface again." Victoria shuddered at Quinn's name. Max couldn't help but think it looked forced.

"Counselors are back, absences are up, emotions are all over the board. It's almost as if we're back at square one."

"And do the kids talk about it, or ask questions, or just internalize it?"

"All the above. It depends on the kid."

Victoria nodded. "Of course. And the teachers?"

"We have the support of administration and if we need a day away, it's granted, no questions asked. Some have needed it, but most are trying to be there for the students. I can't speak for everyone, but I want to show my students that I'm not afraid. Not that it's not okay to be afraid, that's not my intent, but that I'm not afraid to be there."

Victoria leaned closer to Max. When she spoke, her voice was soft, hardly more than a whisper. "Are you afraid?"

Max didn't intend for her voice to be as soft as her mother's, but it was. "Sometimes. I try not to be."

"Oh, baby." Victoria reached for Max's hand and wrapped both of her hands around her daughter's. "I'm so sorry. I'm sorry you're afraid, and I'm sorry you feel you have to hide it. Fight it."

She had hidden it. And fought it. Until she spoke the words, she hadn't even admitted her fear to herself, but it was there, behind the bravado and the fierce determination to keep one person, and one ten-minute segment of her life, from dictating the rest of her life. Max felt her tough outer shell begin to crack and realized her mother wasn't the only one who'd prefer to be inside four solid walls than outside, exposed.

"Tell me, Max, tell me what it feels like. Tell me what goes through your head when you walk into school every day. Tell me what you dream of every night."

Max stared into the yard, not seeing the buds that were just beginning to form on the trees, not noticing the bird that landed on the fence, its head cocked in her direction. A flash from behind the fence, like the sun reflecting off a mirror, went undetected. Through eyes that refused to blink, she instead saw his face, the gun in his hand, his eyes as they scanned the room before landing on her. She saw confusion, indecision, but also determination. And as if watching a slow-motion replay, she saw herself lunge at him.

"I can't let anything about that day go through my head or I wouldn't be able to walk through the doors," Max said.

Her voice sounded far away, as if she were in the next yard, trying to be heard over fifty-mile-per-hour winds. Though she felt the sting in her eyes, they still wouldn't blink.

"When I sleep, I see it all again, every second of it, but it ends differently every night."

"You told me you were talking with a doctor, a therapist. Are you still? You need to let someone help you, baby."

Max felt her head nod. "Yeah, I'm talking to him. He's a good guy, and I think he knows what he's doing, but I don't know that it's helping. Not really, anyway."

"Max?"

Max heard her mother, but she didn't want to answer her. She didn't want to talk, she didn't want to think, she didn't want to do anything but sit and stare and wait for the endless moment to pass.

"Maxine!"

Her mother's voice was louder, more concerned, and more forceful. More motherlike. Max turned. She blinked and let her eyes stay closed until the burning subsided. When she opened them, her mother was only inches away.

Worry etched lines in Victoria's face and creased her forehead. She rubbed at her chest. When she broke eye contact with Max, she looked over her shoulder, looked toward the garage, looked in all directions.

"I'm sorry, Max. I shouldn't have...I didn't know...They promised..."

Before Victoria finished her disjointed thought, before Max could decipher any of it, there was movement in the corner of the yard near the garage. This time, her eyes saw it and tried to focus on it, but at the same moment, there was a noise behind her, coming around the side of the house.

Near the garage was a woman holding a camera up to her face, the lens the size of a 55-gallon drum. Max heard the rapid clicking as the woman got closer. Max drew in a sharp breath and jumped to her feet. Before she could decide what to do, footsteps behind her demanded her attention. Another woman appeared. Max didn't have to know much about fashion to know the dress and shoes the woman wore would cost a month's salary. There was something familiar about the woman. As she got closer, Max noted her flawless complexion thanks to an inch of makeup, her perfectly dyed blonde hair shellacked in place so that not a strand moved.

"What is this? Who are you?" Max demanded.

"Max, maybe we should sit," Victoria said.

"Sit? Why would I sit? What's going on?"

When Victoria wrung her hands and muttered something that sounded like a prayer, things began to fall into place.

"What did you do?" Max hissed under her breath.

"I'm sorry. Really, Max, I didn't know what you'd been going through. I thought we could talk, you could tell your story, I thought it would be okay."

Both the camera-toting woman and the Barbie doll stood looking between Max and her mother. The one with the camera kept clicking. The Barbie doll smiled and smacked her lips together before sidling up to Max and looking toward the camera. With a speed that defied logic, one camera disappeared, and another took its place, this time on the woman's shoulder. She pointed it toward Max.

"Ms. Simmons." The blonde stuck out her hand. "Madison Wilkes. Pleased to meet you."

In what she knew was a childish move, Max thrust her hands behind her back and stepped away from Madison. If she weren't so angry, she might be curious about how the host of the top-rated morning news show in the country decided a teacher in Caston, Wisconsin, merited a trip from New York, but anger won out and Max ignored Madison. Instead, she whirled on her mother.

"You did this? You brought them here? Why?"

"Max, please, don't be angry."

"Don't be angry? You've got to be kidding! I've told you, over and over, how I've been dodging people like this!" Max waved her hand between the two women. "I told you I had no interest in talking to anyone, no interest in being interviewed, certainly no interest in being on TV."

In some part of Max's brain, it registered that her mother's face lost all its color, that there were tears in her eyes, that she trembled from head to toe, but Max didn't care. All she cared about was getting the reporters out of her yard and out of her life, so she spun to face them.

"Get out of here. You have no business being here. I have nothing to say, and I certainly don't want my picture on TV." To prove her point, Max turned her back to the camera.

Madison turned toward Victoria with barely concealed fury. "Ms. Tate, you assured me your daughter was in agreement. You told us she'd welcome the interview, that she'd agree to our terms." Max saw Madison's fist clench at her side. "We paid you in advance."

Max didn't bother concealing her fury. "You what? Is that true? You took money from them? You used me? That's what this has…"

The words wouldn't come. Anger bubbled and was dangerously close to exploding, but behind the anger was a crushing sadness, a devastating sense of betrayal. And it felt all too familiar.

Defeated, Max said, "Get out. All of you. Get out of here."

"Ms. Simmons, I understand that sometimes it's daunting, the thought of being on television, of worrying about how you'll look, of how you'll be portrayed, but I can assure you, we have only your best interests in mind. The country is curious. People want to hear your story. People want to know the woman who stopped a school shooter. May I have just a few minutes of your time? Will you tell me what it was like to look into the eyes of a potential shooter?"

"Get out," Max repeated.

Madison took a deep breath and plastered a smile on her face. "Okay, Ms. Simmons, if you don't want to answer any further questions, perhaps you'll take just a moment and sign the release so we can—"

"NO!" Victoria shouted, then pleaded, "No. Don't. Please."

Max looked between the two. "Don't what?"

Something like compassion showed in Madison's eyes. "I'm afraid it's too late for don't. Ms. Simmons, your conversation with your mother was recorded. Ms. Tate assured us you'd be on board, but I see now that was wishful thinking on her part."

Madison cast her eyes to Victoria whose hand, seemingly of its own volition, reached to fuss with her dress.

"You've got to be kidding. What? She's wearing a wire?" Max stared Madison in the eye but flung a hand toward her mother. "What am I, a mob boss you're trying to get to confess to murder?"

Madison chose to ignore most of what Max said. "We'd like to use the recording to put together a short segment to air next week. Even if you decline the interview with me, we can piece together parts of your conversation with your mother during which you answered many of the questions I would have asked. I'll ask you again to reconsider sitting down with me for a few minutes."

Max was shaking her head long before Madison got to her request.

"Well, then, we will still pay you for your time if you sign a release to use what we've already recorded. Once you sign, you will receive payment. I think you'll be pleased with the amount."

"I don't want money, I don't want to talk to you, and I certainly am not authorizing you to use what you recorded without my knowledge. Or the pictures." Max turned her wrath on the photographer. "I assume you took pictures while I sat here, while I…"

Max looked heavenward and took a long, shaky breath. While I lost it, while I gave in to the fear, while I opened up to someone I thought I could trust. She'd been a fool.

"You cannot use the pictures either. I'm not giving you permission to use any of it. Now, get out of here."

"Many of the pictures were obtained from outside your property. We had permission to be in the neighbor's yard." Madison indicated the yard behind them with a tilt of her head. "We're within our rights to use those photos, though I'd much prefer to work with you on this. Please, let us tell your story the way you want it told."

She seemed nice enough, Max thought, sincere even, but that did nothing to sway Max's decision.

"No. I don't want any part of any of it."

"I'm sorry you feel that way. It could have been an interesting and compelling story, what with the trial coming up."

Max surveyed the group of people in front of her. Madison was clearly disappointed, angry even, but hid it behind a subtle smile and poise that must have taken years of practice to pull off. The other woman had stopped filming and now looked bored. Victoria looked scared to death.

"It's…never mind. If you aren't going to leave, I am." Without another word, Max, with every muscle in her body tensed, walked with a measured gait across the yard and up the stairs to her apartment. Once there, she carefully closed and bolted the door. She filled a glass with water, drank it as if she hadn't had a drop in weeks, set the glass on the counter, then walked to the couch, buried her head in a pillow, and screamed until there was nothing left.

It was an hour before she got off the couch. When she did, she peeled back the curtain on the tiny window that looked out onto the back yard. Not a soul, not any trace of the picnic on the patio in sight. While it was a relief, it didn't help her figure out what she was supposed to do next. An hour of screaming into a pillow had taken her from anger to frustration to helplessness to despair but not to a course of action.

She wouldn't contact Victoria, that was a certainty. Anger didn't begin to describe what she was feeling toward the woman. Or toward herself, for that matter. She knew better, she'd always known better, but she'd let down her guard, and Victoria had moved in for the kill. Max could only wonder if it was because she'd been so desperate for a mother, for someone to care about her, that she'd let down the walls she'd spent twenty years building just because someone pretended to care. If she hadn't seen through the lies because she hadn't wanted to.

She'd always considered herself a good judge of character. She'd always felt that if she could look someone in the eye, she'd be able to see through the bull to the truth. In this case, she'd failed on every account. It was humiliating.

Contacting Ellie or Nicole also seemed out of the question. She'd have to tell them eventually, especially if a story about her, complete with pictures of her in her own back yard, was going to be broadcast within a few days. Right now, though, the hurt was too raw. If she went to her friends, they'd try to soothe, to make everything better, and Max wasn't ready to let go of the mad.

As she looked out into the approaching twilight, words sounded in her crowded mind. *I'm here. If you need me—whenever you need me—I'm here.*

She'd agreed that night at the restaurant, but hadn't expected she'd want to take Beck up on his offer. Did she? Beck wouldn't push. He'd be curious, he would ask a question or two, but when she told him she didn't want to talk, he'd let it go. He'd talk cars with her, maybe let her work on one, he'd make stupid jokes and call her Mad Max, and it might be exactly what she needed.

Deciding giving it too much thought would only lead to changing her mind, Max grabbed her jacket, her purse, and her keys and was out the door and heading for Stevie Ray in under thirty seconds.

The roar of the engine began soothing before she even backed out of the garage. The twelve-minute drive got her to Beck's place just before closing time. Since the garage doors were open, she didn't bother with the office door. The music was on, country as usual. Coupled with the clangs and bangs of tools, and the smells of oil and rubber, it was like a lullaby to Max's bruised and battered soul.

She didn't see Beck. Sven's back was to her, and she'd just opened her mouth to ask him if Beck was around when he spoke to Jake.

"Did Beck tell you if he's coming back tonight?"

"No, but I doubt it." Jake was hidden by a Dodge Ram, but his chuckle came through loud and clear. "He was almost jumping out of his skin when he left. Nervous, but excited."

"Think it will work out for him?"

"You know Beck. He has a way of making things work out."

"But Madison is a pretty big deal. Things might not just fall into Beck's hands this time."

"Ah, Sven, are you forgetting this is Beck we're talking about? Things always fall into Beck's hands."

Max spun on her heel and headed for the exit. She tried to move noiselessly, but it was hard to see where she was going when all she could see was red. She caught her hip on the corner of a tool cart, and the clamor got Sven's attention.

"Hey, Max. Looking for Beck?"

"Not anymore."

"Huh?"

Sven said more, but Max didn't listen. She jogged to her car, unable to get away fast enough.

Not Beck, her brain screamed, and try as she might, Max couldn't quiet it. The beautiful, perfect Madison Wilkes got to Beck too. The pain cut deep, but Max didn't give in to it. She focused on her anger instead. Anger hurt less.

She drove, heedless of where she was headed. The destination didn't matter, only the number of miles between her and Caston. She wondered about Ellie and Nicole. Were they, too, granting interviews, telling stories of their poor, troubled friend who was afraid to stay alone in her apartment, who was so traumatized by the events at school, she'd nearly cut off her hand?

Max didn't want to think that was the case, but she never would have believed it possible of Beck, and she refused to be surprised by anything anyone close to her did, ever again.

It grew dark, and still, she continued to drive. When she pulled into the gravel driveway and stared into the single bulb burning over the garage door, she couldn't say if she'd known it had been her destination, but she knew it felt right.

The door was answered almost before she finished knocking. Skeeter took a moment to look at her, then his shoulders drooped.

"Ah, crap. Victoria," he muttered, and spit on the sidewalk.

"You knew?"

"The details? No. Just knew no good could come of her bein' around."

"Can I stay?"

Skeeter stepped aside and motioned her in. "You know you can. Any time."

"Wanna talk?"

"Not yet."

Skeeter nodded.

"Still sitting on that '71 Mustang?"

"Been waitin' for you."

"Well, here I am."

"Then let's get busy, kiddo."

They worked until Max was too tired to stand. She dragged herself through a quick shower, then collapsed on the bed in what was technically the guest room, but the room both she and Skeeter knew was her room. A few of her things hung in the closet, filled a drawer, and sat on a shelf. It was home. More so than Caston, more so than anywhere she'd ever lived with her dad, more so than anything she'd ever known.

At Skeeter's, she was able to block out everything that hurt, and everything she didn't understand. She closed her eyes, but before sleep could take her, she jumped up again. Grabbing her phone, she opened her email and tapped out a reply; a reply she knew, deep down, she should have sent two weeks ago.

18

When Max drove back to Caston, she did so under the cover of darkness. The weekend with Skeeter had helped soothe her battered soul, but even while they were working on the Mustang, or while they played poker with a couple of Skeeter's friends, or while they watched old Westerns and ate Skeeter's chili, she could never quite stop thinking about all that had happened.

After she'd sent her reply accepting the position in Rwanda, she'd turned off her phone and tucked it in a drawer. She hadn't touched it until she was ready to leave on Sunday night. Still, she didn't turn it on, just dropped it in her purse, then threw her purse in the back seat.

There was no one around when she pulled into her spot in the garage. Good thing, because with a weekend to stew, she knew she wouldn't have been as cordial as she'd been on Friday. Once inside, her apartment seemed smaller than ever, and Max longed for a new beginning. If only the job in Rwanda started in three months rather than fifteen. How she was going to stay in Caston and face a school full of students and colleagues who would see her on television, probably looking helpless and terrified and weak, she didn't know. How she was going to avoid Beck, she also didn't know. And as far as Nicole and Ellie and what to think, and what to do, well, it gave her a stomachache every time she thought about it.

Over the weekend, she'd alternated between being certain there was no way they would have spoken with Madison Wilkes to deciding they probably had. If her mother had, and if Beck had, Madison had probably persuaded Ellie and Nicole to do the same. When she convinced herself they were involved, she felt guilty. When she told herself they would never betray her that way, she felt like a fool. Either way, the feelings weren't good, so at ten o'clock on Sunday night, she turned on her phone.

She ignored the missed calls, the voicemails, and the texts, and dialed Ellie. Ellie sounded as if she'd been asleep.

"Max? Is everything okay?"

"Hold on," Max commanded. Then she added Nicole to the call.

"Hi, Max. What's up?"

"Hold on." She tapped at her phone. "Are you both there?"

"What?" Nicole asked.

"Hmm?" mumbled Ellie.

"Okay, I've got both of you on the line. Here's the deal. Listen, don't interrupt, and then if I was ever any sort of friend to you, tell me the truth."

Max spit out the story as quickly as she could, putting in the details she felt were necessary, leaving out the rest. She told them about her mother's betrayal, about Beck's, and then asked them bluntly, "Did either of you talk to her?"

Max heard Ellie gasp. She heard Nicole moan, soft and low. When neither spoke, she repeated, "Did you?"

"I wish you didn't feel like you had to ask that question. That you know us well enough that there wouldn't be a reason for you to ask it. But I'm trying to put myself in your shoes and imagine how I'd feel, so I can sort of understand. No, Max, I did not speak to Madison Wilkes. I did not speak to anyone else, either. I haven't, and I won't."

Nicole sounded more sad than angry, and Max began feeling the beginnings of regret about the late-night phone call.

Ellie sniffled before she spoke, and when she did, her voice broke. "Oh, Max, I would never...You have to know..." Ellie took a deep breath. "I love you. Tell me how I can help."

Max massaged her temples, trying to beat back the headache that seemed determined to win the battle.

"I'm sorry," Max said, then didn't know what else to say. "I have to go."

She heard both Ellie and Max start to protest before she disconnected, but Max didn't have anything left to give.

Most days, Max was one of the first to arrive at school. On Monday morning, she waited until the last possible minute and ducked into the building with the gang of perpetually tardy students. She hustled to her room to unlock the door for the group gathered outside it, waiting on their delinquent teacher.

Engaging autopilot, she cruised through her day without veering from her planned outline. At lunchtime, because she knew Ellie and Nicole would come looking for her, she hid out in the copy room, taking her time printing worksheets for the coming week. Then, ten minutes before the final bell, she turned her class over to Amanda and ducked out with the excuse of having to get to an appointment with her therapist. She had an appointment, that part wasn't a lie, but she would have made it with time to spare had she left after the last bell. But not ready to face Nicole and Ellie, she stretched the truth and asked Amanda to cover for the final few minutes of the day. Since everyone still went out of their way to accommodate poor, traumatized Max, Amanda didn't hesitate. Did Max feel guilty? Yes. Would she do the same thing again? Probably.

She debated what to tell Dr. Mallick. He'd see through her if she tried to hide the entire incident, but Max figured she could get away without relaying all the dirty details. Talking about what her mother had done didn't bother Max; talking about what Beck had done, did.

Max sat in the same chair in Dr. Mallick's office. Dr. Mallick wore the same shirt, tie, and sweater combination, just with a lighter sweater than he had a few weeks ago. The glasses were the same, the coffee mug was the same, the leather-bound journal, the burgundy Montblanc pen, the desk blotter, all of it the same. Everything was the same, except for Max.

"You seem on edge," Dr. Mallick said once they'd gotten through their customary greetings.

"Do I?"

"Yes."

And then, like always, he waited. Though she knew the game, it was one she couldn't win. She could never hold out more than a minute without answering.

"Wasn't the best weekend."

Still, he waited.

"My mother proved everyone right. She sold me out for a few bucks and her moment in the spotlight."

His eyebrows rose a fraction of an inch.

"She knew I wanted nothing to do with reporters, with interviews, all that crap, yet she made a deal with Madison Wilkes. Know who she is?"

"I do."

"Yeah, I guess everyone does, don't they? My mother ambushed me. Told me she wanted to get together after school on Friday, then got me to talk about what happened at school and recorded the whole thing. There was a woman with a camera hiding across the yard. Madison Wilkes was hiding around the corner, I guess, and then, surprise! They come crawling out of their holes and try to get me to agree to appear on TV telling the whole, sad story of Max Simmons, the teacher who supposedly did some great thing, and that everyone wants to hear from."

"You don't think you did a great thing?"

"That's your takeaway?"

"I think it's a place to start."

"No, I don't think I did a great thing. I think I reacted, and like I've said a hundred times, I don't know if faced with the same situation, I'd do the same thing again. No one seems to want to hear that. They want to think I'm some sort of hero, and I know that's not true."

"There are different definitions of hero. To many, you are a hero. Regardless of what you were thinking at the time, regardless of what you think now after the fact, what you did at that moment can easily be seen as heroic. Do you really not believe that?"

Max began to answer, the same answer she'd given every time someone had thrown around the word hero, but she made herself pause. And think. Did she see herself as a hero? Could she see herself as a hero? If she watched Madison Wilkes interview a teacher who'd stopped a potential school shooter, would Max consider that person a hero? Probably. Then why couldn't she see herself that way?

"I wonder if there aren't two types of people in this world. There are those who with the littlest bit of praise, put on that halo, that badge, and decide everyone should acknowledge them for their greatness. Then there are those who know, deep down, they are no different from anyone else and know that praise is misplaced."

Dr. Mallick offered one of his rare smiles. "Generalities are just that. Generalities. Most people don't fit neatly into one side or the other. I think you know that. You're correct in that some people are eager to accept adulation, and some shun it. Some seek the spotlight, some hide from it. But there's a lot of middle ground, and that's where most people fall. Those people may not want it, but they graciously accept it when it's due, then they're ready to let it go when the fervor dies down. They're okay with both sides.

"Take, for example, the passerby who performs CPR on a stranger;

the underdog who comes out of nowhere and wins an Olympic gold medal; the teacher who stops a school shooter. They are thrust into the spotlight, but that spotlight doesn't last the way it might for, say, a singer who continually tops the charts, one hit after another. Or the scientist who continues to advance the field of cancer research. For those, the praise becomes a way of life and they need to learn to deal with it. How they deal with it, if they deal with it, is another matter entirely, but my point is there are always things in life that take us outside our comfort zone. If there aren't, if we always stay inside our bubble of comfort and familiarity, we stop growing and that's not a healthy way to go through life."

"Is that a long, winding way of telling me I need to be okay with the spotlight? That I have to grant interviews? I have to let people see me and hear me?"

"It's a way of encouraging you to look at why you're so hesitant to be in the spotlight. You don't have to love it, you don't have to seek it out, but why do you fight it? Think about that. For now, let's shift gears and you tell me how you're feeling right now about your relationship with your mother."

Max huffed. "Relationship? Is it a relationship if two people will never again see one another?"

"Is that your plan?"

"That's my plan."

"Have you spoken with her since Friday afternoon?"

"No."

"Has she tried to contact you?"

"Yes. Calls and texts which I have not answered."

"Do you think if you spoke with her, asked her why, you might feel better?"

"I know why. Because it was all about her. It's always been all about her. I should have seen it coming a mile away, and I didn't. I won't make that mistake again."

"What did you do after it happened? Did you talk to your friends? To anyone?"

He knew there was more. How he always knew was a puzzle she hadn't solved, but he knew. Still, Max was determined to deflect.

"I went to see an old friend. Didn't think about the mess all weekend, and it helped."

"That's good. Getting away, stepping back, can clear your head, and help you to see what you can't see when you're in the middle of something. This friend must be someone you trust or you wouldn't have turned to him or her."

"He's the only one I can trust."

Dr. Mallick was good at a lot of things, namely staying calm and showing little reaction when Max said something stupid that she immediately regretted, but as Max watched him, she decided he'd make a lousy poker player. He had a tell, a subtle one, but a tell nonetheless. Across the table, while she wished she could take back her words, she saw his eyebrows rise just a hair above the upper rim of his glasses.

"The only one?"

"Yes."

"Nicole? Ellie? Beck? You can't trust them?"

"I don't know them well enough to trust them."

Max silently congratulated herself on her answer. It was the truth. She didn't know any of them that well. It may not be the whole truth, but it might buy her a reprieve from getting into the whole truth.

"Then this old friend, you've known him long enough to trust him."

"My whole life. He's never let me down, never lied to me, never pretended to be something that he's not."

So much for self-congratulation. Max almost reached for the stapler she saw on the corner of Dr. Mallick's desk. Maybe if she stapled her lips shut, she could avoid saying anything else that would back her into a corner.

"Then the others have let you down? Lied to you? Pretended to be something they're not?"

Max sighed. "Do we have to do this?"

"Do what?"

"Talk about them?"

"Why don't you want to? You've talked about them often. Did something change?"

Max hadn't yet lost her cool in one of her sessions with Dr. Mallick, but she felt herself coming close. She took three deep breaths before she trusted herself to speak.

"One of them did, and I more or less accused the other two."

"I see. We have fifteen minutes. Start wherever you want."

Following her session with Dr. Mallick, Max drove for two hours. She didn't want to go home because she figured Ellie and Nicole, or at least one of them, would show up at her door when she refused to answer her phone. There was also the outside chance her mother would show up, and Max was afraid of how she'd react if Victoria knocked on the door. As far as Beck, he'd called and texted, but still had no idea she knew what she knew. Max figured she had another day, or at least until later that night, before he started to wonder why she didn't answer or respond.

As long as she was in her car, she didn't have to worry about any of them. Over the past three days, she'd given serious consideration to packing up and leaving. As long as she gave Amanda notice, Max felt certain she could get out of her contract. Amanda wouldn't be happy about losing a teacher without warning only a few weeks before the end of the year, but Max held the trump card and playing it was tempting.

The farther from Caston she drove, the more she knew she needed to go back and finish what she'd started. She wasn't a quitter. She'd never been a quitter. She left places when she grew tired of them, but she did so without hurting anyone. She gave notice when she needed to give notice; she said goodbye when she needed to say goodbye. Not once had she packed up and left in the middle of the night because a place or a situation had become too difficult. She wouldn't do it now. She'd finish out the year, she'd leave on good terms, and she'd find a new school where she'd go back to being the Max she was before Caston, the Max who did what she needed to do, who was friendly when others were friendly toward her, but who didn't make friends, and didn't build relationships. Deep down, that was who she was, and she shouldn't have let a couple of girlfriends, a guy who let her use his garage, or a woman who claimed she knew how to be a mother make her think she was anything else.

Max grabbed a burger and fries at a drive-thru. She filled her tank, and like the day before, waited until long after dark to go home. Pleased when she didn't spot an unknown vehicle anywhere in sight, she parked Stevie Ray and plodded up the steps to her apartment. A light glowed from inside, and she shook her head, hoping a light was the only thing she'd forgotten to turn off before she'd left that morning. She'd used the coffee pot, but that turned itself off. She'd gone over her hair with her flatiron. She couldn't remember if that turned itself off, but since the place hadn't burned to the ground, figured either she'd remembered to do it or like the coffee pot, the appliance had taken care of itself.

She was distracted enough with wondering what else she could have forgotten that she'd closed and locked the door behind her before she realized Nicole and Ellie were sitting on her couch and sipping wine. Before Max could find her voice and start demanding an explanation, Nicole beat her to it.

"Don't bother telling us to get out, because we're not going anywhere. And save your indignation about the fact that we're here without an invitation because we don't care. And don't bother looking for signs of forced entry, because it turns out your landlord can be quite accommodating when Ellie turns on her charm. Now, sit down, drink at least half that glass of wine, and then you can say whatever it is you have to say."

Nicole pointed to a third glass of wine sitting on the coffee table. Max drew in a deep breath, held it until she thought her lungs would explode, then let it out while she threw herself into a chair and picked up the wine. She drained it in one long gulp, then slammed the glass back on the table.

"Satisfied?"

Nicole shook her head. Ellie's eyes grew to the size of dinner plates and she looked ready to cry. It appeared they were determined to be as patient as Dr. Mallick because neither one said a word.

"Fine," Max barked. "I'm sorry. I'm sorry about last night. I'm sorry I doubted the two of you."

"And?" Nicole prompted.

"And what?"

They waited her out. Nicole easily, with her arms folded across her chest and a bored look on her face. Ellie, not so easily. She tapped her finger on her wine glass, and looked back and forth between Nicole and Max so many times, Max figured Ellie must be dizzy.

"And I'm sorry I avoided you today? Is that what you want to hear?"

"You're getting closer," Nicole said.

"I wasn't ready to talk to you about it."

Max watched as Ellie looked again at Nicole, who finally gave Ellie a quick nod. Max guessed Nicole had made Ellie promise to keep her mouth closed until Nicole was done playing bad cop.

"You can talk to us about anything. You know we'll be on your side," Ellie said.

"I'm not so good at needing anyone," Max said.

Nicole frowned. "Aren't we past all that? All the 'Miss Independent, I can do everything on my own' nonsense?"

"It's not nonsense, because I can."

"But you don't have to. That's the point," Nicole said.

"Tell us what happened," Ellie said.

"I already did."

"Tell us what you didn't tell us last night," Ellie said.

Max crossed her arms, crossed her legs, and swung her foot as she stared down both her friends. Nicole stared right back. Ellie tried, but Max sensed Ellie wavering and knew any moment she would fly across the coffee table and start hugging.

"I'm going to need a refill," Max said.

Nicole nodded, filled Max's glass, then sat back to listen. So, Max told them.

To their credit, they held off commenting until she finished. Once she did, she could tell neither of them was sure where to begin, so Max got the ball rolling by asking the first question, one she directed at Nicole.

"Can I stop them from using the pictures?"

Nicole lifted her hands only to let them fall. "If you can prove the pictures were taken from your yard without your permission, yes. If, as she told you, most of them were taken from the neighbor's yard with permission from the neighbor to be there, no. If this were some tabloid or some internet troll, I'd say it would be worth it to question whether they had the neighbor's permission, but being this is a national news team, I have to believe they did everything by the book."

"I figured as much. The recording, though, they can't use that, right?"

"Not unless you signed a release, and you said you didn't."

"Of course, I didn't."

"Then no, they can't use that. Whatever Madison Wilkes or the photographer overheard, though, they can use. If she puts together a story, she can say something to the effect of, 'Ms. Simmons was visibly upset when asked about the alleged intruder's statements in court.' If your mother cooperates with them, they can also use her statements about the conversation the two of you had. 'We spoke with Ms. Simmons' mother and she reports that her daughter is having nightmares and every day has to work up the courage to walk into the building where it all happened.'"

"I didn't say those things!"

"I'm just giving you an idea of what might happen. They can't use the recording of your voice, and they can't use what you said on that recording, but they can use whatever your mother tells them." Nicole paused and looked conflicted. "You also have to consider the possibility that they'll ask your mother to be on their show since they couldn't get you. If they put her on TV, there's no telling what she might say. Have you talked with your mother?"

"No."

"Then I think you need to be prepared for that possibility."

"This just gets better and better, doesn't it?" Max took another gulp of her wine.

Ellie jumped in. "Let's forget your mother for a minute and focus on Beck. Have you talked to him?"

"Of course not. Why would I?"

"Because you care about him. Don't you think you owe it to him, and to yourself, to get the whole story? Don't you think there's a possibility you misunderstood?"

"Misunderstood what? I heard them talking, El, and I heard her name. There wasn't much to misunderstand."

"Maybe he was meeting her to tell her to take a hike," Ellie suggested. "He likes you, Max. Why would he betray you like that?"

"Why did my mother betray me like that? Money talks, Oklahoma."

"Ellie's right. You should talk to him, get the whole story, then decide what to do."

"Yeah, I probably won't do that. I've had about enough of people lying to me."

"You need to be sure of what happened before you give up on something that's been so good for you. For both of you. You two were happy together," Ellie said.

"It was just a way to pass the time."

"It was more than that, but let's say it wasn't. You still need to pass the time," Nicole said.

Max hadn't planned on breaking the news until the end of the school year, but as long as they were on a roll, she figured she may as well keep rolling.

"Not for much longer."

"What does that mean?" Ellie asked, and Max heard the fear in her friend's voice.

"I'm leaving. I called Amanda earlier this evening and told her, but I asked her not to announce anything yet. When the school year ends, I'm leaving Caston."

"That seems rash," Nicole said over Ellie's mournful, "Noooo."

"It's not that rash. It's part of why I'm here, of why I'm teaching. It was the plan all along. I just pushed things up a year."

It was so much harder than she'd expected. Watching the realization slowly sink in, seeing the sadness and disbelief on her friends' faces, was so different from anything she'd experienced in any of her other goodbyes. Before, she hadn't cared, and neither had anyone else. Now she cared. Deeply.

"Maybe you could enlighten us as to this plan that you've elected not to mention for the past eight months?"

For as sad as Ellie was, Nicole was equally angry. Her shoulders stiffened and her eyes narrowed as she waited for Max's explanation.

Max decided if she was going to get through the next half hour, or however long they decided they needed to hang around, she'd have to match that anger. Figuring that would be better accomplished on her feet, she stood. It may be petty, but towering over her friends gave her a sense of control. It was her life, and she was the only one who got to decide what she did with it. And no one had to like that decision but Max.

"It's a job. A job I've had my eye on since my second year of college. It's in Africa, helping communities build and maintain reliable water supplies. It's helping farmers learn how to irrigate using less water. It's educating people on some of the technological and ecological advances that will help them survive in what many in this country would see as an uninhabitable climate. It's making a difference. And it's someplace new. I don't stay in one place. I don't know how to stay in one place." Max lifted her arms and waved. "This is proof that if I try, everything around me blows up. As my friends, I hope that you'll understand and support me. It's a new challenge. One I need."

Max continued standing, though the speech had taken more out of her than she'd anticipated. As much as she wanted to fall back into her chair, she knew she needed to at least appear confident or she'd never have their backing.

"Then you're leaving for Africa at the end of the school year?" Ellie's voice pitched higher with every word.

"Not exactly. The position requires two years of teaching experience, middle school level or higher. There's no requirement that the two years be in the same place."

A glimmer of hope sparked in Ellie's eyes. "Then stay. Stay one more year, Max, please? I know you're upset, and you're hurt, and that this has been a year more difficult than any of us could have imagined, especially for you, but starting over will be difficult, too. Here, at least things are familiar. Think back to those first days, those first weeks. We all wanted to quit, leave Caston, and never look back, but we didn't. We stayed and look at us now. We've all grown and learned and found our place. Don't go. Don't throw away all that hard work."

"I can't stay. Too much has happened. There are too many signs telling me it's time to move on. I don't know what my mother's plans are, but if she stays here, I'll run into her. I don't want that. Same with Beck. He's not going anywhere, and this isn't a big town. It's only a matter of time until we cross paths."

"The Max I know wouldn't be afraid of those things. So you cross paths with Beck. It may not be pleasant, but it won't be the end of the world. People run into exes all the time. It's life. As for your mother," Nicole shrugged. "I don't know her, I don't know if her sole intention was to get close to you just to use you, but whether it was or it wasn't, you shouldn't be the one to run. You have ties here, she doesn't. Chances are good, she'll leave. Who knows? She may already be gone. Basing your decision on anything to do with her seems beneath you, and nothing more than an excuse."

Max and Nicole stared, neither wanting to be the first to blink. The more Nicole talked, the more Max's anger built, and she was close to unleashing it on Nicole. As if sensing what was coming, Ellie got to her feet and stood between the two of them.

"Y'all are coming close to saying things you're going to regret. Don't let that happen. We don't want you to leave, Max. Nicole is only trying to point out that maybe some of the things you see as reasons for leaving don't have to be seen that way. Making such a big decision when you're so emotional is never a good thing. You have to give it some time, let the waters settle, and then see how you feel. You certainly can't leave without talking to Beck. I know it seems bad, but you have to consider that there may be an explanation for what you overheard. Basing your decision on indirect information doesn't make sense. If you step back, you'll realize that. Give it time."

"This job is something I want. It's not a whim. I didn't go to school to be a teacher. I think you both figured that out a long time ago. I'm an engineer. I'm teaching because I have to, not because it's been my dream since I was a little girl. I didn't grow up playing school."

"It wasn't my dream either." Nicole may be angry, but behind her anger, Max heard the lingering heartache. "I'm not saying that you should give up your dream, I just don't think it's right to use it as an excuse to bail on us and on everything you've built here. Holding on to your dream doesn't mean you need to run away."

"I'm not running away. I'm leaving. There's a difference."

"Tell me this," Nicole said. "How long have you had the job offer?"

"Two weeks."

"Two weeks. I see. And when did you decide to accept it?"

Max knew she was backed into a corner, but she was determined to fight her way out. "Friday."

"The same day your visit with your mother turned into a lot more than happy hour in the back yard. The same day you overheard what you thought was evidence that Beck was involved. Correct?"

"Yes. And I'm not on trial here, Nic."

Nicole ignored Max. "Why didn't you accept the job immediately upon receiving the offer if it is, as you said, the job you've wanted for years?"

Max tapped her toe on the floor. "Because I wasn't sure I still wanted it. I suppose that's what you want to hear?"

"I want to hear the truth. Is that the truth?"

"It is," Max said on an exhale.

"Then your decision to accept it seems to have been heavily influenced by the events of last Friday. Do you think making a life-changing decision should be based on fear and anger?"

"I don't think I based my decision on fear and anger, I think I based it on what I took to be a sign. What happened was the push I'd been waiting for, telling me that yes, I should follow the dream I've had for years. I let myself get comfortable here. That's new to me, but I won't lie and say I didn't start to like it. Deep down, though, it's not who I am. I know that. Any doubts I had about the job disappeared last Friday. Everything that was confusing is clear."

"Then you're happy? You're confident it's the right decision at the right time for the right reasons?"

"Come on, Nic, enough already! What do you want me to say? I'm not like you and Ellie. For either of you, this would be a life-altering decision. You're not wired the way I am. You don't pick up and leave, then do it again a few months later. I'll go to Africa, I'll do my job, then I'll do something else. It's the right decision for me. I'm sure."

Nicole closed her eyes and breathed deeply as if trying to decide whether she had the will to continue grilling Max. Finally she said, "Prove to us you're not running away. Give it a couple of days, see if a story airs on TV and if so, what sort of fallout there might be, see what happens with Beck and with your mother, and then make your decision. We'll support you whatever you decide, that's what friends do, but another thing we're going to do because we're your friends is help you be sure you're not making a big mistake. Letting you go is the easy route. We'd miss you, we'd be sad, but we'd tell each other we'd keep in touch, and that would be that. Well, we're not going to take the easy route. We're going to be sure you've thought it through because that's what friends do."

Nicole's voice faltered at the end, and she fell back against the couch, clearly out of gas. She broke eye contact, choosing to stare at the wall rather than at Max.

Ellie looked between the two, obviously torn as to where she was needed the most. In the end, she stayed halfway between the two of them.

"Y'all are both right, you know. And don't look at me like that's not possible, because it is. Max, you're right that you are the only one who can decide, or who can know, what's best for you. That's obvious. Nicole, you are right that such a big decision should never be made in the heat of the moment. Believe me, I learned that the hard way when I went and pounded on Vincent's door. When I made the decision to leave home, it was after enough time had passed that I knew it was the best decision for me."

"I already know this is the best decision for me," Max said.

Still looking at the wall, Nicole snorted. Ellie frowned a little but wasn't to be deterred.

"To continue," she said, sounding very much the prim school teacher Max imagined she'd been when she'd played pretend with her brothers and sisters. "Nicole, you are right that Max needs to clear the air with Beck. Not to throw you under the bus, but you know first-hand how something you see or hear can be misinterpreted."

Max saw Nicole flinch and felt a pang of pity for her friend and the misunderstanding that had left Nicole certain Brady was having an affair with his sister-in-law. If she were being honest, Max supposed there were similarities, although Nicole had misinterpreted something she thought she'd seen. Max knew what she'd heard.

"And Max, you may be right about your mother, and for that, I'm so sorry. Normally I wouldn't suggest anyone turn their back on family, especially her mama, but in this situation, I'm in over my head and have to defer to your judgment."

"Thank you," Max said, pleased with the small win.

"So then we can all agree that we've been right about some things, we've been wrong about some things, and what we need to do now is put that in the past and figure out the future."

"Meaning?" Max asked. She noted the fact that Nicole merely shrugged with one shoulder.

"Meaning y'all are friends, and arguing is just plain stupid. Max, can you agree to give it a little more time? You may have already talked to Amanda, but that doesn't mean she's already found your replacement. You have time. Take some."

It was like a knife to the heart when Max saw the desperate clinging to hope in Ellie's expression, and it nearly did Max in. Then Nicole tore her stare from the wall and faced Max. It was more resignation than hope in Nicole's eyes, but a sad resignation.

Max knew right then and there she had to lie and deal with the consequences of that decision later.

"I will take some time," she said.

Ellie let out a breath that would have filled the lungs of a deep-sea diver. Her bones seemed to turn to liquid as she fell back on the couch. A tentative smile touched her lips but didn't quite reach her eyes. She swiveled on the couch to face Nicole.

"And you'll give Max space to make her own decision, then support her, whatever that decision is?"

"That was never in question. Of course, I'll support her. Will you?"

Ellie flinched. "Of course."

Nicole laughed, but it was a sad sort of laugh. "I don't know how this turned into you telling both Max and me what to do. We came here to talk some sense into her, remember?"

"Well, yes, but things took a turn, didn't they?" Ellie waved her hands as if wiping the slate clean. "Right now, all that's important is that we remember we're all friends and that friends support one another. Max, you're going to give your decision some time. Nicole, you're going to give her that time."

"And you?" Nicole asked. "What are you going to do?"

Ellie smiled the first real smile Max had seen since walking through her door.

"I'm going to do what I always do and make sure everyone is happy in the end."

19

Max had to remind herself she wasn't a quitter a dozen times before she walked through the doors of Caston Middle School the next morning.

She'd needed the reminder when her finger had hovered over the keyboard, ready to submit a request for a sub for the next four days. She'd needed another reminder when she'd almost purchased an airline ticket to go to South Carolina that coming weekend to check out the area around Darlington Race Track, and the school district that had posted openings for the next year. And it wasn't so much a simple reminder, more like knocking herself over the head with a baseball bat she'd needed when the calls and texts kept coming from Beck. She'd promised Nicole and Ellie she would clear the air with him, but it was so tempting to block his number and try to forget he existed. Not that she answered the calls or the texts, or the door when he'd shown up at nine o'clock the night before, but at least she hadn't wired her doorbell to shock anyone who pressed it like she'd been tempted to do.

Regardless of what she'd told her friends, in her mind, she'd already left Caston. She may have smiled when Ellie and Nicole had left her apartment, assuring them she wouldn't finalize anything without giving the decision some time, but it wasn't true. While she'd watched them walk down the steps, then disappear as they'd headed down the block to where they'd left Nicole's car, she'd imagined herself walking down the steps for the last time in only a few weeks. When she hadn't been able to sleep and sat with a pot of coffee and her lesson plans for the week, she hadn't been seeing the examples she'd prepared to explain theoretical versus experimental probability to her sixth graders. Instead, she'd pictured engineering lessons tailored toward high school students in South Carolina. Car engines, the mechanics of braking, aerodynamics. The possibilities seemed endless.

While Max knew the school day was the same six hours and fifty minutes as every other day, it seemed twice that long. Maybe she'd ask Dr. Mallick to explain the phenomenon during their next session. She figured it had to do with her emotional state, but maybe if she feigned genuine curiosity, distress even, Dr. Mallick would start talking and she'd be spared some of the soul-searching he normally demanded and that she was definitely tiring of.

As the clock ticked in slow motion toward three-thirty, Max dealt with the normal end-of-the-day chaos without leaving her chair; most of it, without looking up from her computer.

"James, don't forget our deal. If you get any closer to the door, you'll be waiting thirty seconds after the bell to leave this room."

She heard him groan and mutter something that on a different day she may have responded to, but that today she chose to ignore.

"Mackenzie and Kenzie, what's my rule about phones?"

Their high-pitched giggles carried over the din before they answered, in their practiced monotone unison, "You see our phones in class, we won't see them at home."

"Exactly. Put them away. You can wait two more minutes."

"Can we leave early today, Ms. Simmons?"

"Why would I let you leave early, Jace?"

Ever the negotiator, Jace laid out his reasons. "No one interrupted during your lesson. Five different people answered questions, which means we met our goal. No one had to go to their locker to get their homework. And…"

Max looked up when his voice changed to that of a game show host unveiling the grand prize.

"We're your favorite class!" Jace finished with a flourish.

Despite her lousy mood, Max had to chuckle.

"Fifteen seconds," she said.

"Sixty," Jace countered.

"A minute? You'll be out the door and on the bus before the bell rings if I let you out a minute early, then I'll have to answer to Ms. Chapman. No deal."

"Fine. Forty-five seconds."

Jace was a good kid. He may push the limits, but he always knew when to stop, and that, Max appreciated. She looked around the room. They were all good kids. Out of nowhere, a sob rose in her chest and choked her. She clamped a hand over her mouth, mortified.

"Ms. Simmons? Are you okay?"

"Uh, yep. Just thought I was going to sneeze. Crisis averted."

Jace looked at her strangely, as if unsure whether to believe her. Because she knew how to make sure he, as well as the rest of the class, would forget her odd behavior, she said, "Deal. Forty-five seconds, but if I see anyone running, tomorrow you stay forty-five seconds after the bell."

At once, at least three students yelled, "Henry, don't run!" Then the countdown was on.

The language arts teachers were meeting after school, and Nicole had a meeting with her dad's doctor, so Max was spared any further inquisition by her friends, at least for the afternoon. Not wanting to go home, but not knowing what else to do on a chilly and rainy afternoon, Max found herself in her apartment, staring at her phone. So far, she hadn't listened to any of the voicemails from her mother or from Beck. She hadn't read any of the texts, except for the few words she'd been unable to avoid when they popped up on her screen. She found she didn't care what her mother had to say, but the more time that passed, the more she missed Beck, and the more curious she was about what sort of lies he planned on telling her.

Max paced, she ate a half bag of cheese puffs, she even opened her email and debated clicking on links for the bridesmaid's dresses Ellie had sent over the weekend, a task that scared her as much as listening to Beck's voicemails. When she decided ignoring the emails from Ellie was only postponing the inevitable, she reached out a wary hand and clicked.

Through one squinted eye, Max peeked at the first option. The link said sage green, and since Max had no idea what that meant, she was leery. After a minute of studying the model in a flowing gown and with perfectly curled hair through one eye, Max slowly opened the other one.

It wasn't that bad, she decided. At least it wasn't pink. Max had been all but certain Ellie would go with pink. It just seemed like an Ellie color. Max enlarged the photo and studied the dress, then went back to read what Ellie had written.

I love the sage green color, not sold on the scoop neckline, but love the fabric. It comes in other styles, and I'm open to y'all choosing your own style, so don't discount this one because you don't like the neckline.

Max shook her head. Most of it meant nothing to her, other than Ellie loved the color. Why, then, were there other links? Afraid of what she'd find, she clicked on the next.

Pink. Max groaned. She wasted no time closing the photo and searching out what Ellie had to say about that dress.

I always thought I wanted pink, but after looking, I'm just not sure. I included this dress because this is the shade of pink I'd go with if I decide on pink, but I want feedback. What do y'all think?

"No way," Max said, pushing the computer away from her. She'd read, and Nicole had confirmed, that as a bridesmaid, Max was in no way encouraged or even allowed to express an opinion. It was some sort of trap, and one she wasn't going to fall into.

Max drummed her nails on the table while she thought. She could pretend she'd never seen the email, then when Ellie asked about it, play dumb, hope Nicole was there and had something sensible to say, then throw her vote behind Nicole's. But that left open the possibility that Nicole would say something positive about the pink, encouraging Ellie to lean toward the pink.

While Max debated the safest course of action, she realized there were more links embedded in Ellie's email.

"What'd you do, Oklahoma, pick one in every color?"

Terrified, Max started clicking. Shoes, earrings, fancy twisted hairstyles, nail polish colors. Was there no end to the amount of crap she'd have to submit to? When the next click brought up something that looked sort of like a one-piece swimming suit but that sucked in the model's waist and looked like it would result in the wearer certainly passing out from lack of oxygen, Max decided she'd seen enough and slammed shut the cover of the laptop.

She got up to pace again. When three steps brought her to the window, she stared forlornly at the driving rain thinking how much better she'd feel if she could go for a run. Or a drive. Instead, she was cooped up in her tiny space with nothing to do but think about things she didn't want to think about.

Since she couldn't spot even the tiniest break in the heavy, grey clouds, she knew there wasn't a run in the cards anytime soon, so she went to the couch and dropped with a huff. Her phone sat on the coffee table, and Max studied it. She picked it up and twirled it like a top. She played with the kickstand-like lever on the back that at least rewarded her with a satisfying snap every time she lifted it and pressed it back into place. When she couldn't think of anything else to do, she opened up her texts.

The first few from Beck started the way they always did. Something funny, just a word or two to make her smile. One on Friday night asking if she wanted to grab a pizza on Monday evening. A couple on Saturday, checking in and asking again about the pizza. On Sunday, the jokes stopped, and the tone grew more serious. Was she okay? Sick? Did something happen with her mom? That one earned a snort from Max.

Sunday night was the first time he'd asked if he'd done something to upset her.

Max ran the timetable through her head. A couple days of casual texts. He'd grown worried, or suspicious, or whatever it was by Sunday night. She scrolled through the remaining texts. He'd texted twice on Monday, he'd come to her door on Monday night, and he'd texted twice so far today. Determined, she'd give him that, and based on the tone of his texts, worried but maybe more curious.

Knowing it was an exercise in futility before she started, Max read all the texts again to see if she could infer any other feelings or emotions on Beck's part. Anger, because she hadn't responded? Desperation, needing to get in touch with her? Relief, thinking he had a way out of the relationship?

More likely, none of those things, and even more likely, she'd interpreted everything the wrong way because how could you tell from a text?

So instead, she focused on their relationship. They hadn't gotten to the point of discussing whatever it was that was going on between them. If it hadn't been for Ellie's constant talk about Beck being Max's boyfriend, and insisting on calling everything the two of them did dates, Max wondered if she'd look at it as more than friendship. Well, more than friendship, she acknowledged, since she didn't think friends kissed each other the way she and Beck kissed each other. Then she wondered if real couples actually had those conversations like on TV or in the movies where they agreed they were exclusive, or whatever the term was, or where they decided they were officially a couple. Max had no idea. She hadn't asked a lot of questions of Ellie or Nicole about the inner workings of their relationships, and she didn't have any history with long-term relationships of her own to draw from. Mostly she wondered if Beck viewed what was happening between the two of them the same way she did. Maybe they should have had a conversation. Maybe he'd been dating other women all along.

Max hated how much that hurt, but then reminded herself she didn't care. She was leaving, and Beck could do whatever he wanted.

Disgusted with herself for overthinking everything, she threw down her phone and turned on the TV. She took out her frustration on the remote, stabbing at it and flipping through channels faster than they could register. She backtracked when a race scene through the desert caught her attention. It took a minute before she realized she was watching *Mad Max*.

If Max thought things had gotten as bad as they could, Wednesday morning taught her what 'the tip of the iceberg' truly meant.

Her first mistake was turning on the TV while she dried her hair and applied her makeup. She didn't normally watch any morning news programs, but the night before, she'd tuned in to the local news to catch the weather forecast for the rest of the week. In the morning, she realized she hadn't turned off the TV, so she woke it from its sleep mode. When the commercials ended, she found the screen filled with two familiar faces.

One belonged to Madison Wilkes, who sat behind a sleek desk, a properly sober expression on her perfectly made-up face. The other, projected on a screen behind Madison, was the one Max saw every time she looked in the mirror.

Pinpricks of dread started in her cheeks and traveled down to her toes. Her brain screamed at her to turn off the program, but her body refused to obey. The words out of Madison's mouth were like the incessant hum of the drone the neighbor kid liked to fly. It wasn't until the camera panned out and Max saw the man across the desk from Madison that the sounds turned into words. Scholarly looking, dressed in a dull grey suit and boring tie, his oddly high-pitched voice got her attention.

"It's common for people who've been through a traumatic experience to shut themselves in, to shun contact not only with strangers but also with those to whom they are closest. It's a means of self-preservation."

Madison's reaction was appropriately solemn as she nodded. "That fits with what I learned. I had the opportunity to sit down with Victoria Tate, Maxine Simmons' mother, and she detailed examples of times her daughter shunned public places, or on those occasions when Ms. Tate occasionally persuaded her daughter to go to a restaurant or a coffee shop, how Ms. Simmons was nervous, looking over her shoulder and frequently checking the time. Ms. Tate spoke of the nightmares her daughter suffers, of how on many days, it's a struggle for her daughter to do her job. She also said her daughter has anxiety over being a bridesmaid in a friend's upcoming wedding."

Madison turned her head to look away from the man Max assumed was the station's resident expert on crazy people to face the camera. The seasoned television host donned her, 'Isn't that the saddest thing you've ever heard?' expression. "A bridesmaid," Madison repeated. "Something that should be a joyous occasion has become something Ms. Tate said her daughter desperately wishes she'd never agreed to do."

Again turning to her guest, Madison asked, "Is that typical behavior for someone who has been through what Ms. Simmons has been through, Dr. Westrum?"

"Absolutely. Avoiding public places for fear of being exposed, nightmares, no longer finding joy in daily activities or even in special events are all typical experiences for trauma victims."

"We're all familiar with the term Post Traumatic Stress Disorder, or PTSD. Would you say this is an appropriate term in this case?"

"Most definitely. Post Traumatic Stress Disorder was originally used to describe the effects plaguing soldiers returning from war, replacing the terms Shell Shock, or Soldier's Heart. Today, PTSD is a much more inclusive term applying to any situation in which a person is suffering following a traumatic event. War veterans, of course, but also rape victims, child abuse victims, survivors of natural disasters, the list goes on and on. Anyone who was in the school that day, even family or community members who were not inside, could suffer the effects of PTSD. As the person who stopped a potential shooter, some degree of PTSD is almost a given for Ms. Simmons."

"When I was in Caston, Wisconsin, to speak with Ms. Tate, I also spoke briefly with Ms. Simmons; however, she declined to be interviewed or to appear on the show. She was visibly upset by the few questions I asked her. Is it your opinion that if she is called to testify at the trial of the alleged gunman, she will be able to endure the trial? That she will be able to answer the questions asked her about what happened inside Caston Middle School?"

"There is a risk involved in putting anyone on the witness stand. Anyone, any time," Dr. Westrum said. "In the case of someone whom the alleged harmed, it becomes an even trickier situation. Reliving and retelling what happened is likely to bring things back to the forefront, things Ms. Simmons thought she'd dealt with and put behind her. Witnesses suffering from PTSD can, in layman's terms, fall apart on the witness stand. This can either elicit sympathy from a jury or can bring into question the validity of the testimony. Depending from which side you're looking, the prosecution or the defense, this can be a very good thing or a very bad thing."

It was her phone vibrating and bouncing on the tiny vanity that pulled Max from her shock-induced stupor. Her eyes stayed on the TV screen, but her hand clumsily slapped at the counter until it connected with her phone. Knowing it would be one of a handful of people, Max answered without looking.

"Yeah?"

"Turn it off," Nicole said.

"Why? I'm famous."

"Max, turn it off. It's only going to make you angry."

"Hah! You honestly think I'm not already there?"

"Come on, just turn it off. What's to be gained by watching?"

"Don't you think I should know about myself what the rest of the country does? Seems only fair."

Max's phone notified her of an incoming call. She knew who it was before looking.

"Hang on, Nic, seems as though El has her TV on too." Max tapped to switch to the new call. "I can't decide if it's a good thing they used my school picture or if one they snapped while hiding in the neighbor's yard would have been better. What do you think?"

"I think you should turn it off," Ellie said.

"Yeah, Nic's on the other line, and that's what she said, but it's like a tornado bearing down on you, you know? Horrifying, but you can't seem to look away."

"You sound funny, Max. Are you okay?"

"Okay? Are you kidding? I'm so far from okay, I don't know that there's a word for it."

"Turn it off. I'll be there in five minutes." Ellie was pleading now.

"No, I think I'll watch." Max paused for a minute and turned her attention to the TV. "Oh, this is interesting. Did you know that as a woman, I'm more likely than a man to develop PTSD, but less likely to turn to alcohol and drugs as a result? I guess that's good. Or some of it, anyway."

"Max, I'm on my way. Talk to Nicole until I get there."

Max closed her eyes and shook her head, wondering, not for the first time, how this level of madness had become her life. Was she destined for tabloid covers? Maybe a future in reality TV shows? She could be dubbed *The Teacher Who Maybe Stopped a School Shooter,* and make appearances alongside the woman who'd birthed octuplets, or the guy who'd had such a horrible singing audition he'd become a household name for fifteen minutes.

"Are you listening, Max?"

"To you or to the TV?"

"To me," Ellie said, and Max could tell from Ellie's voice, she was jogging as she talked.

"You don't need to come over here and save me, El."

"I'm not coming to save you, I'm coming to visit you. I'll bring coffee, and I'll give you a ride to school."

"I'll take the coffee, but I'll drive myself."

"Turn off the TV, talk to Nicole, and don't leave before I get there."

"Fine, fine, Miss Bossypants. Turning it off."

Max stabbed at the remote and watched the TV go dark. She stared at the black screen, torn between wanting to pretend none of it had really happened, and turning it back on to hear every word. Keeping her promise, she returned to Nicole.

"Still there?"

"Yes. Did you turn it off?"

"Yeah, Ellie made me."

"I'm glad you listen to someone. Are you okay?"

"Why wouldn't I be okay?"

Nicole's sigh had Max moving the phone away from her ear. "Don't be difficult, just answer my question."

Max reminded herself Nicole was one of only a handful of people who really cared about her and unless she wanted that number to become even smaller, it was time to lose the attitude. And the nearly hysterical-sounding voice.

"I'll be okay. Ellie's on her way over here, for some reason."

There was relief in Nicole's voice. "Good."

"What do you two think I'm going to do? Jump out the window? You know I live above a garage and it's only about ten feet to the ground, right?"

"She's being a friend."

"I know."

"Luna is doing that crazy racing around in circles thing again. I should get her outside. Promise you won't turn it back on if I hang up?"

"Promise. I haven't seen Luna in a while. Is she getting big?"

"She is. Come over after school. We'll take her for a walk."

"Maybe."

"Definitely. I'll see you in an hour."

"Can't wait. Do you think middle schoolers watch the news in the morning?"

"They look at their phones in the morning. And in the afternoon. And at night."

"It only takes one of them watching for all of them who are looking at their phones to find out about it."

"Don't worry about it before you have to."

"Yeah, okay."

Max disconnected, then stared again at the black TV screen. The story was probably over. It was the oddest feeling to think that people all over the country heard details about her, and heard a doctor make guesses and draw conclusions about her. Max didn't think it was too much of a stretch to figure at least some of those people were probably now searching the internet for information on her. Curious what they might find, Max's eyes wandered to her computer.

"Don't do it," she warned herself.

As much as she wanted to look, she listened to her own advice and focused on her hair and makeup. Might as well be ready for the next camera pushed in her face.

It was a broken pipe in one of the bathrooms that took the attention off Max that day at school. Two girls happened to be in the room when the pipe beneath the sink cracked and sprayed water with the force of a geyser. The girls became the day's celebrities. The bathroom was roped off leading to a built-in excuse for extending bathroom breaks by several minutes since the kids had to walk to the other side of the building. Rampant rumors about school letting out early because all the water was about to be turned off to repair the faulty sink accounted for most of the chatter and gossip through the end of the day.

Max wasn't anywhere on their radar.

Still, the day was a long one, and though her students didn't bring up the morning news show, several of her colleagues stopped by to offer their support and share their disgust with the unsubstantiated story. By the end of the day, Max wanted nothing more than to go home, but a series of two-word texts from her landlord warned her she'd have a welcoming committee.

Here again.

Sprinklers on.

Bullhorn ready.

Fred had a way with words, and of dealing with pushy reporters. Max decided she'd give it some time and see if Fred would be successful in clearing out the crowd.

Nicole popped in a few minutes after the last bell.

"I'm not letting you off the hook regarding that walk with Luna and me, but I need to ask you to wait about a half hour. I forgot I have a student staying after today to retake a test."

The sort-of promise had slipped Max's mind. Surprisingly, a walk sounded like a good idea, and Luna would serve as a pleasant, if rambunctious, distraction.

"No problem," Max said. "I have some work that's easier done here than at home. Come back when you're ready."

Nicole's jaw dropped a fraction. "You're not going to try to talk your way out of it?"

"Nope. I don't much want to go home since Fred just texted to tell me reporters are hovering again, and I don't have anywhere else to go, so a walk with you and Luna it is."

"Wow. I mean, great. That's great." Nicole looked Max up and down. "Do you have other clothes? You can't walk Luna wearing dress pants and heels."

"I have a gym bag in the car."

"Okay." Nicole took a couple of steps backward toward the door. "And you promise you won't bolt before I get back?"

"Cross my heart." Max did just that.

Nicole nodded but looked unsure.

"Where's Ellie? After the way she clung to me this morning, I can't believe she's not here now."

"I saw her on my way down. Amanda had her cornered discussing the end-of-the-year assembly."

"Ellie's helping with that one, too?"

"She seems to enjoy it." Nicole shuddered and looked horrified at the thought. Max understood the sentiment.

"How are they going to top the last assembly with Brady?"

Nicole smiled, and her whole body relaxed. "No way they'll ever top that one, right?" When Nicole left, she did so with a bounce in her step.

Max busied herself with preparing sets of materials for her engineering students' final project. She counted out straws, measured string, and sorted tissue paper the kids would use to build kites they'd take outside and test during the last week of school. She'd chosen it because it seemed like a fun project and because she knew her students would love the opportunity to go outside, something they were already begging to do most days. Like all the projects they'd worked on over the year, they'd learn from it, even if it seemed like nothing but fun. And that was the best kind of lesson, Max thought, for the kids, and for her.

With a start, she realized how much she was going to miss it. All of it.

The look on the face of a student who'd figured out how to make her balloon car roll smoothly, as well as the look of frustration from one who hadn't, but who wanted to.

The lightbulb moment when variables finally made sense, as well as the rants about how stupid it was that math had letters in it.

The smiles when a test score came back better than expected, and the whispers about how unfair Ms. Simmons' tests, and all tests, were from those who didn't do as well as hoped.

The students who put forth their best effort, who did their homework, who participated in class, who cared. But also those who dreamt up one excuse after another, who tried countless tactics to get out of a test or an assignment, who challenged her every day to hold their attention. The ones who reminded her so much of herself.

Moving to South Carolina, teaching high school instead of middle school, meant things would be different. There was a world of difference between a sixth grader and a twelfth grader. If she'd learned anything over the past eight months, it was that her students, though they might think differently, were children. Many still innocent of the world around them, many with no real sense of life outside their family and their school, especially those without older siblings, Max had learned a lot of the acting out was nothing more than a cry for help when they felt overwhelmed. At the end of the day, most middle schoolers needed their teachers in almost the same way they needed a parent.

She'd been a twelfth grader a lot more recently than she'd been a sixth grader, and Max remembered what took place in the halls of a high school. No longer children, most had figured out their place, their style, their image, at least as far as life during their high school years was concerned. And as far as teachers went, most high schoolers considered them either the bane of their existence or someone who wasn't all that bad and could possibly help them further their goals. But seldom like a parent or someone they really needed.

Max set down the string and scissors and wondered why it all made her so sad. Why the idea of leaving was starting to feel like the wrong decision.

Looking around at her classroom, Max knew she could have done more. Should have done more. A few posters, a half-hearted attempt at a bulletin board featuring some of her students' creations from the day she'd let them loose with rulers and compasses, and, of course, the signs and notes welcoming her back that she'd been persuaded to leave in place, but still a lot of white wall space.

She could have, and should have, done more with her lessons. She could have made them more interesting; she should have worked harder to engage her students.

Before she could sink further into despair and begin questioning every decision she'd ever made, there was a tap on her partially closed door. Expecting Nicole, Max called, "You don't have to knock, Nicole."

But when Max looked up, it wasn't Nicole. In fact, it was probably the two people she'd least expect to see walk through her classroom door. While she gaped, their glances darted around the room, back into the hall, and at each other. It was a toss-up which one looked more uncomfortable and out of place.

"Dad? Skeeter? What are you guys doing here?"

While they continued to shift from foot to foot, both looking ready to make a run for it at the first sign of trouble, the gravity of the situation struck Max.

"How did you get in here? You're not supposed to be able to walk through the doors and wander the halls."

Ellie squeezed between Skeeter and Max's father, causing them both to flinch. Max had the feeling they didn't know which to worry about more, the fact that they were inside a school, or the fact that Ellie was beside them.

"They didn't just stroll in and wander the building, they checked in at the office. I was there talking with Amanda, and I offered to show them to your room," Ellie said. "I gave them a little tour on the way here."

"I bet you did," Max said. Then she turned her attention back to her dad and Skeeter. "You haven't told me why you're here. Both of you."

Skeeter rubbed his hand over the grey stubble on his head. "You weren't at your place," he said as if it explained everything.

"Dad?" Max tried.

Bo Simmons wore a faded Daytona 500 cap over his too-long hair, hair that was as black as Max's, but, she noted, had more grey streaks than the last time she'd seen him. His face was tan, with a few wrinkles around his mouth, and lines around his eyes where his sunglasses would normally sit.

"Wanted to see you. It's been a while."

"How nice of you to surprise Max," Ellie said. "My mama, my daddy, and my entire family surprised me a while back when they showed up and threw an engagement party for my fiancé, Zeke, and me. I just love surprises."

Max tried not to roll her eyes. "I assume you've introduced yourselves, but Dad, Skeeter, this is Ellie Hawthorne, my friend and fellow teacher. Ellie, my dad, Bo Simmons, and Skeeter Curtis."

"Of course we've met," Ellie said with a wave of her hand. "We had lots of time to get to know each other while I showed them around the school."

Max didn't like the satisfied glint in Ellie's eyes. No wonder the two men looked dazed, Max thought, as she imagined the dozens of questions Ellie had likely asked them.

"We ran into Nicole in the hallway, so she knows that you're busy this afternoon. She said to tell you that you can take Luna for a walk whenever you want." Ellie turned her charm on Bo and Skeeter. "It was a pleasure meeting you both. Y'all have fun tonight catching up." With a wink, she added, "See you soon," then wiggled her fingers in a wave and nearly skipped out of the room.

"That one's somethin'," Skeeter said with a shake of his head.

"She is, but she means well. Now, tell me why you're really here."

Bo and Skeeter looked at one another, then at Max. Bo spoke first.

"I saw the news this morning, Maxie. I was going to call you to find out what, exactly, Victoria did, but instead, I got on a plane. Told Skeeter I was coming, he met me at the airport, and here we are. We want to make sure you're okay."

Max had to sit. Her dad didn't fly. Ever. He hated everything about airplanes, and airports, and the very idea of being trapped inside any sort of moving vehicle he wasn't steering. He'd logged enough miles driving across the country to rival a long-haul trucker, and he firmly believed it was the only respectable way of traveling. But he'd gotten on a plane.

"So are you?" her father asked.

"Am I what?"

"Okay. Are you okay?"

"I'm fine. How did you end up here? At school?"

"Told ya," Skeeter said, "we stopped by your place, you weren't there."

"And you decided I'd be here? And that you'd come here to find me?" The whole thing seemed wildly out of character for both of them.

"Talked to your landlord," Skeeter said, grimacing. "After we fought our way past a couple of pushy reporters, and through a heck of a high-powered sprinkler. He told us you weren't likely to be home for a while. 'Course that was after he demanded to see our IDs and darn near frisked us."

"He wanted to be sure we weren't reporters," Max's father explained, then he tensed and asked, "Did your mother really wear a wire and record you?"

Max rubbed her hands over her face. "Yeah, she really did."

"Oh, Maxie Lou, I'm sorry. I should have stopped her from seeing you."

Max dropped her hands away from her face. Anguish had her instead pressing them to her heart. "You knew what she was here for? What she was going to do?"

"No! No, of course not, but I should have come sooner. I should have talked to Victoria. I should have protected you." Bo dropped his gaze to stare at the floor instead of at Max.

Max inhaled, then blew out her frustration with her breath. "You couldn't have known. I didn't know, and I'd been talking with her, seeing her, for weeks."

"Then she's gone?" Bo asked.

"I have no idea."

"Hey, what do you say we get out of here?" Skeeter rounded his shoulders, making himself smaller as if he could hide from everything that had to do with school. "This isn't the place to be havin' this conversation."

"I'd invite you to my place, but it sounds as though there's a crowd. We could go for a drive."

"Actually, we have rooms at a hotel, um, can't remember what it's called, but it's just a few miles from here," Bo said.

Max's spirits soared. "You're staying? Overnight? Really?"

"Yeah, couple nights, maybe. Long as you need us. We got a suite. Big space with separate bedrooms, couple bathrooms, even a little kitchen. That way you don't have to go back to your place, and if you don't want to, we don't even have to go out to eat."

It wasn't often Max found herself on the receiving end of a gift from her father, and she wasn't sure how to respond. When it came to gifts, his plan had always been to ask around, find out what those polled thought constituted a suitable gift for a girl her age, then cajole someone into doing the shopping for him. She'd gotten Barbie dolls when what she'd really wanted was a Razor scooter, an iPod when she'd longed for an outfit like all the other girls were wearing. Her dad had always taken care of her, in his way, but he rarely knew what she really wanted. What she really needed. Until now.

"That sounds perfect. There's a place in town that makes a pizza you'll love. Skeet, you'll hate it, but we'll order a pepperoni for you."

There was a pang when Max recalled sharing that same pizza with Victoria, but she pushed the memory aside and focused on the family in front of her. The family she could count on.

"I'll have to pick up a few things, some clothes, but I'll wait until later. Maybe the crowd will thin."

Her dad held up his phone. "Got that taken care of. That friend of yours took my phone, tapped away at it, then gave it back to me and told me all I have to do is send this text." He looked down and nodded toward the phone screen. "Said she'll take it from there."

Max held out her hand. "Let me see."

Max, I know you'll read this, so let me save you the trouble of arguing. I will go to your apartment, have Fred let me in, and pack up your things. I'm sure I can figure out what you'll need, but if there's anything special you want, let me know. Otherwise, see y'all at the hotel.

Ellie followed, as she always did, with a series of emojis. Max didn't bother trying to decipher them. She handed the phone back to her dad.

"Then I guess that's that. Should we get out of here?"

Skeeter was already on his way to the door. While Max turned out the lights and locked the door, he glanced up and down the hallway as if expecting someone to appear and demand to see his hall pass. "Schools make you nervous, Skeeter?"

"Never much liked 'em. Spent more time tryin' to figure out how to get out of 'em than doin' any work inside of 'em."

Max chuckled. "Sounds like a couple of my students." She threw her arm around Skeeter's shoulders. "Hope they turn out as good as you."

20

Though the room was far nicer, and though they weren't either preparing for or rehashing a race, there was a calming sense of familiarity sitting in a hotel room with her dad and Skeeter, eating pizza and drinking beer. Nicole had delivered the pizzas and the beer, Ellie had dropped off Max's things along with two bags of groceries, and both had left only after Max had sworn she'd call if they needed anything more.

For a couple of hours, they kept things light. Bo updated Max on the latest from the racing world, then laid out his predictions on who would win the regular season and who would qualify for the playoffs. When they argued back and forth about who would win the championship, Max forgot all her worries.

Eventually, almost reluctantly, the conversation turned to all that had happened over the past few months. Max relayed the details of what had occurred inside the school, none of which her dad had heard, and only some of which she'd told Skeeter. She told them about her sessions with Dr. Mallick, and about the welcome she'd received from the staff and the students on her first day back. With disgust and no small amount of embarrassment, she told them about injuring her hand, and eventually, she told them everything that had happened with Victoria.

They asked a few questions, and they both cycled through the emotions Max had endured over the past months: grief, helplessness, anger, frustration, and when they got to Victoria, back to anger.

"She had no right," Bo said, but even as he spoke the few words, his anger melted into despair.

"Have you heard from her?" Skeeter asked.

"She called and texted a couple of times. I didn't answer, or read the texts."

Skeeter nodded and mumbled, "For the best." Her dad looked uncomfortable, and Max recognized the look.

"What is it, Dad? What don't you want to tell me?"

Bo scratched his chin, then pressed his thumbs to each finger and cracked his knuckles in the way he always did when he was nervous. Without speaking, he got up and walked to the closet. Reaching inside, he pulled out his jacket. He carried it with him back to his chair. When he sat, he bunched it on his lap.

"She sent me a letter. It was one of those overnight things. She must have sent it right after everything happened. After she did what she did. When I got it, I didn't know about any of that, but when I saw the news this morning, this made a little more sense."

Bo pulled an envelope from the inside pocket of his jacket. He looked at it, turned it over, then dropped it on the table that still held the pizza boxes and beer bottles. He nodded at it.

"This letter was inside the envelope she sent to me. I don't know how she knew where to send it. She must have done a lot of calling around until someone told her something. Anyway, in her note to me, she asked me to give this to you, said it was important. I set it aside thinking I'd wait until I saw you, then let you decide whether you wanted to read it. As I said, after seeing the news, I figured this must be some kind of apology, or explanation, or, I don't know, more Victoria being Victoria." Bo looked at Max. "It's up to you. I'll throw it away right now and we'll forget we ever saw it, or you can have it."

Max crossed her arms over her chest. "I don't want it."

"Fine."

Bo scooped up the letter, along with the garbage from the table, and dumped it all into the garbage can. Even though the letter was out of sight and Victoria was nowhere near, she still managed what she'd managed to do for years and cast a dark cloud over the room.

It was quiet, with Max lost in her thoughts, and neither her dad nor Skeeter seemingly willing to break the silence. Max wondered how different things would be, at that moment, if her mother had never come to Caston. Or if Max had never allowed Victoria inside her apartment.

First, she wouldn't be sitting in a hotel suite with her dad and Skeeter. The fact that she was, was the only good thing to come out of all the bad. She'd missed her dad, she realized with some surprise.

They weren't close in the way Ellie was close with her parents, calling several times a week and texting in between the calls, discussing what seemed like every decision and every trivial event. Still, Max and her dad had a relationship that worked for them. They both knew they could trust the other to be fair and honest, they understood one another's strengths and weaknesses and together, made a formidable team, and though they both had independent streaks as long as the track at Talladega, they knew they only had to ask, and the other would be there if needed.

Next, she likely wouldn't have seen herself on a national news program that morning. There still could have been, probably would have been, another news story on another day. Maybe not with the pictures, probably not with the first-hand account, but with Albert Quinn back at the forefront of current events, she would have been mentioned along with him.

That led her to wonder whether Madison Wilkes would have followed the story if it hadn't been for Victoria. Would she have tried not only with Beck but with Ellie and Nicole? With Amanda, or some of Max's other co-workers? Would she have tracked down Bo?

Max doubted it. It wasn't a big enough story that someone like Madison Wilkes, or her people who did the grunt work for her, would devote that much time and energy to it. No, Max knew she had Victoria to thank for the headache that pounded behind her eyes and for the sleepless night she knew was ahead. What had made Victoria do it? Max wondered.

"Dad?"

Bo looked surprised when Max spoke, as if he too had been lost in thoughts, maybe memories.

"Why did she leave? All those years ago. Why?"

Max hadn't asked that question as an adult. She had tiny fragments of memories of sitting on her dad's lap, sobbing, and begging to know where her mom was, why she'd left, and when she was coming back. But once she'd realized Victoria wasn't coming back, and once Max had grown up, she'd stopped asking. She'd never gotten an answer, and seeing her father's reaction to her questions, she didn't know if she'd get one now.

Bo cracked his knuckles again, one after the other; he rubbed his bad leg. When he glanced toward Skeeter who nodded almost imperceptibly, a shiver traveled the length of Max's spine.

"She loved you, Max. I never doubted that, and neither should you.

She loved you, but in her way, which wasn't always easy to understand. She never talked much about her childhood except to say she grew up in foster care where she bounced from one family to another, never feeling like she belonged anywhere. The only thing she ever told me about her parents was that her father was dead and she didn't know where her mother was. Of course, I found out later that wasn't true, but by that time, your Grandma Maeve was already in a nursing home. That sort of childhood, I guess, left her not knowing how to really love."

Bo paused and let his head fall back on the chair. He stared at the ceiling, seeming to need to draw strength to continue his story.

"It wasn't the first or the last lie she told me." Bo drew a shuddering breath. "Things weren't always great, but I thought they were good. Victoria, I realized too late, didn't agree. There was a baby. We were going to have another baby. You were going to have a brother or a sister."

It was like she'd jumped into that ice-cold pool at the spa Ellie had insisted they visit. The shock and the frigid chill tingled in her scalp and all the way down to her toes. She hugged herself against it. She watched her dad, waiting without breathing, for him to tell her more, while at the same time wanting to shout and make him stop.

"I wanted more kids. I thought she did too. It's what she'd said early on, so when she told me about the baby, I assumed she'd be as thrilled as I was. That wasn't the case. She was angry. Angry at me, angry with herself, angry with the life which she saw as incredibly unfair. I never told you this, Max, there's a lot I never told you about your mother and maybe that was wrong, but I didn't know how to talk about her without all the anger and the hurt coming through, so I avoided all of it. That probably wasn't the right thing to do, but I didn't always know the right thing to do when it came to you. I'm sorry about that."

Before Max could respond, before she could tell him she knew he'd done his best and his best had been good enough, Bo rushed ahead with his story, as if once he'd started, he couldn't hold it inside a moment longer.

"We met in California, at a race track close to LA. She'd come out for the afternoon with some friends. I was driving then, I won the race, and afterward, she was waiting to meet me. For me, it was love at first sight. I don't think I believed in such a thing before that day, but Victoria was everything I'd ever dreamed of. She was beautiful, confident, full of life, and most of all, she was interested in me."

For the first time since he'd started his story, Bo looked at Max. "She was an actress. Or, she hoped to be. She'd moved to LA, found a few modeling jobs, landed a small part in a commercial, and had dreams of stardom. I believed every word she said, that she'd make it and that she'd be the next superstar. We spent every minute together that we could for those few days I was in California. When I left, we made promises to travel to see each other. We made promises about the future."

Max's head spun. She hadn't known any of it. She'd never known how or where her parents met, she'd had no idea Victoria had been a model with dreams of acting, and she certainly hadn't known anything about a baby. A brother or a sister. It was overwhelming.

More than ever, Max wanted to tell her dad to stop, to keep the rest to himself. She'd gone this long without knowing. Maybe it was best she continue living her life in that blessed oblivion.

"I'm sorry, Dad, I shouldn't have asked. We don't have to talk about this." She reached for the TV remote lying on the table between them. "Maybe we can find a movie. Or do you want another beer? We've got chips, pretzels, all that stuff Ellie brought."

Bo smiled a smile that was so sad it nearly broke Max's heart. When he spoke, it was as if he hadn't heard her.

"We saw each other when we could. Things weren't going well for Victoria in Los Angeles, and she was frustrated. I persuaded her to take a break from it, to come with me and see what my life was like. Not everyone could be happy with the sort of life I was living. I wanted to know if she could.

"She loved it. She loved watching me race, she loved the excitement, she loved seeing the country. We were married before I realized most of what she loved was the idea of me becoming as big a name in the racing world as those she was meeting. Those like Dale Earnhardt who were established and who commanded attention wherever they went, and those like Jeff Gordon who burst on the scene and made a name for themselves in front of her eyes. She always figured that any day, that would be me. And by extension, her. She wanted the attention. She hadn't given up on her Hollywood dreams, she'd just decided to go about things differently. Once I made it, with her at my side, she'd get her face on TV, get the attention of an agent, or a producer, or someone in Hollywood, and she'd start making the movies she'd always dreamed of making.

"Of course, I didn't know that, or realize that, until it was too late. And of course, none of what she hoped for happened. I got hurt, I had to give up driving, and she became bitter. Depressed. The life she'd told herself she loved, she started to hate. She tried with you, and there were good times, but the bad times got worse. I hoped another baby would help, but it did the opposite. She sunk into an even deeper depression. She was angry with everyone and everything. I shouldn't have left that night, I should have known…"

Max had only ever seen her dad cry once, and Victoria had been responsible that time, too. When a tear leaked from his eye and he swiped it away, Max felt like that little girl who'd crawled onto her dad's lap begging for her mother. From across the table, she watched him try to swallow while her own throat burned with the emotion she fought to keep inside. Bo tried to speak, but only managed a choking sound.

"You didn't do anything wrong that night, Bo."

Though Skeeter's voice was soft, it sounded like an explosion in Max's ears. As absorbed as she'd been in her father's story, she'd forgotten Skeeter was in the room with them. Studying him, and wondering at his involvement in all of it, she saw pain in his eyes, as if remembering the past hurt him as much as it did Bo, but she also saw strength. It made her realize, maybe for the first time, how often Skeeter had been that for her, and for her father. Their strength.

"Victoria made her choice," Skeeter continued. "If it hadn't've happened that day, it would have been another. You couldn't be there every minute."

The room was eerily quiet, with only the incessant hum of the heater as a backdrop to the unspoken questions and the unshed tears. When Max couldn't take it anymore, she asked, "What happened?"

Bo waited so long to answer, Max didn't think he was going to, but he drew a breath, then rubbed both hands up and down his face, hard enough that Max could hear the scrape of his rough hands over the two-day stubble on his cheeks. He kept his hands over his face, and his voice was as emotionless as a computer-generated one.

"I had to work late. I came home to an empty apartment and an empty vodka bottle. I'd only been inside for a minute or two, still trying to piece together what might have happened, when the phone rang. She'd crashed the car into a tree and was in the hospital with a whole list of injuries. You were there too, mostly unhurt except for a few bruises and a nasty cut on your hand." Bo's voice dropped to a whisper. "She lost the baby that night."

Max lifted her hand and studied her palm. A scar ran from just below her pinky finger toward her wrist. She'd never known where it came from. Her dad had only told her it was from a cut she'd gotten when she'd been too young to remember. He was right. She remembered nothing of the night, or of the accident. But she remembered her mother leaving.

"When did she leave? It couldn't have been right away."

"No. We tried for a while. Or, I tried, anyway. Something changed in Victoria that night, and she was never the same. Over the years, I've wondered if it wasn't more that she just stopped trying to be someone she wasn't that night. That she didn't so much change as she reverted. I don't know. For about six months we pretended, but she started going out a lot. She disappeared for longer and longer stretches, never telling me where she'd been. One day, while you and I were grocery shopping, she left. And that was that."

Sometimes over the years, Max had tried to remember. Disjointed scenes flashed in her mind, and she never quite knew if she was remembering them in the right order. But she remembered her mom saying goodbye—she figured it must be when she and her dad left for the grocery store—and she remembered the note. The pink note.

The way she'd been protected, shielded, over the years made more sense. While race car drivers partied as much as anyone, and while it wasn't unheard of for a driver to end up on the receiving end of a DUI, it was rare. Since it meant risking their livelihood, most knew better than to take the risk. And most had families. Reckless and drunk driving, combined with putting a child at risk, would equal some serious rebuffing of Victoria at the hands of those that surrounded Max and Bo.

As long as she had her dad talking, Max decided to ask another question. "She told me she sent birthday cards and Christmas gifts. I don't remember any of that. Is it true?"

"She did. For a while. I suppose I could have given the gifts to you without telling you where they came from, but that didn't seem right. Neither did telling you they were from her. Had you been older when everything happened, I would have let you make your own decisions. As it was, you were so young, handing you a gift and telling you it was from your mother would have only made you ask questions about where she was, and when you would get to see her. I didn't have those answers, and my only concern was protecting you from more hurt. If you're angry about that, I'm sorry, but I did what I thought was best."

Funny how that had been Victoria's take on the situation. Almost word for word. It made Max wonder.

"Did she ever contact you? To ask about me?"

Bo looked as if he wished he could give a different answer. "No. But that had nothing to do with you, and everything to do with me. I was the one she didn't want to talk to, not you."

"And you never knew where she was?"

"For a long time, I didn't know. I didn't hear anything. When the cards and packages started coming, they came from all different places. Sometimes California, sometimes New York. Just as likely, anywhere in between. Still, I wasn't sure if she sent them from those places, or if she asked someone else to send them so I wouldn't be able to find her. Eventually, she started coming around again, but I only heard about it. I never saw her. She asked questions about you, I heard about that too, but she didn't get many answers."

"You don't know what she did for all those years?" None of it made much sense, and it bugged Max that she was curious.

Bo shook his head. "At first, I wondered. Whenever we moved, there was a little something inside me that wondered if she'd be there, if she'd come looking for us, but after a while, I realized that wasn't going to happen, and I quit looking."

Max had avoided talking with her dad about her mother for years because it seemed to make him angry. Once she'd been old enough, she'd taken a page from her dad's playbook and turned her feelings to anger. Now, listening to her dad, she realized that underneath his anger, there was a lot of heartache. He'd shoved that away, deep down, to protect her. If he'd shared his heartache with her, it would have taken her a lot longer to move past her own.

"If you don't want to know, I don't need to say nothin', but if you want, I can fill in some of the gaps."

Both Max and Bo turned to gape at Skeeter. He'd hardly said a word, which was nothing new for Skeeter, but in this case, even if Skeeter had been the chatty type, she would have expected he'd want to stay out of their messy family business.

"Fill in the gaps? What're you getting at, Skeet? What do you know?"

Skeeter looked at Max. "You wanna hear this?"

Max lifted her hands wide. "Why not? How much worse can it get?"

When Skeeter raised his bushy eyebrows and frowned, Max braced herself.

"A few weeks after she took off, I hired a guy to find her."

Bo threw himself forward in his chair, leaning toward Skeeter. "You what?"

"Bo, I saw what she did to you. What she did to Max. You were a mess, and Max was upset all the time because you were upset. You two couldn't go on that way, but I knew having her come back wasn't the answer. I wanted to know where she was and wanted to know if there was any hint of her comin' back."

Bo rubbed his hand back and forth over his mouth, muttering as he did so. Max heard words she'd never before heard her dad use. She may be a grown woman, but it scared her.

"Dad?" Her voice didn't sound like her own. At least not like her voice had sounded for years. She sounded like a frightened little girl, and it got her dad's attention. When he spoke to her, his voice sounded like she remembered it sounding when she'd been that frightened little girl.

"Maxie Lou, I'm sorry. Skeet caught me off guard, is all. I'm okay." Bo turned his eyes on Skeeter. "Why didn't you ever tell me?"

"What for?"

"Because…because…I don't know, just seems like you should have."

"No point. If there had been reason to, I would've."

"So?" Max prompted.

"She went back to LA. Tried the acting thing again. Landed nowhere but in a heap of trouble. Took off before it got too bad. Went to New York. Same story, but this time the trouble was more serious, and she landed in jail for a while."

Max couldn't say why the news tore her apart, but it did. Her heart ached for a woman she barely knew, a woman who had done nothing but cause her pain.

"Jail?" Bo asked. He sounded as crushed as Max felt.

"Yeah. Not long. Few months for disorderly conduct and for smashin' up a crappy apartment."

"You didn't just hire someone to find her, Skeet, you hired someone to keep tabs on her. For how long?"

Skeeter shifted in his seat. He wasn't the type to apologize for anything he did. He lived by his own rules and standards, but those rules and standards were set high meaning he rarely got on the wrong side of anyone, so seeing him look as uncomfortable as if he were sitting on a chair full of cactus spines was a rarity.

"Never really quit."

Max watched the blood drain from her father's face. Since her stomach felt as if a twenty-pound dumbbell had just been dropped inside her, she figured her face must look the same.

Bo was the first to find his voice. "Never really quit? You mean to tell me you've had someone following her for over twenty years?"

"Not following, no, but keepin' tabs on her."

"How? Why? You've been paying someone, the same someone, for all those years? That's crazy."

Max had to agree. Skeeter wasn't wealthy. At least, she didn't think he was. And he'd chosen to spend his money trailing Victoria?

"Found a guy way back when. Paid him to find her and watch her. After a while, it wasn't so much a job as it was something he just did. He'd check up on her, make sure he knew where she was, and he'd keep me updated. Kinda got to be friends with him. He's a fan, so more often than not, all he wanted was tickets, or something signed, or to hang out in the infield at Daytona and meet some of the guys."

Bo shook his head, still in disbelief. "That doesn't explain why."

A hint of anger flared in Skeeter's eyes. Another rarity. "What did you expect me to do? Let her come back and have everything start all over again? Once you'd put your life back together, I wanted it to stay that way."

Anger in her dad's eyes wasn't such a rarity, but seeing it directed at Skeeter was. "You stopped her from coming back? You made that decision for me? For Max?"

"You're not listenin', Bo. I said I kept track of her. Watched her to see what she was plannin'. I didn't say I stopped her from comin' back, just that I wanted to know if she was going to."

The reality seemed to hit Bo. "Then she never did try? To come back?"

"Not really. She hung around again after a while. You knew that. But it was more of the same, Bo. She wanted to latch onto the next big thing. Same as always."

Max wasn't sure what was worse, the idea that Skeeter had worked to prevent her mother from coming back to her, or that her mother hadn't tried. Then she looked at her dad and decided it was neither of those, but the way her dad slumped back into his chair under the weight of what Skeeter told him.

"That's how you knew she was coming here to see me," Max said.

"Yeah, but by the time I found out, she was already here. I'm sorry that when it really mattered, I let you down."

"Let me down? You've never let me down, Skeet. Never."

"Shoulda got to you before she did. Might've prevented all this mess."

"Did you know why she was coming? What she wanted?" Max asked.

"No, but I knew it couldn't be anything good."

"Then even if you had told me she was coming, I probably would have talked to her anyway." Max realized it was true, not something she was saying only to ease Skeeter's mind.

Skeeter shrugged. "Maybe, maybe not. Still should've done more to protect you. Worked at it for all those years, then when it was most important, I failed."

The defeated look on Skeeter's face set loose a flood of emotion inside Max. She got to her feet and went to him. They weren't a touchy-feely bunch. Max could recall having either her dad or Skeeter throw their arm around her shoulders a few times, and more often, getting a friendly punch in the shoulder from one of them. As for real, honest-to-goodness hugs, well, another rarity. So Max figured Ellie and all of her hugging, whether it be for something sad, something happy, something exciting, or because it was Tuesday, was to blame when Max found herself throwing her arms around Skeeter.

He tensed before he relaxed and awkwardly patted her on the back. She gave him one more tight squeeze before she eased away.

"You know, Skeet, I am an adult. You don't need to protect me. Neither do you, Dad. I like knowing you're both in my corner, but you raised me well. I can take care of myself."

"Well, 'course you can. Doesn't mean I can't help sometimes," Skeeter said.

"You're right, and I'm grateful that you want to. Both of you. Right now, having you here is the best kind of help I can think of, so thank you."

Skeeter gave Max another awkward pat, this time on her arm. Bo reached across the table and squeezed her other arm. While Max knew they'd never become the hug-happy sort like Ellie and her family, she also knew the three of them had turned a corner that evening, and maybe the occasional hug wasn't out of the question.

Or maybe it was. All three looked from one to the other, not sure what to do or say next. Finally Max broke the tension.

"The 2007 Daytona 500 is on YouTube. We could watch."

"It is? Still say it's the best NASCAR race ever," Bo said. "Turn it on. I'll get some chips."

"What's YouTube?" Skeeter asked.

Max chuckled. "Just watch."

They whooped and cheered, they cringed and criticized, and by the time the checkered flag dropped, they'd forgotten about most everything but racing. Later, when they said their goodnights, and when Max turned out the last light and headed for her room, she threw a look over her shoulder, then doubled back and plucked the letter from her mother out of the garbage.

21

Before Max left for school the next morning, Bo and Skeeter coerced her into making several promises. The first was that she'd spend at least one more night at the hotel. She didn't mind that one since, even with the drama from the previous night, she'd enjoyed her time with them. Next, they made her promise to turn on her phone and leave it on. She pushed back on that. The only calls she got were those she didn't want to answer, but they insisted, so she turned on the phone.

The third thing made her laugh. Skeeter said he wanted to trade cars with her for the day, arguing that Stevie Ray was too recognizable, making Max an easy target for anyone who wanted to get a picture of her or to try to lure her into an interview. Max laughed until she realized Skeeter was serious, then she argued. In the end, after her dad teamed up with Skeeter, she lost the argument. Or, more accurately, she gave up. They didn't often ask anything of her, and if it would provide them some peace of mind, she could give them this.

It was only after relenting that she learned they planned to visit Coot at the track where she'd taken Ellie and Nicole, but by then it had been too late to change her mind. So, when she walked through the hotel parking lot and clicked the key fob to unlock Skeeter's pickup, she paused to pat Stevie Ray on the hood and apologize before climbing into Skeeter's truck.

Since she had a few extra minutes, and since she was in an unrecognizable vehicle, and especially since she was curious, Max detoured past her apartment on the way to school. Assuming interest would have waned, or that something more interesting would have demanded attention, she doubted there would be anyone around. However, when she turned the corner, she spotted the news van, and when she got closer, the reporter standing in the street, just off Fred's property. She laughed but felt a warmness flood through her when she spotted Fred sitting in a lawn chair, hose in hand, waiting.

Deciding the moment was too good to pass up, Max inched the truck closer, then fished her phone out of her purse. When her phone rang in her hand before she could open up the camera, it startled her. Guessing it was her dad or Skeeter checking up on her to make sure she'd kept her word, she was surprised when neither of their names showed on the screen. It was a local number, but one she didn't recognize. Her finger was poised to decline the call when something about the number, or about the time of day, or something else she couldn't quite pinpoint, had her hesitating.

Was it a familiar number? Had she gotten a call from that number before? It wasn't one of the news people who had called previously, because she'd blocked those numbers. Knowing she'd most likely regret it, something made her answer.

"Hello?" Max didn't exactly shout, but her voice was none too friendly.

"Uh, Ms. Sim—, Is this Ms. Simmons?"

The caller sounded young, no older than one of her students. Max's heart thumped in double time. "Yes? Who's calling?"

"Ms. Simmons, it's Reid. I'm sorry, but you said, um, you said I could call if um…"

"Reid." Her heart pounded harder. "Are you okay? Did something happen?"

"I'm not sure." His voice trembled. "I'm okay, but, um, I, there's this kid—"

"Reid, it's okay. You have to tell me if you're hurt, or if someone is threatening you. I'll help you, I promise, but you have to tell me what's going on. Tell me where you are."

"Uh, yeah, okay, um, I'm at home."

"Are you alone?"

"Yeah. My mom and dad are out of town. I'm supposed to get on the bus in a couple of minutes, but I was on my computer and I saw something. I didn't know who else to call."

Max was confused. She hadn't come any closer over the past few weeks to figuring out what was bothering Reid, and though there had been good streaks, she hadn't stopped worrying about him. But he was home, and he was alone. Something on his computer?

"What did you see? You said something about a kid? Did you see someone get hurt?" Maybe some sort of live feed, Max thought.

"No, not yet, but I think he's going to take a gun to school."

At that, Reid choked on a sob. On her end, Max did the same.

"Here? At CMS?" Max had to alert someone. She had to call the police. She had to get to school. Before Reid could answer, she slammed the truck into gear and tore down the sleepy residential street.

"No, he doesn't live here. He lives in Colorado, where I used to live. I've been following him on social media. This one website, it's full of creepy stuff, and that's where he wrote it. I don't know if anyone else knows who he is cuz he uses a different name, but I figured it out. I don't know what to do, Ms. Simmons."

"Okay." Max took a breath. What was she supposed to tell Reid? "Can you call your parents? Where are they?"

"They're probably on an airplane. They're going to kill me. I'm not supposed to do stuff like this on the computer. They always tell me that, and sometimes they check my computer, but I know how to clear my browser, and they've never seen this stuff, but if I show them, they'll be so mad. They'll, I don't know, I don't know what they'll do."

He was spiraling. Max tried to reel him back in while she dodged traffic and, after slowing and taking a quick look, ran a stop sign.

"They might not like what you did, but they won't be mad if you can help prevent something horrible from happening. Um, we need to call the police. Can you hang up with me and call 911? Tell them what's going on, tell them where this kid is, and then, um, then call your parents?"

Max feared she was doing it all wrong. It also finally dawned on her that Reid said it wasn't CMS. She didn't need to break traffic laws to get to school. Still, she had to get somewhere and do something. She slammed on the brakes and made a U-turn.

"Reid, I'm going to go to the police station. Please call 911, try to explain, and I'll go there and try to help in case they have questions or doubts."

"But what do I say if I call 911? I don't know what to tell them."

"Just try, Reid. Hang up, call 911, and do your best. They'll know what questions to ask. You only have to answer."

His voice was shaky when he asked, "What if it's too late?"

"It won't be," Max answered with a certainty she didn't feel. "If we hurry."

"Okay."

"I'm proud of you, Reid. You're doing a brave thing."

Max disconnected before Reid could change his mind. She pressed harder on the pedal and weaved in and out of cars on their way to work, to school, to wherever they were headed, maybe not entirely without their own worries, but without the sort of terror weighing on Max's mind.

The siren behind her didn't register at first. She heard it, she saw the lights in the rearview mirror, but she kept speeding toward the police station. When it finally clicked that it was a police car behind her, she was torn. She could stop, try to explain to the officer what was going on and hope she'd get his or her cooperation, or she could continue speeding and take herself to the police station. Neither sounded like a good choice, but she had to make one. She pressed the pedal even harder.

Two police cars were behind her by the time she screeched into the lot at the police station. As much as she wanted to jump from the truck and start running, she knew better, so she turned off the engine, put her keys on the dash, and waited, nervously tapping her toe while she watched the action behind her in her rearview mirror.

From the car directly behind her, a woman emerged, one hand resting on her gun while she talked into the radio on her shoulder. The second car, Max now realized, was a highway patrol car, and when she saw Marty emerge, she nearly wept with relief.

Marty and the woman stopped behind the bumper of Skeeter's truck to confer. Unable to wait, Max put the keys back in the ignition, lowered the window, and called to Marty. Praying she hadn't made a horrible mistake, she put her hands in the air.

She watched the female officer tense. Marty did the same, but only for a moment before he squinted and relaxed.

"Max? What in the world?"

"Marty, can I get out? It's an emergency."

"Yeah, yeah, sure." Marty turned toward the woman who Max thought still looked skeptical, but who had relaxed a notch.

"I'm sorry. I know I racked up a bunch of tickets, but that needs to wait. I need to talk to someone about a possible school shooting in—" Max realized she didn't know where. Not in Caston, but beyond that, she didn't know.

"What? Where? Not at your school again?" Though poised to take action, Marty looked ill.

"No, not here. I'm not sure where. Colorado?" Max shook her head and repeated, "I'm not sure. A student called me. He's supposed to be calling 911." Max rubbed her hand over her eyes. "I'm not making any sense. Can we go inside? Can we find out if Reid called? I told him I'd try to help. Please?"

The woman looked at Marty who nodded, apparently trying to reassure her Max wasn't completely crazy. When the woman pointed toward the door of the police station, Max started jogging.

Max wasn't sure if the fact that some of those inside the police station recognized her—because they'd met or because her face was far too familiar—helped or hindered her cause. She could tell some took her seriously; she worried some thought she was suffering more effects of PTSD. Regardless, it took several minutes for Max to explain what she knew, and several more for someone to connect the dots and find the officer who was, at that moment, speaking with Reid. An officer had already been dispatched to Reid's home, and another was trying to reach the boy's parents.

Once Max provided what information she could, and once the rush of adrenaline wore off, she stood watching the barely controlled chaos around her and felt helpless. It was a relief when Marty stood alongside her and put a hand on her shoulder.

"They'll get to the bottom of all this."

"I'm not sure I understand what 'all this' is. I'm hoping it's a misunderstanding or some kind of sick prank, but I'm scared to death it's not. What if it's not? What if we're too late? What if this very minute something awful is happening?"

"I learned long ago that worrying never helps."

"Right now, I don't know what else to do."

Marty nodded. "You helped. I'd like to think Reid would have been taken seriously, but it might have taken longer if you hadn't vouched for him and corroborated his story."

"He's telling the truth, or the truth as he understands it. I don't doubt that. He was so scared when he called. If he would have said something sooner, or if I'd asked more questions, made him tell me, we may not be here today."

"Tell you what? He mentioned this before?"

"No, not this, but I knew there was something. He asked questions and said things that led me to believe something was wrong, or that he was afraid of something. It's my fault. I could have stopped this. If I would have acted sooner, we wouldn't be standing here right now. There wouldn't be people in danger. I could have prevented this, but I did nothing."

She was now the one spiraling. It took Marty giving her shoulder a shake to put an end to it.

"That's not doing anyone any good, Max."

"Sorry, but I feel so helpless. Standing here, wondering what's happening, if the police here were able to notify the police there in time. I'm not good at doing nothing."

Marty glanced at the clock that hung over the reception desk. "It's been fifteen minutes since we came inside. An officer will have arrived at Reid's house by now, and someone stayed on the phone with him until that officer arrived. Police wherever it is happening will have been notified. Things are moving quickly, and that's, in part, due to you. You helped."

Max nodded toward the desk. "Will they tell me anything? Is there any reason for me to stay? Am I supposed to leave? I don't know how this works."

"Let me see what I can find out," Marty said, but before he could ask a question, a voice called from somewhere across the room.

"Max Simmons?"

"Yes!" Max's shout startled her, as well as those around her.

An officer approached. He was young, and though he squared his shoulders and tried for calm and professional, the tick under his eye gave him away.

"Ms. Simmons, I'm Officer Channing."

Max shook hands with Officer Channing. Marty introduced himself and did the same.

"The officer on the scene is talking with Reid, but the boy is pretty shaken. We can't reach his parents, and his grandmother, who is on her way to stay with the kids while the parents are gone, is still over an hour away. Reid has an older brother, high school age. Someone may be trying to get in touch with him, but for now, Reid asked for you."

"For me? He wants to talk to me?"

"Actually, he wondered if you'd come there. He's, ah, he's more than a little freaked out. Would you?"

"Of course. Should I just drive over there? I don't know where he lives."

"I'll find someone to take you. Things are crazy, but I'll see if someone is available. Can you go right now?"

"Yes." Then it hit her, and like in a slapstick comedy, she slapped her hand to her forehead. "I'm supposed to be at school. They've got to be looking for me. I can't believe no one called me."

Max reached for her purse, only to find it wasn't hanging over her shoulder. She patted her jacket pocket but didn't find her phone.

"My purse. My phone. I don't know what I did with them." Max looked around wildly as if both would appear in front of her eyes.

"Probably in your truck," Marty said.

"My truck? Oh right, the truck. I need to call."

"I could take care of that for you, if you'd like," Officer Channing offered. "And I'll get someone to take you over to the boy's house."

"I can do it," Marty said.

Officer Channing hesitated as if unsure what protocol dictated but then nodded. "That should work. I'll let the chief know. He wanted to talk with you, Ms. Simmons, but he's about ten minutes out, and I think that talk can wait. The boy needs you more." He nodded at Marty. "Yeah, that should work. I'll get you what you need."

Three minutes later, Max was speeding across town in Marty's patrol car. She'd grabbed her purse, so in an attempt to distract herself, took out her phone. A missed call and a voicemail from school. She knew she should call herself instead of relying on Officer Channing to take care of her business, but she didn't trust herself to explain the situation without falling apart.

Marty didn't talk but glanced over at her every few seconds.

"I'm okay," Max said.

"You're not, I'm not, no one involved is okay right now, but I hope you can hold it together when you talk to that boy. He's going to need someone he can trust and who can be strong for him."

"You're right. Of course, you're right. I'm making it seem as though this is somehow about me. I don't mean to. I'll do better. I'll do better for Reid."

"Hey, Max, that's not what I meant. You have every right, every reason, to be upset and scared. This is about you. Your student called you because he trusted you. So, yeah, it's about you, and it would be unnatural if what's happening didn't affect you, even more than it affects others."

Max could only mumble a half-hearted reply.

"We're here," Marty said. "Are you ready?"

Max was already on her way out of the car. "I'm ready," she said and hoped she could back up her words.

It seemed like days, possibly weeks, had passed when Max finally parked Skeeter's truck in the hotel lot that evening. She didn't even know how to rank the day she'd just had on her list of terrible days since she'd experienced the highest of highs, the lowest of lows, and dozens of emotions in between, all in the span of a few hours. Wherever it ranked, it had left her exhausted, mentally and emotionally drained, and wondering if life would ever seem normal again.

Max rummaged through her purse as she walked through the lot, searching for the room key card she knew she'd tucked inside that morning. When she got to the front desk and hadn't found it, she decided it must have fallen out when she'd dropped her purse in the mad dash to Reid's front door.

"Hi," she said to the bored-looking woman behind the desk. "Sue," she added when she spotted the woman's name tag. "I can't seem to find my room card. Any chance I can get another?"

"Sure," Sue said while she tapped at the computer in front of her. "Room number?"

"Ah, I don't remember. I wrote it on the card. Third floor. It's a suite."

Sue looked up to shake her head at Max. "That's not safe, you know. Anyone who finds that card can get into your room. "

"Yeah, you're right. Didn't plan on losing it, though."

"No one ever does," Sue said, with another shake of her head. "Name?"

"Max Simmons. The room is under Bo Simmons, I think."

This time when the woman looked up, the boredom vanished from her expression.

"Max Simmons. You're the teacher who stopped the shooter. I recognize you now. My niece goes to your school. Thank you. Thank you for what you did that day."

"Oh, I—"

"You protected all of them, all those kids."

"How is your niece?"

"It was rough at first, but she's better. Or she was before he was back in the news because of his court date. My sister said Ari had a bit of a setback, but she'll be okay."

"I'm glad to hear it."

"Here you go," Sue said and handed Max a room card. "If you need anything else, let me know."

"Thank you, and I will."

"Thank *you*," Sue repeated.

Too tired to face the stairs, Max jabbed the button for the elevator. While she waited, she wondered if actual famous people hated their lives because being recognized, even once in a while, got old really fast.

Her dad and Skeeter weren't there, but that didn't come as a surprise since she'd scanned the parking lot on her way in looking for Stevie Ray and had come up empty. Reminding herself that both her father and Skeeter were perfectly capable drivers, she tried to relax. Thirty seconds—and four laps around the room—later, she knew that wasn't going to happen.

Max debated going for a run, but with her body rebelling at even the few laps around the hotel room, she knew the idea was futile. She considered a soak in the hot tub, but she didn't have a bathing suit, and the idea of sitting in a tub with a bunch of strangers was far from appealing, so she discarded that idea as quickly as the first. What she wanted, she realized, was to talk to someone. Someone she could trust, someone who would understand, someone who would care. When she'd become the sort of person who wanted that, she didn't know, but somewhere along the way, it had happened.

She hadn't yet told Ellie or Nicole about her morning. Amanda knew, since Officer Channing had called her and Max had filled in a few abridged details when she'd gotten to school, but aside from those few words with Amanda, Max hadn't discussed what happened with anyone. The fact that she'd chewed her nails down to the quick told her she needed to.

Skeeter and her dad would likely be back before long, but after the previous night, Max didn't relish the idea of having another talk on a sensitive topic again any time soon. Nicole and Ellie would make time for her, she knew that, but Max felt like the only conversations the three of them had anymore were depressing ones. Max had an appointment scheduled with Dr. Mallick the following week. She could probably push it up, but what she was feeling was more of a 'right now' kind of thing rather than a 'how's Friday at three o'clock' kind of thing.

Try as she might, she couldn't keep herself from thinking of Beck. She flexed the fingers that were still frustratingly stiff. Whether it had been while working on a car, while on a drive or a walk, or even while he'd been at her side during and after the ordeal with her hand injury, she'd always enjoyed his easy way of talking, the patient way he listened. She missed it. She missed him.

Already a few days ago, she'd realized that she'd overreacted. That she'd jumped to conclusions. That she'd been so hurt by what her mother did, she'd expected more of the same from everyone else. That she hadn't given him a chance to explain, and that that had been unfair.

Even if she heard the worst, he deserved to tell his side, and she deserved the chance to tell him what she thought of his choices. Running from the situation had been the coward's way out, and not at all like her.

While she weighed the pros and cons of calling him, her phone rang.

"*Think* of the devil," Max muttered. She wavered only a moment before answering.

"Hey."

"You answered. I was starting to think you never would."

"Same here. Are you at work?"

"Home. Just walked in the door. It's been—"

"Can I come over?"

"Yes, but do you want to tell me what's been going on? Why you haven't answered any of my calls and texts?"

"Not really."

"Then by all means, come on over. This should be fun."

Max ignored his sarcasm and disconnected. Not giving herself time to reconsider, she grabbed her bag and was out the door in less than a minute, but she made sure she had the key card.

"Nice to see you, even though you look as if you'd like to stab me."

"That may be a bit extreme."

Max pushed past him and into his living room. She liked his house. The main floor was mostly one, large open space with a big kitchen that looked into the living room. Wood floors throughout with rugs to soften the look. Comfy, brown leather furniture, and a TV that was large without being ridiculous mounted above a gas fireplace. An oversized island in the kitchen, something she'd always thought accomplished nothing but getting in the way, but that she'd come to love after sitting on the tall stools that surrounded it, eating the steaks Beck grilled, or sharing a smoothie after a run.

What was missing were the dogs.

"Where's your murderous posse?"

"In the yard."

"Ace won't open the gate so Indie can escape and terrorize the neighborhood?"

"Gave them both new bones. That should buy me some time."

"Hmm." Twice Max had helped Beck chase Indie around the neighborhood. They'd tromped through neighbors' yards, sprinted across streets, even followed the dog onto porches and decks, and all the while, Max would have sworn Indie was laughing at them. Max wasn't eager for a repeat performance.

"So, how have you been? It's been a while."

"Not great."

Max looked out into the yard where both dogs were, for the time being, gnawing on their bones. She scanned the kitchen counters, letting her eyes rest on the stack of mail. She craned her neck to peek into the mud room.

"Are you going to tell me what's wrong, or are you here just to prowl around my house?"

Max whirled on him. "Don't you think you should go first?"

Beck lifted his hands. "I don't know what I'm supposed to say. You've been mad about something for days, ever since I went to Madison—"

Max drew in a sharp breath.

"What?"

"You're admitting it? Just like that? No lies, no excuses, nothing?"

"I have no idea what you're talking about. Admitting what?"

That you went to Madison's! Unbelievable," Max muttered to herself. Deciding she'd heard enough, she headed for the door.

"Hold on a minute. What, exactly, is wrong with that?"

"You can't be serious. And I can't have this conversation."

"What you can't do is walk out of here without telling me what I did that was so wrong. It was business."

Max stopped and turned to face him. "Business? That's what you're calling it? Nice."

"Yes. Business. Last week, and again today. I told you, I just got back, but I think it's taken care of, at least for now."

"You talked to her again?"

"I had to. Things got complicated."

"Complicated? For you? What do you think it's been like for me?"

"I know things haven't been easy for you, but I'm not sure how my business made your life any more complicated."

"You can't honestly believe what you did wouldn't affect me!" Max raked both her hands through her hair, frustrated enough, and angry enough, to tear out every last strand.

"What did I do?" Beck's tone matched Max's in both volume and frustration level.

"You just told me you talked to her! More than once!"

"Who?"

Out of patience, Max yelled, "*Madison!*"

"Who in the world is Madison? I don't—"

Beck stopped shouting, but his mouth stayed wide for a moment as if frozen. Slowly, millimeter by millimeter, his mouth turned into a grin. A big, know-it-all grin. Max had the almost uncontrollable urge to wipe it off his face. Because she was afraid she might try, she turned again to leave, but when Beck chuckled behind her back, she changed her mind once more.

"You think it's funny?"

"That you're jealous? Yeah, I do."

"Jealous? I'm not jealous, I'm mad!"

That only served to make his grin even wider. "Ah, yes, Mad Max."

"Seriously, what is wrong with you? If you think this is all one big joke, then I think we have nothing more to talk about. Don't call, don't text, just leave me alone."

Max had the door open before Beck spoke. "If you would have listened, you would have heard me say I went to *Madison*. Madison, not Madison's. Madison, as in the capital of Wisconsin. Madison, home of the University of Wisconsin, and home of Millicent Beauregard, an eighty-something-year-old-woman who just sold me her chain of six auto repair shops. So, while I'm sure there's plenty wrong with me, it's probably not what you've been thinking. And I'm pretty sure I don't even know anyone named Madison."

Max stared at the floor while she digested the words. She tried to remember what she'd overheard Sven and Jake saying when she'd stopped by Beck's garage.

Madison is a pretty big deal. Things might not just fall into Beck's hands this time.

Are you forgetting this is Beck we're talking about? Things always fall into Beck's hands.

She'd just been blindsided by her mother and Madison Wilkes. Hearing the same name at Beck's, it hadn't exactly been a stretch to assume it was the same Madison. Still, she supposed it wasn't impossible that she'd made a mistake. That she'd jumped to conclusions.

Swallowing what little remained of her pride, she looked at Beck. "Then you didn't talk to her? You swear?"

"Who?"

"Madison Wilkes."

"Who is Madi...oh! Wow. That's what this has been about? You thought I talked to that woman from the news? The one your mom talked to? The one who did the story about you?"

"Yes."

"Max." Beck dropped his head and shook it. He blew out a giant breath before he said, "Why would I do that?"

"Money. That seems to be why my mom did it. Or a moment of fame? I don't know why people do the things they do."

Beck walked to her and reached for her, but Max backed away.

"Okay, not yet, huh? Well, then let me say that I didn't talk to anyone about you, I wouldn't talk to anyone about you, and if you can be mad about something that didn't even happen, maybe I should be mad about what did happen. You accused and convicted me without giving me a chance to defend myself. You ignored me for days, left me wondering what I'd done to hurt you, and instead of maybe letting me help you through everything you've been going through, you wasted your energy on being mad at me. Pretty unfair, Mad Max. Makes me not want to give you the gift I brought you from Mad— from my trip."

"You got me a gift?"

"Not so fast. I think you owe me an apology."

Beck tried again, and this time Max didn't refuse his arms when they wrapped around her. All the anger flowed out of her.

"I'm sorry. That day when it all happened, when my mom set me up and had Madison Wilkes and her photographer there to interview me, after it was all over, I went to see you. I wanted to talk to you. I overheard Sven and Jake before they saw me, and they said things like, 'Madison is a pretty big deal,' and 'He was almost jumping out of his skin when he left. Nervous, but excited.' What was I supposed to think except that you were the next in line to tell the world all about me?"

Beck hugged her tighter. "I didn't see the news story, but after I heard about it, I watched part of it online. I tried to call you, I texted you. I knew you had to be upset, so when you didn't answer, I gave you space, never dreaming the reason you didn't answer was that you thought I was involved. You should have had more faith in me."

Though it felt good to have Beck's arms around her, she wriggled free. She needed to look him in the eye.

"You're right. I should have. I'm sorry I didn't. I was more upset than I care to admit after what my mother did, so when I went looking for you, and when I heard what I heard, I convinced myself you were just one more person I couldn't trust. One more person who was going to hurt me. One more person I'd let get close enough that they *could* hurt me."

"I'd never hurt you. Challenge you or tease you, yes, but hurt you? Never. I hope you know that."

Max nodded. "Can we sit? I don't know how much longer I can stand. It's been quite a day."

Beck led her to the couch where he sat and pulled her down next to him. Max settled in and rested her head on his shoulder.

"Are you mad at me?" she asked.

"Nah. I'm going to forget about the news angle and how you doubted my integrity, and instead remember this as the time you got jealous of some woman named Madison.

Max chuckled. "Fair enough."

"Now," Beck said as he ran a lazy hand over Max's hair, "tell me what happened with your mom."

"Are you sure you want to hear it? It's not a story with a happy ending."

"I gathered that much. Tell me. You'll feel better."

So Max did, and an hour later, she felt better. And she was starving.

"I don't suppose you want to feed me? I haven't eaten anything today."

"Nothing? Why not?"

"Um, that's another story."

"Let me get the dogs inside, then you can tell me that one, too. How about tacos?"

"Perfect. I'm going to quickly call my dad to tell him I'll be out for a while, then I'll help in the kitchen."

That one eyebrow shot up.

"Another part of the story."

"Sounds like it calls for a bottle of wine. What goes with tacos?"

22

While Beck cooked the meat, Max sat at the island chopping lettuce and tomatoes, shredding cheese, and fending off the dogs.

"You'd think they hadn't seen me in a year," Max said when, after fifteen minutes, their excitement level still hadn't waned.

"They missed you."

"Right." Max watched as Indie jumped straight up in the air, high enough that her eyes were level with Max's. "I still can't tell if she likes me, or if she wants to take a chunk out of my face."

"She likes you." Beck looked over his shoulder at Indie who had started to growl. "At least I think so."

Max was glad when Ace got a little too close and Indie decided to focus on him. The two darted across the room, snapping and growling at each other.

"That's okay?" Max asked with a dip of her head toward the tangle of dogs.

"Yeah, they're just playing. Ace will tire of it soon enough and put Indie in her place."

"Interesting dynamic they have."

Eventually, the dogs wore themselves out. Ace crawled onto his bed, Indie followed and snuggled up next to him, and they both slept the sleep of the innocent. Max knew better.

After Max and Beck had both eaten two tacos, Beck said, "Ready to talk?"

"I suppose, if you're ready to listen. It's a lot."

"I'm ready."

Max started by filling in some of what Madison Wilkes said during her story. Beck didn't say much, but a vein in the side of his head throbbed when Max relayed some of Dr. Westrum's analyses. He reached over to hold her hand when Max's voice thickened while telling him how her dad and Skeeter had shown up at school and whisked her away to a hotel. And he closed his eyes, shook his head, and breathed out, "No, no, no," when she told him about the call from Reid.

"It was awful, Beck. It was like I was living it all over again, but this time, there was nothing I could do."

Beck's grip on Max's hand tightened. "I haven't listened to any news today. What happened? Was anyone hurt?"

"No. Because Reid called, the police got to the boy in time. It's impossible to say if he would have acted, but he had a gun in his backpack."

"He was at school? With a gun?"

Max shook her head. "He was on his way to school. The police caught up with him between his home and the school, just walking along like any other day."

"So the police were just in time. Geez, just think…"

"I know," Max said. "If Reid hadn't called, if he'd waited, if he hadn't looked at this kid's posts this morning, so many ifs. I don't know if Reid understands how important what he did really was."

"But you saw him. Reid. He asked for you, and you went to his house, right? How's he doing?"

Hearing Beck use Reid's name made Max realize what she'd done, and it added to her feelings of failure.

"I shouldn't have told you his name. He's my student. I shouldn't have used his name. Beck, you can't breathe a word to anyone. I have a duty to protect his privacy. There are rules, and there's just plain decency. I shattered both."

Beck cupped Max's cheek to gently lift her head until she was looking at him.

"It's okay. You don't have to worry. I won't say a word. He's a child. I'd never do that. Besides, I'm not much of a gossip anyway."

That earned Beck the hint of a smile.

"How is he doing?"

"He was okay when I left him. Still sort of in shock, I think. My gut tells me it's going to get worse for him before it gets better. That's how it was for me. Things sink in and you realize what could have happened.

"Once his grandmother got there and after I told her what I knew, I left. I had one text this afternoon from the grandmother thanking me and telling me Reid was 'holding up.' I didn't want to bug her by texting back and asking a bunch of questions, so I'm not sure what she meant by that."

"You haven't heard any more from the police here in Caston? Or from Marty?"

"No, but I wasn't directly involved. They don't owe me any information."

Beck looked like he wanted to argue that point, but refrained.

"I'm guessing this is the student you mentioned to me before? The one you thought had something he wanted to tell you?"

"Yes."

"How did he know what the kid was planning? It was posted online?"

Max shrugged with one shoulder. "Yes, on social media, but on a really dark social media site. Reid's new this year. From what I've pieced together, it seems like this kid was very popular at Reid's previous school. I don't think he and Reid were ever friends, but when Reid moved away, he started following some of his former classmates on social media to keep up with what was happening there. I don't know how it all transpired, but this kid started posting strange things, and it got Reid's attention. Somehow, Reid followed this kid's trail to a pretty dark website where this kid was active. Reid started monitoring the posts. Today things took a turn."

Max put her hand behind her head and rubbed, trying to ease the knot in her neck. When Beck took over, she sighed with relief.

"Like I told you, Reid talked to me a few times over the past couple of months. He never quite got to the point, but he asked some questions and hinted at things, things that concerned me at the time, and that now make sense. I knew he was worried, I could tell he wanted to tell someone something, but as I'm learning is often the case in the mind of a middle schooler, he was afraid. They're afraid of the stigma that comes from telling. They're afraid of being wrong. They're afraid of doing anything that means they'll be noticed, singled out. This morning when Reid called me, he said he was afraid to tell his parents because he knew he'd get into trouble for being on that website. Still, in the end, he did the right thing, the brave thing, and spoke up. Who knows what might have happened if he hadn't?"

"He's obviously a good kid who has a good teacher. You deserve credit too, you know. You gave him a safe place to talk. When you sensed his reluctance, you didn't press, but you left the door open for when he was ready. You even gave him your phone number. Not everyone would have done that. Without you in his corner, it's possible he wouldn't have spoken up."

"I'm not looking for praise or thanks, I'm just glad he did what he did."

They were both quiet. Max looked out the sliding door that led to the back yard. Darkness was creeping in, casting long shadows. The leaves hadn't fully popped, so the trees looked dark and lonely and sad.

Max wondered how Reid was doing, if his parents were home, if his grandmother was still there, and if Reid felt safe. And she wondered about the other boy, the one in Colorado who'd thought something was bad enough, or unfair enough, or maddening enough that bringing a gun to school was the only solution. She wondered about his family, what they were going through, if they'd get the boy the help he needed, if they'd ever be whole again.

That led her to think about her own family. Or what passed for her family. Both of her parents were only children, so Max never had aunts, uncles, and cousins. Her dad's parents died before she was born; Max's mother had kept her own mother's existence hidden for years, and by the time Max learned of her grandmother, it was too late for much of a relationship since a stroke followed by other illnesses had left her grandmother in need of round-the-clock care available only at a nursing home.

She had her dad and Skeeter. She'd always had them, and even if it wasn't a typical family situation, and even if her dad hadn't always acted like Max might have wanted, she had them to support her when she needed them.

Max turned her head to look at Beck. She knew he had an older sister, she knew his parents were divorced but that he was close with both of them, but beyond that, she didn't know much. Did he have a big family, the kind Ellie had with cousins around every corner, uncles looking out for him, and big Labor Day picnics? Did he have support when he needed it?

It made her think about leaving Caston, and about leaving him. About how unfair it was to come to his house, to let him comfort her, to feed her, to listen while she unloaded all her emotions. When she left, would he miss her? If he did, would he have someone to help him through? Or would he find someone? Would he focus all his time and energy on his business?

Then it hit her, and she sat up straighter. Her selfish concerns vanished as she focused on him.

"You bought a chain of auto repair shops?"

He grinned. "I did."

"Why didn't you tell me? I mean, you mentioned it, or how would I know, but why did you let me blabber all evening and not tell me more? It's huge news!"

"Seemed like you needed to blabber, and I didn't mind waiting."

"I'll tell you I'm sorry the entire evening has been focused on me, because I truly am, but I'm hoping we can move past that because I have so many questions."

Beck waved his arm. "In the past. Ask away."

"How? Where? Why? Oh, just tell me everything."

"Let's see. I bought a chain of six shops, they're all located in Wisconsin, and they were all owned by Millicent Beauregard and her husband. He died a few years ago. She's been trying to hold the business together, but she's past retirement age, and neither of her children has any interest in running things. Millicent and her husband ran a successful business for years, but Millicent has been struggling since she's been on her own, and the business was in trouble."

"Isn't that risky? Buying a failing business?"

"I checked out all the locations, met with all the managers, looked over her financials, had my lawyer look at all of it, and in the end, decided it won't take much to get things back on track. The structure is good, it just needs a little reinforcing. I'm looking forward to the challenge."

Max chewed on her lip and debated asking her next question. "I know it's none of my business, and you don't have to go into detail, but I'm curious. How can you afford to buy a business? One with six locations? All those employees, and all that overhead?"

Beck shrugged. "You can ask. I inherited some money from my mom's parents a couple of years ago and I've been looking for the right investment opportunity. I also worked out a deal with Millicent where she's financing part of the sale, and where she'll keep a small stake in the business for the first two years. It's a good deal for both of us."

"How will you do it? You work twelve-hour days at your shop here."

At that, Max spotted the first shadow of doubt, of concern.

"Yeah, that's going to be tough. At least, at first. Sven and Jake know about it, and they're both capable of doing all the work required, but I'll have to hire another person. I'll have to spend some time at all the shops, get to know the people who work there, determine what needs to be done as far as updating and replacing equipment, hiring or firing, all of it. Remember that buddy I told you about who has the 2014 Camaro he doesn't know how to take care of? Tibbs?"

"Yeah."

"Tibbs may not know much about cars, but he's a whiz when it comes to running a business. He's bought and sold several of his own and has guided at least a dozen people through doing the same for themselves. He's made enough money that he could retire at thirty, but he'd be bored. I talked to him about working with me. Handling some of the business side of things. He hasn't given me a definite answer, but I could tell he's interested. Assuming he agrees, it will take a lot of the pressure off."

"And if he doesn't?"

"Then I'll have to find someone else. I know I can't do it all on my own, at least not right away."

"Wow, Beck, I had no idea you were considering anything like this."

Max didn't like the sadness that came with that realization. Something so important seemed like something he would have mentioned.

"When I made the first trip to see Millicent about the sale, I gave it maybe a ten percent chance of amounting to anything. We both thought about it, then when we spoke again, after we hashed out some details, I realized the idea wasn't all that far-fetched." Beck paused and seemed to debate how to continue. "I, ah, I did try to call you and talk to you about it. I stopped by, but we never connected."

Max closed her eyes and tipped her head back to rest on the couch. She wondered when she'd last wanted to undo time as much as she wanted to undo the past week. She kept her eyes closed when she whispered, "I'm sorry. I'm sorry I wasn't there for you. You've been there for me so many times, and the one time you needed me, not only was I no help, I was a distraction."

"I wanted to bounce the idea off of you, that's true, and wondering what I did was something of a distraction, but in the end, it worked in my favor."

Max rolled her head toward Beck and opened one eye. "How's that?"

"Millicent is surprisingly observant. She noticed a difference in me from the first time we talked and when I went back to see her this time. It took her only one guess to determine the change had to do with a woman."

Both of Max's eyes opened wide. "You discussed me?"

"In only the most general terms. She gave me some sound advice, then we moved on and talked business."

"Advice?"

"Give you space and get you a gift."

"That's right. You mentioned a gift."

"Sit tight," Beck said, standing and heading for the stairs. He was back in less than a minute with his hands behind his back. "I didn't have time to wrap it."

"That's okay." Max leaned, trying to look around Beck.

"Millicent's instructions were, 'No flowers, no chocolates, nothing easy. It has to be meaningful, and it's best if it makes her laugh.' I was stumped until I was checking out the area where the shop in Madison is located and happened upon a really fun store."

"You've got me curious."

"It's not a big deal," Beck said, then pulled his hand out from behind his back.

It was meaningful, no question about it, and it made her laugh a deep belly laugh. But when Beck put the shiny baton in her hands, it also melted her heart.

"They're staying through the weekend," Max told Ellie and Nicole Friday after school.

Ellie nodded. "That's what Bo told me when I texted him this morning."

Max could only stare. "You're texting with my dad?"

"Of course."

"Why?"

"Because I like him, and because I'm hoping to see him again. I invited both your dad and Skeeter to dinner tomorrow. I was hoping to have them, and you and Beck," Ellie turned to Nicole, "and you and Brady. It's been a while since we've done anything like that, but he said he thought he had plans."

"I see. Then I don't have to tell you about the party, because you already know." Max got up to leave. "Hope to see you there."

"What? What party? Max Simmons, you sit right back down and tell me what in the world you're talking about!"

291

"You seem to know everything before I do. How is it you don't know about this?" Max asked, with her sweetest, yet phoniest, smile fixed firmly on her face.

"Nicole, do you know what she's talking about?"

"No idea," Nicole replied, but she looked like she didn't much care, one way or the other.

Ellie threw her hands in the air. "How can I be there if I don't know anything about it? Tell me what y'all are planning! I'll want to bring something, and I'll need time to put it together."

Max enjoyed watching Ellie squirm but took pity on her. "Beck is having a barbecue on Saturday. He's celebrating a new business venture. Saturday evening, at his place. He told me to tell you not to bring anything. I told him that would never work. He said to bring whatever you want."

Ellie looked as though she might explode from happiness. "A party, at Beck's, to celebrate a new business? Isn't it wonderful that it coincides with your daddy being in town?" Ellie's eyes twinkled mischievously.

"Quite the coincidence, yes," Max said.

"What sort of business?" Nicole asked.

"He bought a chain of repair shops. I'm sure he'll tell you all about it at the party. Assuming you'll be there? You and Brady?"

"Sure. At least, I think so. I don't have any plans, and I don't know of anything Brady has going on. Sounds like fun." Her frown, and the worry in her eyes, didn't add up to her words.

"Is something wrong?"

"No. Well, yes. Well, no, not exactly wrong." Nicole's frown deepened. "My dad's house went on the market last week. The realtor texted to tell me we got an offer today."

"And that's not good news?" Max asked.

"It is, sure, but I don't know, I guess I didn't think it would happen this fast. I thought I'd have more time to get used to the idea. Once the house is sold, it'll be like that part of my life is over. My childhood, all the memories. It seems weird that it's ending."

"But it's not really ending," Ellie said. "You'll always have those memories. Nothing and no one can take those away."

"I know that, but driving by and seeing someone else living there? That will be hard. And even though Nate said he was okay with me selling the house before he gets back home, I can't help but worry that one day he's going to regret not getting a chance to say goodbye."

"Boys are different in that way," Ellie said. "They don't get as emotional about things like this. He'll be okay."

Ellie did what Ellie always did and hugged Nicole.

"You're probably right," Nicole said when she pulled away. "I'm making a big deal out of nothing."

"It's not nothing," Ellie said. "It's hard when things change, when you know they'll continue changing, but you have to look ahead, not only back."

"Then I probably need a party, right?"

Max sensed Nicole also needed a change of subject, so obliged. "Five o'clock tomorrow. Beck is hoping to grill and since it still gets pretty cool at night, he thought earlier rather than later."

"Yes, yes, back to Beck," Ellie said. "It's cute how you skimmed over the fact that just a day or two ago, y'all weren't speaking. Or you weren't speaking to him, at any rate. Care to fill us in on what happened?"

"I decided it was time to talk to him, so I did. Turns out it was a misunderstanding."

"You don't say," Nicole mumbled.

"Then he didn't talk to Madison Wilkes?"

"He didn't. He went to Madison as part of this business deal. Seems I heard the name and perhaps jumped to conclusions."

"I can think of a dozen things to say to that, but I'm too happy to dwell on the negatives," Ellie said. "So moving on. A party tomorrow. It seems like Beck wants to get to know your daddy. Is there something we should know?"

"You never quit, do you?" Max said, but she couldn't stop the nervous flutter in her belly. She'd never admit it to Ellie, but she'd also wondered about Beck's timing. She focused on Ellie instead of the niggling worry. "The only thing you need to know is Beck's address. I'll text it to you."

"And you never answer a question, do you?" Ellie shot back. "Fine. I'll figure it out for myself tomorrow. I look forward to it."

All Max could do was shake her head. "I'm leaving now. I'll see you tomorrow."

"Max, before you go, I wanted to ask you about yesterday morning," Nicole said.

Max stilled.

"Did something happen? You weren't here at the beginning of the day, then later I saw you talking with Amanda. You looked upset. I tried to find you after school yesterday, but you were gone before I got to your room. If it's none of my business, that's fine, but do you want to talk about anything?"

Reid hadn't been back to school, and on the list of things Max was currently worrying about, he was near the top. She hadn't decided what to tell Ellie and Nicole, or even if she should tell them anything, but since she knew they'd either find out on their own or get it out of her eventually, Max made a snap decision. Their input on how to deal with Reid when he did come back couldn't hurt.

Instead of answering Nicole, Max simply closed Ellie's classroom door. They rarely closed the door, so the action got her friends' attention.

"Can we sit?" Max asked as she dropped into a desk chair.

Without hesitation, without questions, Nicole and Ellie each pulled a desk close.

When Max started her story, and when Nicole reached to clasp one hand and Ellie the other, their strength strengthening her, Max knew she'd made the right decision.

23

If the weather was any indication, Beck's impromptu party was destined to be a success.

Max, bundled in a robe and a cup of steaming coffee in her hand, stood on the small balcony outside the hotel room and took a deep breath of fresh spring air. It was still cool, but the forecast was for seventies by afternoon. The sun was rising in a cloudless sky, the grass was greener than it'd been the day before, birds chirped and sang and flitted from tree to tree as if they hadn't a care in the world.

Max wished she could say the same.

She'd barely slept, and her cares were becoming too many to track. Somehow, a reporter had found her at the hotel, and somehow that reporter had learned of her involvement in 'preventing yet another school shooting.' Based on the way he'd worded his questions as Max had pushed by him and into the hotel lobby, she'd determined he didn't have any names or even the location of the suspected incident. She had no intention of filling in any of the blanks for him. When the reporter followed her inside the hotel, and when Max spotted Sue at the desk, she'd taken Sue up on her offer of help. Max had been able to duck into the stairwell while Sue had effectively waylaid the reporter.

No updates from or about Reid added to Max's worries. Not that she expected a call, exactly, but she'd hoped for one. Or an email, or a text, or anything from anyone letting her know how Reid was doing.

Ellie had succeeded in adding fuel to the burning question Max already had about why Beck had thrown together a party so quickly.

And on top of everything else, she still hadn't told anyone she was leaving Caston.

The door opened behind her. Bo joined her on the deck, his own cup of coffee in hand.

"Nice morning," he said.

"It is."

They stood side by side, sipping their coffee and watching the birds. A squirrel appeared and dashed up a tree trunk only to scamper back down and do the same on a half dozen more tree trunks. He seemed as confused as Max.

"Are you still planning on going for a run?"

"Yeah. I should get going."

"No rush, just wondered if you wanted to join us for breakfast."

"If you're not in a hurry. I can be ready in an hour if that works."

"That works. Skeeter is making another pot of coffee. He doesn't do anything unless he's had at least three cups, so we've got time."

Max nodded and reached for the door.

"You okay, Max? I heard you up during the night, and you've seemed distracted."

"I'm okay, but I have some news. We'll talk over breakfast."

An hour later, Max, Bo, and Skeeter were in the hotel restaurant, drinking more coffee and eating from the endless buffet. Max had told herself she'd stick to oatmeal and fruit, but somehow the plate in front of her held a made-to-order omelet, two pancakes swimming in maple syrup, and four strips of bacon. She plucked a strawberry from the bowl of fruit that sat alongside her plate, pretending it made up for the rest.

"Skeet decided he's going to drive me back to Alabama. Saves me from getting on another plane, and Skeet gets to see Tack."

Just the mention of Tack Morehouse made Max smile. He had the biggest, softest heart of anyone she'd ever known, but hid it behind salty language he claimed he'd learned as sure as he'd learned how to captain a ship and fire a gun during his stint in the Navy. He was responsible for more than a couple of groundings when she'd tried out some of that language on her father.

"Tack's there? You didn't tell me that. How is he?"

"Same as always. I think this is the third time he's come out of retirement. I don't know why he keeps pretending he'll ever give it up. The day he stops breathing grease and exhaust fumes will be the day he stops breathing."

"Does that mean you're coming out of retirement too, Skeeter?"

"Nah, unlike that old fool, I knew when to call it quits. Maybe I'll talk some sense into him, but I doubt it."

Max's smile grew bigger. Skeeter and Tack were as close as any two people Max knew in her big racing family. When they got together and started telling stories, they always drew a crowd.

"Think you'll stay around Talladega for a while?" Max asked her dad.

"Now that you mention it, I'm thinking about heading back to Darlington."

"Darlington? Really? That's a coincidence."

"How do you mean?"

She had her opening, and she'd promised herself she would tell her dad and Skeeter about her plans. Even so, the words wouldn't come.

"What is it, Max?" her dad asked.

She drew in a breath and spit out the words before she could talk herself out of it. "I'm looking at applying for a job around Darlington for next school year. Then, a year from July, I'm going to Africa for a job."

Her dad tilted his head and studied her through narrowed eyes. Skeeter's mouth twisted as if he wanted to say something, but thought better of it.

"Africa," Bo finally said. "To teach?"

"No, not exactly."

Max explained the job. When she heard herself touting its many positives, and when she stressed how it was something she'd wanted for years rather than a snap decision, she wondered whom it was she was trying to convince.

"It sounds like quite the opportunity. I'm not sure how moving to South Carolina fits in, though," Bo said.

Max tried to read her dad's eyes, but he did a good job of keeping them averted.

"A change of scenery," Max said with forced enthusiasm. "Staying here after what happened at school would be hard. I don't like being recognized, and I don't like being known as the teacher who stopped a school shooter. I prefer anonymity."

Bo nodded. "What about your friends? You three seem close. And what about Beck? I've gotten the feeling there's something there."

Bo's face pinked. They'd never been good at talking about personal stuff. Seemed they still weren't.

"He's got businesses all across Wisconsin now. Who knows how much time he'll spend in Caston? Besides, if we want to see each other, we can. Most people don't hate airplanes the way you do." Max tried to smile, but couldn't quite manage it.

"If that's what you want, then I'm happy for you," Bo said. "Proud of you, too."

"Thanks. Um, I haven't exactly told—"

"I'm sorry to interrupt."

Max looked up to find Sue standing alongside their table.

"Hi, Sue."

"That man is in the lobby again. I can keep him out of the dining room since he doesn't have a reservation, but I can't kick him out of the hotel since he's technically not doing anything wrong. I don't want him to bother you. When you're finished here, give Tasha a wave." Sue pointed to a teenager who was clearing tables. "She'll take you through the kitchen and to the service elevator so you can avoid the lobby."

"What man?" Skeeter and Bo asked at the same time.

"Thank you, Sue. I appreciate it."

"It's nothing," Sue said, with a flick of her wrist. "Enjoy your day and let me know if I can help with anything else."

Sue disappeared just as quickly as she'd appeared. Max gave her dad and Skeeter a quick explanation. Both looked toward the door and out into the lobby, but the reporter was out of view.

"I'm finished if you are," Skeeter said, already getting to his feet while looking over his shoulder.

Her dad was on his feet just as quickly, and the two headed toward Tasha.

Max ate her last bite of bacon, then followed.

Scattered across Beck's yard were people talking and laughing, meeting and catching up. Enjoying themselves. Max watched from the patio, wondering why she wasn't doing any of those things.

Ellie had Beck cornered and was clearly grilling him as only Ellie could. Max didn't have to be close enough to hear the innocent-sounding questions to know they would serve to get every last detail out of Beck. Max considered going to Beck's rescue but decided he was a big boy and he could take care of himself.

In another part of the yard, her dad and Skeeter were talking with Beck's father. Max hadn't known Jim Dawson was going to be at the party, but it turned out to be a nice surprise for her dad and Skeeter, as the three seemed to have no shortage of things to talk about.

Sven and Jake were there, as were several other friends of Beck's, including Tibbs. When Max snuck out to get a peek at his Camaro, she had to shove her hands in her pockets to keep from popping the hood. She hoped if Tibbs took the job with Beck, one of the perks would be that the car would receive the care it deserved.

Nicole had texted Max earlier that afternoon saying she and Brady might be late because Brady had something to take care of on the way to Beck's place. They weren't there yet, so Max didn't have Nicole to serve as a buffer between Beck and Ellie's barrage of questions. Max had just pulled her phone from her pocket to check the time when she spotted Nicole and Brady, hand in hand, coming around the side of the house.

Max lifted her hand and waved. Nicole waved in return, then grabbed Ellie by the arm as she and Brady passed her, and pulled her across the yard toward Max. And Max hadn't even had to ask.

"Welcome," Max said, then wondered at the huge grin on Nicole's face, and the dazed look on Brady's.

"I was talking to Beck, you know," Ellie said when Nicole finally let go of her arm. She smoothed the sleeve of her lightweight pink sweater. "It was a little rude to literally pull me away."

"I have something to tell you. Both of you."

"Your house? The sale is final?" Ellie guessed. "Congratulations."

"No, I mean yes, I think the sale will go through, but that's not it."

"Is it your daddy?" Before Nicole could answer, Ellie looked at Brady. "Oh! News on the Dragonthea movie?"

"El, maybe let her tell us?" Max suggested.

Ellie sniffed but pressed her lips together.

"I...Brady and I...we..." Nicole seemed suddenly nervous.

"I've got this," Brady said, and lifted their joined hands, twisting his wrist to display the diamond on Nicole's finger.

Ellie's squeal stopped conversations from one side of the yard to the other.

"You're engaged!" Ellie stretched onto her tiptoes to wrap her arms around both Nicole and Brady. "I'm so happy for y'all!" Ellie squeezed them both again before easing back and wiping at her teary eyes. "Let me see, let me see," she said, as she reached for Nicole's left hand. She rotated Nicole's hand in one direction, then the other. "Stunning. Simply stunning. Oh, my goodness, isn't this just the best news, Max?"

"It is. Congratulations." Max hugged Nicole because it seemed to be expected, then rather awkwardly did the same with Brady.

"When? How? Tell us!" Ellie said.

"On the way over here, actually," Nicole said, appearing to still be in something of a state of shock.

Some of the glee vanished from Ellie's face. "On the way over here? In the car?" Then she caught herself and smiled wider than ever. "That must have been just the sweetest."

"No, not in the car," Nicole said.

Brady took a step back from the group. "I think I might go find a beer. Is Zeke here?"

Ellie nodded. "Over there, talking with Jake, one of Beck's employees, who, it turns out, went to high school with Zeke. They both played football. Go tell Zeke the news. He'll be so happy for you."

Ellie practically pushed Brady away, then once he was gone, said to Nicole, "Now, tell us the entire story, and don't leave out a thing."

"She might not want to tell us everything," Max said and earned herself a withering look from Ellie.

"I still can hardly believe it," Nicole said. "I was completely surprised. Honestly, Brady gave me no indication that he was planning to ask me."

"Oh, that's the best way," Ellie said. "I have friends who expected it and guessed right down to the day, time, and place. It's still exciting, and special, and beautiful, but I think being surprised is just so much better."

Max didn't think it would be well received if she said she'd suspected Brady was planning to propose, so she stayed silent.

"Last night, when I told Brady about Beck's party, he hesitated for a minute before saying he'd love to go, but asked if we could leave early because he had a stop to make on the way here."

"Ooh, it's already exciting," Ellie said.

"When we left, I asked him where he had to go, and he told me he wanted to check out a spot for a scene in his book. He's never asked me to do something like that with him before, something for research on a book, so I was preoccupied with asking him questions about the story."

"Perfect," Ellie said. "He picked a topic interesting enough to keep you distracted. Very clever."

"Because I was distracted, I didn't give much thought to the fact that we were at Franklin Park until he stopped and parked. We were at the top of the sledding hill."

Ellie sighed and pressed her hands to her heart.

"He said he needed to check the view from the top of the hill so he could get an idea of how far he could see from that height or something like that. Anyway, I still wasn't paying much attention, I was busy trying to figure out how that worked into a story about dragons, when he led me to the spot that, last winter, I'd told him was the starting point for the best route down the hill on a sled."

Max was pretty certain Ellie was holding her breath now. If the story took much longer, Ellie might pass out.

"When I finally took notice, I saw a path down the hill made of rose petals. Hundreds, thousands, of pink rose petals from the spot at the top all the way down to the bottom. Brady took my hand, walked me down the path, and when he stopped he said, 'It was right here that I realized I was in love with you. We'd just crashed spectacularly, I was lying flat on my back, you were asking me if I was okay, and I knew. I almost made a fool out of myself and told you right then and there, but we'd only just met, and I knew you'd think I was crazy.'"

Nicole looked at her hand. "Then, before I knew what was happening, he was down on one knee and holding a ring. The most beautiful, most perfect ring I could ever imagine."

Ellie made all sorts of sighing and cooing noises, and Max thought her friend might actually melt into a puddle. While Max wasn't quite as overcome, she had to admit, it was a pretty spectacular job on Brady's part.

"It is perfect, Nicole. The ring, the proposal, all of it. Perfect." Ellie hugged Nicole again. "I'm so happy for you."

Now Ellie and Nicole were both wiping their eyes. Just as Max wondered how she could either generate some tears of her own or find a reason to make an escape, Beck joined their group.

"I just heard the news." Beck hooked his thumb in the direction of the makeshift bar. "Brady's walking on air over there. I'm happy for you guys."

Beck gave Nicole a one-armed hug.

"Thanks, Beck." Nicole's face was back to looking like it was going to split in two, her smile was so big.

"I asked Sven to go to the liquor store to get some champagne. We'll have a celebratory toast."

Nicole's smile dimmed. "No, Beck, this is your day. It's about you, not us. So, congratulations on growing your business. From what Max told us, it's an incredible step forward."

"Thank you. I'm excited about the possibilities. Tell you what, we'll make it a dual celebration."

Nicole's eyes pleaded for help when they found Max's, but Max just shook her head and said, "I think that sounds like a great idea. There's a lot to celebrate today."

Max figured it was only Nicole's unwillingness to let anything put a damper on her day that had her backing down. Under any other circumstances, Nicole would have slipped into lawyer mode and talked her way into getting what she wanted. Instead, she smiled and nodded.

"Okay, thanks, Beck. And thanks for having us today. This is quite the spread."

"I can't take much credit for that. When I first started negotiating this deal, I went to a friend, Tibbs, for some advice. I commented to him that if it went through, I'd have to throw a party. His wife, Cheri, that's what she does. Plans parties for people."

Beck shrugged as if that made as much sense as Tibbs owning a 2014 Camaro and not taking care of it.

"I guess Tibbs and Cheri had faith in me because things were mostly in place. When I called Tibbs and told him about the deal, he said all I needed to do was give Cheri a date and time, and she'd handle the rest. I bought some beer, but other than that, she did everything."

"She plans parties? All kinds of parties?" Nicole asked.

"I guess."

Nicole scanned the yard. "Which one is she?"

Beck pointed. "Over there. Blue and white shirt. Sven is back. I'm going to check that he got everything. Ladies." Beck tipped an imaginary hat.

"Huh," Nicole said, as she narrowed her eyes at Cheri.

Max could see the wheels turning. Ellie apparently could as well, because she gasped and grabbed Nicole's arm.

"No! I know what you're thinking, Nicole, and no. You cannot turn over everything wedding-related to a party planner! No matter how wonderful, and how capable she may be, you need to do it yourself. That's what makes it all so wonderful. Looking at venues, deciding on colors, taste-testing food and cake, choosing a theme for the decorations, designing bouquets with all your favorite flowers, the music, the layout of the tables, the seating charts. Surely, you don't want to miss out on even one bit of that."

It wasn't Max's wedding, and she was ready to find Cheri and beg her to take over every last detail. If Nicole's dazed look was any indication, she had the same thought.

"I'll help. Max and I will do what brides—"

Ellie's face turned red enough to clash with her pink sweater. "I didn't mean to presume...I don't know what your plans are...I can help with whatever you need help with," Ellie finished and stared at the ground.

Nicole put her finger under Ellie's chin and lifted it so the two were looking at each other. "I want you to be my bridesmaid." She turned and looked at Max. "I want you both to be my bridesmaids. Of course, I do. I was going to go about asking a little differently, but will you? Will you be my bridesmaids?"

Ellie forgot everything else. She bounced in place as she repeated, "Yes, yes, yes."

Max felt queasy. Two weddings? Two times she'd have to look at dresses, attend parties and showers, *plan* parties and showers, smile and say a toaster was the most wonderful toaster she'd ever seen, that the yellow dress with the bow was the most wonderful dress she'd ever seen?

Then it hit her: she wouldn't be around. She wouldn't be around to help with planning and prepping, with parties and presents. She'd be a thousand miles away. Depending when the wedding happened, she might be on the other side of the world.

"Max?"

Max smiled and prayed she looked sincere. "Of course, Nic. Of course."

"Thank you. Both of you. I'm also going to ask my sister-in-law, Jayne, and my friend, Skye. Of course, I don't know if either will be able to do it. Skye's in California and my brother still has over a year on his contract in Japan."

"I'm sure it will all work out," Ellie said when a cloud of concern settled over Nicole.

"I hope so," Nicole said. "Still, dealing with all the details involved in planning a wedding isn't really my thing. I don't think it could hurt to talk to Cheri."

Before Ellie could begin her list of reasons why doing so would be a mistake, Max elbowed Ellie, then nudged Nicole toward Cheri.

"Go," Max said.

"But—" Ellie started after Nicole.

"Let her do her wedding her way." Ellie still looked like she wanted to protest, so Max brought out the big guns. "She doesn't have a mother or sisters to help her. She may not even be able to talk over her plans with her father since she's told us he's getting mixed up more frequently. Her situation isn't the same as yours. If this is how she wants to do it, we need to support her."

Ellie was immediately chagrined. "Oh, my stars. You're right. How could I be so insensitive? Do you think I hurt her feelings? I have to go apologize."

"I think the best thing you can do is listen to what she says after talking with Cheri, then tell her she made the right decision, whatever that decision may be."

"Absolutely. I can do that." Ellie tilted her head and smiled at Max. "Just look at you, knowing all the right things to say when it comes to a wedding. And you acted like you didn't have the first clue."

"I still don't have the first clue when it comes to weddings. I'm simply learning how to better deal with you."

Ellie threw her head back and laughed. "Oh, Max, you say the darnedest things."

Since she hadn't asked recently, Max figured she should. "How are your wedding plans coming?"

"Very well. Thank you for asking."

Max cringed but soldiered on. "Have you decided on the dresses yet?"

"As a matter of fact, I have."

"Oh, yeah? What color?"

"For heaven's sake, don't look so scared. I think you'll be happy. Actually, out of all the girls, the color will suit you best."

"Oh?"

"Yes. Since we've decided the wedding is going to be in the winter," Ellie paused and laughed. "I can hardly believe I said those words. Who would have ever thought I would have a winter wedding? No one, that's who. It was always summer, with everything green and blooming. Or, if that wasn't possible for some reason, fall, with all the beautiful fall colors. But here we are. A December wedding."

"And the dresses?"

"Right, the dresses. Green, Max. A beautiful emerald green that will match your eyes like the color was made for you. With your black hair and your skin tone, you're going to look like a model walking down the aisle." Ellie sighed. "The color will work for Nicole and Hayley, but Char is going to hate it."

Ellie flicked her wrist. "But I can't please everyone, can I? And it's not as if I'm in love with the peachy color I'll be wearing next month for her wedding. Peach with my skin tone? Now that is an atrocity."

"So, green?"

"Yes, Max, green."

"Okay. Good to know."

The two watched Nicole shake hands with Cheri, then lean in and hug her.

"It looks like that went well," Max said.

"Yes, it does, and yes, I'm fine with that."

"When do you think they'll get married?"

"I don't know. I don't think they'll try to squeeze it in before next year, do you?" Ellie looked more distraught than she had at the idea of Nicole using a party planner.

"That would be bad?"

"No, not bad, just quick. Though I suppose if she has someone planning everything, it would be possible." Ellie began chewing on her nail.

"Relax, Oklahoma, she's not going to step all over your wedding."

"I'm not worried. She can do whatever she wants as far as a date, of course."

Since Max couldn't offer any assurance as to what date Nicole would choose, Max decided a change of topic was the safer route.

"Pretty great proposal, right?"

"Amazing proposal. How sweet that Brady took her to the exact spot where he first knew he loved her." Ellie sighed. "I know exactly when and where I first realized I loved Zeke."

Max stopped listening because her eyes locked on Beck's and all she could think was that she knew exactly when she'd fallen in love with him, and the realization hit her with the force of an eighteen-wheeler speeding down a deserted Montana highway.

It wasn't the moment on the dance floor when he'd sung in her ear. It wasn't when he'd taken her to dinner, listened to her talk about her mother, and promised he'd be there for her any time. It wasn't even when she'd learned the truth, that he hadn't spoken with Madison Wilkes, and when she'd realized how wrong she'd been because, deep down, she'd known he'd never do something like that.

No, it was when they were in his truck, and he was driving her home after sitting at the hospital with her for hours. Rather than quiz her on what the nurse had told her as far as caring for her hand, and about the follow-up appointment with the surgeon, he'd made jokes.

Sure, she'd wanted to throw either herself or him from the truck, and yes, she'd cringed with embarrassment when he'd told her in detail how she'd asked him to go to Ellie and Zeke's engagement party with her, but still, that had been the moment. Whether because of the drugs or because she'd been humiliated by his report of her behavior, she hadn't realized it then. Now, though, it was clear.

She was in love with him.

And she was leaving.

They feasted on the spread the caterers provided. They listened as Beck gave more details on his business venture, thanked everyone for being there, then toasted the newly engaged couple. When it got chilly, they gathered around the portable patio heaters that Cheri had thought to have delivered along with the tables and chairs.

The party didn't show any signs of winding down, but Max wanted to do just that. She snuck into the house, away from the crowd, and tucked herself in the corner of the couch in the nearly dark living room.

The job in Rwanda was a dream come true. She wanted the challenge, and she wanted the change of scenery. She wanted to be where no one knew who she was. Where no one knew anything about her.

That evening again, when she'd met Beck's friends, Sven's and Jake's girlfriends, it had been more of the same. The shock they'd tried to hide when it clicked and they realized who she was. The questions they'd asked that she didn't want to answer, and those that they bit their tongues in order to keep from asking. She'd gotten a text an hour ago from Marty warning her that he'd overheard talk about her involvement in preventing another school shooting that afternoon when he'd been at State Patrol headquarters. That told her word would spread sooner rather than later, and that rather than the questions dying out, they'd ramp up again.

If she'd ever been more confused about her life, she didn't know when.

Max closed her eyes and curled up against a pillow. If her dad and Skeeter weren't there and depending on her for a ride back to the hotel, she'd sneak away from the party. She was trying to figure out how to go about telling them it was time to leave when something landed on her legs. Shocked, Max opened her eyes and bolted upright. Two eyes stared back at her.

"Geez, Indie, you scared the heck out of me."

Max patted the dog on the head. It was all the invitation Indie needed. She walked over Max's legs and wiggled and turned until she'd nestled herself against Max's chest. Once Indie settled, Ace jumped up on the couch and tucked himself in the crook of Max's knees, his head resting on her calf.

"Look at you two, not trying to eat me at all. Thanks, guys, I needed this."

Max gave Ace a rub, hugged Indie, then told herself she'd take five minutes to soak in the comfort they seemed determined to provide.

She closed her eyes and was asleep after two.

Later, when voices woke her, it took her a moment to remember where she was. It was much darker outside than it had been when she'd sought refuge in Beck's living room, and Max was forced to acknowledge the possibility existed that she'd slept through a good portion of the party. While lights had been turned on in the kitchen, her couch in the corner of the living room was still hidden in the shadows. Max blinked and tried to get her eyes to focus.

There seemed to be a crowd gathering. The rustling and the clanging, the sounds of cabinet doors opening and closing, told her clean-up was well underway. Feeling guilty, and more than a little embarrassed, Max shifted, trying to get up without disturbing the dogs. A low rumble came from somewhere deep inside Ace, and Indie wiggled until she wedged her head back underneath Max's chin.

"Okay, just another minute," Max whispered.

She rubbed her cheek over Indie's head and ran her fingers over Ace's.

"I can't believe she's still asleep in there," Max heard her dad say.

"You know, I think she's just plain exhausted." This time it was Ellie. "It's been a rough stretch for her, hasn't it? She doesn't want to let on, but ever since that man showed up at school and barged into her room, it's been one thing after another."

"Do you think she's okay?" Bo asked. Max heard a level of concern in his voice she hadn't heard up to that point. Concern he hadn't shared with her.

"I know she will be," Ellie answered. "Your daughter is about the strongest woman I've ever met, and let me tell you, I know some mighty strong women. She doesn't like to ask for help, or to show any weakness, so she's been trying to get through everything that's been thrown at her all on her own. Sometimes when it seems like she's not okay, it only means she needs to lean on someone, just a little bit, and she'll be okay again. We've tried to be there for her, y'all are here now, and that's what she needs. Support that doesn't seem too much like support."

Eavesdropping, even when she was the topic, felt wrong, but Max was too curious to stop them. She knew she ran the risk of hearing something she didn't want to hear, but she also knew she might hear something she'd never otherwise hear.

"I told Max I'm glad she has the both of you," Bo said, and though Max couldn't see, figured he was talking to Ellie and Nicole. "You're right when you say she's not very good about asking for help, but I get the feeling you give it, regardless."

"We try," Nicole said. "Sometimes it's a fight."

Bo chuckled, then even Skeeter joined in. "Our Max likes a fight. She can be stubborn, but it's usually for a good reason."

Finally, Max thought, someone on her side. The next voice Max heard was Beck's.

"Stubborn? That's a fact. Did she tell you she almost didn't let me take her to the hospital when she nearly sliced off her fingers?"

"She didn't tell the story quite that way, but let's say I read between the lines," Bo said.

"We're getting her used to the idea of having friends," Ellie said. "We've introduced her to slumber parties and spas, and she introduced Nicole and me to y'all's world of racing. I imagine she told you about our trip to the race track?"

This time, Max heard both her dad and Skeeter snicker.

"We heard," Bo said.

"Yes, well, it just goes to show that Max has come a long way since I first met her. Nicole, could you ever imagine the Max we met last fall being a bridesmaid in two weddings?"

Max decided maybe eavesdropping on a roast of yourself wasn't such a good idea. She shifted Indie out of the way and started to get to her feet. When she heard her dad, she froze.

"She's going to miss you ladies. Folks always say they'll keep in touch, but that rarely happens. With the weddings, she'll have a reason to come back."

Max didn't breathe. Based on the silence from the kitchen, she wasn't sure anyone else did, either.

"Then she's leaving." There was a sad sort of resignation in Nicole's voice.

Ellie joined in. Instead of resignation, Max heard desperation.

"But she said she'd give it time, that she would put her decision on hold. Whether she'll admit it or not, she made that decision in the heat of the moment, and that's never a good idea. She can't, she just can't go to Africa."

"She just told us. This morning. I, ah, I didn't know it was a secret. She didn't say. Skeet, she didn't say, did she?" Bo stumbled over his words and Max didn't have to see him to know he'd be viciously cracking his knuckles.

Max had to go out there, she had to say something, she had to fix it. But then there was another voice, and this one was flat, devoid of any emotion. All Beck said was, "Africa?"

24

The drive was mostly silent unless tension was factored in, in which case it was as loud as a rock concert. Her dad and Skeeter were staying one more night at the hotel, but Max needed to be alone. Max went inside with them long enough to grab her things. She assured her dad she wasn't upset and was noncommittal when they asked her to join them for breakfast the next day.

Once she was alone and driving back to her apartment, the volume amped up when the replay of what was said in Beck's kitchen sounded over and over inside her head. She'd disappointed every single one of them.

Nicole and Ellie had both mumbled their pseudo-sincere congratulations to try to dispel some of the awkward silence in Beck's kitchen. Max knew they'd expected her to change her mind, especially since she'd worked things out with Beck.

Her dad, though he hadn't said much, clearly felt Max should have told him not to discuss Africa, or South Carolina for that matter, with anyone. And she should have, she'd meant to, but they'd been interrupted at breakfast. Skeeter, who hadn't commented earlier that morning when Max had broken the news, said only five words. Five words to which she hadn't had a reply. 'Thought you'd found your place.'

And Beck was disappointed in the person he felt he knew, and now was certain he didn't.

Max plodded up the steps to her apartment. The cold, lonely space that greeted her felt emptier than any place she'd ever lived. More so even than the spots she'd landed for only a few weeks, or those places where she and her dad had slept on mattresses in the basement of a friend's house, even the rusty trailer without running water where they'd camped one hot summer in Florida. Right now, she'd take any of them over the apartment full of the ghosts of mistakes, missed opportunities, and regrets.

She threw her duffle bag on the bed, then dropped down alongside it. Every bone in her body ached with exhaustion, while every brain cell fired at top speed, trying to find an answer that wasn't there. After she'd stared at the ceiling for two hours, she dug out the sleeping pills she'd been prescribed following the incident at school but had thrown in a drawer and hadn't touched since. She held the bottle in her hand for ten minutes before she gave in and swallowed one.

It was hot and humid, a typical summer day in South Carolina, and Max wondered why she'd been so eager to return to it. She felt the sweat drip from her temples, trickle under her arms, and roll down her chest. She tried to lift her hand to wipe her forehead, but her hand was so heavy the effort proved too much, and she gave up. Instead, she turned her head one way, then the other, but found every movement sent screaming waves of pain from the front of her skull around to the back.

She heard a far-off rumbling, faint but familiar. An engine, but as she listened more closely, she wondered why it started, then stopped, then started again. Someone revving the engine repeatedly, she decided, and wondered who'd be getting an earful for goofing off. With some surprise, Max realized she could feel the vibration as if she were standing next to the car, but she couldn't remember going to the track. And it was dark. She wouldn't be at the track at night, would she?

Then it stopped, and the only sound was her ragged breathing. Even that, she realized, hurt. Every shaky breath that shuddered out of her lungs sent tremors through her body and fired up the jackhammer that seemed to have taken up residence in her skull. When the engine started up again, Max whimpered. Determined to find the source of the noise, she again turned her head, and only then realized her eyes were closed.

With a gargantuan effort, she opened one eye. The blinding sun was like a lightning bolt straight to her brain, and she clamped the eye shut, willing the burning to ease. She waited a minute, then tried again. After several tries, she finally opened her eyes enough to realize she was lying on her bed, in her apartment in Caston, with the sun shining through her tiny window directly into her face. When the noise started again, and she felt the vibrations throughout her head, she slid her hand across the damp sheets until she reached her phone.

Lifting it enough so she could see the screen, she squinted and saw Ellie's name. Not surprised, and definitely not ready, or able, to talk to Ellie or anyone else, she dropped the phone. Once it quit ringing, she lifted it again to check the time. She closed her eyes, blinked three long blinks, and looked again.

"No way," she croaked.

No way it could be one o'clock. If the sun weren't blinding her, she'd be certain it was one in the morning, not one in the afternoon, because that meant she'd been asleep for over twelve hours. She never slept for twelve hours.

The sleeping pill. She remembered taking the sleeping pill. Regretting her decision and vowing to never make the same one again, she tried to sit up. When the entire room spun, she fell back against the pillows, only to have her head split in two. Though it took all her energy to do so, she put one hand on each side of her head, trying to ease the pain. That's when she realized her head not only had likely split in two, but it was on fire. When she tried to swallow, she found the fire had spread to her throat.

"No," she moaned.

Max did not do sick well. She rarely got sick, but when she did, she was a terrible patient. This had been confirmed numerous times by both her dad and Skeeter. She always apologized once she felt better, but if they honestly expected her to eat when her stomach felt like she was riding a rollercoaster, or to drink when her throat had been scraped raw by a pack of vicious wolves, or to answer when they asked her for the thousandth time how she felt, then really they were to blame, not her.

She took inventory. The sheets were indeed sweat-soaked, as was her T-shirt. Her skin hurt everywhere the T-shirt or the sheets touched. Her head was home to a drum line, her throat was probably bleeding, and she felt like she could sleep for twelve more hours if only someone would get her some water. Ice-cold water that she could hopefully somehow swallow, but if that proved impossible, that she could dump over her body to bring her temperature down from boiling.

Slower this time, Max eased herself to sitting, then standing. With one unsteady step after the other, she made her way to the kitchen sink. She opened the faucet to blasting, then while she waited for it to get cold, pulled a glass from the cupboard. Though she was thirsty enough to drink a dozen glassfuls, she had to work up the courage to take a single sip. Even when she filled her mouth with water, she held it there, guessing swallowing was going to hurt like the devil.

She was right, and she knew the icy water had been a mistake. Dumping it, she exchanged it for lukewarm. This time, she pressed her fingers to her throat while swallowing and it seemed to ease the pain, if only a little. She managed a few swallows before giving up. Instead of dumping water over her head, she opted for a cold rag for her forehead. She filled a water bottle, made a stop in the bathroom where she found some ibuprofen, put on a dry T-shirt, then hobbled back to bed where she tried to find a dry spot on the sheets.

Before she could lie down, there was a knock at the door. Since there was no one she wanted to see, she ignored it, but the knocking only intensified.

"Max? You in there?"

Even groaning hurt her throat, but Max couldn't help herself. She knew she couldn't ignore her dad.

"You're sick," Bo said when she opened the door.

He sounded more disappointed than worried.

"Yeah," Max whispered, and when her throat screamed, tried nodding. That hurt worse.

Skeeter stood on the step below her dad. He leaned to look around Bo's shoulder, then frowned at Max. "You don't look good, kiddo."

Rather than responding, Max settled for stepping back and waving them inside. They both took a minute to look around, then in unison, nodded and accepted what they saw.

"Can I get you something to eat? Or drink?" Bo asked.

Max narrowed her eyes and stared him down.

"I guess some things never change." Bo directed his comment to Skeeter who shrugged in reply.

Max waved her hand toward the couch. She took the chair. Since she was suddenly freezing, she wrapped the blanket that hung over the back of the chair around herself to stop the shivering.

"You didn't answer the phone, so we thought we'd say goodbye in person," Bo said. "Thought you were mad about last night, but this is probably why you didn't answer."

"Probably," Max said, then winced.

"Hurts that bad?" Skeeter asked.

Max gave him one nod.

"Used to like ice cream when you had a sore throat," Skeeter said. "Have any?"

This time, it was one shake of the head.

"Could go get some, if you want."

"No, that's okay."

"I don't want to leave you alone when you're feeling this lousy," Bo said.

"I'm fine."

Bo responded with a snort. "You're not, but I know how much you like hovering."

Max raised her eyebrows. It made her think of Beck and his infuriating ability to raise just one. She made herself focus on the hellfire in her throat, as that was less painful.

"Sorry for spilling the beans last night. It didn't dawn on me that you might not have told your friends. They didn't take the news very well, did they?" Bo didn't wait for an answer. "Have you talked with any of them?" He continued his one-sided conversation by answering his own question. "No, of course you haven't. You can barely talk."

The fact that Max was grateful for whatever sort of plague she'd contracted since it meant a reprieve from having to talk to any of them made her question her sanity.

When she watched the looks Bo and Skeeter threw one another, even her fever-addled brain knew something was up. "What?"

"What?" Bo said.

Max was familiar with his avoidance tactics. She was also angry that he made her spell it out when every word made her want to give up talking for good.

"What don't you want to tell me?"

"Nothing. I'm only worried about leaving you when you're sick. I was thinking we should stick around another day or two."

If she hadn't been certain doing so would feel like she'd swallowed glass, Max would have laughed. Her dad's body language made it clear he wanted to do nothing of the sort. She knew how twitchy he got when he was away from cars and a race track for more than a day or two, and he was already on day five.

"Go. Ellie will somehow divine the fact that I'm sick and will smother me."

"I could call her," Bo offered.

Max did the single head shake thing again. "She'll know."

"It was good seeing you."

And just like that, her dad was on his way back to Alabama.

"You too."

"You still thinkin' you'll head to Darlington this summer?" Skeeter asked.

He seemed to regret his words almost before he finished speaking them. Max again wondered at their secrecy, or avoidance, or whatever it was, but she was too tired to put in enough effort to demand an answer from them. Instead, she settled for another nod.

"Should we go get you something before we leave?" Bo asked. "You know you need to be sure you're eating and drinking. Maybe some of them sports drinks you used to like when you were sick."

Orange Gatorade. Had to be orange. The time her dad had forgotten and brought red, Max had thrown a fit. It was a wonder he still spoke to her.

"I'll be fine. Ellie," she repeated, and Bo nodded.

"Then we should probably hit the road. Thinking about stopping in Indy or Bristol on the way, seeing who's around."

Max managed a weak smile. Her dad and Skeeter deserved a trip to catch up with old friends, and they deserved to enjoy themselves instead of worrying about her.

"Tell everyone hi."

"You sure you're gonna be okay?"

"I'm sure, Skeet. I'll call tomorrow and prove it."

"You be sure you do that," her dad said. He leaned over and hugged her. Though it felt kind of awkward, Max held on a second longer than was necessary.

Skeeter patted her on the shoulder. "I'm gonna stop by on my way home. I'll call and let you know when."

"Thanks."

They stumbled over a few more awkward goodbyes, then Bo and Skeeter were out the door and on their way. Max only made it as far as the couch, where she cocooned herself in the blanket and fell into a restless sleep.

When she woke next, it was to more pounding on her door. She had no concept of how long she'd been asleep, so figured it could just as likely be her dad and Skeeter back to tell her something they'd forgotten as it could be anyone else.

The ibuprofen must have kicked in, because it hurt a little less to get up, a little less to swallow. The room spun less when she sat up than it had earlier.

"Max, I know you're in there, I saw both your cars, so you might as well open up because I'm not going anywhere until you do."

There was no way she had the energy to deal with Ellie. It was tough on a good day; sick and operating at maybe ten percent, impossible. Still, she'd learned it was best to get it over with sooner rather than later. Max cracked the door and squinted into the sun.

One peek was all it took for Ellie's expression to change from ready to scold to ready to comfort.

"You're sick. I was afraid that might be the case."

When Ellie took a step forward, Max sighed and pulled the door open wide.

"Why?"

"Because yesterday you alternated between pale and flushed. At first, I thought it was excitement, or maybe nerves, but then you went and fell asleep in the middle of the party." Ellie shrugged as if that explained everything.

Max threw off the blanket because she apparently was back to the sweating portion of the program. She eased onto the couch, then leaned to rest her head on one pillow and used the other to fan herself.

"Oh, dear." Ellie put the back of her hand against Max's forehead, then repeated, louder, "Oh, dear."

"That bad?"

"Have you taken your temperature?"

"No."

"Do you have a thermometer?"

"No."

"Do you want me to ask Zeke to come over and check on you?"

"No."

"Have you eaten?"

"No."

"Maaax," Ellie said in her best, bossy voice.

"Can't. Hurts."

"How about drinking? You need to get enough fluids when you have a fever."

"Hurts."

"Okay, then this is what you're going to do. You'll eat soup. You'll drink. You'll rest. It appears you're feeling warm right now?"

Max nodded once.

"And I would imagine a short time ago, you were freezing like you were standing outside during a Wisconsin blizzard."

Another nod.

"Right. When you're sweating, you'll drink something cool. When you're shivering, something hot. Do you have any tea?"

"Let's save ourselves time and assume the answer to all your questions is going to be no." Max had to massage her throat, but the pain was worth it when she got an eye roll from Ellie.

"Then I'll go to the store. Honey lemon tea, with some real honey to add to it. That will help your throat. What about something cold? Do you have a preference?"

"Orange Gatorade."

"Aw, isn't that sweet? That's the same thing Coltie likes when he's sick." Ellie patted Max on the head like she would a small child. "What about your medicine cabinet? Do you have any throat lozenges? Aspirin or ibuprofen?"

"Had some. Gone."

"You know what? I'll just buy everything."

Ellie went to the kitchen sink and turned on the tap. Max closed her eyes while Ellie banged around, opening and closing doors. In the couple of minutes Ellie was out of sight, Max dozed off. Her eyes fluttered open when Ellie was once again standing in front of the couch.

"Here. Drink some water. Then go over to the sink and gargle with the warm salt water I left there for you."

Max crinkled her nose. "No."

"Yes. It will help. Are you going to be okay while I dash to the store?"

Max nodded. "Can I expect Nic to bang on the door in a few minutes?"

"No, I talked with her earlier and convinced her you were okay. I confess, I told a little white lie and said that I had spoken to you and that there was nothing to worry about."

Max raised her eyebrows.

"She got engaged yesterday. I remember that feeling, and I want her to hold on to it, and enjoy it, for as long as possible. Today she should think of nothing but the fact that she's going to marry the man she loves."

"Nice of you," Max croaked and meant it. "You don't have to be here either."

Ellie clicked her tongue. "I do. I'll be back as soon as possible. One last chance if you have any requests."

If Ellie was going to make her eat, Max figured she may as well enjoy it. "Strawberry ice cream and macaroni and cheese. And no celery in the soup."

Ellie tilted her head and smiled at Max. "Bless your heart. You and Colt could be best friends."

By Monday evening, Max felt better. The fever was gone, and she could swallow without wanting to cry. Since Ellie had forced Max into a trip to urgent care the previous afternoon, strep had been ruled out, meaning Max could go back to work as soon as she was fever-free for twenty-four hours. Max wanted to round up and go back on Tuesday, but Ellie, in typical Ellie fashion, had served as the go-between and given Amanda all the details. Max would return to school on Wednesday.

She'd spoken with her dad and Skeeter and had been relieved to learn neither of them was sick. She knew Beck had also avoided the bug, but only because Ellie had spoken with him.

He'd called on Sunday while Ellie was making soup. Max had been sleeping and never heard her phone, but Ellie had answered, filled in Beck on Max's situation, and learned he and Tibbs were leaving that evening to tour the newly acquired businesses. They'd be gone until Wednesday.

Since she'd had plenty of time to think, Max had spent a fair amount of time debating whether she would have answered Beck's call and, if so, what she would have said. She still had no answer. He'd texted wishing her a speedy recovery, but had said nothing else.

Max felt like she was right back where she'd been a few days ago. She and Beck were at odds, the people she cared about most were disappointed in her, and she didn't know how to fix any of it.

Since she'd finally reached a point where she couldn't sleep anymore, she needed a distraction. She opened her computer, thinking perhaps her sub had emailed with questions or comments. Within the lengthy list of emails, most of which she could scan and delete, she found a short note from her sub reporting that things had gone well. She opened and read a couple more, then one from Reid's mother caught her by surprise.

Ms. Simmons,

I'm sorry I haven't been in touch sooner, but please know my negligence in no way diminishes the amount of gratitude both my husband and I have for the way in which you responded and helped Reid. I hope that soon we will have a chance to speak face to face and fill one another in on more of the details surrounding what happened last week.

Until then, I have a favor to ask of you. Please be assured that Reid is unaware I am contacting you, so if my request is something with which you are not comfortable, Reid will never know I asked.

Would you be willing to speak with Reid before he goes back to school? We are looking at Wednesday as his first day back. The past five days have been challenging for him, but he has handled the questioning by Caston police and a detective from Denver as well as we could have hoped.

Max stopped reading. She supposed it made sense that someone from Colorado would want to speak with Reid, but she hadn't known it had already happened. She remembered what it had been like for her, the relentless questions that, even though those doing the questioning had tried to be considerate, brought back every detail, every minute, every fear. She remembered how she'd wanted to beg them to stop asking the same questions over and over, and let her try to forget. Instead, she'd done her best to answer every question, look at the situation from every possible angle, and try to do her part to ensure justice would be served.

But Reid was only thirteen.

Still, he's nervous about his return to school now that it seems the news has leaked locally. He doesn't know what to expect from his classmates or from his teachers.

My husband and I thought that perhaps you would have some insight for him, some wisdom, some words that we don't have since we've never been in his place. Or yours.

If you're not comfortable speaking with him, I understand completely. If you would be willing to speak with him, I can arrange to meet you wherever and whenever it is convenient for you.

Thank you for your consideration, and thank you again for all you did for Reid.

Max read one line again. *The news has leaked locally.* She hadn't watched TV or looked at any news online for the past two days. She'd suspected after encountering the reporter at the hotel, but she hadn't given it much thought since.

Max didn't hesitate. She typed out a reply to Reid's mother, offering to meet the next day. She may have screwed up everything with Beck and with her friends, but she still had a chance to do the right thing with Reid.

* * *

Max had suggested they meet at the lake, thinking it would be better than sitting at a restaurant staring at each other across a table. The trail that wound around the lake meant they could walk. The ducks and the geese that called the lake home could provide a distraction. As could the playground. Who didn't like to swing? And if all else failed, and Reid was still uncomfortable, Max had an ace in her pocket. Or rather, at the end of a leash.

It was a sunny day with only the gentlest breeze. The beautiful day worked wonders in helping Max shake off the lingering aches and general sluggishness the virus had left her with. Max checked the time and, with only a few minutes until Reid and his mother were scheduled to arrive, coaxed Luna back toward the parking lot.

Nicole had been more than happy to let Max take Luna out during the day. Max hadn't shared the details, had only said she felt like getting outside since the forecast looked good, and she owed Luna a walk.

Luna was thrilled with the idea. She wasn't as thrilled with the leash, which she repeatedly tried to bite as Max tried to walk the pup along the path, but they were slowly coming to an understanding.

Nerves knotted in Max's stomach when she saw a shiny, black BMW pull into the lot, park, and Reid get out. She'd rehearsed some things to say to Reid, but depending on his state of mind and how their conversation went, knew she may be on the wrong track entirely.

Max recognized Reid's mother, Betsy, from conferences earlier in the year. She was impeccably groomed, stylishly dressed, and carried herself with the same confidence Max remembered from their earlier meeting, but Max sensed Betsy's unease and worry, even from a distance. She glanced repeatedly between her son and Max as if unsure she'd made the right decision.

Max lifted her hand in a greeting. At her side, Luna wiggled and strained against the leash as Reid got closer. As Max had hoped, Reid's face lit up and he hurried forward, dropping to his knees and playing with Luna.

"Hello, Ms. Simmons."

Betsy held out her hand, and Max shook it.

"Hello. Hi, Reid."

Reid glanced up only long enough to utter, "Hi," then returned his focus to Luna

"That's Luna."

"Is she yours?"

"No, she belongs to a friend."

"Thank you again for agreeing to meet us," Betsy said, and again cast a tense glance at Reid.

"Happy to do it," Max said.

When Reid paid no attention to either Max or his mother, Max motioned with a nod toward the path. Betsy nodded her agreement.

"Want to walk Luna with me, Reid?"

"Can I, Mom?"

"Sure. I'll wait right here." Betsy pointed toward a picnic table just off the path.

"Okay."

Max handed Reid the leash, and the two began walking.

Reid glanced over his shoulder. "My mom thinks I should talk to you."

"She told me."

Reid asked a few questions about the dog. Max reminded him to hold tight to the leash when a squirrel scampered across the path. They were a quarter mile into the walk before Reid took his eyes off Luna.

"Why aren't you at school today?"

"I had some sort of virus. Knocked me out for a couple of days. I'm going back tomorrow."

"Me too, I guess."

He didn't sound thrilled with the idea, but he did sound like he wanted to talk. Max relaxed some, thinking that, for once, things might be easier than she'd expected.

"You don't want to?"

"I don't know. Not really."

"Why not?"

Reid looked up at Max. "You probably know why not."

"The attention? The questions?"

"Yeah."

"I didn't like that part either. Still don't."

"What am I supposed to tell people?"

"Only what you want. There's no rule that says you have to answer questions you don't want to answer or give any more information than you're comfortable giving."

"Except with the police."

"Well, yes, except with the police. Did they ask you the same questions about a hundred times?"

"Yeah. They tried to ask them different ways, but it was still the

321

same questions."

"That seems to be how they do things. Kind of drove me crazy."

Reid nodded, then got quiet. Max, determined to let him set the pace, followed suit and pressed her lips tight.

They'd walked for a few minutes before Reid asked, "What am I supposed to say when people ask me how I knew what to do?"

"What do you mean?"

"Like, everyone seems to think I did this really great thing. That I took all the right steps, in just the right order, and stopped a kid from doing something horrible."

Reid stopped and when he looked up at Max, she saw him losing the battle against the tears. "I don't know if I did the right thing. I don't know how to answer their questions because I don't know that I made the right decisions. Like what if I would have said something earlier? What if I would have told someone this kid was on that website and saying some scary stuff? Could I have kept him from even getting out of his house with a gun? That would have been better than the way it happened. Could I have done something that would have meant someone would have helped him? And I could just as easily have waited too long, and he could've made it all the way to school before the police caught him. Then it would have been my fault for not acting fast enough. I feel like people are treating me like I'm some kind of hero, and I'm not! All I did was disobey my parents, go on some sketchy website, and then finally call you when I got really scared. That's not stuff a hero does, that's stuff that a screw-up does."

When Reid finally paused, his face was blotchy, he was trembling, and he was gasping for breath. And Max was afraid she was in way over her head.

Max took a breath and gave herself a minute before responding. It was uncanny listening to him. He'd told her, at times word for word, what she'd been telling Dr. Mallick, Beck, her friends, anyone who insisted she talk. Their experiences, though different, were still very similar. And that meant she knew how he felt, and she realized seeing him hurt was far worse than any hurt of her own. Unsure if she was doing the right thing, she reached out an arm. Reid hesitated, but then let her hug him.

"You know, I could stand here and tell you that you are a hero, that you did all the right things, that you handled the situation as if you'd followed a guidebook, but we both know that's a bunch of bull. You reacted. You didn't plan it. If you had to do it again, you don't know if you'd do it the same way, or if you'd be able to do anything at all. And that's okay."

Reid took a deep, shuddering breath, then pulled away. He looked at her with a mixture of curiosity and what she thought might be gratitude. Or relief.

"I get it, Reid, because I felt—I feel—exactly the same way. When people insist on calling me a hero, I want to scream."

"Really?"

"Really."

"But you talked to us. In school. It seemed like you knew what you were talking about when you told our class about doing the right thing, and being brave, and saying something if you see something. "

"Yeah, I guess I did, but that doesn't mean I think I did everything right."

Reid took a minute to pet Luna, burying his face in her fur, then started walking again. Max followed.

"I think because you'd been through it, when you told us to speak up, to say something, it meant more. We'd heard that before, all the stuff parents and teachers have been telling us since we were little kids, but I don't think most kids listened until you said it."

"I'm glad you think it helped, but I don't know that I did anything special."

"It helped me do what I did."

The way he said it, more simply, more matter-of-fact than all the other things people had said to her, hit her harder than all the fancy words she'd heard over the past months. The conversation was turning into a lot more than Max had bargained for. She'd hoped to help Reid, and maybe she was, but she found herself thinking he was helping her more than she was helping him.

"If I could do it, then you can do it. Even if you don't feel like it's one hundred percent true, all the things people are saying, try to understand that they mean it, and to them, it is true. Hero means different things to different people. To those that you directly helped, you are a hero, Reid."

Max made a mental note to thank Dr. Mallick because she was pretty sure she'd just plagiarized him.

"Have you talked with a therapist?" Max asked.

"Yeah. My mom and dad made me. I didn't want to, I told them I didn't need to, but they made me. I have to go again on Friday."

Max ordered herself not to grin. "I didn't want to either but it helps.

It might not seem like it, and you might feel uncomfortable, but it helps."

Reid nodded. They wandered along the path, both watching Luna jump and snap at a fly that followed her, until Reid stopped. He stared at the lake for a while, watched as a pair of ducks flew overhead, then corralled Luna and wrestled with her. Max waited. She'd learned to read the signals from him, and there was more he wanted to tell her, but he hadn't worked up the nerve.

"Do you think they'll listen to me?"

"Who?"

"Kids at school."

Max wasn't sure where he was headed. "About what?"

He took a breath, and the words came in a rush. "I was thinking that I should, like, do more. Like I should try to explain to other kids that sometimes telling is the right thing to do."

"I think that's a good idea and a brave thing to do. Do you want to talk to our class? Whenever you're ready?"

"Maybe, but…"

His cheeks flushed, and he looked down at Luna. Max was glad she'd brought along a distraction.

He kept his eyes down and said, "I thought maybe a video. I could post it online. Probably no one would watch, but even if one kid did, and if that kid then did the right thing, it would be worth it. Kids at school would probably make fun of me, but I decided I don't really care."

Now Max was the one who had to look down at Luna. Reid was braver than she was, Max realized with no small amount of shame. A thirteen-year-old boy, only days removed from his harrowing ordeal, was already searching for ways to put his experience to use, to help others. What had she done? She'd hidden, she'd felt sorry for herself, and she'd run.

When she looked up, she realized Reid was watching her, waiting for a response. Knowing kids could spot a phony a mile away, Max hoped they could also recognize sincerity.

"Reid, I think that is probably the most amazing idea I have ever heard. I don't think it would be possible for me to be prouder of you."

A sort of renewed energy followed Max home from her talk with Reid. Sure, her list of problems she had to deal with and messes she had to clean up was lengthy, but they no longer seemed as overwhelming.

She may not have all the solutions, but she felt like they might be within reach. Her goal had been to help Reid, and she thought she had, but she knew without a doubt that he'd helped her.

Reid had echoed things others had been telling her for months, but hearing the words from a thirteen-year-old made them more believable. Though Reid was a good kid, and a considerate one, he had no vested interest in trying to make her feel better, or in trying to make sure he said all the right things. He simply spoke his mind, and by doing so, opened Max's eyes.

While she prepped for the next day and the eleven that followed until they reached the end of the school year, while she tidied her apartment, while she scanned online news sites for what details she could find about the incident in Colorado and any mention of Reid, while her mind was on any number of things, in one small corner of her brain, an idea was growing.

Max knew better than to focus too hard on it. If she sat down and planned, or researched, or put too much thought into it, she'd either talk herself out of it, or she'd let it bog her down. Instead, she kept her mind busy with anything else, and let the idea take root.

Still not a hundred percent, Max found she was tired much earlier than what she'd normally consider bedtime. Deciding that listening to her body was the smart thing to do, she showered and got ready for bed. It wasn't until she searched for her favorite moisturizer and came up empty that she remembered she'd tossed the duffle bag she'd had with her at the hotel in the closet without unpacking it.

She retrieved the bag, tossed the dirty clothes in the laundry basket, and found her moisturizer. Before she folded the duffle to tuck it back on the closet shelf, she checked the outside pocket.

Max was proud of herself when the letter didn't rock her the way it would have a month ago, or even a day ago. She was proud that, unlike the note she'd found on her table after her mother left following their first visit in Max's apartment, the sight of this one didn't drop her to her knees. Still, she wondered how after so many years, the slant of her mother's writing, the way Victoria added a loop when she wrote the capital M in Max, was still like a knife to Max's heart.

With the letter in her hand, and her hand hovering over the waste basket, Max reconsidered. If she read it, she could put it behind her, once and for all. If she didn't read it, she may always wonder. Something had made her pluck it from the hotel room trash. Some part of her, she supposed, was curious.

Max sat on the couch and when she wrapped herself in a blanket before opening the envelope, knew very well she was doing it to try to somehow shield herself from whatever was inside. Telling herself there was nothing that said she had to read the whole thing, that if she didn't like what she read, all she had to do was tear it up and throw it away, Max started reading.

Max,

After what happened, I know my words won't mean anything to you, but I have to tell you I'm sorry. I'm sorry for what I did, and I'm sorry I hurt you.

I was never as brave as you, Max. I've watched you over the past few weeks, and you are so very brave. Not just what you did at school, but what you do every day. The way you fight for what you think is right. The way you protect those around you. The way you go after what you want. No, I was never that brave, and I never will be. All my life, I depended on my looks, or on the man I was with to get what I wanted. Now, my looks are only a memory, and I've burned too many bridges to have any of the men I once cared about care about me.

It's no excuse, but all I can say is I was desperate. I foolishly thought that if I could have just one more chance, if I could get myself back in front of a camera, someone would see me, and remember me. I was full of such delusions of grandeur that when I first spoke with a rep at the network, I asked for a professional copy of my interview. I had it all figured out. I'd send it to an old friend—at least he used to be a friend—who makes documentaries to prove how I've changed and that I could do serious roles. It would be a new start for me.

Clearly, I was a fool, and clearly, I made a horrible mistake.

I swear to you I tried to undo what I'd done, but it was too late. I refused to appear live in their story, but I'd already signed a release for them to use what they recorded, and what I'd already told them. Oh, how I wish I could take it all back.

The only silver lining to come out of all of this is that I got to spend some time getting to know you. I know, it's something I should have done years ago, but I will always be grateful that I got to do it, and even if it was too late, I will hold on to my memories of the time I had with you.

And what memories they are! You have made a home for yourself, Max. That's something I didn't know if you'd ever be able to do growing up the way you did. It worried me that like me, and like your father, you'd never be able to settle in one place and be happy there, but it was clear to me that's exactly what you've done. You've made friends, you love your job, you have Beck in your life, and you're happy. You're content.

I don't know if you've realized it, but you refer to Caston and your apartment as home. Not always, but the times when you let your guard down, when you were relaxed and we were chatting about everyday things, you used that word. Home.

To most people, home is a word that's used indiscriminately to describe wherever they may be resting their heads, but I can almost guarantee it's not a word you used growing up. Your father never had a place to call home. He never referred to anywhere we stayed as home. He tried after you were born, but I ruined that and afterward, he never settled anywhere for long. Hearing you use the word means you've found home, and more than anything else, that's what I want for you. I want you to know the sort of life where you have a place to call home.

That doesn't mean you can't have adventures. You can, and you will. That's as much a part of you as the motor oil I sometimes think runs through your father's veins, and therefore, through yours. Yes, you'll have adventures, but you will have home.

Again, I am so very sorry that I screwed things up so horribly, but I'm also so very happy that I got to know you, if only a little.

Be happy, be brave, be home.

Because she didn't know what to think, and because she didn't want to try to figure it out, Max folded the letter, slid it back into the envelope, and tucked it into a drawer. Then she went to bed, exhausted. She closed her eyes and tried to turn off her brain, but it refused to cooperate, and that beginning of an idea started to grow.

25

Kids jumped and shouted and hugged their friends. Papers fluttered and littered the hallway. Shrieks pierced her eardrums while at the same time a booming, deep bass pounded as if it was coming from inside her. It was the last day of school, the last minutes of school, and it was a free-for-all.

Max knew she was supposed to try to maintain some semblance of control, but she didn't have it in her to correct or reprimand or otherwise put a damper on the pure joy that was the start of summer vacation. Let them run, let them blast their music, let them be kids, she thought, then her practical side took over, and she prayed no one got hurt.

"Bye, Ms. Simmons!" Jace waved at Max as he ran past. He jumped on the back of his best friend, who then carried Jace, piggyback, down the hall.

"Bye, Jace," Max said to his back.

"Have a good summer, Ms. Simmons!" Kenzie's and MacKenzie's voices sounded in unison.

"You too."

Gradually, the volume dropped, the sea of bodies dwindled to a trickle, and the discarded papers settled. Max took a deep breath, then let it out slowly. It was an odd experience. Nine months ago, she'd longed for this day. Now, she had pangs of regret, of loss even, thinking that her time with the group of students she'd come to know and care about was over. They'd move on, she'd move on, and their time together would be nothing but a memory. A good memory for them, she hoped, but one she knew would fade as they moved on to new adventures.

Max didn't need the eyes in the back of her head to know Ellie and Nicole were coming up behind her. She turned and braced herself for the barrage.

"I cannot believe you didn't tell us." Ellie had her hands on her hips and a frown on her face. "I can't believe Amanda didn't tell me. I was in charge of the assembly, after all."

"I asked her not to say anything."

Ellie acted as though Max hadn't spoken. "When she said she needed some time for a special presentation, I thought, well, I don't know what I thought, but I certainly didn't expect that!"

"I thought you liked surprises, Oklahoma."

"I do. Usually." Ellie's expression softened. "Oh, you're right, I do like surprises, and this was an incredible one. I'm so proud of you, Max. Still, a heads-up wouldn't have been the worst thing."

"I'm proud too. And surprised. I wouldn't have expected you to agree to something like that," Nicole said.

Max waved them into her room and pointed them toward desks. Like so many times before, Max thought. The three of them gathering after school to rehash their days, to share their triumphs, their frustrations, and their fears. Max knew she wouldn't have made it through the year without the two of them, even if Albert Quinn hadn't barged into her classroom with a gun. She was grateful to Ellie and to Nicole, and she knew without a doubt they'd stay friends, no matter what. But she couldn't think about that.

"I didn't agree, at first," Max said. "Amanda approached me with the idea a couple of months ago, and I refused. Not really my thing, you know, being in the spotlight."

"We know," Ellie said. "But you changed your mind."

Max nodded. "Reid, and all that happened with him, made me change my mind."

"And now Reid St. Martin is the recipient of the first-ever Max Simmons Award for Bravery," Nicole said. "It has a nice ring to it."

It still felt odd, still sounded odd, having her name attached to an award, but she'd been determined to have Reid recognized for what he'd done. Word had spread over the past ten days and most everyone heard some version of the story, but Max wanted the details, and Reid's part, clarified. Reid had balked, the same way Max had balked at the idea of the award, but when Max explained the other part of her plan and what it would mean if he agreed to that, the award hadn't seemed like such a big deal.

"I tried to get them to call it the Caston Middle School Award, or something like that. I was overruled."

"It's perfect the way it is," Ellie said. "I've got to say, you could have knocked me over with a feather when Amanda called you up to the microphone, and especially when you walked up there! I thought maybe she'd sprung a surprise on you, but when I saw how confident you looked, I knew something was up. I thought maybe you were going to explain that you're leaving Caston."

Max decided to ignore that for the moment. "I'm not great at speaking in front of people. I hope I didn't sound too nervous. Or ridiculous."

"You sounded confident," Nicole said. "Anyone listening knew without a doubt that you believed in what you were saying. The kids were squirrelly, summer vacation was starting in only minutes, but they paid attention to what you said about Reid. It made an impression, even if it didn't seem like it."

"The kids always listen to you, Max. They're going to miss you next year. Everyone is going to miss you next year."

Again, Max ignored Ellie.

"Reid did a great job, didn't he? If there's a silver lining to come out of his experience, it's that he's gained so much self-confidence. He went from being shy and hardly willing to speak in class to standing up in front of the entire school and encouraging them to be brave in whatever sort of situation they might find themselves."

"You made such an impression on him," Ellie said. "That's why he was able to do what he did. I guess next year it will be students in South Carolina that will benefit from all you have to give."

Nicole whispered a one-word warning. "Ellie…" Ellie fell back in her chair and crossed her arms over her chest.

"I guess Amanda is having a permanent plaque made that will be displayed outside the office, and each year, she'll add the name of the student who gets the award. The students will get a smaller version to keep for themselves."

"Too bad you won't be here to see it," Ellie muttered.

"So I was thinking, if all goes according to plan and the video happens, we could show it at the fall kick-off assembly. Reid will get his plaque, and we can talk about what went into making the video, and what we hope it accomplishes."

"Remember the assembly when you thought volunteering for the dunk tank was a good idea?" Ellie laughed, but it sounded hollow. "I wonder who will volunteer next year?"

"Ellie, are you listening to Max, or do you have your replies planned out ahead of time and ready to go?"

Max thought Nicole might have learned a thing or two from Ellie, as her voice held the same sort of scolding that Ellie's often did.

"I heard her," Ellie said. "She said they'd show a video at the assembly, Reid would get his plaque, then something about telling what went into making—" Ellie stopped, and a hopeful, yet guarded, excitement sparkled in her eyes. "We?"

"Yes. Reid and me."

"But you're leaving. How can you and Reid—"

Nicole interrupted Ellie. "You're staying?"

"I'm staying."

Ellie stayed in her chair just long enough to gasp, then she flung herself at Max. "Really? You're really staying? You're not just saying that so you can make a getaway without a teary goodbye?"

"No, but that would have been a good idea."

Max felt another set of arms go around her. "I'm glad, Max," Nicole said. "I'm so glad. I was trying to be supportive because I promised I would be, but it's been hard. You belong here. Ellie and I knew that all along. What made you realize it?"

Max gave both of them a squeeze before easing out of the group hug.

"It's kind of a long story. Are you sure you want to hear it?"

"Of course, we're sure," Ellie said. Nicole nodded her agreement.

"Okay, then. It was a lot of things that separately might not have meant much, or enough, but together, seemed like too much of a sign to ignore."

The way in which Ellie and Nicole sat, waiting to hear more of Max's story, was exactly what she would have expected, Max realized, had she given it any thought. The two women who had become the best friends she'd ever had were so different, yet both so perfect.

Nicole had her legs stretched straight, her shoulders were relaxed, and she smiled easily. She looked relieved, probably that she wouldn't have to deploy the ammunition she'd stockpiled and had at the ready in a last-ditch effort to persuade Max to stay. And Max knew that ammunition would have been well-researched, and vast.

Ellie looked as tightly wound as a clock. Her hands were folded in her lap, but her fingers tapped unceasingly. Ellie's lips were pressed so tightly together they'd turned white. Max knew that Ellie, too, had plenty to say, but unlike Nicole, there was no way Ellie would be content to keep silent.

Max loved them both like sisters.

"It was Reid that first made me reconsider. When I talked to him that day at the lake, I was blown away by how he'd come to terms with what he'd been through, and how he had already decided he wanted to try to make something good come of it. He was so much braver than I was. When I wanted to hide and run away, he wanted to put his face out there for everyone to see, his words out there for everyone to hear.

"Then, believe it or not, it was my mom."

At that, Ellie's hands grasped the edge of the desk, she sat as straight as an arrow, and it became impossible for her to stay quiet.

"You talked to her? When? Why didn't you tell us you were going to do that? We would have been there for you."

"I know, and thank you, but no, I haven't talked to her. I read a letter she wrote shortly after she left Caston. She sent it to my dad, and he gave it to me when he was here. I didn't plan on ever reading it, but…" Max shrugged.

"She said a lot of things I'm not yet ready to deal with, but in between all of that, she said some things that struck a chord. Things I wasn't able to ignore. She said the thing she was happiest about after spending time with me was that I'd found a place to call home."

A satisfied "Hmm" escaped from Ellie's pinched lips.

"I may not be ready to forgive Victoria, but I do have to admit that until I read her words, I didn't realize that they were true. The idea of home might not sound like much to either of you, but it's different for me. I've never had a place that I've called home. Ever. Now, it seems like I finally have one, and since that's the case, it seems kind of stupid to leave."

This time it was Nicole who interrupted.

"Then I guess I have to be grateful to Victoria. That's hard because of the way she hurt you, but I can put some of that behind me and focus on how she helped you. Do you think you'll get in touch with her?"

"That's the next part of my story. The video I mentioned? That was Reid's idea initially. When we spoke, he said that he wanted to do something to try to help other kids who might find themselves in a situation where they have to speak up. He talked about making a video and posting it on social media, despite the teasing he figured would come with it. I was already so proud of him, but that just about floored me.

"My mother made an off-hand comment in her letter about a producer she knows, and I took Reid's idea and built on it. I want to turn his story, and my story, into more than just a video. I want it to be a documentary. I may be dreaming, but I'm going to try. I'm going to ask Victoria to put me in touch with this producer and see if he will consider making a film out of our stories. It would be a public service kind of video. We can't pay him, but hopefully he sees it as a goodwill sort of thing and something that might get him some publicity."

"Oh, my stars!" Ellie said. "Max, that's incredible."

"It's just an idea at this point. I hope it works, I'll do my best to make it work, but it's still a long shot."

"Ellie's right. That's incredible. Telling your stories, your way, you'll make a difference."

Nicole reached for her hair and twirled it around her finger. She pulled her lip between her teeth. Max knew better than to interrupt.

"I'm going to talk to Brady. If things don't work out with the person your mother knows, maybe he can talk with the people who want to make his movie. If they're not the right people for the job, maybe they can point us in the right direction. One way or another, we're going to get this done."

"Daddy has a colleague who's an entertainment lawyer. I can get in touch with her if we need her help."

Us. We. Just like that, she wasn't alone in her endeavor, but part of a team. And just like that, Max was certain that team would get the job done. Her gratitude threatened to overwhelm her.

"I don't know what to say. I didn't tell you expecting your help."

"Max, you—"

Max held up a finger to stop Ellie. "But, thank you. That's the correct thing to say, right?"

Ellie smiled and nodded.

"There's another reason—or two reasons—I'm staying in Caston. You know I never had real friends before coming here. I didn't even know how to be a friend, at least not the sort of friends you both are. You were patient with me, you showed me things and introduced me to things that I'd never had, and against my better judgment, it seems I've decided I like the idea of girlfriends. Somehow, I lucked out and got the best on my first try. I figured I'd better stick around because I'm sure I'd never get that lucky again."

Tears glistened on Ellie's cheeks. Nicole used a finger to dab at her eyes.

"We've come a long way, haven't we?" Max asked. "Remember those first few days when we all wanted to run? That first happy hour when El made us list three positives from our week and it was so hard? All the times when we were certain we were doing everything wrong? I never would have made it without the two of you."

"And look at us now," Nicole said. "Ellie, you've become everyone's favorite teacher, and have become a one-woman entertainment committee handling everything from the assemblies to the spring dance to getting matching T-shirts ordered for the staff."

"Oh, that stuff is easy. What about you? That Ellis Island Day you organized? The kids are still talking about it. And you're so good with them, one on one. Look what you did for Katie. You don't talk about it, but I know you were coming in early at least once a week to give some of your students extra help."

Nicole shrugged off the praise. "It wasn't much, just a few minutes here and there. Nothing like Max. Stopped a school shooter, got an award named after her, and is probably going to end up becoming a movie star. We pale in comparison."

"Knock it off," Max said. "How about we agree that we've all done more than we ever thought we could do?"

"Agreed," Ellie said.

"Agreed," Nicole said.

Memories played through Max's mind like a movie on fast-forward. The orientation when they'd met, the slumber party at Ellie's, the nights at Scooter's, the pizzas they'd shared when they'd worked hours after the last bell, the weekend at the spa, the afternoon at the race track. The laughs, the tears, the support, the friendship. Max had no idea why she'd ever thought she should leave.

She marveled at the fate that put them all in the same place at the same time, but then her heart gave a little lurch. What if, after finally making the decision to stay, her friends decided to leave? There were things that could easily take one or both of them away from Caston. She wanted to ignore the questions and simply enjoy the feeling of accomplishment at what they'd done, and relief at the long summer ahead, but she had to know.

"Do you ever think about going back to Oklahoma?" she asked Ellie.

Ellie tipped her head and gazed upward. "I'd be lying if I said it never crossed my mind, but, Max, you hit the nail on the head when you said this seems so right. Y'all are here, Zeke is here, and I'm happy here. I never expected this would be where I'd land, but it's become home. The perfect home. And if Caston turns out people like Nicole and Zeke, two of the most amazing people I know, then I'd be plumb crazy not to want to raise my kids here."

Max nodded her agreement while Nicole blushed and shook her head.

"And Nicole?" Max said. "Now that your dad is settled, do you think about finishing law school?"

"Actually," Nicole said, and the little lurch in Max's heart turned to a thud. "I told you that the district superintendent is a friend of my dad's. Out of the blue, he called me a few days ago and asked me about my plans for the future. He knows I left law school to come home, and he asked if I had plans to return. Long story short, he said that I'd have the backing of the district if I chose to do so. He talked about a reduced teaching schedule if I chose to take online classes to finish my degree, and he also said that the district is going to be looking to hire a lawyer in the next few years. He said he'd like to talk more to me about it after I've had time to think things over."

"Nicole, that sounds like the ideal scenario," Ellie said. "How do you feel about it?"

"It's a lot to consider. I mentioned it to Brady. Like you, he thinks it sounds ideal, so we'll see. I'd more or less given up on the idea of going back to school, and I'd reached a point where I was okay with that, but I can't deny that what he proposed is exciting. It might work."

When Nicole grinned, Max saw a sparkle in Nicole's eyes, a sparkle that, up to that point, only Brady had evoked.

"Honestly, Nic, it sounds great," Max said. "A 'best of both worlds' sort of thing."

"For all the fretting we did about this year, and about this town, and about most everything, look how perfectly everything turned out," Ellie said, then she turned to Max. "And while we may be the perfect friends, I wonder if there's not another reason you decided to stay?"

A warmth and a sweetness flooded Max, as sure as if she were sipping a mug of rich hot chocolate.

"Maybe," Max answered.

"Speaking of Beck," Nicole said, "how did he react to the news you're staying?"

"Actually," Max looked at the clock on her classroom wall, "I'm telling him in twenty minutes."

"What?" Ellie and Nicole shouted in unison.

"I didn't know for sure until a few days ago. There were things I needed to take care of, and Beck was out of town. More of my long story. Maybe we can finish it another time? I shouldn't be late."

Ellie waved her hand toward the door. "Go! Go make Beck the happiest guy in Caston. We have all summer to hear the details."

There was so much more she wanted to say to her friends, but Ellie was right. They had all summer. And all the days that followed.

The note stuck to Beck's front door had just two words. *Back yard.* Max pulled it from the door, then followed the directions. Since Beck had hardly stopped moving long enough to eat or sleep in the past two weeks, Max expected to find him poring over paperwork or stabbing at his laptop. She wouldn't have been completely surprised to find him taking apart an engine. When she saw the patio table covered with a pale pink tablecloth, an enormous vase filled with tulips in its center, and a bottle of champagne chilling in one of those silver buckets that she'd only ever seen in movies, she was not only completely surprised, she was confused.

"What's all this?"

"A celebration."

Beck took one of the champagne flutes from the table, filled it, and held it out for her. He filled a second, then lifted it in a toast.

"Congratulations on finishing your first year of teaching."

Max clinked her glass with his, then took a sip. The bubbles skittered on her tongue as if they were as nervous as she was. Before being face-to-face with him, it had seemed easy. Fun, even. Now it seemed anything but easy. She couldn't help but wonder and worry if what she was so eager to tell him would elicit anything more than a shrug.

They'd talked a few days after his party, and she'd apologized that she hadn't told him about leaving Caston before her dad spilled the beans. Beck had asked a few questions about her plans, then talked in general terms about staying in touch and seeing each other, but then he'd changed the subject. At the time, Max had been relieved he hadn't made things difficult. Now, she second-guessed everything.

"I know the feeling of the last day of school as a student. There's not much better. What's it like as a teacher?"

"Kind of the same. Sweet freedom."

Beck smiled. "Sit." He pulled out a chair.

Max would have preferred to pace, but she sat. She went to take another sip of her champagne, only to find the glass empty. Beck didn't ask, just poured. Max took a sip, then decided she needed to ease into the bigger conversation.

"How's work?"

"Busy, but Tibbs and I came to an agreement yesterday, so that will take some of the pressure off."

This time, Max lifted her glass. "Then congratulations to you, as well. I know how much you were hoping it would work out with him."

"After three weeks without him, I wasn't hoping, I was praying. I figured out pretty quickly I wasn't going to be able to do it all on my own. Had he turned me down, it would have meant searching for someone else, and I wouldn't have known where to start looking."

"How about in Caston? Are Sven and Jake staying on top of the work with you gone so much?"

"They're pulling a lot of overtime. I owe them, big time. I put out some feelers at the tech school hoping I might be able to hire someone, at least part-time, but no luck yet."

Max saw her opening. "I have the summer free. I'm pretty good at oil changes."

"Hah! I wish I could hire you." His smile turned sad. "Have you heard back about the job in South Carolina?"

"I did. Scheduled an interview for next week."

"Hmm. Congratulations, once again."

"Un-scheduled it a few days ago."

"It will be high school instead of middle school?"

"Un-scheduled it a few days ago," Max repeated.

"You what? Why?"

Nerves had her stomach doing backflips. She had to stand, had to move, had to take her glass with her to keep her hands busy. She sipped, then spoke.

"What would you say if I told you I changed my mind?"

Max stole a quick glance to try to gauge Beck's reaction but didn't give him a chance to answer. His expression was remarkably blank.

"Some things happened in the past week. I thought I was so sure about what I wanted, but then..." Max shrugged. "Things."

She gave him a recap of what happened with Reid, told him about the letter from her mother, and paced and sipped.

"A thirteen-year-old is brave enough to face what happened to him, to try to turn it into something good, and my answer is to run? I finally realized I was using my history, my life of never staying in one place, as an excuse to run from everything that seemed hard, and that's not who I am.

"I also tried to tell myself that the friendships and the connections I've made here were only temporary. That they weren't enough to make me want to stay. When I slowed down enough to listen to myself, I knew I'd been lying to myself."

Max refilled her glass herself and avoided eye contact with Beck.

"Still, I'd made a commitment to a job that, at one time, I really wanted. I had to make sure if I changed my mind, I wouldn't be leaving them in a predicament. I spoke with the woman I interviewed with last year. She was very understanding, and she kind of laughed at me. They have a list of applicants a mile long."

Max's pacing came to a sudden halt. "Where are the dogs?"

She looked at Beck for the first time since she'd started her story. The tiniest smile—or maybe smirk was a better term—twitched at the corners of his mouth.

"Inside. I didn't want them to spoil what I had planned." Beck waved his hand over the table.

Max's eyebrows cinched together as she tried to decipher Beck's expression and his words. He gave her nothing, so, more nervous than ever, all she could do was continue. She told him about the award, and about her idea for the video. It was easier talking facts than feelings.

"When I told my principal I'd changed my mind, there was more laughing. Honestly, I started to get a little tired of it. She said she hadn't considered looking for my replacement because she knew I'd 'figure out what I wanted.'" Max mimed air quotes. "At least Ellie and Nicole seemed surprised."

Max didn't know what else to say. She'd expected, or at least hoped for, more of a reaction from Beck.

"So if you need some help this summer…"

"Sit down, Max."

"Huh?"

"Sit down. Please."

Max didn't like the calm, cool, and collected vibe she was getting from Beck. She got the feeling that he knew something she didn't, and that didn't sit well.

"Fine," Max said and sat.

"More champagne?"

"Is there more?"

Beck lifted the bottle. "Some."

Max looked at her empty glass. "Did I drink it all?"

Beck just smiled and filled it.

"Is it my turn to talk?"

Max signaled the go-ahead with her glass.

"First, you're hired. I'd never find anyone better."

So far, so good, Max thought, and nodded.

"Next, your news makes me very happy, but I was never going to let you leave."

Her nerves disappeared when indignation filled every available space inside her.

"You weren't going to *let* me?"

When Beck chuckled, a hint of anger began to bubble. She really was tired of laughter at her expense.

"I had no intention of letting you leave *me*. You may have left Caston, but you weren't going to leave me."

"Oh."

"That's what this was all about. This is only phase one. Depending how difficult you were, there were several phases to follow."

"Oh?"

"Indeed. Indie and Ace even had roles in phase three."

"Now I'm curious."

Beck reached for Max's glass, took it out of her hand, then kept her hand in his.

"I wasn't about to lose you, Mad Max. I've known that for quite some time. I've been waiting for you to catch up."

Max's heart began to thump. She wondered if Beck felt her pulse race in her wrist.

"It seems I'm in love with you, whether you like it or not."

"I don't not like it."

"You told me so many times that you can't stay in one place, that it's not in your blood. I was prepared to provide evidence that you can, in fact, put down roots, that you already have, but it seems a middle schooler and your mother have done some of that work for me."

"Before you go any further, there are a few things I need to tell you."

"Shoot."

"I can't cook."

"I know."

"I like to watch Hallmark Christmas movies. All of them. Even the reruns."

"I'll deal with it."

"And if you tell anyone that, I may have to kill you."

"Understood."

"Sometimes I just need to drive a car. Fast."

"So do I. We'll take turns."

"And just to be clear, I said I'll *try* staying in one place, but that's never worked for me before. The day might come when I need to leave."

Even as she said the words, she felt, more than ever, that they weren't true. She wanted home, and she wanted Beck.

"I think you're wrong, but you'd know best."

"Okay, then just one more thing."

"What's that?"

"I love you."

The smirk that she'd gotten so used to disappeared. In its place was a smile that melted her heart. Beck stood and took Max with him. He pulled her close.

"I've been waiting to hear those words since that day I drove you home from the hospital. You were so tired, and I know your hand hurt much more than you let on, but you fought me every step of the way, you matched me barb for barb, you were determined not to let me get the upper hand, and for some reason, that's what did it. I knew there'd never be a dull moment with you, Mad Max."

"Well, that's funny, because that's the same time I knew. You drove me crazy, you teased me mercilessly, and when I thought about it later, all I remembered was that I knew I was in love with you."

"I'd say we should toast this profound realization, but you may have had enough."

"I don't think a toast will do me in."

"In a minute."

Beck leaned close. His lips grazed hers once, twice, and Max thought she'd go mad. She put her hands behind his head, pulled him toward her, and pressed her lips to his. Max decided she could happily stay right there, standing in Beck's back yard with the combination of the late afternoon sun and the heat from Beck warming her as deliciously as if she were back in the hot tub at the spa. She might have to suggest that spa to Beck...

Max pulled away.

"You said something about this being phase one. I'm curious what else was in store had I put up more of a fight."

Beck poured the last few drops of champagne into their glasses.

"To you staying in Caston. To us. To the future."

Max tapped his glass with hers and sipped. "I like how that sounds, but those other phases?"

Beck chuckled. "Okay, if you insist. Phase two was a fancy song and dance number I'd been working on for a couple of weeks. My top hat and cane are inside."

Max laughed. "I would have liked to see that."

"Phase three involved Ace and Indie. They've learned some slick new tricks. Ace has a tux and Indie an evening dress on right now."

"They've been alone all this time. You honestly don't think they've eaten the other's costume?"

"I remain hopeful."

"Next?"

"Phase four focused on your stomach. I have your favorite pizza from Scooter's warm in the oven, and I have those dark chocolate salted caramels you love."

"I still want that stuff."

"I figured you would."

Max kissed him again. "You think you know me so well."

"I do."

"Fine, then which phase did you think would be the winner?"

"The last one. Phase five."

"There's a phase five? How can you possibly top the first four?"

"Phase five was a question. Just a question. One I got permission from your father to ask you when the time was right, but that I'm going to hold off asking until I can make it special, and until you're not crying."

"I'm not crying."

Beck merely raised that single eyebrow and used his thumbs to dry her cheeks.

"There may be fluids leaking out of my eyes, but that's allergies. Another thing I have to mention. I have allergies. Terrible allergies. They make my eyes water."

"Then I'll wait until your allergies clear up."

"Thanks. I appreciate that."

"I love you, Max."

"I love you, Beck."

Beck put his arm around Max and she leaned her head onto his shoulder. So many thoughts, so many emotions, so many things Max knew that one day, down the road, she'd spend some time analyzing, but for now, she was content.

She was happy.

She was home.

If you enjoyed reading *Finding Home*, please help other readers find and enjoy it by leaving a review on Amazon or Goodreads or wherever you review books. Just a few words will do and will be very much appreciated.
Thank you!

Also by Margaret Standafer:

I Know an Old Lady

The Misty Lake Series:
Misty Lake
The Inn at Misty Lake
Misty Lake in Focus
Anchored in Misty Lake
Sunset Over Misty Lake

The Caston Teacher Series:
Leaving Home
Coming Home
Finding Home

Margaret Standafer lives and writes in the Minneapolis area with the support of her amazing husband and children and in spite of the lack of support from her ever-demanding, but lovable, Golden Retriever. It is her sincere hope that you enjoy her work.

To learn more about Margaret and her books, please visit www.margaretstandafer.com

Manufactured by Amazon.ca
Bolton, ON

33155711R00203